CONTENTS

Prologue
1. The Maverick   2
2. The Journal   14
3. Nebraska   21
4. Awakening   28
5. Tin Soldiers   46
6. Fish for Life   56
7. Cowboys and Indians   93
8. Abnormalities   119
9. Ranch Life   146
10. Urban Cowboy   187
11. Young Love   201
12. Mikhail   237
13. Winter   293
14. Dawning   310
Acknowledgements   330

PROLOGUE

I grew up in the shadow of a mysterious land. Although the Sandhills were a mere forty miles away and West Virginia's size, I knew very little about them.

My dad told me Sandhills stories that sparked my curiosity but, at the same time, dampened my desire to venture there. One day, he came home from ice fishing in the Sandhills to unfold the traumatic events as he cleaned a heaping pail of perch. He and a neighbor drove a hundred miles up to Willow Lake on that bygone winter day. They eased the family sedan right out onto the thick ice to provide shelter from the subzero air. Gerald, his fishing partner, put on his cotton chore gloves with the tiny plastic knobs for grip, grabbed the ice spike, an old axle with a sharpened tip, and went to work chopping the first hole.

Gerald, a big man, sent the chunks of ice flying as he stabbed away. Dad was busy getting a fishing pole ready when the sound of chopping turned to silence, and then a string of expletives filled the air. Gerald stood with his empty hands facing upward, looking down at the spot where his ice pick disappeared. "I lost the pick," he grumbled. The lake water had splashed up and instantly froze on his knobby gloves, making them "slicker than snot on a doorknob." He got down on his hands and knees and peered down into the water. "I can see it down there. It's standing up, stuck in the bottom." Then he took off his gloves and coat, rolled up his shirt sleeve, reached down as far as he could, and grabbed the axle. What a stroke of luck! They were able to fish all day, occasionally ducking into the car to thaw frozen fingers and fishing lines.

Dad enjoyed telling another Sandhills story that gave me the creeps. On their way back from South Dakota, my parents decided to stop at the Valentine National Wildlife Refuge for some fishing. He turned off Highway 83 and followed Spur 16 to Hackberry Lake, where he parked to survey the situation. A wide cattail hedge stood between him and open water. Boatless, he took off his shoes and socks and started wading through the poison ivy and bullrushes, out to where the water licked at the billfold in his back pocket. Open water was still beyond casting range, so he turned around to slog back through the cattails. About halfway back, he looked up to see a six-foot bull snake stretched across his path. Dad hated snakes. When he got back to the car, he jumped in, wet pants and all, and sped off, never looking back.

I had minimal personal experience in the Sandhills before high school graduation. I faintly recall driving up to the Nebraska National Forest at Halsey a couple of times to chop down our Christmas tree. I also recollect the highway that wound through the endless hills and valleys en route to the Black Hills. We learned at an early age that the Middle Loup River, which flowed by our hometown of Arcadia, originated in the Sandhills. I marveled at the volume of water in that river and wondered why it never ran dry.

Growing up, we understood that The Wild West

began with the Sandhills, just on the other side of Anselmo, Nebraska, at the sign that read "Range Fires are Dangerous." We heard stories of real-life cowboys and possibly even some Indians who lived in those hills. Old-timers would say, "Those are some tough folks up there; it's rough to live out in the middle of nowhere like that." I got the impression that people who lived in the Sandhills could survive just about anything.

Then, in my late teens, male hormones kicked in, giving me the curiosity and courage to venture into the Sandhills. Like the 18th-century French fur trappers, I explored new lakes and rivers from my canoe. I discovered the native forests lining steep canyon walls along the Dismal River. I found fountains of pure water boiling out of the sand, increasing the river flow by the mile. And oh the lakes! They teemed with fish and fowl like no other place on earth.

Uncle Jim moved a trailer house to Big Alkali Lake in Cherry County a few years later, and through his influence, I started a fishing guide business at age thirty-two, specializing in the Sandhills' natural lakes. Five years later, I started working for a deer hunting outfitter in the western Sandhills. In these guiding experiences I watched each client go through a mind transformation when immersed in the wilderness of water and dunes. I've learned things about the Sandhills that go beyond science. I've experienced spiritual awakenings that affected my theology. I learned that the Hills have a mysterious way of manipulating the soul.

One day a few years ago, I realized that I needed to write a book about the Sandhills. Nebraska's famed author, Mari Sandoz, assumed this task many years ago and handled it so eloquently. But even her prowess with a pen couldn't fully describe the deep mystery of this land. The Sandhills consist of a unique set of ingredients that I can write out on a recipe card, but you cannot fully appreciate them unless you taste them mixed and cooked. Photographers have tried to catch it in pictures, but they lack the gentle whisper of wind through the grass or the orchestral underscore of marsh birds. To create a literal sample of the Sandhills, I must attempt the near-impossible and appeal to all your senses while gently plucking the strings of your heart and soul.

We have the opportunity to read various non-fiction books about the Sandhills. Historians have documented life in the early days, and filmmakers produce docudramas depicting contemporary ranches every few years. There have even been some fictional works with Sandhill settings. These are all excellent resources, but a vital ingredient still seems to be missing.

To do proper justice to the Sandhills, I will sprinkle cold-hard facts and a few sprigs of poetry into a warmhearted story about a young man named Jack, who decides to escape the clatter of the city in an attempt to find his purpose in life. Jack is a fictional outsider who comes to experience real-life places in the Sandhills. You, the reader, can pull on his biking shoes and ride along with him as he cycles the hills. Along the way you will learn all sorts of interesting facts about ourselves and this world we live in.

About now, many scholarly eyebrows are raising. Mixing facts with fiction goes against the rules. But as the poet Ocean Vuong states, "The rules, like streets, can only take you to known places."

As you read along, you will discover that this story could be used as a textbook, covering a spectrum of scientific studies from anthropology to zoology. It's also a history book dealing with many little-known incidents from the last 150 years. All these facts, though, will be cleverly placed in an engaging narrative.

My hope is that you will enjoy discovering the countless secrets of the Sandhills along with Jack as he pedals his way across this immense land. My ultimate goal with this book is to dish up a slice of this region that gives you a genuine taste of its mystique. Thank you, and enjoy! –John Hunt

But ask the animals, and they will teach you, or the birds in the sky, and they will tell you; or speak to the earth, and it will teach you, or let the fish in the sea inform you.

−Job

1. THE MAVERICK

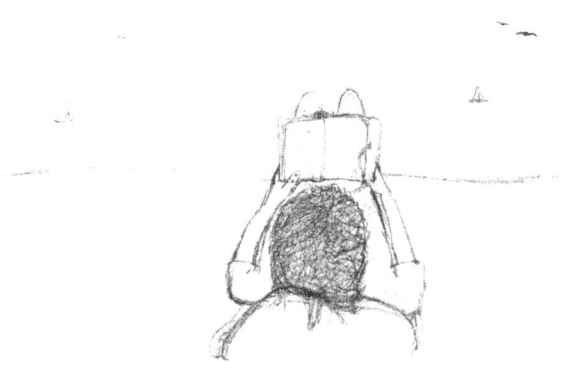

Narrow tires sank deeply into the sand as a lanky-framed youngster struggled to push his bike across the beach to the water's edge. The turquoise water of Lake Michigan quietly slid in and licked the Chicago shoreline on that warm June evening. Jack Harris unstrapped his bike helmet, shook out his mop of red hair, and felt the cool lake breeze evaporate the beads of sweat from his forehead. The sun-warmed sand beckoned his body to rest awhile. Pulling off his backpack to prop under his head, he closed his eyes and let the screeching of distant seagulls carry him off to another place.

Jack's world up until now was missing something. He grew up in the city and experienced pretty much everything that it had to offer. Humanity hustles through the brick and steel canyons back there, but out on the lake, he could slow down and turn loose his sense of wonder. Mysteriously, the sand and water allowed him to envision life beyond the streets of Chicago.

Jack pulled a worn book out of his pack and sat up in the white sand to read. He thumbed through the pages until he found the entry. Then he silently read the handwritten words.

I think maybe I've discovered what's important in life today. It's not about fame and fortune. It's not about being comfortable. It's not about enjoyment, status, or who I know. I helped a cow give birth today. I watched it take its first breath of air and suck its first drink of milk from its mama. Then the little fellow shut his eyes in contentment as the warm milk found its way into his slowly growing little tummy. I marveled at this new little life, standing wobbly kneed in the sand. Life is about finding contentment in simple things.

Jack looked up from the book, out across Lake Michigan with the setting sun warm on his back. He mulled over the word "contentment." He may have been content when he was younger, like the time he bought his first bike. All was good until the chain started popping off. Then it became a nuisance, just like his job, which was tormenting him now. "There has to be more to life than this," he muttered softly to himself as he restlessly dug his feet into the warm sand. "Somehow, someday, I'm going to figure out what it is," he vowed as he turned back to the urban confines of his home.

The apartment where Jack and his mom, Shelly, lived was plain but comfy. They had lived in places like this all his life. He and his mom were pretty close since he never knew his father, and he had no siblings; she did her best to prepare Jack for manhood.

Shelly managed to get Jack through the difficult years of puberty. His high school years passed too quickly, and the day she feared was now upon them. He seemed more restless every day. She wanted a fulfilling life for Jack but wasn't ready to be alone.

Over pizza that night, Jack worked up the courage to propose an idea to his mom. "What would you think about me leaving for a year?"

Shelly was caught off guard by Jack's question. She ran through all the possible reasons why her son would want to leave home but was at a loss for words. Her only response was, "Why?"

"I don't know for sure," was Jack's reply. "I just need to go figure something out, I guess." Shelly silently pondered these words. She thought back to when she was nineteen and restless. She wanted her son to be happy but didn't want him to get hurt either.

"Where are you thinking about going?" she asked, half fearing his answer.

"Nebraska," Jack replied.

"What on earth are you going to do in Nebraska?" she mused.

Jack shrugged his shoulders and reached for his backpack. Then he pulled out the old book and tossed it on the table.

"Isn't that Farley's old journal?" she asked.

"Yeah, and he lives in a place called the Sandhills. This journal could help me find him."

"I'm sorry, but doesn't that sound kind of crazy?" asked Shelly.

Jack paused and tried to come up with the right words to convince his mom. "Crazy or not, I feel like this is something that I have to do."

Shelly just raised an eyebrow and dropped the conversation.

Later, alone in his room, Jack googled the Sandhills. He had never traveled west of Chicago, so this journey promised to be a new and exciting adventure. According to the map, the closest part of the Sandhills to Chicago was west of a city called Norfolk. He then googled Greyhound and found a bus route starting at $135.00. "Wow, I can afford that... and the trip is only twelve hours and fifty minutes!" His excitement built as he realized that this trip could be so simple.

Jack went to bed that night, envisioning the months ahead. "I'm leaving the only life I've ever known. I want to find Farley and have him show me the things he wrote about in his journal: the cities in the sky, the backward flowing river, the ten-mile-wide crop circles, and the boiling cold water springs. I want to learn how to ride a horse. I want to hunt a mule deer. I want to go to the place where the silence is deafening. I want to lay out under a billion stars and listen to the coyotes sing. Most of all, I want to find answers to these questions that keep haunting me." Jack drifted off into pleasant sleep with the familiar sound of cars and sirens wafting through the walls. The following day Jack got out of bed with a new resolve and wrote out his preparation list.

1. Quit his job as a bicycle courier.
2. Draw out most of his life savings in cash.
3. Buy a bus ticket.
4. Convince mom.

Peddling to work, Jack thought about the job that

he started while in high school. It wasn't a terrible job, but it didn't bring him a great deal of satisfaction. He felt even less essential when he turned in his two-week notice. "You can quit today. There's plenty of other kids wanting your job," was the reply.

"One down and three to go," he exclaimed as he hopped on his bike and headed to the bank.

Jack walked up to the bank teller, gave her his account number, and asked what his balance was. She looked it up and said, "One thousand, eight hundred twenty-six dollars and thirty-two cents."

"I'd like to keep my account open but want to draw out seventeen hundred in cash."

"Okay, I'll be right back."

When she turned to leave, Jack remembered a story from history class about the six Chicago gangsters who committed the nation's largest bank robbery. Using machine guns and revolvers, they got away with two and a half million dollars from a bank in Lincoln, Nebraska.

"I guess this is my little way of returning some of the money to Nebraska," he chuckled out loud.

"What's that?" inquired the teller returning with the money.

"Oh, nothing," replied Jack awkwardly as she counted out the money, stuffed it in an envelope, and handed it over. Jack turned and headed across the bank lobby to the front doors with his life savings folded in half and tucked securely in his front pants pocket. Step two accomplished, he thought to himself as he swung a leg over his bike and took off down the street.

The Greyhound station was far enough away that Jack decided to postpone his ticket purchase. He was a little unsure about his mom's reaction to this big adventure anyway. She didn't exactly give him her blessing, but she'd had a day to think it over. "Tonight's the night," thought Jack as he turned his bike east toward Lake Michigan.

Jack thought about his bike as he traversed the traffic. The bike gave him a sense of freedom. It gave him the means to escape his troubles for a while. As he pumped the pedals, he was siphoning the vexations out of his mind and scattering them down the road behind him.

He pedaled on until an opening appeared ahead, signaling the edge of the city. He could see green grass ahead and beyond that, blue water that reached the eastern horizon. This place was Jack's escape. And it served its purpose well, until recently. Now, it only seemed like a stepping stone to higher ground.

Sitting out on the sand with his shoes off, Jack pulled the journal out of his backpack and randomly sifted through the pages. He picked out words as he skimmed along. Foreign words like "snow snakes," "sun dogs," and "yuccas" caught his eye. It seemed like the Sandhills were on a different planet instead of only a couple of states away. Farley had a way with words that seemed to draw the reader into the writing place and time. As Jack read, he could almost reach down and pick "the arrowhead" out of the sand between his toes. He heard the water lapping against Farley's fishing boat as he steered it through the reeds and up onto the sandy beach of Big Alkali Lake. A parent killdeer ran across the sand with its fluffy babies on long, toothpick legs close behind, screaming, "killdeer! killdeer! killdeer!" Jack awoke from his reading when he realized that the birds he was hearing were seagulls and distant sirens.

Jack remembered his mom and pondered the words that he would say to her later that night. He didn't want to hurt her or make her feel unappreciated for the love and care that she had given him. Other than a couple of her friends, he was all she had in this life. She didn't say much about her childhood. All he knew was that she moved to Chicago about the same time that he was born.

Shelly did her best to bring Jack up with all the advantages she could afford. He attended public school, where he developed an obsession for basketball. Academically, Jack shuffled through with interests in history and geography. He had friends who have since moved on. Girls were annoying mysteries. All in all, he could say that he had a happy enough childhood.

But the tender age was behind him, and now it was time to move on. Jack didn't realize that becoming a man was going to be so complicated. Tough questions constantly plagued him. How can I make a living? How can I be happy making a living? What kind of father will I be someday? Will I ever be content? On and on, the questions rolled through Jack's mind as he sat through another Lake Michigan sunset.

On his bike ride home that evening, Jack decided to be honest with his mom and pour out the questions that had been milling through his mind. He hoped that she would understand.

Shelly spent the day thinking about their conversation the night before. She had lunch at the park where she noticed a half-grown robin hopping along the ground. It must have gotten the courage to test its wings and jumped out of its nest. She hoped that a cat wouldn't find it struggling along. As she watched, she couldn't help but think about Jack's words to her. He was in the same predicament as this little bird. He needed to move on to the next stage in life, even if it meant hardship to body and soul. Realizing that this is a necessary part of life, she decided to let him go.

The apartment that night had a heavy feeling, much like the atmosphere just before a mid-western thunderstorm. Jack arrived with an unsure "Hello," and his mom returned the greeting. Jack dropped his pack on the floor and headed to the bathroom to wash up for dinner. As he dried his hands and face, he glanced in the mirror and rehearsed his opening line to his mom. Suddenly, it sounded all wrong. What was he going to say? His mind spun in incoherent circles as he walked back out to the dinner table. Jack sat and stared at his plate as his mom brought a salad bowl to the table and sat down.

"I decided that you're right," Shelly said, breaking the silence.

Jack glanced up at her with a puzzled look.

"About what?" he asked.

"About going to Nebraska," his mom replied. "I want you to spread your wings or kick up your heels; whatever you need to do to move on in life." Jack sat back in his chair to digest his mom's words.

"You mean that?" he asked.

"I mean it," she replied. "But I need you to promise me one thing," she added.

"What?" replied Jack.

"I want you to come back alive," she answered.

Jack's face broke into a huge smile. "I promise!"

Suddenly, Jack's oppressive sky opened up, and

the dark, heavy clouds rolled away. He had his mom's blessing! The final and most challenging quest of the day was so easy! "Thanks, mom!" he said as he jumped up, hugged her, and ran to his room to make plans. Shelly sat for a while at the table and wondered what just happened. She just turned her son loose. He's just like one of those maverick calves that Farley wrote about in his journal, "running and jumping the whole durn pasture the second you turn him out," she mused to herself.

    The following day, Jack hopped on his bike with a list of stuff to buy. First, he needed to outfit his bike with cargo bags, or panniers, as the salesperson called them. A pup tent and a lightweight sleeping bag were tops on the list. He would need a lighter to start fires, a mess kit, and some liquid soap. He would need a water bottle. He was pretty sure that all adventures require a rope, so he threw in a small coil. He purchased a fishing outfit nestled neatly in a small plastic case. Then he found a slingshot with the advertised power to kill a rabbit. He also bought a knife that looked like it would butcher whatever animal or fish he could find to cook. He made a mental reminder to watch some YouTube videos on preparing a fish and a rabbit. He left the sporting goods store $184 shorter but felt secure owning the tools needed to survive the Sandhills.
    Next, he went home to pack his clothes. Jack figured summer in Nebraska is just as hot as summer in Chicago, so he picked out some shorts, tee shirts, socks, and underwear. If he was still in Nebraska when winter hit, he could purchase a coat and jeans. He was used to

cold weather growing up in Chicago, so he wasn't too worried about it.

Next, he went online and purchased his bus ticket. The instructions required him to wrap his bike in a tarp for transportation in the belly of the bus. The tarp might come in handy later. The bus ticket cost $164.00, leaving him $1,352.00 for food and necessities until he could find a temporary Nebraska job.

His bus departed Chicago on Friday morning, so he had a day and a half to make final preparations. He watched some survival videos on the internet: how to build a fire, how to clean a fish, how to cook a fish, how to dress a deer, what to do in a bear attack, and how to set a broken bone. Then he oiled his bike chain and checked it over for maintenance issues. He listed all the possible things that he needed and packed each one carefully into the new panniers. He debated over the razor, thinking he might just let his young whiskers grow, but decided to bring it along. When he started strapping everything on his bike he thought about rain, and realized that the tent and sleeping bag needed a waterproof bag, so he made a quick trip back to the sporting goods store. He picked up a plastic tarp to wrap his bike in for the bus trip while he was there. Back home, after several hours of work, he stepped back to admire his ride. "All systems go," he announced with an air of finality.

Friday morning, Jack crawled out of his bed to the smell of bacon. Shelly rose early to send her son off with a home-cooked breakfast. Jack walked out and sat down to fried eggs, bacon, and french toast.

"Wow, this looks good!" exclaimed Jack.

"Might be a while before you get another home-cooked meal," replied Shelly.

"Yeah, I might get tired of granola bars before this trip is over," sighed Jack as he dug out his checklist to go over everything one last time with his mom.

"Just take care of yourself, and call me once in a while," said Shelly.

"Don't worry, I will," Jack replied as he got up to give his mom a bear hug goodbye. He then checked his pockets for his billfold and phone, strapped on his backpack, pushed his heavily laden bike out the door, and headed down the hallway to the elevator. Shelly yelled one last, "I love you," as he walked away.

"Love you too!" Jack yelled over his shoulder, "See ya later!" And just like that, he was gone.

Jack had two ways to get to the bus station. He could pedal the three miles or set his bike on the front rack of a city bus. Everything would have to be removed from the bike and carried on the bus to do option two. He decided to pedal to the station, plus he wanted to test out his fully loaded ride.

He arrived at the station an hour before departure, which gave him time to take all the packs off and wrap the bike with the tarp. He discovered a use for his rope when he went to secure the tarp. "All those MacGyver reruns come in handy," he said to himself as he cinched up the rope and tied it off.

Jack's bus finally arrived, and he slid his bike and duffle bag into the belly compartment, making sure that they would ride okay, then he boarded the bus with his backpack and panniers; these would ride in the seat beside him. In a few minutes, the bus took off, winding its way through traffic to Interstate 88, heading west out of Chicago. As the Chicago skyline dwindled behind, Jack already started feeling different about life. He entertained the thought that to find himself, he must first get lost. Little did he know how true these words were going to be.

2. THE JOURNAL

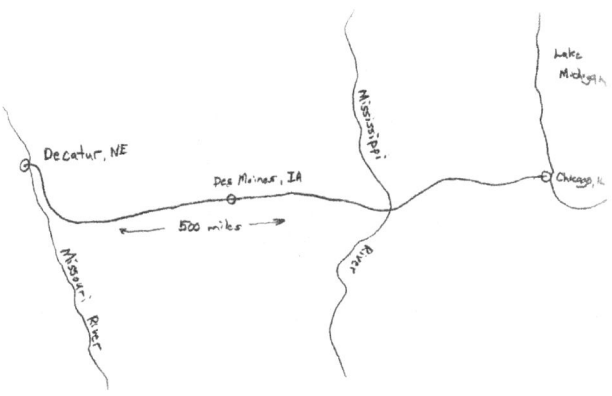

J ack settled back in his seat and watched the rows of corn strobe past in the hot June sun. His bus trip would take him right through the middle of our nation's breadbasket. Iowa and Illinois are ranked one and two in corn production in the U.S., followed by number three Nebraska, the Cornhusker State. This trip would also take him across the Mississippi and Missouri Rivers, the two longest rivers in the U.S. Jack gazed at the eternal fields of corn and soybeans and pondered how different it would be to live out here, away from the city and all its people.

    The man across the aisle stared at his phone as the miles clicked by. Jack wondered if the guy made this trip so often that he didn't care what passed by outside the bus window. Out of contagious reaction, Jack pulled out his phone and checked for messages. This little device would be his only lifeline to the world that he was leaving behind. He wouldn't say that he was addicted to social media, but then again, neither would the guy across the aisle. Jack started thumbing down through the bottomless feed, and the miles clicked past. The next time he glanced up from the screen, he noticed that the bus was crossing a long bridge; he glanced out the side window at the mighty Mississippi. Wow, I almost missed it, he thought to himself.

Putting the phone away, Jack looked out the window for a change in scenery as the bus entered Iowa, but only saw more cornfields. While digging around in his backpack for a granola bar, he felt Farley's journal, pulled it out, and set it in his lap. As he munched down his snack bar, he felt the leather binding of the old book. A thin strap tied the book shut. Opening it, he found only hand-written print and a few pencil doodles —amateur artwork with sketches of cabins and pine trees and fish and deer with enormous antlers. Farley seemed to draw from his heart as he pondered the words inside. Jack read the inscription written in pencil on the first page.

Dear Jack, you're just a little suckling now, but by the time you read this book, you will be working your way into manhood. Maybe your mom will find a good man to help you through the tough years of growing up. I'm sure your mother will do the best she can, but there are certain things that only a father can teach. I don't know much about being a father, but I was once your age, so I may understand what you're going through—best Wishes, Farley Hayes.

Jack had read this inscription many times since his mom presented the book to him on his thirteenth birthday. Each time though, he felt the same yearning to discover the writer behind those words. Although the book didn't include Farley's photo, Jack pictured a tall, salt and pepper-haired man topped by a worn-out old cowboy hat. He had a horseshoe mustache with pure white tips. The cowboy drove a rusty old pickup truck that looked overworked in its prime years. He was a little stooped himself from too many years of hard labor. But behind all this rough exterior and a pair of bifocal glasses sparkled the kindest eyes. These were the eyes that spotted the mama deer rearing back on its hind legs and thrashing at the coyote that was attempting to kill her fawn. They were also the eyes that peered down the open sights of his Winchester 30-30 as he squeezed off a round at that coyote, scaring him into the next county. The old gentleman filled the journal with stories like this.

Farley told stories about the wild weather in the Sandhills, like the sunny day when a tiny tornado hit his fishing boat square in the middle and sucked a plastic grocery sack out of the boat, spiraling it up and up until it disappeared into the clouds way up in the sky. He figured it probably dropped somewhere in South Dakota. Then there was the evening when he topped a rise with two fishing clients from Pennsylvania and straight in front of them was a massive twister rolling across the hills. The easterners were thrilled to see their very first real-live tornado. Farley turned on the radio to listen for weather warnings, but the area was too remote to report.

Farley was a man of many ambitions who spent

some years in the military before settling down on a Nebraska Sandhills ranch. Between cattle chores, he spent time creating wooden wonders in his carpentry shop. He loved showing off his beloved Sandhills, and people came from all over the nation to hunt and fish with him.

Jack flipped to the second page of the journal and started reading:

> When I first came to the Sandhills, I viewed this land like everyone else who didn't grow up here. People who traveled through told stories of a vast expanse of wasteland devoid of people and life. "Nothing but open range and cows," they said. I got a job on a cattle ranch smack dab in the middle of these hills after my hitch in the Army, and it didn't take me long to find out that my first impression of the Sandhills was dead wrong.
>
> The bulk of the world contains hard, straight horizons which delineate cold, calculated logic. But here, it's much different. The soft curves of the Sandhills form a relief of Eve in the glory of her young innocence. This environment, pure as a snowflake, leads us to take an honest look at ourselves.
>
> Grass and living creatures have turned these dunes into a lush Garden of Eden. Animals run around totally exposed in the treeless environment yet seem to flourish. Even the boundless undulations of the hills themselves dance in the evening sun.
>
> Just below the surface of the sand flows the lifeblood of the Sandhills. The ground absorbs each precious raindrop like a sponge. This water is stored in the sand, bringing life to the grass on the hills. Water seeps out of the sand in the lowest spots and forms lakes and rivers, which bring aquatic life to a region once considered a desert.

The twenty-some rivers and creeks that flow out of the Sandhills are the world's most constant-flowing streams.

For some reason, the living creatures grow to extreme size in the Sandhills. Bluegills as big around as the bottom of a five-gallon bucket swim around the lakes. I once saw some bullfrogs that looked large enough to swallow a pop can. I guided a hunter from Georgia who hesitated on shooting a whitetail buck because he thought it was an elk. I guess that fish and animals grow proportionate to the space they occupy, and the Sandhills cover 20,000 square miles, approximately the area of West Virginia or Lake Michigan.

The sun from heaven above and water welling from deep below gently endow these everlasting dunes with life beyond explanation.

At this point, Jack looked up from the journal and contemplated the magnitude of his journey through the Sandhills. Farley didn't mention the town or county where he lived. How would he ever find him in an area that large? His mom was no help, only saying that Farley was a good man, but nothing else. He hoped to find more clues in Farley's journal that would point to his whereabouts.

Jack glanced out his window at the endless fields and wondered why Farley didn't write about corn. Are there no fields in the Sandhills? He remembered a story about haystacks and searched through the journal until he found a page titled "Prairie Hay" and started reading.

In the summertime, we put up hay for the long winter months ahead. The Sandhills are more than just hills. Thousands of years ago, before the grass could take hold, the prevailing northwest winds swept all this sand into massive dunes. Between each dune is a low, flat valley that has ample water just below the surface. This myriad of valleys form the hay meadows that grow tall grasses that we cut and stack for feed in the winter.

Usually, starting in July, cattle ranchers don their farmer hats and head out to the hay meadows. Up until a few years ago, they cut the hay with sickle bar mowers pulled behind all colors of antique-looking tractors. Many of these tractors had dual tires installed to help them float over the soggy ground. The soft ground sometimes forms waves that billow ahead of the tractor in the treacherous low spots. After the hay dried in the sun for a few days, it was raked into windrows using the same tractors pulling dump rakes or wheel rakes. Next, homemade motorized sweeps pushed piles of hay to the slide stacker. The slide carried the hay up and dumped it into a giant removable cage. This process required countless hours from several helping hands.

Nowadays, the hours are reduced considerably with the use of windrowers and balers. One man can more efficiently do the job of four or five back then. The winds of change are sweeping over the Sandhills.

Jack wondered about Farley's statement. What changes were happening in the Sandhills? Were they good changes or bad? Will I find it the way that he wrote about? These questions ran through Jack's mind as the bus departed I-80 and continued west on I-680 on its westward route to the Missouri River.

The bus glided along, past more fields bordered by cottonwood and oak trees. The hills seemed to be getting more significant, with artificial terraces cutting the areas into bizarre shapes. Then, the highway rolled down between some wooded bluffs and onto a broad valley. Jack had arrived at the Missouri River, and over on the other side was his destination state. Ahead was the spot where the Mormons crossed the river on their walk to Utah back in the mid-1800s. Before the bus crossed the river, it turned north on I-29 and went 40 miles upstream. Then it turned back west on a state highway which led to a bridge over the Missouri River. Jack felt a surge of excitement as he looked down at the same river that Lewis and Clark traveled in their expedition to find a passage to the Pacific coast. Then Jack snapped back to the journey at hand as the bus rolled past the big green sign stating, "Nebraska...the good life".

3. NEBRASKA

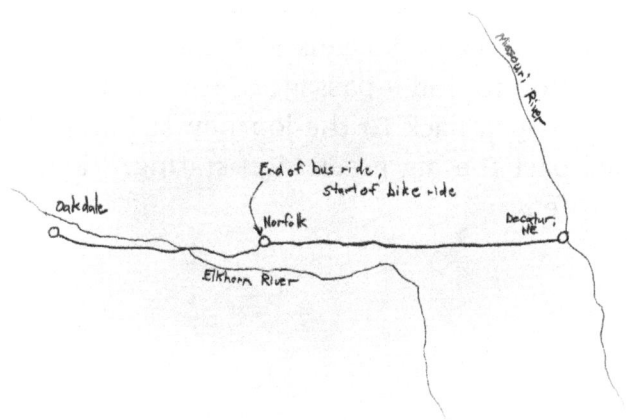

Jack watched with curiosity as the bus drove through the small town of Decatur, Nebraska. What a different life these folks must live compared to Chicago. No taxis. No skyscrapers. No people, at least none that he could see, just a few cars parked in front of a handful of stores. The houses were so spread out compared to urban Chicago. Before he knew it, the bus was back up to speed in the rolling fields.

Every mile or so, the bus drove past a residence along the two-lane highway. Jack could spot the farmhouses from a distance since they all had a line of trees planted around them. The trees protect the houses from the winter winds that howl across the open fields. Most of the farms also had large, round, steel structures nearby. Jack figured that these stored the crops. The tall, rectangle-shaped buildings housed all their tractors. Each farm looked to Jack like its own little kingdom, surrounded by a vast, green lawn.

Every ten or twenty miles, the bus would slow down momentarily for another small town. Each town had a main street, sometimes paved with bricks. Jack could see billboards for a bank, a bar, a cafe, a grocery store, and sometimes a lumberyard. What curious, sleepy little towns these were.

Once in a while, the bus drove past some large pens of cattle. No grass grew in these pens. If the wind was right, Jack could detect his first whiff of cow manure. He figured that he might as well get accustomed to that odor. Farley said, "It smells like money."

The bus turned onto highway 275, and Jack realized that he was nearing the end of the line when he saw the sign that read Norfolk 24 miles. He also remembered Farley's note about the correct way to pronounce "Norfolk."

If you say "Nor-folk" or "Nor-foke" or worse, then people will know that you're not from around here. The town's original name was "North Fork" since it was on the Elkhorn River's North Fork. The original settlers shortened the name to "Norfork," but when the post office filed for the town name, they somehow misspelled it as "Norfolk." If you say "Nor-fork," then you will fit in just fine.

Jack went through his checklist one more time to make sure that he wouldn't forget to purchase last-minute provisions. Granola bars and water topped his list. He made a mental note to ask a store clerk if he might be overlooking something. He could feel a little surge of adrenaline as the city came into view. The bus pulled into the station and rolled to a stop. Jack gathered his packs and shuffled to the door. The sun was sinking low over the city as Jack waited anxiously at the side of the bus to retrieve his bike from the belly storage. He started feeling pangs of helplessness as he pulled the tarped bike from the compartment and dragged it to his pile of baggage. Suddenly, it seemed like his whole life lay in a heap in the middle of the parking lot. The sun was going down on his euphoria as reality set in.

Jack gathered himself, unwrapped his bike, strapped on the bags, and headed west, searching for a park where he could spend the night. A few blocks later, he decided to stop at a convenience store to ask for directions. When the cashier heard his predicament, she said, "Oh, I know where you need to go. Turn south on First Street, and follow it a mile and a half to the Elkhorn River. Before you get to the river, you will see a sign for the Cowboy Trail parking lot. Turn in there and follow the bike trail up the river, and it will take you right to the Ta-Ha-Zouka Park campground."

"Thanks," replied Jack, and he turned back for the door. He hopped on his bike and continued west, following the lady's directions. Fifteen minutes later, he arrived at the Cowboy Trailhead and turned onto it. By now, it was getting dark, but street lights lit the trail enough to see. A few minutes later, he arrived at the campground, dropped twelve dollars in the self-pay station, and then selected a spot to put up his tent.

The campground was well lit, so he didn't have any trouble setting up his pup tent. When he rolled his sleeping bag out, he could feel the anxiety start to melt away as he crawled into the little cocoon. "This is great," he muttered to himself as he lay listening to his first Nebraska quiet. "So this is what it's like to hear nothing." After a few minutes, he could detect a high-pitched buzz. It grew louder, sounding like a remote-controlled airplane. Jack knew the sound of a mosquito. Chicago ranks as one of the most mosquito-infested cities in the U.S. "Great. I forgot to buy mosquito repellent," he muttered to himself. He slapped his forehead and wiped freshly drawn blood along with the squished insect from his skin. "The little bugger must have flown in while I had the tent door open. I guess they have mosquitoes in Nebraska too."

Jack lay and listened to the sounds. He wondered at the curious belching sound made by the nighthawk in flight. While in a dive, its feathers create a sound like the "brrrt" from an A-10 Warthog Gatling gun. This peculiar bird zipped erratically over his tent, snatching moths out of the air. In the distance, he could hear the slight gurgle of the Elkhorn River. Other than a far-off dog bark, all was quiet in this corner of the world. Eventually, the sandman overcame the excitement of the day, and Jack drifted off into peaceful sleep.

At the slightest hint of morning light, the robins started singing. Their song was loud enough to rouse Jack from his first night's stay in Nebraska. He lay and wondered what the birds were communicating. They seemed to be telling each other important news about their day ahead.

An hour later, Jack glanced at his watch for the tenth time and decided to crawl out of his sleeping quarters. "It's not even 6:00 in the morning, and I'm getting up... weird." The sun quickly followed him up and started drying the night dew from his tent. Jack wandered down to the water and watched it gurgle past. The Elkhorn was nothing like his home river. The Chicago River is more like a canal with steel walls and imperceptible flow. This Nebraska stream was shallow with sandbars and a very noticeable current. He wondered if he could catch a fish for breakfast. He envisioned a nice trout on a stick over an open fire, like in the old western movies. Then he remembered that he hadn't purchased a fishing license yet. "One more thing to buy this morning," he mused.

He ate a granola bar back at his tent and then rolled up his sleeping bag and stowed it in the waterproof duffle bag. Then he rolled up and packed his tent. After strapping everything to his bike, he headed north into town to find a store. Luckily, he didn't have to pedal far. A mile and a half up the road, he came to a superstore that carried everything he needed. He bought bottled water, more granola bars, mosquito repellent, a fishing license, and some apples. He also bought a road map, hopped back on his bike, and headed south to the Cowboy Trail.

The Cowboy Trail is a hike/bike trail built on the abandoned Chicago and North Western Railway. Jack figured on taking this trail as far west as possible and then divert onto the paralleling highway. According to his map, this trail passes through several small cities en route to Valentine, 195 miles west. He could stop in each town and ask for the whereabouts of Farley Hayes. Finding Farley looked to be an adventure.

The trail started as smooth concrete but quickly turned to gravel. It was straight as a train track through fields of corn and beans. Then it turned south, crossed the Elkhorn river, and turned back west again. A stretch of flat farm ground lay between Jack and his first glimpse of the Sandhills.

Ahead lay an endless road rising nearly 3,000 feet in elevation to the western Sandhills' highest peaks. Yesterday's bus ride carried him from 500 to 1,500 feet above sea level, a change approximately the Trump Tower's height. His bike ride ahead would be equivalent to ascending the tallest skyscraper in Chicago, the Willis Tower, two times.

Jack's destination was the town of Neligh, 36 miles to the west. He pedaled along the gravel path as the morning summer sun grew hot on his back. The month of June is the month of growth in Nebraska. The long hours of daylight fuel the crops to stretch quickly skyward. Seeds planted just a few weeks ago were by now rows of leg-high corn.

Ten miles up the trail, Jack came to Battle Creek, named after a proposed attack of Nebraska Militia and the U.S. Army on a Pawnee village back in 1859. The Pawnee chief surrendered before the battle could take place, though. The train tracks arrived in the young town of Battle Creek in 1879, in its westward push for the gold rush in the Black Hills.

Proceeding up the old railroad trail, Jack came to more whistle stops every six to eight miles. Meadow Grove, Tilden, and Oakdale; each quiet little town had its gas station convenience store where he could stop and get a snack and a cold drink.

Shortly after departing Oakdale, Jack noticed an opening in the trees to his left. The land beyond rose to the horizon in slight grass-covered undulations.

Scattered about on these strange mini hills were green, spear tipped rosettes topped with a staff of creamy flowers. He pondered at this new sight, not realizing that he gazed upon soapweed "yuccas"- the trademark plant of the Sandhills. He finally reached the eastern tip of a drift of sand that stretched from here to forever.

4. AWAKENING

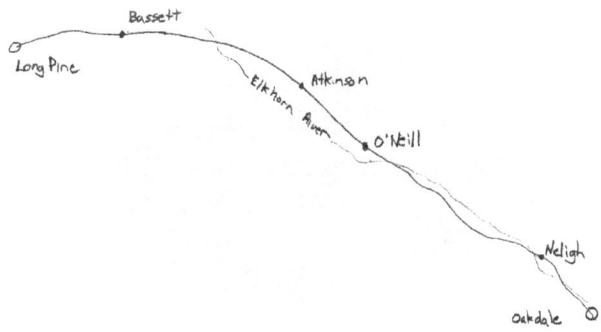

Jack's first encounter with the Sandhills was nothing more than a side-glance as he cycled along the Cowboy Trail. As quickly as it appeared, it vanished as he crossed the Elkhorn River. The Elkhorn on the east and the Niobrara River farther west loosely form the hills' upper boundary. Most of the water in these rivers flows from the giant Ogallala Aquifer lying beneath the Sandhills.

Mid-afternoon, Jack pedaled the final gap of this thirty-seven-mile leg into a town called Neligh. At the east end, he found a park with a hot shower for a $5 fee. Spotting a shade tree, Jack decided to set up camp for the night. He stowed his sleeping gear inside the tent and headed into town to find something to eat.

After stuffing his young appetite with pizza, he cycled around town to experience the area's culture. Spotting a black sign in front of some well-kept old buildings, he coasted over and discovered a historical marker that described Neligh's water-powered flour mill. The mill, now a museum, operated for nearly 100 years, grinding corn and wheat grown by area farmers to be marketed all over the United States.

A strange newness swept over him as he traveled back in time to this world so different from his. Life here seemed to run in slow motion, stretching minutes into moments and months into seasons. He puzzled over this bizarre sensation as he hopped on his bike and headed back to camp.

Back at the tent, he grabbed his backpack and fishing kit and rode down to the river. "At least this part is like Chicago," he determined as he got off his bike and walked down to the water with his backpack. He constructed his fishing rod from the travel kit and attached a lure. He made a few casts into the river current and then set the rod down for a break. "Fishing's the same too," he groaned as he plopped down under a tree on the riverbank.

His mind picked up where it left off back at the old flour mill. What caused that weird feeling? Farley wrote about the Sandhills' capacity to alter a newcomer's temperament. He wasn't even in the Sandhills, yet he sensed a change already. Jack pulled out Farley's book and opened it to a page titled *Resensitizing*.

I've witnessed many newcomers to the Sandhills. People show up from all over the U.S. and sometimes other countries to hunt, fish, or experience ranching. I see a change come over them as each day passes. They arrive with their internal clocks set on urban standard time, much different from Sandhills time. They also show up with their five senses tuned to the city and go through a mild shock as they step into this vast sea of sand and grass.

Eyes accustomed to buildings, streets, and trees search for familiar sights but see only hills and grass. Ears desensitized by mechanical sounds, hear nothing customary. The stillness on a calm day can be deafening to a person desperate for noise. Noses familiar to exhaust fumes readjust to ultra-fresh air. Feet and legs trained to walk on hard surfaces find the soft sand challenging. Taste buds freak out in their virgin experience with wild plums and chokecherries.

Jack paused for a minute to look out over the water. Considering Farley's words, he noticed the smell of the river. The lush aroma drifting off the water hinted at vitality. Life hung in the air, attracting creatures to the water's edge. Jack watched a curious mink scamper past his shoes in its erratic jaunt upriver. Then he noticed little silver flashes in the water. Schools of fathead minnows filed upstream, possibly alarmed by the mink. The river contained all sorts of life. Jack just needed to wake his senses to see it.

Most significantly, one must adjust to the expanse of unpopulated space. People in the city are used to seeing lots of other people. Out here, you could walk, ride a horse, or even drive a car for an hour and not see another soul. If you happen to see someone, it's only logical to stop, shut off your engine and chat for a spell. Neighbors who live miles away probably converse more face to face than city folks who live a few feet apart.

Adjusting to the wide-open spaces takes some time. Urban foreigners come to the Sandhills knowing only street numbers. They don't understand the concept of giving directions in enormous numbers of miles and compass points. One must learn a sense of direction and adapt to long drives in this part of the world.

Jack looked up as an old pickup truck rolled past the road above and stopped upstream. An older man got out and said something to his wildly barking passengers as he slammed the door shut and then pulled a fishing rod and bucket out of the back. The man in bib-overalls picked his way down to the river and shoved a rod holder into the sand. Then he opened a glass jar from the bucket and fished something out to put on his hook. Baited up, he gave the big old rod a swing and watched his hook and sinker plop into the river. Then he stuck the pole into the rod holder and sat down on the bucket.

Jack glanced at his tiny travel fishing rod and wondered if it was adequate. His fishing experience thus far in life was limited to city park ponds. His mom admirably tried to help him fish, but she didn't have the expertise to teach the art. Farley described experiences he had as a fishing guide, but he didn't disclose any secret tips. He was going to have to learn on his own.

Suddenly, the dogs went wild in the old truck, jumping up and barking out the window openings. Their master was fighting a fish! Jack watched in awe as the gent leaned back against his arched rod. A large tail flopped out of the current and threw a spray of shiny beads across the water. Minutes later, the fish bellied out onto the sand in front of the old fisherman. Then he reached down, grabbed it behind the head, and hoisted it up to admire.

Jack couldn't take it any longer. He had to find out how the fellow did it. He packed up his stuff and rode up alongside the truck to watch. The dogs now had a new reason to bark, and the man, sensing a change in their voice, turned around and discovered his young spectator.

"Hello, sonny. Didn't see ya sitting there," he exclaimed.

"Just saw you catch a fish," Jack responded, " and I was wondering how you did it."

The old man glanced back at his rod tip and said, "Nothing special." Then reconsidering Jack's question, he added, "Except for my bait, it might be kind of special."

"What's special about it?" asked Jack.

"It's my secret recipe. Catfish love it," replied the old man. He stood up and pulled the jar out of the bucket. "You start with fresh chicken guts, add some anise oil, and let it simmer in the sun for a few days. The smell takes a little getting used to."

Jack felt his stomach somersault as he stared at the contents in the jar. He could only imagine what it smelled like and braced for the lid removal. Thankfully though, the old fisherman put it back in the pail.

"You're not from around here, are you?" asked the man as he sat down.

"No, I'm from Chicago," replied Jack.

After a pause, the old man said, "Chicago? What are ya doing here?"

Jack thought about this question for a minute and answered, "I'm searching for something, I guess." After another pause, "I'm looking for someone. His name is

Farley Hayes. You wouldn't happen to know him?"

"Never heard of him," replied the old man, "But I hope ya find what you're looking for." He felt around in all his pockets and then exclaimed, "Dang it all to heck! Where's my cigarettes? Must've left them in the truck." He begrudgingly got up from his stool and shuffled up the bank. When he tried to open the truck door, though, it was locked shut. "Dang it! I told you kids not to lock this door again!" Two pairs of hound dog eyes stared innocently at him through the glass. "You guys unlock this door right now!" The dogs just looked at him.

"I might be able to reach through the opening and unlock the door," offered Jack.

The old man looked at Jack's long skinny arms and said, "By golly, you just might. Go ahead and give it a whirl." Jack got off his bike and eased up to the truck window, not knowing what to expect from these big, boisterous dogs. "Now, you guys leave his arm alone." Jack looked at the man to see if he was kidding, but he seemed serious. He strummed his fingers on the glass to test the dogs, and they just sat, expecting a treat for good behavior. They looked innocent enough. Jack put his right hand in the opening, prepared for quick withdrawal. Nothing. He slowly reached downward, eyes locked on the closest dog's eyes. He groped for buttons on the side of the door, pressing each one gingerly. At last, he heard a thud as the doors unlocked, pulling his arm quickly out of danger.

"Got it!" exclaimed Jack.

"Thank you... I didn't get yer name." the old man said as he stuck a gnarly fist out to shake hands with his Good Samaritan.

"It's Jack," as Jack once again reached his right

4. AWAKENING | 34

hand out to the unknown.

Later that evening, after a long hot shower, Jack ate a couple of granola bars and an apple and then retired to his tent. It's time to plan for tomorrow, thought Jack, pulling out his phone and road map. He Google searched a satellite map of northern Nebraska and found Neligh. Following the Cowboy Trail westerly, Jack discovered the trail washed out between Neligh and Clearwater, so the new route hopped onto Highway 275. Looking at the map, he would bike through hundreds of big green circles en route to O'Neill, forty miles west. Sleep came easy on this, his second night in Nebraska.

The robins were at it again early in the morning, but Jack ignored them to get another hour of sleep. He packed up and headed into town for some pancakes, then hit the road west. He decided to try out the highway to Clearwater, avoiding detours on the Cowboy Trail.

As Jack started pedaling up the highway, he noticed that motorists were giving him a strange signal. About every fifth driver raised his index finger as he went by. Jack took it as a friendly gesture since they didn't show signs of road rage.

Highway 275 was smooth, with paved shoulders to ride on. It paralleled the Elkhorn River, with no hills to climb. As Jack cycled west, he noticed all the cropland on his right, but the south's terrain turned to grassland. Small lakes started showing up in the fields of grass. Jack was looking for this change in topography. It was how Farley described the Sandhills.

Jack made a pit stop in Clearwater and then again in Ewing for lunch. Mid-afternoon, he reached O'Neill, his destination for night three. He stopped at a station with a shop to do maintenance on his bike. So far, it was holding up. He replenished his water supply and headed south to find the Carney Park campground, his home for the night.

Summer Sunday afternoons in northern Nebraska are for picnics, relaxing, and rodeo. Weekends without a sanctioned rodeo spell roping practice for the hard-core cowboys. When Jack wheeled into the campground, he noticed several pickup trucks with horse trailers parked nearby. He was about to get his first taste of cowboy life.

Jack rode through the campground, looking for a spot to camp. He stopped under some trees by the rodeo arena, pitched his tent, and then biked over to watch the action. Gazing through the steel bars at the riders inside, the action instantly caught his fancy. He'd seen cowboys on TV and read about them in books, but never witnessed them in real life. This city kid was spellbound.

The cowboys rode effortless circuits astride big, beautiful horses, chasing a plastic calf on skis that trailed behind a four-wheeled ATV. The cowboys took turns roping the horns on the fake steer, twirling big loops as they cantered past. Man and beast seemed to be one, with the sole purpose of catching that runaway calf.

As he watched, it suddenly became apparent that some of the cowboys weren't boys. One was smaller in stature, with blonde hair flipping out from under her hat. Jack's eyes fixed on her as she galloped past. She wore blue jeans and a long-sleeve shirt, just like the rest of the guys. Some men wore Stetsons, and others wore ball caps; she sported a white straw hat. She appeared to be about his age, maybe a shade younger. This slight cowgirl captivated Jack with her graceful confidence.

Then, too quickly, the show was over. The cowboys rode out of the arena and headed down the lane to their horse trailers. Jack had to think fast. He remembered Farley's comment about how Sandhillers stop on the road to say hi. Jack quickly pedaled around the arena and positioned himself between the cowboys and their trucks. Then he casually rode toward them and stopped on the side of the trail to let them pass. He greeted each one as they rode by, but no one stopped to talk. Then, surprisingly, two cowgirls brought their horses to a halt alongside Jack and his bicycle.

"I noticed you watching over at the arena. You look like you're not from around here," spoke the blonde.

Jack, distracted by her naturally stunning eyes, tried to think up an intelligent question. "I'm Jack... I'm from Chicago. I was just wondering why you were throwing a leash on the pretend cow."

The girl smiled and introduced herself, "I'm Savannah, I'm from Hyannis, and this is Dusty, glancing over at her friend. We're practicing breakaway and team roping for the high school rodeo."

Jack floundered for another brilliant question and came up with, "Don't you have any real sports, like basketball, in Nebraska?"

Savannah smiled again and responded with a spunky yet polite, "Yeah, we have basketball, but rodeo is the REAL sport." Then they rode off.

Jack biked downtown to get a hamburger and mull over his short but sweet encounter with a real cowgirl. He rehashed his conversation with her as he munched down his french fries. Did his words sound stupid? Did he sound like he was making fun of her sport? If so, she seemed to take it very well. Where did she say she lived? High Anise, or something like that. He typed it into his smartphone, and Google asked, "Did you mean: Hyannis Nebraska?" Then he checked the distance and was astonished to discover that she lived 215 miles west of here. Who would drive that far to practice? He decided that Nebraskans were pretty serious about this thing called rodeo.

Back at the campground that evening, he called his mom and recounted all his adventures over the last two-and-a-half days. She was glad to hear his voice and sounded happy for him. "Just be careful, Jack. Nebraska dangers are different from Chicago dangers." He said everything was going great and promised he would take care of himself.

An older couple sat at a picnic table across from Jack's campsite. Curious about this young man with nothing but a tent and a bicycle, they struck up a conversation. "Where are you headed?" the husband asked.

"The Sandhills," replied Jack. "Where are you headed?"

"Montana...Washington, way out west," replied the man. "We started from our home in Tennessee."

"Sounds like a long trip," offered Jack.

"Yes, three weeks. Are you from around here?" asked the man.

"Chicago. Everyone here seems to know that I'm not from Nebraska. Do I look that much different than them?" asked Jack.

The couple looked him over closely, and the man concluded, "You might be a little more sunburned, and you're not wearing blue jeans."

"And you're skinny," added the wife. "Maybe you just need to get a Husker ball cap."

The couple chuckled over their observations, and then the man grew serious and asked, "Did you know it's supposed to storm tomorrow?"

Jack shook his head, "I guess I need to pay more attention to weather forecasts."

"I wouldn't want to get caught in a storm on a bicycle. It's bad enough in an RV. Keep an eye on the sky."

Jack heeded this bit of sobering news and decided to do some planning for the next day. He had never weathered a thunderstorm outdoors. Farley wrote about the weather in his journal, so Jack pulled it out and flipped to the thunderstorm page.

I learned a respect for weather on April 20th, 1974. A stiff south wind swirled up a tornado that we stood and watched from our front porch for over an hour. It approached from the southwest, growing taller by the minute. At one point, the primary tornado had two tails spinning circles around it. It looked like a giant taffy pulling machine, with the candy clump being grass and dirt. It veered to the east a couple of miles from our farm, hitting a dairy, and then proceeded to chop the town of Arcadia in half. I will never forget watching the chunks of sod and cow pies falling from the sky and the sound of cattle bawling from their trauma.

Jim, my old fishing buddy, told of a tornado that hit his neighbor's house on a Sunday afternoon back in 1953. First, it destroyed the home and took the life of a bachelor, then it traversed a few hills and struck the Madsen home.

Mr. and Mrs. Madsen, their son, two daughters, and five grandchildren were all killed; their bodies scattered across the hillside. Jim said he still gets a sick feeling in his gut, thinking about the child's finger he found while helping clean up debris the next day.

Summer storms can turn a pleasant day into chaos in just a few minutes. Severe thunderstorms can have life-threatening wind-driven hail and lightning, not to mention tornadoes. It's best to learn how to read the sky to avoid catastrophe.

Thunderstorms usually occur in the late afternoon or evening, following a day with a stiff south wind. Often the skies are sunny in the morning; then, some high-level fish scale-looking clouds form out of the blue. These "musky scales" foretell storms to come. These clouds will disappear as quickly as they begin, so you need to be watching for them. Later, you will see cumulonimbus clouds forming. These are puffy-sided clouds that build straight up; I call them "towers of power." If they build up east of you, don't worry about them. But if they build to the west, watch out. When the cloud grows tall enough, it flattens out and forms an anvil top. If a round dome punches out through the top of the anvil, be doubly concerned. You now have a supercell thunderstorm.

Lightning is the deadliest feature of summer storms. Cows reaching through a barbed-wire fence for greener grass during a thunderstorm have a death wish. I've heard of multiple cows dying in one strike. Don't run for the shelter of a lone tree during a thunderstorm; it's a lightning magnet. Get as low as possible and stay away from metal.

We get hailstones the size of softballs in some of the supercell thunderstorms. Even more destructive, though, are the smaller, saucer-shaped stones driven by 70 mph *wind. This kind of hail will strip the bark from a tree. I got caught by a freak hail storm in the middle of a lake with a couple of eighty-year-old gentlemen while fishing one day. A small cloud came over from the southwest and looked like it might rain. I told the fellows to don their rain suits, which they were in the process of doing when I heard a big sploosh in the water a few yards away. Then another one. Hail! I grabbed the only protection that I could find, a big rubber landing net, and told the guys to huddle as I held it over their heads. Luckily, we didn't get any direct hits.*

  Jack closed the book and stewed over Farley's weather stories. He didn't figure severe weather into the equation when planning this trip. He pictured himself out on some lonely stretch of highway, desperately seeking shelter from the wind, hail, and lightning. Then a thought entered his mind. He could take refuge under a bridge. Now, he could rest easy, knowing he had a plan for tomorrow's uncertainty.

  Monday morning dawned bright and clear with a south breeze. Jack cleared camp and packed his panniers for the day's ride. He bid farewell to his Tennessee neighbors and rode into town, following his nose into a restaurant that smelled of sausage and coffee. He enjoyed an excellent hot breakfast. The patrons glanced at him, much like a meager church congregation observing a stranger walk up the aisle. He thought about his conversation the evening before about his unfamiliar appearance to the locals. To fit in, he might have to visit a clothing store. But that can wait; this day, he has many miles to cover, and possible bad weather.

  Jack continued his journey on Highway 20, preferring the paved surface to the graveled trail. The wind picked up as he traveled northwest. The previous two days were relatively calm, which made for easy cycling. Today was different. The stiff southerly crosswind created a new struggle with keeping the bike on course. Jack settled in for a long, stubborn ride.

Nineteen miles up the road, Jack entered the town of Atkinson. He made a quick pit stop and continued on the next ten-mile stretch to Stuart. Here, the highway curves and points straight west, making it even more challenging to fight the south wind. Ten miles later, he cycled past the tiny town of Newport, continuing to Bassett. He noticed the fish scales high in the sky on this twelve-mile stretch, and a little shot of adrenaline entered his muscles, boosting his strength to fight the wind.

Bassett is situated on and around a rare rise thus far on the Cowboy Trail. Highway 20 climbs the east side of town and then coasts down past a school and football field on its way to an intersection with Highway 183 and 7. Jack spotted a gas station at this intersection and pulled in for an afternoon break.

Jack went in and inquired about a good camping spot in the area. "Long Pine State Recreation Area, if you're headed west," replied the friendly cashier. "Just watch out for the storms."

"Thanks, I'll do that," said Jack as he headed back for the door with a handful of snacks. "How far is it?"

"About ten miles," replied the cashier.

Jack stepped back out into the summer heat and stretched his tired legs. He figured that he had ten miles left in him and the campground sounded inviting. He took a look at the sky and noticed that it was getting darker to the west. Above was a high, triangle-shaped cloud that pointed east. He didn't realize that this was the anvil's forward point on a building supercell thunderstorm.

Back on the road, Jack noticed that the wind was subsiding a bit. He was thankful for the cloud cover and more relaxed travel. The Cowboy Trail, which strayed off north for the last twenty miles, suddenly showed up again. Farm ground still dominated the countryside, making him wonder if he would ever escape this flatland.

A few miles from Long Pine, Jack noticed the sky ahead had changed into multi-colored bands. Against the horizon was a sheet of steel gray, topped with a layer of bluish-black. Above this was an expanse of green clouds. Jack picked up his pace again with another shot of adrenaline. This time he was pedaling for life.

The cloud bank loomed large in front of him, and flashes of lightning lit up the darkening atmosphere. Thunder rolled across the prairie, warning its creatures to run for cover. Jack could see pine trees now and started thinking about protecting himself. He remembered Farley's counsel against taking refuge under a tree. The highway started curving down into a forested canyon but still afforded no shelter. Finally, he spotted guard rails just as the wall cloud hit, shoving a blast of wind that nearly toppled him. He jumped off his bike and pushed it behind the guard rail to the bridge ahead. It seemed like he would never reach shelter as large wind-driven raindrops pelted him in the face. Then the highway and earth separated and formed a concrete bunker for Jack and his bicycle. He made it to the Pine Creek bridge just as the heart of the storm hit.

Jack huddled against the concrete abutment under the bridge's center as sheets of wind-driven water whipped through the grass below. It was raining so hard that he couldn't see the creek just a few yards away. Then it started hailing. White stones were bouncing across the ground, even under the bridge. Leaf-covered branches, sheared off by hail, flew past. The din was so loud that it almost drowned out the crashes of thunder. Jack shut his eyes and prayed for deliverance. A few minutes later, the wind subsided. Then the hail stopped, and the lightning moved off to the east. A little while later, the rain stopped, and all was quiet except the dull roar and distant thunder of the retreating storm. Jack stood for a minute and listened to the forest come back to life after the onslaught. As he watched the creek carry off ping pong ball-sized hailstones, he concluded that thunderstorms are necessary and very active ingredients in nature's formula.

Jack pushed his bike back to the highway, noticing how the sand soaked up the rain. Back on the road, he stomped his feet, and the sand fell off. "Cool. I don't have to worry about muddy shoes," he muttered to himself as he swung back on his ride. At the top of the hill, he spotted the sign for the Pine Creek State Recreation Area. He turned off the highway and headed south to the park, and turned back east. He coasted down, past numbered campsites to the bottom of the canyon. The few vacationers he saw were assessing damage from the storm. He was thankful that he didn't have camp set up yet; the hail might have shredded his tent.

He picked out a campsite on a grassy knoll just above the stream and parked his bike. Then he walked back up to the pay station and put in eight dollars for his night's stay. Back at the campsite, he cleared some fallen tree limbs from the spot for his tent. He noticed the fire pit and wondered if he could start a fire with wet branches. The thunderstorm and melting hail had cooled the air temperature nearly thirty degrees, making a bonfire sound comforting.

He noticed the fire pit next door had a stack of unused firewood, so he hauled it over and piled it up to dry a bit. Then, he went looking for some kindling-something that he'd seen in the movies to start fires. He dug down under a large pine tree and pulled out a clump of old needles that felt only slightly damp, which he placed in the pit. Next, he snapped some dead sticks over the tinder. But when he held his new lighter underneath, the pile only produced a tiny whiff of smoke. He needed some dry fuel. Then an idea struck him. He walked up to the bathroom and borrowed some toilet paper. Placing it under the pine needles, he touched a flame to it, and voila! He had a fire that lasted about ten seconds. Back at the restroom, he rolled off a much larger fire source. This time he meant business. The paper blazed under the needles, drying them to ignition. An hour later, Jack was sitting back to a crackling fire.

Jack got out his cook set and a package of soup for his evening meal. He just needed to add water and set it on the fire grate, stirring occasionally. The soup heated quickly, and Jack enjoyed his first meal cooked over an open fire. By the time he cleaned up supper, he was almost too tired to set up his tent.

He slept well until the middle of the night when he woke to the sound of distant thunder. "Oh no, not again," mumbled Jack as he watched far-off flashes cut through the blackness. He lay and listened, but thankfully, the thunder didn't get any louder. "Storm must be going somewhere else." Then he drifted off to sleep again.

The sun's rays cleared the canyon's east rim, pushing the deep shadows away long before Jack stirred the following day. He lay in his cozy quarters and listened to the warm tranquility of Pine Creek. He figured the last time that he felt this snug, he was in his mother's womb. His state of euphoria carried him back to the good times in life, memories so fond that they gave Jack a lump in his throat and a tear in his eye. When he finally snapped out of his trance, he wondered what that was all about. This was his second mind aberration of recent. "Must be one of those secret things that Farley always wrote about," whispered Jack, breaking the stillness.

5. TIN SOLDIERS

The frontiers must be well guarded. — Matthew Henry

Stomach grumbles eventually forced Jack out of the sack on this bright Tuesday morning. He mounted his bike, hoping to find a place to eat breakfast. His map showed a town called Long Pine a couple of miles to the southeast, so he pumped his bicycle up the hill to the park entrance and took a left. Soon he came to a tee where he turned east and crossed an old bridge where he glanced down and spotted his campsite, nestled in the curve of the stream. The road took him past cabins for rent, and soon he entered the village.

Long Pine seemed different from the other towns that Jack had biked through so far. He rode past older houses painted in various colors. Some had picket fences, some had dog houses in the back yard, and most had a shade tree or two out front. But a couple of things seemed peculiar. Each home had well-manicured lawns, except for the spot under a slightly rusted pickup truck parked out front. The vintage trucks appeared to be no more than yard ornaments. As Jack cycled down the streets, he began to wonder if anybody lived there. It reminded him of movies depicting mock towns set up to test an atomic bomb detonation's effects. Everything was in place, except people.

He turned south on the main street and slowly rode past the aging businesses searching for a restaurant. He rode past a lumberyard and a post office. A couple of cars sat in front of the grocery store, so he stopped and entered. The sales clerk, noticing this young, out-of-place stranger, said, "Hi, can I help you?"

"Yeah," Jack replied. "I was looking for somewhere to eat. Is there any place in town?"

"There is, but it isn't open until ten. It's the Sandhills Lounge two doors south."

Jack glanced at his watch. 8:30. He couldn't wait an hour and a half to eat, so he wandered down the store aisles, looking for breakfast. He stood and studied the AR-15 rifle on display with a $599 price tag. That's something he'd never seen in a grocery store back home. He settled on a package of powdered donuts and paid the cashier. "Is there anything to see around here?" he asked.

"Have you been to the old railroad bridge on the Cowboy Trail yet?"

"No. Is it far from here?" replied Jack

"Go two blocks south and take the trail west a half a mile. It's pretty cool."

"Thanks, I'll check it out. And, in case you're wondering where I'm from, it's Chicago."

The clerk smiled at Jack and replied, "Welcome to Nebraska!"

Jack followed the old trail to the bridge and parked his bike. The view from atop one of the highest bridges in the state was spectacular. Pine Creek originates from the Seven Springs, flowing out of the

Sandhills a few miles south of town. These springs produce some of the purest water on earth, filtered naturally by sand. Over the years, the creek cut a canyon to the Niobrara River fifteen miles to the north. The steep walls of the valley are forested with pines and cedars. Ash and oak trees dot the meadow below. Jack leaned against the rail and ate powdered donuts as he took in the pristine summer morning.

When Jack finally decided to mount his bike again, he grimaced in pain. The previous day's ride took its toll on his legs. He decided to stay another day and explore this intriguing slice of paradise.

Back in town, Jack rode the nostalgic streets, curiously studying its unique charm. On the east side, he discovered a building that looked to be an abandoned schoolhouse. Someone artistically adorned the two-and-a-half-story brick building, making it look more like an asylum. Next to the street, all the way around the perimeter, were stone columns wrapped in barbed wire. On top of each post was a white pebble. These stone pillars guarded each side of the cement walk leading to the front door. Jack's eye followed this trail to the sign above the door, which mysteriously read, AND ONE TIN SOLDIER RIDES AWAY.

Long Pine School

Glancing at his watch, he headed back to Main street and the Sandhills Lounge. He'd always envisioned entering a western saloon, like Matt Dillon, but feared that he looked more like Barney Fife. The place was empty, except for a man behind the bar, who glanced at Jack and said, "Hi, can I help you?"

Jack sauntered up to the bar and said, "Yes, I was wondering if you serve breakfast."

The man smiled and replied, "I can cook you a hamburger if you'd like."

By now, Jack was hungry enough to eat a skunk, so he said, "Yeah, that would be great!"

The bartender left for the kitchen, and Jack had a seat, glancing around the room. The bar top immediately caught his eye. It was a thick wooden slab cut from the center of a tall pine tree. The slab's front edge was the irregular face of the tree, with the bark peeled off. It gave the room a rugged, no-nonsense feel.

The sound of ground beef hitting the hot skillet shifted Jack's stomach juices into overdrive. The bartender returned and continued their conversation.
"Are you biking?"
"Yes."
"Where are you headed?"
"The Sandhills."
The bartender considered this answer, then asked, "Anywhere in particular?"
"I'm looking for a man named Farley Hayes. Have you heard of him?"
"Doesn't ring a bell. Do you know where he lives?"
"All I know is that he lives somewhere in the Sandhills."
"That's a pretty big area. You may have to narrow it down a bit."
"He writes about lakes, wild animals, and cowboys. Does that narrow it down?"
"Sounds pretty much like the entire Sandhills." With that, the bartender went back to the kitchen and returned a moment later with a big juicy hamburger and fries.
Jack wolfed down his meal while they made small talk about the previous evening's storm, Chicago, and cycling. He appreciated the friendliness of the people in this part of the world. As he paid his tab, he told the bartender, "Thanks for the best tasting hamburger I've ever eaten!"
"You're welcome, and good luck with your endeavor!"
As Jack rode out of town, he remembered the old school and the slogan above the door. He kicked himself for not inquiring about it back at the bar. Mysteries have

always intrigued him, and this one had him baffled. He filed AND ONE TIN SOLDIER RIDES AWAY into his memory bank for future reference as he pedaled back to camp.

Back at the campsite, Jack sat at the picnic table and studied his environs. The swift-flowing stream was the focal point of the painting before him. Deciduous and coniferous trees filled most of the canvas with lush green clearings along the stream banks. Above all this was a canopy of blue sky laced with white cumulus clouds.

Jack was in the mood to read. He pulled the table under a shade tree, topped it with his sleeping bag, and stretched out on it. He opened Farley's journal and sifted through the pages until he spotted a title that caught his interest.

Guardians of the Hills

The cattleman is a unique individual. Mostly, he wears the symbolic white hat, which he removes in the presence of ladies. He respects his fellow man with an extra firm handshake while looking him in the eye. In short, he lives by the Code of the West.

* Live each day with courage.
*Take pride in your work.
*Always finish what you start.
*Do what has to be done.
*Be tough but fair.
*When you make a promise, keep it.
*Ride for the brand.
*Talk less and say more.
*Remember that some things aren't for sale.
*Know where to draw the line.

Sandhill ranchers take the last entry of the Code a step further. They have drawn a seven hundred thirty-mile imaginary line around their beloved Nebraska hills and stand guard against anyone posing a threat to their domain. They are proud of their land's pristine beauty and threaten the use of whatever force necessary to keep it that way. Anyone messing with their water, scenery, or Code of ethics is lumped into a culture of unwanted people that they label as "crazies." Sandhillers keep a wary eye on environmentalists, industrialists, or just about anyone who doesn't make their living raising beef.

The term, Castle Doctrine, dating back to 17th century English common law, states that an Englishman's home is his castle. Matthew Henry, an 18th-century minister, wrote in his Commentary on Exodus 22:2, "Every man's house is a castle, and God's law, as well as man's, sets a guard upon it; he that assaults it does so at his peril." Using this doctrine as a guideline, Sandhill residents collectively guard their 20,000 square-mile "castle" with an invisible yet widely respected force.

In 1884, a vigilante committee known as the "Regulators" captured a young horse thief named Kid Wade. He stole thirty horses on the Niobrara river north of Bassett and fled west to the Black Hills. He circled back east, following the White River to the Missouri, which he followed downstream to Niobrara. Moving upstream, he started selling the horses to farmers. But when a man suspected him, he escaped to Iowa. The Regulators traced him to LeMars and set a trap for him—seizing him at gunpoint. They brought the young horse thief back to the scene of his crime at Carns on the Niobrara. They took him to Long Pine, then back to Carns, and then to Bassett. Just after midnight on February 8th, a dozen masked *and armed men hijacked the prisoner, took him outside of town, and hung him from a railroad whistling post. Later, Kid Wade's father showed up at Carns, threatening to prosecute the vigilantes. His mutilated body was found buried, with his feet sticking out of the ground.*

It's a more civilized world today, but Sandhill ranchers still live in areas so remote that law enforcement officers may be an hour or more away. The mere threat of vigilantism not only wards off potential crimes, but it brings a sense of security to these isolated residents. Winchesters and nooses are no longer a threat, but these days, aircraft and AR-15 rifles provide a more sophisticated security blanket.

In the century following the murder of Kid Wade, numerous other bad men were mysteriously culled out of the Sandhills. In 1987 Ralph Quador drove his Cadillac from California to purchase a ranch near Almeria. The farm economy was in a slump, and he managed to buy up 17,000 acres of grassland at the depressed price of $100 per acre. He quickly made enemies of area folks through his surly attitude and selfish business dealings. He knew nothing about cattle but proceeded to brag about his ranch being the largest in Loup County. So when he was found dead in bed with six .22 caliber bullet holes in his head on January 24th, 2000, no one seemed alarmed or dismayed. His killer was never convicted.

Jack pictured Winchester-toting horse riders leading Kid Wade through the snow past this very spot. Then he remembered the AR-15 for sale at the grocery store. Still nagging him was the mysterious saying above the entrance to the old schoolhouse. He pulled out his phone and googled "And One Tin Soldier Rides Away." Wikipedia describes a song written by a couple of Canadians in the Vietnam war era.

One Tin Soldier

*Listen people to a story
That was written long ago,
'bout a kingdom on a mountain
And the valley folks below.
On the mountain was a treasure
Hidden deep beneath a stone,
And the valley people swore
They'd have it for their very own.
Go ahead and hate your neighbor,
Go ahead and cheat a friend.
Do it in the name of heaven,
You can justify it in the end.
There won't be any trumpets blowing,
Come the judgment day,
On the bloody morning after
One tin soldier rides away.
So the people of the valley
Sent a message up the hill,
Asking for the buried treasure
Tons of gold for which they'd kill.
Came the answer from the kingdom,
With our brothers we will share,
All the riches of the mountain,
All the treasure buried there.
Now the valley cried with anger,
Mount your horses, draw your swords
And they killed the mountain people,
So they won their just rewards
Now they stood before the treasure
On the mountain dark and red*

> *Turned the stone and looked beneath it*
> *Peace on earth, was all it said.*
> *Go ahead and hate your neighbor,*
> *Go ahead and cheat a friend,*
> *Do it in the name of heaven,*
> *You can justify it in the end.*
> *There won't be any trumpets blowing*
> *Come the judgment day,*
> *On the bloody morning after*
> *One tin soldier rides away.*

Songwriters: Brian Potter / Dennis Earle Lambert
One Tin Soldier lyrics © Universal Music Publishing Group

Jack read and reread the lyrics to the song and then listened to it, trying to fit it with Farley's writings. He imagined a tin soldier riding off into the hills after a confrontation between the valley people and the mountain people. It seemed this guy was the only one left standing after a needless war. Perhaps he represents a rancher who tried to fight off the crazies who came seeking the Sandhills' hidden treasures. But when they discovered the plain reality of the prize, they turned and marched away, leaving our soldier alone again in his beloved land. All this conjecture left Jack feeling a little apprehensive about his venture into the hills. What if the Sandhillers don't accept him? But then he remembered that Farley moved into the Sandhills, where they treated him with respect. Maybe if he lives by the Code of the West, all will be well.

6. FISH FOR LIFE

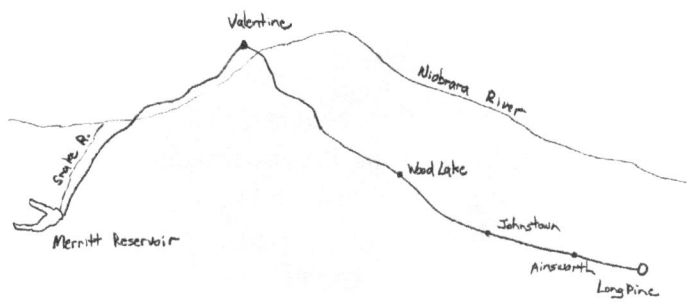

Shouts from an excited youngster shattered the lazy June afternoon stillness. Jack looked up from his picnic table to see a young boy run up the creek bank with a fish flopping on the end of his line. "I caught one, I caught one!" exclaimed the lad as he ran to his campsite. Watching the parents glory over the young man's accomplishment, Jack resolved to learn how to fish.

In a few minutes, he had his pack rod constructed and ready to cast. He fingered through the assortment of small lures and decided on a pink jig with a white plastic twisty tail. Not sure how to tie a proper fishing knot, he settled on a couple of overhands and cinched it down tight. He cast the lure into the swift, crystal clear water at the creek bank, watched it sweep downstream, and then reeled it back in. After a dozen or so casts, he decided that he must be doing something wrong. Peering into the water, he could see lots of pebbles but no fish—it looked like he was going to have to find one.

Moving slowly downstream, he studied every square foot of water, looking for a fish. At an inside curve of the stream, a large log paralleled the shore. The tree caused a current break, and in the quiet water underneath, Jack spied some movement. There, blending in with the pebbles, was a brown trout, undulating slowly to hold its position against the flow. Jack excitedly made a cast in the fish's direction and watched in disbelief as it shot downstream, spooked by his arm movement overhead. Fishing was going to be more challenging than he expected.

Around the corner, Jack spotted another log in the water a few yards downstream. This time he wasn't going to scare the fish. Keeping his distance, Jack eased up to the water's edge and aimed a cast toward the log. Unfortunately, his lure landed on wood, and when he tried to jerk it off, his line snapped, leaving a pink and white ornament on the old water-logged cedar stump. He needed to learn how to tie a better knot.

He googled fishing knots back at the picnic table and sat down to watch videos demonstrating everything from blood knots to the improved surgeon. Finally, he found a video titled "Palomar- Simplest and Strongest Fishing Knot in the World." He watched the video a couple of times and then tried tying one himself. Using another lure out of his pack, he tied it on using the Palomar knot, and to his amazement, he couldn't snap it off with his hands. "Time to get serious," he muttered as he rose to sneak back down to the stream.

He decided to go back to the original log and see if his fish was back. Sure enough, the trout was at its favorite haunt, waiting for some unsuspecting critter to happen by for his lunch. This time Jack eased up to the edge and slowly held his pole out with the lure dangling six feet below the rod tip. He looked like a cat sneaking up on a mouse as he reached out an inch at a time, eyes locked on the fish. The little jig touched the water with the finesse of a mosquito landing on an ear lobe. The jig settled into the current a yard upstream of the fish and disappeared from view behind the log. Suddenly, the trout shot from its ambush position and nailed the lure, peeling line as it sped downstream. He didn't adjust the reel's drag control before he started, and the fish swam at will, undaunted by Jack's furious reeling. When he realized that he wasn't making any headway, he grabbed the line, wrapped it around his fist, and started backing up the bank. The trout leaped from the water a couple of times, the second one landing out on the bank as Jack scrambled back down to pounce on it. "Yeah!" Jack yelled as he clutched the squirming fish to his chest and ran back up the bank, glancing over at the neighbors. "My first fish!"

Jack knelt beside his flopping catch and looked it over. It was about a foot long with a yellow belly and ringed spots down its iridescent side. It was the most beautiful fish that he'd ever seen—and hopefully, the most delicious. Here was his chance to cook a trout over an open fire, as he'd seen on the internet.

First, he needed to clean the fish. By the time he found his knife, the fish had expired in the hot June air.

He remembered his only prior experience with this sort of thing—dissecting a frog in high school biology class. The videos that he watched back at home described trout as the easiest fish to clean and eat. He just needed to open the belly and slip the guts out, and it's ready to cook. Once done, he walked to a hydrant, rinsed the fish off, and then returned to camp to build a fire.

The summer sun had the wood dried out after the previous night's rain, and soon he had a fire going. He walked down to the creek and cut a green willow stick to shove down the fish's throat and into the body cavity. Then he positioned it over the fire to cook. Slowly rotating the fish, he checked it periodically to see how it was doing. He pushed a fork from his mess kit into the thickest part of the flesh, and when it flaked off the bone, he figured it was ready to eat. He pulled the stick out and dropped the fish into his mess kit bowl. Peeling off the blackened skin revealed tan-colored meat that resembled tuna but tasted more like salmon. In a few seconds, he devoured the entire fish and glanced back down at the stream, wondering how long it would take to catch another one.

Jack spent the rest of the day poking wood into the fire and fishing. By sundown, he was exhausted; living off the land was pretty intense. The three fish he managed to catch and consume didn't match the calories he burned in the process; he needed bigger fish.

After sunset, Jack listened to the resident wild turkeys flap up to their night roosts, then he slipped down to the creek with a bar of soap and a wash rag. In the silent darkness, he slid into the frigid spring water, trying not to yelp in shock of instant cold. Twenty seconds later, the shivering boy was back out in the warm summer air, quickly drying off and sneaking back to his tent to get dressed. The warmth of his sleeping bag never felt so good as he listened to the quiet of another Nebraska night.

Dawn brought with it an urge to hit the road again. Jack took down camp and packed it securely on his bike for the day's journey. He regretted leaving this little piece of heaven on earth but knew he had to move on. In a few minutes, Jack was back on Highway 20, heading west again. Eight miles later, he cycled into the town of Ainsworth, stopping only long enough to purchase a breakfast sandwich and carton of orange juice at the gas station.

Ten miles west, Jack rode through Johnstown, a village of sixty-one people that started with the railroad back in 1883. A few miles further, Jack rode out of the cornfields and onto a vast prairie; he was entering ranch country.

The highway curved and aimed northwest for its thirty-three-mile approach to Valentine. Jack rolled along, noticing how the houses were stretching farther apart. He could now ride several miles and not see a single residence. He was getting his first real taste of the Sandhills.

As the summer sun grew higher and hotter on his back, he was thankful for the breeze born from his forward progress. The weather was much like back home in Chicago. It was a little warmer here, but the air was also dryer, so it felt the same. He occasionally glanced at the sky, looking for the telltale signs of a storm. The vast, blue expanse beckoned him on.

Jack turned north off Highway 20 at Wood Lake and rode up Main Street until he came to a shade tree to sit and enjoy a sports drink. The sign said the town had a population of sixty-three. He sat for a minute and compared small-town Nebraska with metropolitan Chicago. These people were of the same human race as the ones where he grew up. They must have the same purposes in life too. They indeed aspire to a fulfilling existence, just like in the big cities. He watched a flatbed ranch truck rattle up the street and then looked over at his trusty old bicycle, which was looking increasingly out of place. There didn't seem to be much need for bicycle couriers in the Sandhills.

Glancing at his map, Jack noted that he would pass through one more town before Valentine. Arabia sounded like a strange name for a community in this part of the world. He did a quick search and discovered that the founder compared the local soil to the sands of the Arabian Desert. The town consisted of a post office and rail station to load cattle until the 1950s. The buildings sifted away when semi-trucks took the place of trains to haul livestock.

Jack knew he was nearing the end of the Cowboy Trail and the scenic bridge over the Niobrara, so he decided to exit the smooth highway at Arabia for the final ten-mile span into Valentine. He stood up, stretched, and mounted his bike.

By now, the sun hovered straight overhead, pushing air temp well into the 90s. Jack pulled out another water bottle every few miles to stay hydrated. He feared that his supply would run out before seeing civilization again. He was riding across the largest underground aquifer in the world, fretting about his water supply.

Lifeblood of the Sandhills

Jack rode past cow herds scattered about the rolling hills and others bunched in the sandy areas around a windmill tank. To this point in life, he only knew that cows were the source of milk and hamburger. These odd creatures didn't pay much attention to the passing cyclist. He planned to understand them better before this adventure was over.

The miles stretched on as the road took him deeper into the hills. When he spotted a sign over an adjacent lane that read Arabia Ranch, he exited onto the Cowboy Trail, which ran along the highway's north side. He rode past the slight remains of Arabia, then the trail split off and headed north through a valley passage. He rode past expansive hay meadows and over the headwaters of Fairfield Creek. From the looks of the trail, he was sharing it with cows and cowboys. He was slowly immersing himself in the land.

The old rail bed now paralleled the highway again with two and a half miles between them. Jack felt isolated from civilization as he pedaled across the vast sea of grass. Clear, black water dotted with willow trees filled the ancient ditches. He could hear frogs croaking and bellowing love songs somewhere down in their watery haunts. At times he was surrounded by so much water that he wondered if he took a wrong turn and was cycling through the Florida Everglades.

Then, surprisingly, he was next to the highway again. He pedaled through another abandoned railroad town called Thatcher and followed the road another four and a half miles to the Niobrara. Dense forest marked the upper rim of the river canyon, warning Jack of a sudden change in topography. A pine aroma filled the air in his lungs as he neared the valley. Then the ground abruptly disappeared from under Jack as he rolled out onto the old wood and steel bridge.

Near the center of the quarter-mile-long bridge, Jack stopped to admire the scene. He stood 148 feet above the river bed and watched how the current sculpted underwater dunes in the water below. The panoramic view infused with the incense of pine and aquatic freshness held him spellbound.

At the end of Jack's repose, he realized that his mom would enjoy a picture of this. He leaned out over the rail and snapped a selfie with the river in the background. Seconds later, Shelly sat at her desk in Chicago and smiled at the grin on her son's face. "Looks like you're having a good time; love you," she texted back. Jack grinned again and sent her a "love you too."

A couple of miles up the trail, Jack rode into the

warmhearted town of Valentine. The sign subtitle read Small town Big adventure; he just entered the Mecca for outdoor adventurers. This city marked the end of the line for today's fifty-five-mile ride. North, up Main Street, looked to be the town's hub, so he headed that direction, watching for a suitable establishment to stop and get recommendations.

This town seemed to have more activity than the last several. Cars traveled in both directions as Jack rode north. The stores looked kept up and busy. Soon, he spotted a sign across the street that caught his eye —Young's Western Wear. He swung across, parked his bike, and went inside. In a few seconds, a store clerk was at his service. "Can I help you?"

Jack turned his gaze from the racks filled with boots and hats to the blue jean-clad lady before him. "I hope so," replied Jack. "I'm looking for a place to camp tonight, and your store looked interesting, so I came in to look around."

"Please do," replied the clerk. "We have a city park with camping—north on Main Street, just outside of town."

"Thanks, I'll check it out. I was also wondering about other things to do in the area and maybe a good place to eat."

"The Peppermill is a good place for a steak. And we have lots of things to do around here; canoeing and fishing are very popular."

"Do you know of a good place to fish?" inquired Jack with a bit of anticipation in his voice.

"Merritt Reservoir seems to be popular... and it's only about twenty-five miles away."

"Sounds good. I'll give it a try." Then Jack realized

that there was a good chance that Farley could frequent this store. "One other thing—you wouldn't happen to know a man named Farley Hayes?"

The clerk thought for a moment, then shook her head. "No, can't say that I've heard of him." Then she could see the speck of disappointment in Jack's eye. "Is he someone that I should know?"

"Probably not, I guess. I'm not sure where he even lives."

The clerk was perplexed. This young man standing in front of her looked very out of place in his biking shorts and big-city mannerisms. Now he's inquiring about a man that he doesn't seem to know. She decided not to pry any further. "Make sure to ask if you need any help," she said, then turned to another customer.

Jack wandered up and down the aisles, enjoying the cool air and smell of fine leather. Someday shortly, he hoped to dress in clothes like this. Then, maybe he would fit in.

The city park lies at the bottom of a valley formed by Minnechaduza Creek. Jack set up his tent near the creek, then used the public shower. Donning his last clean shirt, he headed back into town to find the steak house. Way down on the southeast corner, he spotted a large sign that read Peppermill Restaurant and Lounge. Under this was another marquee sign that read, "Trump called us stupid but delicious." Jack pondered this statement as he went in to order the heftiest steak and potato on the menu.

After a delectable meal, Jack went across the road to a shopping mart for supplies. He stocked up on granola bars, a couple of sports drinks, and water. Back at camp, the sun was dipping low in the northwest. He had a few minutes to reflect on the day's events before turning in for the night. His excursion thus far was going well, and he was looking forward to Merritt Reservoir and the hungry fishes within.

Jack rustled out of the sack at the first hint of daylight and prepared for his first plunge deep into the hills. His destination was a lake formed in 1964 when the United States Bureau of Reclamation constructed a dam on the Snake River. Farley described Merritt Reservoir as "tucked away in the northern Sandhills, much like a large uncut diamond, hidden in a sharecropper's field." Jack felt a surge of adrenaline as he pumped his bike pedals up the hill and into town.

Main street was quiet at this early hour except for the local coffee shops. Jack rode through town and stopped at a gas station on Highway 20 for a breakfast sandwich. He asked the attendant directions to Merritt, and he said, "Go west a couple of blocks and turn south at the brown sign."

Within minutes Jack was out of town, riding south past an airport runway. The road curved west and followed the north rim of the Niobrara River valley. Signs of civilization grew farther apart as he ventured west. Then he came to a road sign warning of a steep grade ahead. He coasted down into the river bottom and marveled at the scene where he was silently gliding. Dark green hardwoods dotted the pristine meadows along the river. The early morning sun glinted off the bodies of whitetail deer as they flagged away from this sneaky intruder of their world. Redtail hawks perched on dead tree limbs, waiting patiently for the sun to dry the dew off their feathers before starting a morning hunt. Just before he crossed the river bridge, a lone coyote slunk across the road in front of him, looking as if it just robbed a chicken coop. A kingfisher scolded him and flew downstream as he pedaled across the bridge. He shuddered to think about missing all this had he been driving a car.

Then came the long climb out of the valley; a car wouldn't be so bad now. When He topped the south rim of the canyon, he noticed a definite change in the landscape. Jack could see nothing but countless round-topped hills interspersed with yuccas looking south from the road's high points. He parked his bike, walked over to the shoulder, and kicked the soft ground. Sand fanned out in front of his tennis shoe. He reached down, picked up a handful, and let it sift through his fingers back to the ground. Jack could imagine sand on a seashore or a public beach back on Lake Michigan, but not out here in the middle of a continent. Nothing about this was logical. He felt as though he was entering the great unknown.

The road kept at a southwesterly course, first lateraling the Niobrara, then the Snake River. Jack wasn't aware of the history, some old and some new that he was cycling past on this particular stretch of road. Like the sacred Indian burial grounds near the two rivers' confluence, the outlaw hideouts down in the Snake River canyon, and Nebraska coach Tom Osborne's favorite trout fishing haunt straight below that western skyline.

Then Jack was riding alongside a concrete channel full of water. The canal was the main reason for building the reservoir- water to irrigate all those fields he left behind. Jack figured he must be nearing the dam.

Then he saw it- the first piece of level ground he'd seen since entering the Sandhills. The earthen dam filled the gap between the Snake river canyon walls. Just a little further up the road, Jack topped a hill overlooking the lake. He pulled to the side and soaked it all in. "Farley was right; this truly is a diamond in the rough."

Merritt Reservoir is near full-pool at the start of summer, meaning it hasn't drawn down from irrigation. The lake before him took on the color of the blue sky above, sandwiching the hills on the other side that tapered down to a point that split the lake into two arms. A small island with a tree stood out from this spot. Willows and cottonwoods grew on the shoreline in places. The distant sound of boat motors carried across the corrugated surface. Seagulls and pelicans were working the water near the dam. But what struck Jack most was the marine smell that signifies the distinctive life that water brings.

Jack spotted a business establishment just up the road and decided to check it out. The sign on the front of the building read Merritt Trading Post Resort, where pickups pulling boats sat at gas pumps. Behind this store stood a restaurant with "Waters Edge" written on it.

Jack stepped inside the store's front door and paused to look at a display of photos; happy anglers proudly held massive fish for the camera. Inside, he delved into the wondrous sights of a bait shop. A large aerated tank full of lively minnows first caught his eye: Then foam minnow buckets and coolers, life jackets, sunglasses, and bag chairs. The first aisle contained colorful chartreuse and orange lures resembling baitfish and others with no natural features. Then, he came to recognizable items like hooks and bobbers and other things foreign to him, like bottom bouncers and planer boards. The last aisle contained food staples like potato chips, bread, granola bars, and cooking oil.

The neighborly man behind the counter noticed Jack staring bewildered at the lure display and asked, "How's it going?"

"Good!" replied Jack, "I just got here, and I'm a beginner fisherman. Do you have any advice?"

The man grinned and replied, "Yeah, get your hook in the water! Seriously though, what kind of fish are you after?"

"I have no idea. I caught some trout a couple of days ago in Long Pine Creek. What kind of fish are in this lake?"

"Just about everything you're going to find in Nebraska, except maybe trout. You have to fish the river on private land below the dam to catch them. Do you have a boat?"

"No, I'm traveling by bike."

"Harley?"

"No, a bicycle."

"Oh wow, where are you from?"

"Chicago."

"Are you kidding me? That's awesome! What brings you to Cherry County?"

Jack thought a second, never sure how to answer this question. "Life quest, I guess. You wouldn't know a man named Farley Hayes?"

"No."

"I didn't think so. Anyway, I sure would like to catch a fish like the ones on your bragging board."

"If you want a boat, we have rentals, or you can

just fish from the bank."

"I've never operated a boat, so I guess I'll fish from the bank. I'm going to camp too. Do you know a good spot?"

"Any of the campgrounds along the south side of the lake should be good for fishing. The water's high and the bluegill are spawning, which draws the predators into the smaller bays."

"What are the predators?"

"Pike, bass, and sometimes walleyes. Do you need bait?"

"I have a few small lures that came with my fishing kit. Do I need anything else?"

"You can catch panfish on small jigs or spinners, but nightcrawlers work best. We also have minnows and leeches."

"What are leeches?"

"Just a minute and I will show you." He went to the back room and returned shortly with a couple of small styrofoam containers. "Here's what a leech looks like," he said as he opened the lid and showed Jack the contents. They looked like brown blobs packed in water. "The easiest way to put one on your hook is to let one attach to your finger, then run the hook through the side of its sucker."

At this, Jack's eyes grew large. He didn't grow up with leeches and nightcrawlers. He didn't have the proverbial creek that flowed through the childhoods of time past, complete with tree forts and unexplored wilderness. His childhood consisted of pavement and hustle. He was entering a strange new life indeed.

"I'll stick with the nightcrawlers. Is there a trick to hooking them on too?" Jack inquired.

"Break 'em in half. Then they're easier for bluegill and perch to eat, and they go farther."

Jack figured that he could handle that. "I'll take a carton."

"Do you have a way to keep them cold? They won't last long in the heat."

Jack couldn't carry a cooler on his bike. "What should I do?" he asked.

"Keep them in the shade as much as possible. You can always come back for more when they're gone," the storekeeper said with a grin.

Jack paid for the crawlers and started to head for the door. "Good luck!" the man said with a voice of sincerity. "Catch a big 'un!" Then, with a final thought, he added, "And watch out for the cactus; it's murder on bike tires!"

"Thanks!" Jack exclaimed as he walked out the door.

Back in the rapidly warming sun, Jack wrapped his bait container in a dirty tee-shirt and stuffed it in his backpack. He then pulled onto the road and headed south to find a campsite along the lake. He came to the first one almost immediately, where he swung in and made a quick circle past a boat ramp and a large parking lot full of pickups and boat trailers. He parked his bike and strolled around the campsites, stopping on the hill above the parking lot to pick something off the toe of his shoe. "Ow!" he yelled as he tried to jerk the tiny cactus from his finger. The green demon, the size of half a Tootsie Roll, with barbed needle points that jumped from one contact to another, held his utmost attention until he finally brushed it off on a tree trunk. "Not camping here!" he exclaimed as he walked back down to his bike.

Jack continued southwest along the lake, checking each campground as he went. He spotted a shower house in the Cedar Cove area. "That will come in handy later," he thought to himself as he rode past. He was three miles up the lake by now, and the road turned south as it wound around the Boardman Creek arm. He pulled onto a side road marked Beed's Landing. "Interesting name," he thought as he rode toward some trees at the base of a steep bluff. At first, he wondered where the lake was as he rode through the campground. All of a sudden, the trees opened into a sharp drop into a hidden bay. The second he saw it, he knew this was the place. He coasted off the road and onto a small peninsula surrounded on three sides by water. The campsite, which consisted of a picnic table, a fire grate, and a young shade tree, filled the entire point. This spot looked like the perfect place to make home.

In a few minutes, Jack had his tent erected under the shade tree. The buffalo grass carpeting the campsite was well worn from the feet of previous visitors. Anxious to get a line in the water, he had camp set up in record time.

Jack constructed his pack rod, still sporting the jig he used to catch trout back at Long Pine. Large boulders lined the bank around the peninsula to prevent wave erosion. Jack crawled down, sat on a flat rock, and made a cast into the clear water. He slowly reeled the lure in, expecting a monster fish to engulf it. Nothing. Another cast. Nothing. And so it went until he figured he must be doing something wrong.

Back in the shaded recesses of the south cove, Jack noticed some other fishermen. From the sound of their conversation, they were having some success, so he worked his way closer to see what they were doing. Nearing them, he watched a mom and her two kids casting orange and yellow bobbers to the center of the tiny cove. The bright-colored floats bobbed until a fish grabbed the bait, pulling them under the surface. The kids were so intent on their fun that they didn't even notice that they had a spectator edging ever closer.

Jack studied their system each time they reeled in to check their bait. Finally, he couldn't take it any longer, so he walked over to talk to them. "Looks like you're having some luck," he offered as he approached the family. "I was just curious, what are you using for bait?"

"Nightcrawlers," exclaimed the young boy. "The fish love 'em!"

Just then, his little sister squealed as she reeled with all her might, "I got one!" She drug the fish flopping onto the mowed grass as her mom went over to help unhook it.

"What kind of fish is it?" asked Jack.

"Bluegills," the boy answered. "And they're biting pretty good!"

The mom brought the fish down to put in the basket tethered to the shore. First, she held the fish up for Jack to examine. The almost round shape caught his eye first. It looked like a drink coaster with a mouth on one side and a tail on the other. It had a dark orange belly, and its back was dark green with faint vertical bars extending down its yellowish side. Its beautiful coloration made Jack think that this should be an aquarium fish. "Are they any good to eat?" he inquired.

"They're the best," the mom answered. "We fillet

them, bread 'em in cracker crumbs, and deep fry them."

"That sounds delicious," Jack drooled, remembering how long it had been since he wolfed down his breakfast sandwich back in Valentine.

Just then, the boy interrupted in a half-whisper, half exclamation, "I'm getting a bite!" His bobber twitched a couple of times and then stood still. "Rats, he must have left." Suddenly, it disappeared below the surface, and the boy jerked back on his pole to set the hook. After a fight, he battled the fish to the bank and proclaimed with excitement, "It's a bass!" He grabbed the foot-long fish by its lower lip and proudly hoisted it up for everyone to see. "I caught a bass!"

Sensing Jack's curiosity in fish, the boy held it up for him. "It's a largemouth bass," he explained. "See how big his mouth is?" as he positioned the fish so that Jack was looking right down its throat.

"Wow, he does have a big mouth," Jack affirmed. Then he looked the fish over from head to tail. It was shaped more like a trout, with a white belly and moss-green back. But what caught his eye was the distinct, broken horizontal line that appeared airbrushed down each side. This fish, which was in the same scientific family, looked nothing like the bluegill.

Then the boy did a perplexing thing. He stepped to the water's edge and set the fish in, swishing it back and forth, and then released it back to its watery home. "Why did you let it go?" Jack asked. "Aren't they good to eat?"

"Dad never keeps the bass. He says they're just for the fun of catching and releasing for the next guy. Besides, they taste like moss," he replied using his best grownup voice.

Jack marveled at this youngster's skill and knowledge of the outdoors. He must have a dad who taught him well. Now, this kid half his age was teaching him. He suddenly became acutely aware of the importance of a dad.

"Didn't your dad come with you?" Jack asked, not seeing anyone else around.

"Yeah, he and his buddy left in the boat before we got up this morning. They should be back pretty soon."

Jack watched the boy open his nightcrawler container, pull one out and pinch it in half. He dropped one half back in the box and threaded the other wriggling part onto his hook. Before he could cast it back to his hot spot, though, Jack asked to see his setup. The plain hook held the bait at the end of his line, which dangled six inches below a small lead sinker. A bobber clamped on the line a couple of feet above the weight. Jack didn't have any tackle like this in his pack. "Could I borrow a set of the things you're using?" he asked. "I promise to return them."

"Yeah, I have a bunch," the boy replied as he opened his tackle box. He rummaged through the compartments and picked a couple out for Jack. Then he cut the lure off with a pair of fingernail clippers and tied on the hook using the same knot that Jack learned a couple of days ago. He then squeezed the split shot weight on his line a few inches above the hook. Last, the boy dug around and found a bobber. "This keeps your bait from sinking into the snags," he said as he clipped it on at the proper height. "You can experiment with depth by sliding the bobber up and down your line. Do you need some worms?"

"No, I have worms," Jack replied. "Thanks for your

help... I'll give this a try."

"Good luck!" the boy said as he went back to his fishing.

Jack walked back to his campsite, opened his backpack, and grabbed a granola bar and the worms. Then he looked around for another place to fish. To the north was a much larger cove with willow trees shading the back end. It looked like another good spot, so he headed in that direction. As he walked along, he noticed some movement on the ground ahead. A tiny creature scurried toward the rocks and stopped to look at him. It was a small green lizard called a six-lined racerunner. As he crept closer for a better look, the lizard disappeared under the riprap.

Under the shade of willows, Jack studied the quiet, clear water in this hidden lagoon. The reservoir had receded a couple of feet below full-pool due to irrigation, leaving a small rim of sand on the shoreline. The sweet perfume of blooming smartweed filled the air. This aquatic weed grows like lily pads in the water and then becomes amphibious, sending long rope-like runners out on the beach. The runners had crinkly leaves and pink blossoms. He found a big opening in the smartweed and decided that this looked like an excellent place to fish.

He opened the worm container and peered in at the tangled mass of nightcrawlers. If a ten-year-old kid can do this, so could he. Gingerly, he grasped one between his thumb and index finger. As he pulled to remove it from its cousins, it started pulling back. The harder he tugged, the stronger the worm became. Finally, it popped free. Now came the dubious task of breaking it in half. He gripped the now, fully awake worm with both hands, pinching tightly with fingertips. When it snapped in half, the two pieces went into hyper-drive, writhing out of his grasp to the ground. He pounced on the two squirming chunks and threw one back in with its buddies, snapping the lid shut behind it. He threaded the tail half on his hook as the boy showed him, leaving a couple of inches wiggling below the point. He was ready to cast this irresistible meal into the home of hungry fish.

Carefully, he swung the bait out to the center of the opening. He didn't want to risk snagging in the tangle of floating smartweed. The bobber landed with a gentle plop and turned upright when the weight below tightened the line. Jack watched with anticipation as the rings from his cast retreated to the weeds.

This style of fishing required a bit more patience. Jack sat down in the sand after a couple of minutes without a bite. He remembered how his mom used to say "Patience" when he couldn't wait for dinner to finish cooking when he was half-starved. Thoughts of food reminded him of the granola bar in his pocket. He dug it out and peeled the wrapper back. Just as he took a big bite, his bobber did a little dance. He jumped up and gave his rod a jerk to set the hook, just like the kid did. Then he reeled furiously to bring in only a worm. He tossed the bait back in the water, disappointed in his missed opportunity. Immediately, the bobber started dancing again and dipped below the surface. Now, he waited a couple of seconds to set the hook. When he pulled back, he could feel resistance; he just hooked his first Merritt fish! He recognized it as a bluegill when he pulled it from the water. It was about six inches long, much too small for a meal, so he removed the hook and let it go. He was after something larger for supper.

The afternoon flew by as Jack honed his skills at bluegill fishing. Before he knew it, the sun was touching the trees atop the giant bluff on the west shore of the Boardman. Suddenly, the bluegills in his fishing hole started acting strangely. In unison, they flew up out of the water as if they were fleeing from something. The next time it happened, he noticed a large, torpedo-like vee on the surface. Then he remembered the bait shop man's words, "the predator fish will come shallow to feed on bluegills." Jack felt a little squirt of adrenaline enter his system, increasing his heart rate considerably. "If the predators are feeding on bluegills, then I just need to hook a bluegill for bait," he said quietly to himself.

After the commotion died down, the bluegills started biting again. Jack hooked one, but this time he didn't reel it in; he was going to let it swim erratically around the pool, hopefully enticing that predator back. He sat back in the warm sand and waited.

The small bluegill towed the bobber around the opening, with Jack steering it away from the weeds until it was tired. Then it just lay helplessly finning in place. Jack imagined what it looked like from the fish's perspective. The little guy was probably down there, nervously glancing in every direction, waiting for the inevitable; every dark shadow seemed to be moving, then, one dark shadow started growing closer, picking up speed, and whoosh! Jack's bobber raced across the open water, headed for the underwater labyrinth below the smartweed. The behemoth fish shot through the roots unimpeded by Jack's wimpy outfit. Jack held on for life. Then, seconds later, his rod went limp. When

Jack reeled in, he had only a bobber dangling on his line. His fish of a lifetime was gone.

Gathering up his gear, he headed back to camp, dejected. He sat at the table and looked at his little fishing rod with the missing hook. He realized that he would never be able to catch a big fish with it. Then he heard a voice coming up from the south cove, "There you are. I've been looking for you." Jack turned around and saw his little fishing buddy walking his way. "We were wondering if you wanted to join us for a fish fry."

"Fish fry?" Jack questioned.

"Yeah, we're frying up all the bluegill, plus some fish that Dad caught this morning. Can you come?"

Jack's attitude suddenly brightened. "That sounds great! I'm starving." He grabbed his fishing rod and followed his new friend to their campsite. "By the way, my name's Jack. What's yours?"

"Keaton. We're from North Platte. Where do you live?" the boy replied.

"I'm from Chicago."

"Holy cow, how far away is that?"

"Only a couple of states away."

"I noticed your bike. Do you have a car too?"

"No, just the bike."

"Wow," Keaton exclaimed as they entered his family's campsite. "Hey everybody, this is Jack."

Keaton's mom smiled and said, "Hi Jack, we met this morning. I'm Steph." Keaton's little sister shyly pushed her baby stroller past with a dog in it.

"This is my sister, Kara, and our dog, Russell."

"Hi Jack, I'm Randy," Keaton's dad said as he held out his hand that wasn't holding the frying ladle. "Are you hungry?"

"I'm starving, and that fish smells delicious!" Jack exclaimed.

"Good! We cooked plenty," replied Randy. "Grab your plates, guys!"

Jack was almost overwhelmed by the welcome he received from this family. They acted as if he was another son. He heaped a pile of golden fillets alongside a scoop of coleslaw on his plate. Keaton's mom was right; the bluegills were delicious. Munching them down with this family helped him forget his sorrow over the lost fish. They got acquainted as they ate, learning some highlights of each other's lives.

"Hey Dad, tell Jack about what you saw this morning," Keaton interjected between mouthfuls.

"Oh yeah, that was pretty wild," Randy replied. "I was fishing the flooded trees on the Boardman, and a critter came swimming across in front of us. At first, I thought it was a beaver, but it swam too awkwardly. When it crawled out on the other side of the bay, it shook itself off and ran up the hill. It was a bobcat!"

Jack's eyes grew wide. "I've never seen a bobcat. How big are they?"

"About the size of a coyote," Randy replied. "The crazy thing is… cats hate water. It must have had a pressing reason to swim across the lake."

"Maybe it was learning how to dog paddle," Steph quipped. Kara giggled at this thought as she reached down to give her begging dog a morsel.

"How about you, Jack? Keaton tells me that he got you set up to catch bluegills. Did you have any luck?" asked Randy.

"Yeah, I caught some small ones, but then a monster fish moved in, and I tried to catch him. He ate my bluegill and took off real fast. Then he broke my line. That's why I brought my pole over to see if I could borrow another hook."

"Let me see your pole," Randy said, reaching across the table. Jack handed him the tiny outfit. "You're gonna need a lot bigger pole if you want to land a northern pike."

"Is that what it was… a northern pike?" Jack asked with sudden intensity.

"I'm sure it was," replied Randy. "They are at the top of the food chain. They can eat just about anything in and on top of the water."

"It's a good thing a pike didn't try to eat that bobcat," joked Keaton. "They might have had a wrestling match!"

"I can set you up with a pike rod if you'd like," Randy offered, watching Jack's eyes for a reaction.

"That would be super!" Jack replied excitedly. "I would love to catch that fish!"

They all pitched in and cleaned up supper; then Randy went over to his arsenal of fishing rods leaning against their camper. He grabbed a long, heavy pole with a spinning reel. "This one should do the trick. It even has a steel leader attached."

"What's a steel leader?" inquired Jack.

"It's this nine-inch length of thin braided steel, just above your hook to keep the pike from cutting your line with its razor-sharp teeth."

Jack picked up the pole and felt its heft. "Wow, this feels like it might give me a chance against that pike. Thanks for letting me borrow it!"

In the meantime, Keaton found a couple more small hooks for Jack's bluegill pole. "Do you care if I fish with you tomorrow?" he asked.

"That would be good," replied Jack. "Maybe between the two of us, we can land that fish."

Jack thanked them for their hospitality, and then, like in the previous campgrounds, he asked to plug in his phone to charge overnight. They were happy to oblige and wished him a good night's sleep as he left for his campsite. He went to bed that evening with a renewed determination.

During the night, a great horned owl chose a perch not far from Jack's tent. Its hoots were loud enough to wake him from a deep sleep. He lay and listened for a while; then, curiosity drew him from the sack. He unzipped the tent and crawled out to have a seat at the picnic table. The crescent moon had set not long after the sun, leaving only the stars to give light, and oh what light they did give! For the first time in his life, Jack gaped at the spectacle overhead. The Milky Way reached up from the hill across the bay, forming a band of light that mirrored in the glassy water. The Big Dipper was twice as big as he ever imagined in the northern sky. He followed the imaginary line from the cup's outer stars to find the North Star, a trick he learned in science class. He'd forgotten the names of other constellations scattered across the inky backdrop.

The romantic setting encompassing Jack stirred up scenes from The Adventures of Tom Sawyer. The young Tom fantasized about leaving home to become a swashbuckling pirate so that he could return someday and sweep his true love off her feet. Jack didn't have a "Becky Thatcher" back home, but there was the cowgirl who so caught his fancy a few days prior. This thought wasn't his first of Savannah since that memorable afternoon. The image slipped freely into his mind of her powder blue eyes and golden hair tucked perfectly under her Stetson hat. Just then, the owl bellowed out a string of hoots that floated eerily across the bay, ricocheted off the steep bluff, and echoed back to Jack, snatching him from his reverie. Reluctantly, he went back to bed.

A southerly breeze kicked up with the sunrise as Jack lay and wondered what to do about breakfast. He was getting tired of granola bars, and there weren't any nearby gas stations. The lonely young camper pictured his neighboring family gathered around a propane stove, frying bacon, scrambled eggs, and pancakes. They were so gracious to invite him to supper last night, but he didn't want to wear out his welcome by showing up hungry again. Then he remembered his fishing mission; granola bars it is.

He slept with his two fishing rods, having nowhere else to stow them overnight. Pulling them out, he laid them on the table to do a quick inventory of his tackle. First, he needed to catch the bait. He opened the carton of nightcrawlers and quickly swung it away in disgust. They died in the heat yesterday and were ripening into a stinky glob of soup. Going to plan B, he tied the little jig with the plastic trailer onto the bare end that the pike bit off. He now had a lure dangling under a bobber. "Looks like it should work," he said to himself as he gathered the two poles and headed to his secret fishing hole.

Everything was just as he left it last evening at the far end of the lagoon. The south wind created some wave action out on the Boardman, but it was still pretty quiet in this protected bay. Jack leaned the pike rod up against a willow and then made a cast with the other pole. The bobber swayed with the gentle undulations coming through the weed patch. Jack settled back to watch.

Either the fish didn't like his lure, or they weren't biting. Jack waited patiently for an hour. Just when he was wondering if he should try something else, he saw someone heading his way. "Hey, Keaton, over here!" he exclaimed, just loud enough for his little fishing buddy to hear, but hopefully not so loud that he scared away the fish.

Keaton walked around the lagoon to Jack's spot. "I was beginning to wonder if I could find you. It's kind of hidden back here. Are you having any luck?"

"Nothing so far. I think maybe I need some worms. Mine all died."

"I brought some... and I also brought a landing net. Dad said we might need it."

Jack reeled his line in to exchange the jig for a hook and worm, hoping that it would entice the bluegills. Baited up, they both started fishing, and it wasn't long until bobbers began dancing. Jack reeled in a bluegill, and they went to work, rigging the pike rod for action. They impaled the baitfish under its dorsal fin with a large hook and heaved it to the center of the open pocket.

"Now I guess we just wait for Mr. Big," said Jack as he sat down in the sand, rod in hand.

"Yeah, he should be by anytime," replied Keaton, plopping down in the sand next to Jack.

A few minutes passed, then Keaton broke the silence. "How come you're biking so far from your home?"

Jack thought for a second. "I don't know for sure. I guess I just needed a change of scenery."

After a minute of silence, Keaton piped up again. "Isn't it kind of scary being so far away?"

"Well, it's certainly different. Chicago is nothing like this."

"What's it like... living in a big city?"

Jack had never answered a question like this. He thought for a while and came up with an answer. "In the city, there's a lot more noise, traffic, and people. It's hard to get away from people. The houses are super close together. I live in an apartment with my mom."

"Oh." Keaton dug his heels into the sand, mounding up a pile in front of his outstretched legs. "We live in a city too, but nothing like Chicago."

A few more minutes passed without conversation. Some seagulls squawked overhead.

"We have seagulls in Chicago," Jack said, breaking the silence. "And a great big lake."

Keaton perked up with this information. "Is it good fishing?"

"I don't think so. At least, I never heard of anyone catching a fish there."

Keaton mulled this over as he dug deeper into the cool sand. "What good is a lake with no fish?"

"I see sailboats on it sometimes."

"Oh, that might be fun."

Another long pause ensued. Jack thought about this kid and how lucky he was to have a dad. The closest thing he had to a father was the notebook in his backpack. He felt like he was getting closer to Farley every day, though.

"What's it like... having a father?"

Now it was Keaton's turn to ponder a brand new question. After some thought, he answered, "Dad brings us on these fishing trips and teaches us about the outdoors. He knows a lot about fishing, hunting, and camping. At home, he's pretty good at mowing the lawn."

"I didn't grow up doing any of those things," Jack replied with a sound of regret in his voice.

Jack laid back in the sand and looked up at the sky. "See those clouds up there? The ones that look like fish scales?"

Keaton looked at the muskie scales overhead. "Yeah, I see them."

"A man that I know says that those clouds come before a thunderstorm."

"Oh really? I didn't know that."

Jack felt pleased to teach Keaton something about the outdoors finally. Something that his "dad" taught him.

Suddenly, the rod lying across Jack's torso jerked toward the water. Jack got a better grip on it and held on. The water erupted as a monster fish stampeded through the weeds, heading for the main lake. Jack jumped to his feet and clutched the pole with both hands. The reel's drag was screaming as the line peeled off yards at a time.

"What should I do!? Jack hollered in total confusion.

"Hang on! I'll get the net!" Keaton yelled back.

The monster pike left a trail of cut stems and leaves as it ripped through the weed bed. Jack held the long pole high, and the taut line jerked free of the weeds as the fish was now in open water. Keeping the rod as high as possible, Jack quickly walked toward the mouth of the lagoon to try to catch up with the fish. After a thirty-yard run in the first few seconds, the fish slowed to catch its breath for its next lunge.

Jack could feel every swing of the fish's massive tail as it powered away from the shore. He hoped the heavy line would hold and not snap like yesterday. The fish turned and headed straight at him now, which produced a great deal of slack; loose line can cause the hook to drop out on its own. Just as it neared the shore where the boys were standing, the pike whirled around and went on another drag-ripping run. This time though, it didn't go as far.

Fish and fisherman continued the back and forth tussle, each time getting a little closer to shore. When the fish swam by just out of reach, Keaton exclaimed: "Holy Cow! He's huge! He's too big for the net!"

The pike finally played out, and Jack led him up to shore, where it rested while Jack and Keaton figured out a plan. The fish was twice as long as the net opening. After much deliberation, they decided to net it tail first. But when the hoop touched its tail fin, it shot back out to open water. Slowly, Jack swam it back in. This time Keaton put the net under its midsection and lifted it with all his might. The pike curled down into the rubberized net, which stretched enough to accommodate its folded body. Jack held the rod under his arm and helped Keaton haul the fish out of the water and up the bank.

"We have to show dad!" Keaton burst out as they lugged the writhing brute and fishing rods toward camp. The pike had retired by the time the two excited fishermen strode in. "Look what we caught!" proclaimed

Keaton.

"Oh my Goodness!" shrieked Keaton's mom. "That thing's huge!"

Keaton's little sister and ever-present companion, Russell, walked over to see the fish. Kara looked from a distance as the dog walked up and sniffed it. "Come on, Russell," as she gave the leash a little tug, "That fish might bite you."

"I'm going to call your Dad," Steph said as she pulled out her phone. "He's gonna want to see this."

The two anglers had the fish lying in the grass, figuring a way to pry open its mouth to remove the hook. Pike are notorious for clamping down on their prey to the bitter end. "Dad has some jaw spreaders in the boat. I've seen him use them on a pike; maybe we can use a stick." But every makeshift pry they found snapped in half. "We need a screwdriver," Keaton concluded.

Moments later, Keaton crouched beside the fish with a ten-inch, number 2 flat-tip. Sticking it between its jaws, he pried them open with a grunt. "Wow, their mouths are really strong." They could now see the razor-sharp teeth inside. "Dad says that pike teeth are so sharp that they cut a quarter-inch before they touch anything. I don't want to find out how sharp they are."

Jack tugged on the line, and to his amazement, the hook inside was loose. He wiggled it back and forth as he pulled, and the tackle slid free, bluegill and all. "He wasn't even hooked! He just wouldn't open his mouth to let go!" Jack exclaimed.

Jack retrieved the phone that he left charging overnight and asked Steph to take a photo of him holding the fish. He spread his hands a couple of feet apart and slid them under its belly. Then the proud fisherman hoisted it up like a forklift for the camera. He didn't need to pose a grin; it spread naturally across his face. A minute later, at a desk in Chicago, Jack's mom instinctively broke into a similar smile.

Soon, they could hear the sound of a boat motor heading their way. "I bet that's Dad," Steph assumed. The boat slowed and pulled to the shore below their campsite.

"Yep, it's Dad!" Keaton said, excited to tell him the story. "Hey Dad, we caught a monster!"

Randy lashed his boat to a tree and walked up the bank to the campsite. "What's this I hear about a big fish?"

"Come look!" Keaton yelled, motioning his dad over.

"Holy Moly! That's a big pike," Randy bellowed. "I can't believe that you guys caught him." He pulled out the tape measure in his hand and stretched it from the tip of its lip to the end of the tail. "Thirty-nine inches. Now let's see how much he weighs." He inserted the large hook of a digital scale into the bottom of its gill slot and hoisted it up. "Take a guess," he uttered.

Keaton, wanting to show off his familiarity with big fish, guessed "Ten pounds."

"How about you Jack, what's your guess?"

Jack had no idea what to guess. "Eleven pounds," he offered, figuring Keaton was in the ballpark.

"How about sixteen and a half pounds," Randy announced with a grin. Everyone in the circle around the fish gasped in amazement. "Wow, this is one healthy fish."

Randy laid the fish back down and went to get

his fillet knife. "We need to clean him soon." Gathering some zip lock bags and his knife, they picked up the fish and headed up the hill.

The fish cleaning station was a pretty impressive structure. A gable roof covered a large stainless steel table. In the middle of the table was a square hole. A water hose hung from a swiveling arm above. They laid the fish out on the table, and Randy went to work.

"Pike are excellent to eat, but there is a trick to cleaning them," Randy said in his teacher's tone. "They have a row of Y-bones down their back straps that need to come out." First, he cut behind the gills from top to belly. Then he started down the backbone, head to tail, slicing the fillet off. Then he ran his knife between the skin and meat, taking the skin off. Next, he laid the fillet, inside facing up and belly toward him. He chopped about five inches off the tail, washed, and threw it in the bag. Next, he cut down the lateral line that separates the belly meat from the back strap. The belly section was cut into frying size portions, washed, and put in the bag. "Now, all I have left is the back strap. This is the tricky part." He laid the remainder of the fillet, skin side up and lateral line toward him. Starting at the head end, he made an incision about halfway down on the thickness, from head to tail, cutting only about an inch deep. "Can you hear my knife on the bones?" he asked. "I can feel the Y-bones on the bottom side of my knife tip." Then he picked up the strap and cut a small circle around the bones at the head end. Gripping the Y-bones with his right fingers and the fillet with his left, he pulled the strip of bones out, like zipping open a coat. He tossed the strip of bones into the disposal hole and cut the remaining ribbon of boneless meat into three-inch frying lengths. "And that's how you clean a pike," he said as he flipped the fish over to do the other half.

Jack watched the whole process in amazement. He wondered if he would ever be able to do this himself. It looked like something that required a lot of practice. When Randy finished, they washed the table, ran the garbage disposal, and threw the carcass into a designated container. "Don't ever throw a carcass this big in the grinder. It will plug it up," Randy said as he washed his hands to leave.

When they turned around to head back down to their campsite, they noticed the darkening western sky. "Looks like it could storm," Randy said with a tone of uneasiness.

Still coated with yesterday's road grime and today's fish slime, Jack remembered the other campground shower house. He walked back to his quiet little peninsula and grabbed his soap and towel. Soon, the cyclist headed out to the highway. Turning north, he got a better view of the western sky. It was getting darker by the minute. His pace quickened with each side glance.

Jack temporarily put the building storm out of mind as he lathered down in the stream of hot water. He didn't remember showers ever feeling this good at home. Maybe it was the smell of pine trees wafting through the gable vents, or perhaps it was just the feeling of washing two days of sweat from his skin. When he dried off, he almost hated to put his dirty clothes back on. Then a brilliant idea struck him. He would let nature wash his clothes!

Back outside, the sky was turning a greenish

shade of black. Jack jumped on his bike and fought the increasing wind back to Beed's Landing. He feared a gust would toss him off the road and into a cactus patch, leaving him with two flat tires and nowhere to escape the wicked storm. At last, the frantic cyclist turned off the highway and rode straight at the wall cloud scraping the top of the bluff across the bay. He pedaled like he never pedaled before. The northwest blast arrived as he jumped off his bike and jerked his backpack off. He fumbled the zipper open and poured his dirty clothes out on the table, where they immediately blew off toward the lake. He chased them down and picked up rocks as he went, bringing them back to the table. Spreading them out, he piled rocks on them to hold them down. In the wind, he could hear someone yelling his name. It was Randy, calling him to take shelter in their camper. He did a quick once-over to make sure everything was secure and then sprinted for the RV. Huge drops pelted him in the back as he reached the door, which opened before he could grab the handle. Randy ushered him in and slammed the door shut.

 Jack glanced around the camper at the facial expressions of his newfound friends. Steph had a genuine look of relief that Jack escaped the storm. Keaton was calculating how big the next gust would be and whether it would blow the camper over. Kara was clutching Russell to her chest and singing a lullaby. Randy was at the window watching the bedlam outside, looking like a captain tossed about on the raging seas. Jack stood in the middle of this beautiful crew, feeling like this was the exclamation point to the two best days of his life.

7. COWBOYS AND INDIANS

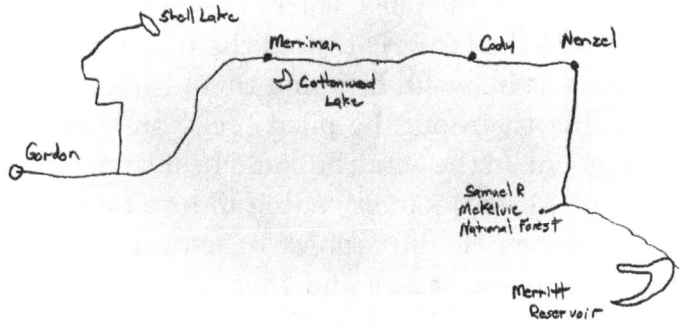

Summer storms are fast and furious. One minute you're hanging on for dear life; moments later, the sun is chasing the clouds away to the east. Jack's stay at Merritt Reservoir turned out to be a memory for the ages. He found it difficult to part ways with his newly adopted family from North Platte. Alone again, he stayed a couple more days, exploring the vast array of coves and bays. The warm sand, occasionally shaded by flowing willow trees, the sweet fragrance of water and summer blooms, and the pleasant sounds of youngsters frolicking along the shoreline: all this reminded Jack of a storied paradise called the Garden of Eden.

But he knew it was time to move on. His visits for fresh nightcrawlers had been a morning routine at the bait shop. Before leaving the lake, he stopped and asked for directions to continue his journey west.

"Cross the dam and head west on the oil road. It will take you through the McKelvie National Forest and eventually back to highway 20. There's a nice campground right along the road," said the man behind the counter."

"Thanks, I'll try that," Jack replied. "I need to grab some snacks too," he said as he picked out a handful and headed back to the counter.

"Good luck on your trip, and I hope you find your friend," the man said as he rang up the food items. "Do you have water?"

"Yeah, I filled my bottles at the campground pump. Thanks for all your advice. I hope I can come back someday; this is a beautiful place!" Jack bid farewell with one last glance at the trophy fish on the board, satisfied that he was able to conquer one of those giants.

Jack cycled across the dam, taking care not to steer off the road as he gazed out across the water. Heavy white pelicans stood at the water's edge, watching him with a suspicious eye. A momma killdeer and her brood of chicks ran single file on long, toothpick legs across the wavy concrete. Seagulls were screaming "Fish, fish, fish!" out in the deep water. The road curled north, up over a brush-covered hill, and back into the endless sea of grass.

Jack negotiated some hills and rode past a large brown sign that read, Samuel R. McKelvie National

Forest. He looked in every direction but couldn't spot the forest. Maybe they considered the numerous yuccas as trees. Several miles west, the road slithered across wetland marshes with small, dark blue lakes. Long-legged herons, known to the old-timers as shitepokes, stood in the shallow water along the edge where they patiently waited for a fish or frog to happen along. One stood so close to the road that Jack spooked it into flight. It took off with a raspy squawk, causing Jack to smile at the saying, "Sing like a bird." Singing like a heron would not be a compliment.

After a dozen or so miles, the road came to a stop sign. Jack could finally see some pine trees to the west and south. The signage said that this was Road 16 F, and he needed to take a left to Steer Creek Campground. The road started south and then bent back to the west, where he promptly arrived at the campground. It was still morning, but the shade under the giant ponderosa pines looked inviting.

Jack cycled the loop through the forested campground and stopped at a picnic table near the road. The place was all his. After a short siesta under the whispering pines, he walked over to an information sign and noticed the Blue Jay hiking trail. Interested, he started on the mile-long path traversing over Steer Creek, through the pines in the valley, and then crossed the road south. He was now in the wide-open, treeless Sandhills. For the first time, Jack was tasting the magical savor of being alone on foot in the grass-covered dunes.

Jack wandered into a hidden blowout slightly off the path where he discovered tiny flowers of deep purple and intense yellows hugging the warm sand. He wondered how wildflowers showed up this far from anywhere. It was as if he were standing in an eternal expanse planted by the hand of God.

Back at the campground, Jack grabbed his water bottles and walked over to the hand pump. After three or four strokes on the long handle, water gushed out of the spigot, allowing him to fill a bottle with one hand while pumping with the other. Amazingly, the water tasted the same as that purchased in a store.

Jack ate one of his granola bars since it was approaching noon, then hopped his bike to continue his journey. But he stopped immediately; his front tire was flat. A sudden wave of panic washed over him. He had an emergency hand pump with him, but what if it leaked out as fast as he pumped it up? He dug the pump out and went to work, filling the tire up. He detected a tiny hissing of air, adding to his dismay. His only hope was to head north and find a place to repair it.

He stuffed the pump into a pouch to easily access it and proceeded onto Road 16 F. Nenzel, population twenty, was eighteen miles north. He doubted if a town of that size would have a tire repair shop. If not, he would continue west on Highway 20 until he found one.

Every three miles, he stopped to firm up the spongy tire. An old ranch truck approached from behind and ground to a halt beside him at one of these pit stops.

"Are you having troubles?" came the gravelly voice through the open passenger window.

"Yeah, I've got a flat tire," Jack replied, quietly hoping for some assistance.

"I'm headed into Valentine if you need a ride," the voice offered.

Jack jumped up from his pumping, not willing to miss this opportunity. "I sure could use a ride to get this fixed."

The tall, lean, slightly hunched cowboy crawled out of the cab and shuffled around back to drop the tailgate. "If you can find the room, slide yer bike in here, and I'll shut the gate on it."

With some help from the old cowboy, Jack hoisted the bike atop a mound of feed sacks, buckets, and various fencing tools. The man slammed the tailgate shut and stuck his hand out. Jack, by now, had learned that the handshake was common Nebraska courtesy.

"Name's Webb Williams."

Jack reached out and placed his comparatively childlike hand into the steely grip of the older man. "I'm Jack Harris," he replied, trying to hide his grimace.

"Glad to meet ya," Webb growled as he shook Jack's hand back and forth like a pit bull shaking a rag doll. "Let's git to town."

They crawled into the cab, slammed the doors, and took off on yet another brand new adventure. Jack was riding with a real-life cowboy in what smelled like an authentic ranch truck. The combination of cow and horse manure, along with oats, hay, and animal medications, reminded him of the zoo back in Chicago.

"Yer not from around here, are ya," Webb surmised, breaking the silence.

"I'm from Chicago."

"Chicago, what the h*** are you doin' out here on a bicycle?"

"It's a long story, I guess," Jack replied, still not knowing a way to verbalize the real reason. "One thing for sure, I'm looking for a man named Farley Hayes."

"I've lived in the Sandhills my whole life, worked lots of ranches. Never heard of him."

The truck crossed the Niobrara river valley on their way north.

"You fixin' to stay here a while, or are you just passin' through?"

Jack thought about this question a moment and then figured that this was as good a time as any to pour out his heart.

"Farley Hayes wrote a journal about the Sandhills. He says some secrets can only be learned by those living here. I'd like to stay long enough to discover them."

After a deep pause, Webb broke the silence, "This guy—Farley, he's right. Over the years, I've seen lots of people come out here from all sorts of places. They git here with their brains spinning like a bucking bronc. These hills have a way of smoothing out our way of thinkin'." Webb stretched a gnarly hand past Jack's nose and pointed out the side window, "Ya see those fence posts streamin' past along the road ditch?"

"Yes."

"Count 'em for a mile. I'll tell ya when to quit."

At sixty miles per hour, the fence posts whizzed by the truck pretty fast. Jack did his best to keep count, all the while wondering why he was doing it.

A minute later, Webb told him to stop counting, "Did you see that herd of antelope back there?"

"No, I was counting fence posts. Was there really a herd of antelope?"

"Yep, and you missed 'em. That's how folks are when they first come to the Sandhills. So busy counting fence posts that they miss the big picture."

Jack looked back out his side window again, this time shifting his focus from the nearby fast-moving posts to the distant hills, which were sitting still as a picture. "Wow, I've never noticed that before," he uttered. This bit of cowboy wisdom seemed helpful. A few miles up the road, Jack had already forgotten the number of fence posts that he counted, but he sure would like to see another herd of antelope.

Shortly, they rolled to a stop at the junction with Highway 20, next to the tiny town of Nenzel. Jack eyed the row of old buildings, looking for signs of life.

"Does anybody live there?" Jack inquired, taking advantage of his tour guide.

"Yep, a few kin of George Nenzel." Webb glanced over at the curious look on Jack's face, "George started the town back in 1899. All the towns along here came and went with the railroad. Some are still hangin' on; some died a long time ago. The ones that are still livin' have too much grit to die."

Jack felt sadness, thinking about the life slowly draining away from a bustling town, reducing it to a pile of weathered boards atop foundations sculpted by hopeful hands in another era.

"Ranchin's a lot different than it was fifty years ago. A big ranch used to have seven or eight families living on it, jist to git all the work done. Now days, that same ranch might have two. It takes people spendin' money to keep these towns alive." After a pause, Webb added, "The Indians used to come down from the rez, but not so much anymore. Must've built their own stores."

This observation steered Jack's interest in a new direction; he'd never met an Indian.

"Are there still Indians around?"

"Lots of 'em, a few miles north on the Rosebud and Pine Ridge."

Jack envisioned savage, loincloth-clad warriors astride big appaloosas, circling a hapless wagon train. The chief always wore a bonnet of eagle feathers that flowed several feet behind. And just when things were going to get ugly, the U.S. Cavalry would come charging on the scene.

"Kinda sad, what we turned the Indians into. You know, compared to what they used to be," Webb reflected. "Before white man, tribes came from every direction to hunt the Sandhills' buffalo. Pretty crazy to think they could kill that big animal with lil ol' sticks. Then along we come, killin' off the buffalo and shippin' the Indians out of state. The Cheyennes were the last Indians to use the Sandhills—hid all winter in a valley west of here. They were runnin' from the army after escaping a prison camp down in Oklahoma."

By this point, Jack was so immersed in the conversation that he forgot his bike trouble. He barely noticed the miles clicking by as Webb told stories about battles between the Pawnee Indians and the Sioux. Then he told the story about two Pawnee Indians who were working as scouts for Luther North. They ran on foot fifty miles a day to keep up with Luther, who was on horseback. On the final day of the trek, they challenged each other to a foot race. On that hot July day, they ran eighty-five miles in twelve hours.

"Boy, they must have been pretty tough back then," Jack exclaimed.

"Everybody had to be tough back then, even the whites," replied Webb. "Some Sioux Indians caught up

True story! the Martin brothers

with a couple of kids on horseback and pinned them together with an arrow. They managed to escape and hide out under some hay. They both survived—with no doctor. Now that's tough."

Jack tried to imagine an ordeal like that. It made his troubles look pretty puny.

"Speaking of tough, have ya ever heard of the Great Cowboy Race?"

"No."

"Longest horse race in history—one thousand miles from Chadron to Chicago—yer hometown. We just drove over the trail they took. Doc Middleton, the ol' horse thief himself, was one of the contestants. Took 'em pertinear two weeks to do it—ended up at Buffalo Bill's Wild West show at the World's Fair, right next to Lake Michigan. I believe that was back in the 1890s."

Jack absorbed each story as Webb shelled them out. Unfortunately, they were nearing Valentine.

"I sure appreciate the ride," Jack said as they slowed for the town. "I don't know what I would've done without it."

"Think nothin' of it," Webb replied. "We gotta watch out for our neighbors out here."

Webb pulled the truck into a filling station.

"They fix tires here. I'll help you unload yer 'sickle."

They hopped out and pulled the bike out of the back, then Webb did a dreadful thing: he stuck a fist out for a farewell handshake. Jack gritted his teeth and toughed through it. Then the old cowboy was gone.

Thirty minutes later, Jack was back on the highway, retracing his path west. He marveled at the difference between riding in a truck at sixty-five miles an hour and pedaling a bike in the open air doing twelve. Sights missed before popped now. A creek flowed along the highway to the north that he overlooked before. After a few miles, it crossed under the road where a sign read Minnachaduza Creek. This name sounded like Indian; he was sure that Webb could have told him its meaning. He hoped to run into more guys like Webb in the future. His flat tire turned out to be a blessing in disguise.

Another land feature caught Jack's interest as he rode west. To the north, the land was angular and table-topped. To the south were the unmistakable rolling waves of the Sandhills. Once again, a water stream was the shoreline between sand and clay. Just past the small town of Crookston, Minnachaduze Creek angled northwest while the road headed straight west. Soon the hard-land ridges grew farther away, leaving him out to his sandy sea.

At the town of Kilgore, he was less than five miles from the South Dakota border. Then he rode past Nenzel, where he and Webb had entered Highway 20 from the forest. He noticed several road signs that read Bridges to Buttes Byway; he was on the scenic two hundred mile stretch of highway that connects the high bridges near Valentine to the famous high buttes overlooking Fort Robinson. Seven miles beyond Nenzel, Jack approached another town. A large, white water tower displayed the town name, CODY. Then he spotted an orange billboard that caught his eye: © MARKET, Student-Run Grocery Store, Open Monday-Saturday. Another sign out front stated: NEBRASKA'S ONLY STRAW BALE SUPERMARKET. These postings sounded intriguing.

Jack parked his bike outside the stucco building and entered the Circle C Market. Inside was a modern, neatly stocked store, slightly larger than a gas/convenience mart. The pine planked ceiling drew his eye to a large sign painted high on an interior wall: It's More Than A Store. It's Our Future! Jack remembered Webb's statement about these small towns surviving on grit. This store appeared to be a good example.

"Can I help you," a youthful-sounding voice asked.

Jack glanced over at the young lady at the register and wondered if she was one of the students running the place, like the sign out front stated.

"No, I'm just curious about your store," Jack replied. "Do you attend a college near here?"

"High school."

Perplexed by her answer, Jack asked, "Are you saying that high school students run this store?"

"Yeah, with a little help from the school and some volunteers."

"That's pretty awesome." Jack glanced around the store, then asked, "Where do you keep the straw bales?"

This time the girl looked puzzled. Suddenly, she broke into a smile, "Oh, we don't sell straw bales! They're inside the walls," she exclaimed, pointing at the front wall.

At this point, Jack was almost afraid to ask another question for fear that he looked dense, but he just had to know, "Why are straw bales in the walls?"

"Insulation."

"Oh, of course. I wasn't thinking."

The salesgirl giggled and said, "That's all right; we get that question a lot."

Jack turned and walked down the aisles, looking for something besides a granola bar to eat. He picked a can of Spaghettios, a bag of corn chips, and an apple. Back at the cash register, he asked the young clerk if there was a park in town.

"Yeah, right behind the store," she said, pointing north.

"Thanks. This is a pretty cool idea—this store."

"Yeah, it is pretty neat. Thanks for shopping!"

Jack stepped out into the late afternoon heat and crawled on his bike. He rode north over what used to be the railway and arrived immediately at a park with a table under a shade tree, where he prepared his evening meal. The young traveler spent the rest of the evening relaxing and reflecting under the guardian shadow of the Cody water tower.

The following day he hit the road early to beat the intensifying summer heat. Jack appreciated the desiccating effect of the sand, absorbing the morning humidity to a more comfortable level. A few miles out, he spied a group of animals with unnaturally white markings. Antelope! He coasted to a stop to watch, which made them nervous. The lead animal broke and ran for the distant hills, pulling the rest with him. They ran fast and effortlessly, hardly slowing down for the fence that they crawled under single file. Once past the barbed wire, they accelerated to full speed in a flash. It was a fantastic exhibit of survival.

It's a twenty-four-mile stretch between Cody and Merriman with very little traffic. Jack whiled away the time, counting cars and cowherds. Twice, he thought he caught glimpses of deer silhouetted on hilltops. After his talk with Webb, he started extending his focus beyond the city norm. In this open land with no trees, every creature depends on far-reaching vision. He wondered how many coyotes were sitting out there watching him ride silently past.

Just as Merriman's water tower came into view, Jack spotted a sign that read Cottonwood Lake State Recreation Area. He pulled onto the gravel road leading a short distance south to a park nestled in the wedge of a three-quarter circle lake. A single row of large cottonwoods rimmed the lake's outer perimeter, staging this cinematic rendition of a Saharan oasis.

Jack followed the road to a concrete boat ramp and parked his bike. He walked down to the water and peered in, looking for signs of life. Through the clear water, he spied some bluegills sitting above round spawning nests in the sand. The lake bottom in the spawning beds resembled the surface of a chinese checker board. Without hesitating, he scrambled to assemble his fishing rod.

While he cast his little jig into the bluegill hole, a dark-colored truck pulled to a stop behind him. The door opened, and a uniformed man stepped out and strolled down the bank to him.

"Having any luck?" The man asked.

"Not yet. I just got here, though," replied Jack, glancing at the badge on the man's shirt.

"Are you biking?"

"Yes." Jack wondered what this inquiry was about and if he was possibly doing something wrong.

"Just thought I'd stop and check your fishing license. You are over sixteen?" the officer asked politely.

"Oh, yeah, my fishing license." Jack pulled out his billfold and picked through the compartments, thankful that he remembered to purchase one while in Norfolk. He quietly sighed with relief when he found it. "Here it is."

The officer studied the license and stated, "Chicago?" with a tone of amazement. "Did you ride all this way?"

"No, I took a bus to Norfolk, but I rode the rest."

"That's still a pretty good ride. Where are you headed?"

"Not for sure. I'm checking out the Sandhills." Then Jack thought of something, "You wouldn't happen to know a Farley Hayes?"

"No, can't say that I do."

"He must live in another part of the Sandhills," Jack supposed.

The conservation officer detected a tone of disappointment in Jack's voice and asked, "Is there anything I can do to help? I have ways to find people."

Jack glanced his way with a sigh, "I've tried everything. The Farley Hayes that I know isn't listed anywhere on the internet."

"Do you have a general idea where he lives?"

"No, just somewhere on a ranch in the Sandhills."

"That's a pretty big area, but give me a minute, and I'll see what I can find."

The officer retired to his truck for a few minutes while Jack continued to fish. He was thankful for the man's help but held little hope that he would discover anything. He returned in a few minutes with his findings.

"I didn't locate anyone that matches that name description in the Sandhills area. Is it possible that he moved away?"

"I don't know for sure. I don't even know if he's still alive."

The officer pondered this statement but decided not to push the issue any further.

"Which direction are you headed?"

"West, is there a good place to camp in that direction?"

"Depending on how far you're riding... Shell Lake would be the closest."

"How far is that?"

"As the crow flies, less than twenty miles. By road, it's more like forty—and several miles are gravel. It's worth your time though."

"Sounds good. Is it hard to find?"

"It is a little tricky; maybe I should draw you a map." He sketched out a detailed map with a road that made a big sweep to the southwest, north, and back northeast. "Pay close attention to the forks in the road up in this area; signs are pretty scarce." He tore the sheet of paper from his tablet and handed it to Jack.

"Thanks!"

The officer wished him luck and then took off in his truck. Jack had ridden twenty-four miles that morning, and the giant cottonwoods looked inviting for an afternoon siesta, so he figured Shell Lake could wait for tomorrow. He made camp and settled in for a relaxing day.

He caught some eating-sized bluegills, and he craved fresh meat, but he had no way to fry them to a golden brown as they did back at Merritt. He wondered if he could cook them whole, like trout over an open fire. After a fashion, he had a crackling fire and a willow cooking stick.

The bluegill were more willing to bite than trout, but it still turned out to be a long process. Two hours later, Jack was still catching and cooking. He found out that bluegill, unlike trout, were covered with inedible scales that needed to be peeled away with the skin after cooking. They tasted good, though, with a bit of salt sprinkled over the white flesh.

After dinner, he kicked back in the shade and watched the flames die down in the fire ring. He remembered a poem in Farley's notebook about fire rings, so he pulled the journal out to revisit it. Farley's hand-printed poems were not his own; he transcribed them from other books, noting the authors at the end.

Rings

Along the meadow's edge
Old green grass rings appear.
They tell of campfires burned,
When cowboys gathered here.

They would collect the fuel
From dead and fallen trees,
To ready evening camp
Against a late spring freeze.

With bedrolls on the ground
And horses tended too,
They'd each submit to sleep,
Expecting crystal dew.

As they awoke to stars,
All fading with the night,
The sky off to the east
Would glow in dim, cold light.

A frosty morning calm
Would seize their aching bones.
Perked ears of the horses
Would catch their murmured moans.

To a nest of tinder,
From striking flint and steel,
A spark would birth a flame,
For coffee and a meal.

A helpless babe at first,
But slowly it would grow,
Igniting twig and branch,
To set the camp aglow.

The offspring given life,
From mating steel and stone,
Would feed on gathered fuel,
Until its flame had grown.

Racing through the kindling,
Both arrogant and proud,
The youthful blaze, enticed,
Would pop and crack aloud.

Heat it generated
Defended from the cold
And warmed the wrinkled hands
Of cowboys growing old.

Unsplit wood resisted
The adolescent's race.
It, too, would turn to ash,
But at a slower pace.

They'd drink cowboy coffee,

Poured from a boiling pot,
As flames reduced the wood
To embers glowing hot.

Replaced by steady heat,
More comforting and tame,
The arrogance and pride
Would decrease with the flame.

In time, each hand would pause
To silently admire
How much like life it was,
The slowly dying fire.

From dead and fallen trees
A homage had been made,
Assuring next year's green,
Where once just ashes laid.

This ritual unplanned,
They carried out each spring.
They found that birth and death
Were both bound to a ring.

The cowboys, old, are gone.
Their blazing flames have died,
But somewhere in our young
The stone and steel reside.

Along the meadow's edge
Fresh green grass rings appear.
They speak of recent flames,
As cowboys gather here.

—Kip E. Sorlie

Jack lay and pondered the words of this poem. He thought about the old cowboy who so graciously helped him yesterday. Did Webb go through a time of pride and arrogance in his younger years? He supposed that we all do to a certain extent. Then Jack wondered about himself. Was he like a twig, sparking a hot, short-lived fire? Or was he more like the unsplit log, burning at a slower rate in life? He guessed only time would tell.

The rattle of cottonwood leaves and the bright, shimmering water lulled Jack into a rare afternoon nod. He woke up twenty minutes later, completely disoriented. For a second or two, he had an out-of-the-body experience, forgetting where in the world he was. Then reality slowly fell back into place as the amnesia wore off. He looked around at his little oasis as if he were transported there in a time warp; he recalled this same sort of surreal ambiance back at the old flour mill in Neleigh.

After lazing around all afternoon, Jack hopped his bike and rode into nearby Merriman. He stopped at Buckles Service, bought a cold drink, and then biked around town, looking for life signs. This town, too, was showing its age. The brick buildings on Mills Street that once bustled with commerce now stood deserted. The houses had the same feel as the ones back in Long Pine. Old boats and campers weathered along the few streets. The stately trees looked as old as the houses that they protected. An aging brick structure that once was a school skulked in the southeast corner of town.

Dry creek, flowing a healthy stream of water, cut through the middle of town en route to Cottonwood

Lake. On the west edge of town, Jack crossed the highway to a wandering street that connected a few more houses. Some looked lived in, and some didn't. At the east end of the road, Jack turned north on highway 61 and rode past a few more houses to the end of town.

He spied one more street going east at the outskirts and swung in to investigate. It started gravel as it curved around an old steel building. Then it turned to asphalt and extended straight as an arrow as far as he could see. Finally, he came to a lane that led off the pavement to a sign that read St. Elizabeth Cemetery. He continued down the road and cycled to a dead-end turnaround. Something seemed strange about this road to nowhere. He headed back in the direction he came from and noticed an orange windsock next to the steel building. Suddenly, he realized that he was biking down an airport runway! He stopped to gaze back at the cemetery and determined this was the only road into it. He tried to picture an airplane aborting its landing due to a funeral procession. There was something about this nonconforming, no-nonsense way of doing things that made Jack smile.

He rode back to camp, stopping to get some snacks at the gas station. He spent the rest of the evening fishing and bracing for the evening onslaught of mosquitoes. He learned that it's best to be inside his tent when the skeeters come out at dusk.

The following day, Jack crawled out and packed for the forty-mile ride to Shell Lake. He was soon on Highway 20, heading west again. Ever since Valentine, the highway had been leading almost straight west. About four miles past Merriman, the road took a turn to the southwest, heading for Gordon. About ten miles from Gordon, Jack rode out of the Sandhills onto flat farm ground again.

The Sandhills' footprint is shaped roughly like a bluegill, with its mouth southwest of Alliance and its tail, two hundred sixty-five miles east near Oakdale. The tip of its pectoral fin is near Gothenburg on the Platte River, and a forward-leaning dorsal fin reaches into South Dakota, north of Gordon. Jack's destination, Shell Lake, is just behind the dorsal fin's front spine, about halfway up.

He turned north off Highway 20 and biked the straight section roads of agricultural land. Once he reached the hills again, the road went back to its typical Sandhill fashion, winding along between the dunes. He referred to his hand-drawn map at each fork to stay on track.

Just when he wondered if he was hopelessly lost, he rode past a small sign that said Shell Lake. Soon, he spotted water glimmering through willow trees. The road turned southeast and squeezed between the trees and a big hill as it led to the lake's far end. He rode past a boat ramp with a dock at the halfway point. At the south end, he turned around and rode back to the boat ramp. The grass under a large tree near the ramp looked like a good spot to build camp. Jack was excited to finally rough it at a camp with no tables, water, or bathroom; thankfully, he filled his water bottles that morning.

After he set up his tent, he walked out on the dock and started fishing. He quickly realized that angling here was much different than at Merritt. Moss beds filled the lake, making it impossible to cast from the shore without snatching a big clump of green coontail. A narrow trail of open water where the boats came and left presented the only fishable water. Surprisingly though, he felt a tug as he swam the little jig down the slot. He swept the unfamiliar fish onto the dock and tried to grab it, but he quickly dropped it, clutching his bleeding palm under his arm. Yellow perch go into a defensive mode, flaring their razor-sharp gill covers and needle-pointed dorsal spines when pulled from the water. Jack learned a painful lesson to grab a perch head first, pressing the gills and dorsal fin down tightly.

He studied the curious-looking fish, noting first the dark green vertical bars that ran down the length of its body. It had bright orange pectoral fins and a yellow underbelly. It was shaped more cylindrical than bluegill. He managed to unhook it without getting skewered again and tossed it back in the lake.

Jack studied the shore across the way and wondered how long it would take to hike around the lake. The sun was still straight overhead, and the days were long, so he made the decision. He packed a couple of waters and started north.

He walked the road to the entrance and then continued on a two-track around the lake's north end. Cattails and bulrushes prevented any casting from the bank, so he kept walking to the end of the trail in the northeast corner. Then he left the beaten track and ventured south into the unknown. A large hill on the east side of the lake sloped down to the shoreline, providing easy walking on the sparsely covered sand.

He stopped to try a few casts at a spot where the hill sloped steeply into the water. As he plodded through a bare sand patch, he spied a painted turtle struggling up the slope. It left an unusual trail behind:

a zigzag furrow in the sand, bordered on each side with frantic scratch marks. Curious about what this turtle was up to, he sat down and watched its painfully slow progress. At a spot with a little south slope, the turtle stopped and laid its throat on the sand. Then it crawled a bit further and did it again. It must have found what it was looking for because it started digging with its back legs, pushing sand out from under its tail into a pile behind. The soft sand moved quickly, and it soon had a hole about three inches deep. Then, to Jack's amazement, it started laying eggs. The turtle found an excellent, warm sand incubator.

Jack left the little lady to her work and stepped down to the shore. He could see open water past the short spike rushes along the edge. It was time to take off his shoes and socks.

Wading out to thigh-deep water, he could cast and retrieve without hanging up. On his third cast, something grabbed the jig and surged off for cover. He let the large fish have its way until it spun and headed another direction, with Jack reeling up the slack. Then it exploded out of the water and tail-walked across the surface, shaking its head violently. After a long, hard-fought battle using his tiny fishing outfit, he was able to lead the fish back through the sparse rushes to the shore. He recognized the fish as a much larger specimen of the largemouth bass that his buddy, Keaton, caught back at Merritt. He reached down and pried his thumb into its lower jaw, as Keaton taught, and hoisted the three-pound fish up to admire. He felt utmost satisfaction surge through his body as he held the fish out in triumph. Then he popped the lure free and released the fish back to the water.

Jack worked his way around the lake, stopping whenever he found an open hole in the weeds. The hill to the east tapered down to a green meadow at the south end, where a small stream flowed from the lake down an old artificial dike. He jumped across the creek and was soon back on the road home.

By the time he reached camp, he was hungry enough to eat a fish raw. He rummaged through his provisions and found three granola bars, a few sticks of beef jerky, and a bottle of water. Store-bought snacks would have to suffice tonight.

Jack leaned back against his shade tree and looked out across the lake. A pair of trumpeter swans cruised side-by-side toward the other shore. Noisy coots worked in a loose group out in the middle, tipping bottom's up, searching for mossy tidbits. Then he shifted his gaze to the big hill behind the camp. The sun dipped toward the west and cast a welcome shadow on this side.

Unconsciously, he stood up and started up the hill. He figured it was time to see what it looked like from the top. He was in the best shape of his life; still, he found breathing difficult in this higher elevation as he scaled the steep hill.

When he reached the summit, he turned and gaped at the surrounding vista. The lake was a large, blue oval below him. He could retrace his earlier circuit, spotting the distant sandy spot where the turtle laid her eggs. The setting sun cast deep shadows in the thousands of dips and crevices as far as he could see in every direction. He stood in awe, painting a mental picture of this landscape for future recollection.

A mosquito snapped him back to reality, and

he loped back down the hill, covering eight feet per lunge. The soft sand gave way with each landing, and he was back at camp before another bite. He grabbed his repellent and dove into the tent. He figured that he could brush his teeth in the morning after the mosquitoes went back to bed.

That was Jack's first night away from any sign of humanity. There were no street lights or distant highway traffic. He wondered how far away the closest person was, probably at some remote ranch house, tucked away in the hills. After several distant coyotes howled out their echoed harmonies, he drifted into uninhibited sleep.

Morning brought a renewed energy to Jack's journey. According to the map, he would complete his westward travel and start south along the Sandhills' western fringe. His provisions ran out the night before, so he skipped breakfast and broke camp. Gazing over the lake one last time, he said goodbye to another beautiful hideaway.

A growling, hungry stomach urged Jack toward Gordon. His map didn't show many dirt roads, so to be on the safe side, he retraced his previous day's path back to Highway 20. In an hour and twenty minutes, he rolled into town.

First, he rode past tractors: antiques on the left and brand new ones on the right. Then he spotted a war helicopter. A sign below the old bird read: AH-1 Cobra Helicopter, A MEMORIAL TO ALL VETERANS THAT HAVE SERVED TO KEEP OUR COUNTRY FREE DURING TIME OF WAR. Gordon American Legion. Next door was the Antelope Creek Cafe, and he could almost smell the coffee and bacon. He parked and hurried in to indulge his hollow stomach.

    Jack wolfed down a stack of pancakes, a side of bacon, and scrambled eggs. He was afraid to overdo, though, since he had a day's ride ahead.

    He stopped at a gas station next door with a sign out front saying, coffee—39 cents a cup. He went inside to buy water and snacks for the day and noticed that the people inside didn't look like cowboys. The men and women had straight, black hair and dark brown eyes set in broad, high cheekbones. Deep, weathered wrinkles etched the older faces. He suspected that he was in the presence of some true Native Americans. He pulled in to buy a couple of apples at a grocery store on the west side of town and encountered more people with the stereotypical Indian features. He concluded that he was a cowboy wannabe entering Indian territory. Things were getting interesting.

8. ABNORMALITIES

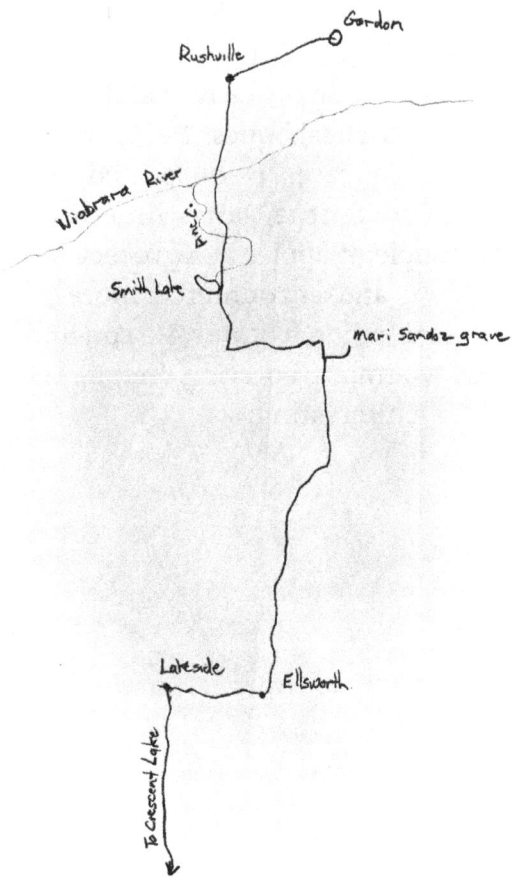

J ack's journey started on the northeast border of the Sandhills. He was now nearing the northwest corner, where he chose to take a hard left at

Rushville onto Highway 250. This road cuts down to Lakeside just inside the western fringe of the Sandhills.

He'd cycled two hundred eighty-seven miles from Norfolk to Rushville. His side jaunts to Merritt and Shell lakes amounted to another eighty miles. Now heading south, he calculated that he'd traveled one-third of his journey. This milestone caused him to measure how he was adjusting to this radical change in lifestyle. The Sandhills, patient, yet potent, were working their magic on him.

Jack had no idea what bizarre spectacles lay before him. He spotted a hill ahead in the distance and wondered if he was about to leave the flat farm ground again. Sure enough, topping the rise, the lonely traveler entered the inviting grass-covered curves of the Sandhills. Six miles later, he once again coasted into the Niobrara River valley, which looked different here. Bare grass slopes replaced the pine-covered canyon walls. Cottonwoods and cedars grew randomly along the river. Compared to the magnificent flow under Valentine's high bridge, the stream looked as if a deer could leap across. Jack rose and started pedaling up the long climb out of the valley, figuring that this great river's headwater was not far away.

At the top, he saw a large flat area ahead. The road stretched straight and long as far as he could see. He even rode past some cornfields. Then he was in the hills again, then another flat, and then hills again. Confused by this hodgepodge terrain, Jack found himself freewheeling down into another deep valley. This one looked just like the Niobrara basin a few miles back, except it was almost treeless.

A sign that read, Pine Creek, marked a ribbon of

water flowing through a large tube under the highway. Jack braked to a stop and studied the clear stream below. Something about the water was all wrong. Then it occurred to him that it was flowing backward! Every stream that he'd crossed thus far flowed generally east. Unless he got turned around on that flat stretch of highway, this creek was flowing straight west. It wasn't just a meander in the stream bed either; the entire valley, as far as he could see, pointed toward the Rocky Mountains and the Continental Divide. This brain-teaser had him so baffled that he pulled out his compass to verify that north was still behind him.

  He rode through the hills a few miles and then came to another large valley. This one was also perpendicular to the road, just like the last two. Large willow trees grew in the ditches at the bottom with a sign reading Pine Creek. Jack stopped again and checked the stream; it was smaller and flowed from west to east like it was supposed to. He surmised that the creek did a U-turn in the hills and passed under the road at these two spots. Something out there must be impeding the creek's easterly flow.

  A couple of miles farther, Jack spotted a blue lake surrounded by cottonwoods and pines off to the right. A sign along the road said Smith Lake State Recreation Area. He'd traveled fifty-three miles since leaving Shell Lake early that morning, and this looked like an excellent place to spend the night. He turned off and rode west, looking for a campground. First, he came to a boat ramp where he saw a man and woman fishing off the dock. He was curious about the fishing here, so he pedaled over to chat with them.

  He swung off his bike and started down the

floating boat dock to the fishermen, who turned in surprise at the sound of footsteps.

"Didn't hear you drive up," the big man with a tattered old cowboy hat exclaimed with a jolt.

"Yeah, the bike's pretty quiet," Jack replied.

At this, the couple both turned and gave Jack and his bike a once-over.

"Are you having any luck?"

"Just a couple bluegills," the man replied. Then, curious about this skinny youngster, he inquired, "Where'd you bike from?"

"Norfolk."

The man contemplated this as he watched their conspicuous red and white floats bobbing way out in the lake.

"I'm really from Chicago," Jack added.

Again, the man and woman both turned to look at him.

"Yer a ways from home."

"Yeah... quite a ways."

They exchanged small talk, feeling each other out for irregular behaviors that undoubtedly come from backgrounds so different. Jack attempted to explain his journey in a manner that would make sense to a cowboy but wasn't sure how it sounded. When he said he was out to discover the Sandhills' secrets, he could sense the man's ears perk up.

"Are you lookin for some REAL secrets... the kind that you won't find in a book?" he asked.

Jack glanced at the earnest look on the man's face.

"Uh... yeah, sure," he replied with slight hesitation.

"If you have time tomorrow, I can show you

some," the man said matter-of-factly.

Jack thought for a second and then replied, "Yeah, I have time... where should I meet you?"

"Be right here at four-thirty in the morning; I'll be coming this way."

Four-thirty in the morning! Jack pondered this announcement with great angst. Why on earth would he want to meet this total stranger at such an unreasonable hour?

Impulsively, he replied: "I'll be here... my name's Jack."

"I'm Wyatt, and this is my wife, Lacy," the man countered as he stuck his hand out.

"Glad to meet you... see you here in the morning," Jack said as he shook his hand with all the grip he could muster. "Good luck with your fishing!"

"Thanks... see ya in the morning."

Jack returned to his bike and continued around the lake, looking for a place to set up camp. He rode past a small pine tree forest that extended up a hill to the north. The road curved around to the west and led to the south shore, where the campsites were situated. A parkland pine forest encompassed the southwest corner, creating a Canadian feel to the lake. Jack instantly fell in love with this place.

He set up camp under a pine tree and dug into his food provisions, preparing for a short night's sleep. As it turned out, he spent the night checking his watch between brief lapses of fitful slumber. Every possible scenario crossed his mind that might happen when morning finally arrived.

At 3:55, he decided that this was close enough; he squirmed into his clothes in the tent confines and then sprayed down with mosquito repellent. Then he zipped open the tent fly and crawled out into the fresh air of western Nebraska.

Even in the darkest hours of early summer, a faint light rotates from the northwest quadrant of the sky to the northeast. Jack pedaled around the edge of the lake in the night glow, wondering what critters were out there, watching this silent human glide past. The pine forest outside the road looked like jagged black lairs to who knows what kinds of predators. He hurried to the rendezvous point.

The boat dock was a dark jetty onto black glass, reflecting the stars above. Jack walked out to the end and sat down to wait for Wyatt. When the echo of his footsteps died off, he started noticing the night sounds. Bullfrogs bellowed out their reverberant hums from the shoreline rushes. A night hawk nearly reproduced the sound with its lightning-fast dives in the dark sky above. Mosquitoes buzzed past his ears, desiring his blood but not liking the repellent. A cathemeral killdeer ran, scolding loudly at his parked bicycle. Then way off in the distance, a lone coyote barked, triggering a canine musical that spread like gossip across the vast hills.

The sounds of nature carried Jack's mind off to his new happy place, where he was all alone with his thoughts. His reflections were clear, unobstructed by the turmoils of our mechanical world. Free to think this way, his existence opened before him, like a flower opening its petals to the life-giving sun. Purpose in life, which was so clouded before, now seemed close at hand. He could almost reach out and grasp this journey's intent when a new sound broke the silence—Wyatt's ranch truck.

The old 4X4 pulled into the boat ramp parking area and stopped with the headlights pointed at Jack and his bike. Wyatt got out and exclaimed, "Didn't know if you'd show or not... this early in the morning."

"I wouldn't miss this opportunity," Jack replied. "What should I do with my bike?"

"Let's throw it in the back of the truck," Wyatt replied. "We can unload it when we get to the ranch."

They loaded the bike, pulled on the highway, and headed south.

"How far are we going?" Jack questioned.

"Not very far from here... but it's going to take some time. We need to get there by sun-up if you're gonna see it."

Jack's curiosity intensified with this statement.

"Is it some sort of wild animal?"

"Nope." The cowboy paused and let Jack stew a little longer, then continued, "Some folks call it looming... we just call 'em mirages."

This statement took Jack by total surprise. Mirages were not one of the possible secrets that ran through his mind during the night. He sat back in his seat and pictured movie scenes of a man dying of heat exposure, staring through solar waves at an imaginary oasis, only to stagger into nothing more than a hallucination.

"Are these mirages real?" Jack asked.

"Real as the nose on your face," Wyatt replied.

The truck had turned off the highway and was on a narrow black-top, moving east. Then it turned back north on a bumpy road that almost tossed Jack airborne a few times. The lane seemed to go on forever, but they topped a rise and entered a yard with a large dog.

"We can drop your bike off here," Wyatt said.

The morning was lighting the sky as they drove north out of the ranch yard. They stopped where a barbed-wire gate swooped across the sand trail.

"Com'ere, I'll show you how to open this one, then you can get the rest," Wyatt said as he crawled out. Jack followed him to the gate and watched the cowboy unlatch a hook attached to a steel bar from the barbed wire. He swung the lever toward him and let it fall, then grabbed the post and pulled it from a wire loop near the ground. Then he dragged the gate in a big arc away from the truck and dropped it. He drove through the opening and got back out to show Jack how to shut it. The whole process looked pretty simple.

At the next gate, Jack hopped out and waddled through sugar sand to open it. He remembered the clip on top and set about the process of unlatching it. The metal snap had a spring tongue that needed to be depressed to unhook it off the barbed wire. He squeezed it in but struggled to get it off the wire.

"Push the lever toward the gate," he heard from the open pickup window.

He tried this, and the hook popped right off. Then he made the fatal mistake of letting loose of the lever, which sprung around and hit him in the chest with the force of a twenty-ounce hammer blow. He temporarily dropped to the ground, clutching his ribs, feeling for broken bones.

"Are you all right?" came the voice from behind.

Jack gingerly felt his torso over and found nothing broken. "Yeah, I'm all right," he replied, more embarrassed than hurt. He got up and pulled the post out of the wire loop, and swung the gate open.

Wyatt pulled the truck through, and Jack dragged the gate back into place, where he reversed his steps to shut it. The trickiest part was correctly positioning the lever back on the post to torque it back around. This time, he held on with all his might as he brought the bar around to latch it. Hearing the click as the c-clip secured the tightening lever to the gate, Jack felt a twinge of victory. Then he looked up and realized that he shut himself on the wrong side of the fence. Wyatt tried to wipe a smile off his face as Jack finally crawled back in.

Two gates later, the sun was about to poke over the giant hills to the east. Wyatt pulled to a stop where the two-track went over a pass.

Jack looked around at the crazy, wild terrain they were sitting in. If the Sandhills were an ocean, the western third is overwhelmed with rogue waves compared to the swells in the central and the east's tranquil seas. He watched in awe as the sun started casting rays across the hilltops, bringing stark contrast between the deep shadows and sunlit slopes.

Then Wyatt stepped out of the truck and motioned Jack to do likewise. He walked around to Jack's side and leaned against the hood.

"Take a look at the western horizon," he said, pointing across the hood.

"What is that?" Jack inquired with a gasp.

He was looking at a bluish object floating in the sky over the hills to the west.

"That's the town of Hemingford... thirty-five miles away," he answered.

"But how is it hovering up in the sky like that?" Jack asked, not believing his eyes.

"There's a long, scientific explanation for it called

looming. It has to do with the sun's rays bending around the earth's curvature. When the situation's perfect like it is right here, for a few minutes, that town not only moves up into the sky, it looks a lot closer than it is. Here, take a look through my binoculars."

Jack peered through the glass and relayed all he saw, "There's a water tower, and some large white grain bins, and trees. Did you say that town's thirty-five miles away?"

"Yep, pretty amazing, huh," Wyatt replied.

"It looks like it's only five miles away through these binoculars," replied Jack in astonishment.

View across Mirage Flats

"Take a look at that hillside over there," Wyatt said, pointing at another hill. Jack swung the binoculars to the slope that Wyatt indicated and noticed some light tan-colored animals.

"I see them. Are they deer?"

"Yep, Mule deer."

Jack watched the herd grazing up the sunlit hill for a few moments, then looked back at the mirage city. He couldn't find it anywhere, though. "Where did the town go?" he asked.

"Back behind the hills where it belongs," Wyatt replied. "It's time to move on."

They jumped back in the truck, and Wyatt turned it around, heading back south. He turned east at a crossroads in the sand trails and followed a long valley a couple of miles. At the end of the valley, the path meandered up a hill to another gate. This one barely stuck out of the ground due to sand drifting on the windswept hilltop. Jack struggled to open it, and they continued east, down a steep hill and onto a sizable oval-shaped valley. The flat bottomed valley with a windmill in the middle was surrounded in all four directions by massive hills. Wyatt drove across the flat, clawed his way up the east side, and parked high on the north slope. Here again, he stepped out of the truck with Jack following.

"Look real hard and see if you notice anything peculiar," Wyatt said.

Jack studied the landscape, which was not unlike counting waves on a windswept Lake Michigan. The hills rolled on forever in every direction with no sign of humanity other than the windmill. After a few minutes, he conceded, "No, I guess I can't see it."

"Ye'r standing right in the middle of it," Wyatt said.

Jack looked to the ground all around the truck but

still couldn't see anything out of place.

Wyatt walked a few yards away and stepped into a slight depression. "Come over here," he said to Jack.

Jack went over and stood next to the cowboy.

"Now tell me what ye'r standing in."

Jack looked down and asked, "A low spot?"

"Yep. Now follow that low spot down the hill," he said, pointing west.

Jack did as instructed, and something suddenly appeared in front of him. Two parallel lines about twenty yards apart went down the hill, arched across the south side of the big valley, and continued up the hillside on the other end where they curved over the top, miles to the northwest.

"Now turn and look the other direction."

Jack did a one-eighty and looked the other direction, amazed to see the very same set of lines arching to the northeast and out of sight miles away. He imagined these lines continuing around to form a circle. "Wow, this is like a ten-mile diameter crop circle. Did aliens cause this?"

Wyatt laughed and replied, "No, but it's an interesting story. Back when people first started ranching out here, prairie fires roared across these hills with nothing to stop em. So they hooked a plow behind a team of horses and dug these twin furrows around their ranch. The wind drifted the loose sand out of the furrows and piled it on the side, creating the terrace that you're standing in. It's a big fire break created by horses and nature. Would you believe that you can see these lines from outer space? Check it out some time on a satellite image."

Ancient fire break furrows

Jack immediately pulled out his phone, which thankfully had one bar on this hilltop. He recorded a waypoint so that he could find this spot later.* This was something that he could show his mom when he returned home to Chicago.

Wyatt walked over and plucked a flower petal off a blooming yucca and popped it in his mouth. "Ever try one of these?" he asked.

Jack watched with interest to see if he was serious. "No... I guess not."

"Try one and tell me what they taste like."

Jack stepped to the nearest plant, picked a thick, fleshed, whitish pedal, sniffed it, and then stuck it in his mouth. One chomp and he instantly recognized the flavor. "Peas!"

"Yep, the Indians used these for lots of things:

they boiled the seed pods to eat, made brushes, rope, and mats out of the stems, and used the roots for shampoo and laundry soap. That's why we call 'em soapweed. Out west, they used this same kind of soap to catch fish—it poisons 'em."

Wyatt headed back to the truck and announced, "I've got one other thing to show you... hop in,"

They bounced back down the hill and crossed the valley, this time taking a trail that veered off to the northwest. They had driven for miles on the barely visible tracks, which had Jack hopelessly lost in the never-ending hills and valleys. He was amazed at Wyatt's ability to navigate this impossible terrain. Jack gripped the truck's grab bar for dear life as they climbed almost straight up, in axle-deep tracks. Then they were on top, winding through the blowouts and yuccas.

"That's Ted's buffalo fence," Wyatt pointed out with a hand motion to the right.

"There's buffalo out here?"

"Yep, but you rarely see 'em. Mr. Turner doesn't overgraze the land."

"Are you talking about Ted Turner, the billionaire?"

"Yep, the largest individual landowner in Nebraska... he's trying to preserve the land in its pristine state."

Jack looked at the buffalo pasture and compared it to the cattle ranch that they were driving across. It all looked the same to him.

Wyatt maneuvered down into an expansive valley and pointed the truck north. He drove around the hill base, and a white object came into view. Jack eyed the curious artificial structure as they approached.

"What is this?" Jack asked as they parked and got out.

"This is an old Kincaider's cellar," replied Wyatt.

"What's a Kincaider?"

"A homesteader after the Kincaid Act of 1904 passed. The government gave six hundred forty acres free to anyone willing to file a claim and live on the land for five years."

Jack walked around the old cellar, then crouched to peer inside. Over the years, sand had sifted in and filled it level with the ground. It looked like a good hideout for animals.

"I wonder how long he lived here," Jack mused.

"Probably long enough to be considered a landowner. Then, like all the others, sold out to the large ranches and left for an easier life. There's an old sod house still standing three miles south, filled with sand like this—still has three dresses hangin in a wooden closet. I'd like to know the story on that one."

Jack tried to imagine raising a family in such an isolated area. There were no stores, no hospitals, no electricity—just sand, yuccas, and wind. "It would take a pretty self-reliant man to live out here," Jack concluded.

"Wasn't just men... a young lady built herself a shack down towards Hyannis and lived in it to get her place." reflected Wyatt. This statement was almost more than Jack could swallow. He couldn't comprehend the physical and mental toughness it would take to survive in this environment. "Yessir, the folks out here come from pretty hardy stock."

They crawled back in the truck and headed for the ranch house. Jack contemplated Wyatt's assessment of Sandhillers as they jostled their way across the hills and valleys. He thought about the cowgirl, Savannah; did she come from hardy stock too? He always figured that a kid had to be tough growing up on the streets of Chicago, but out here, it's a whole different kind of toughness—less show and more grit—the kind of grit it takes to open and shut these barbed-wire gates.

When the big dog welcomed them back at the place mid-morning, Wyatt asked, "Can you find your way back to Smith Lake from here? I have a few chores to do."

Jack made a quick attempt to retrace their earlier path in the dark. "I think so," he replied with a reassuring voice.

"It's pretty simple. You'll come to two tees in the road. Take a right at both of em, but wait here a couple of minutes; I'm going to send something with ya."

Jack watched the cowboy duck into the front door of his home and then swung his gaze across the yard. Various sized pens stood in the shelter of a cedar tree grove that encased the northwest side. He spotted some chickens in one of the wire enclosures. Below this, goats were roaming around in a larger pen. The goat-sized dog stood with his tail wagging beside the car door, looking either friendly or hungry—Jack couldn't decide.

After a few minutes, Wyatt appeared again with a couple of sandwiches in his hand. "Here, take these... there're no cafes out here," he said as he handed them out to Jack.

Jack took the sandwiches and said, "Thanks! I'm getting pretty hungry."

As he swung on his bike, Wyatt added, "I just thought of another thing you should see before you leave this part of the Sandhills. We have a famous author that grew up in this area, and she's buried a few miles east. Her name's Mari Sandoz."

Jack, being a bit of a history buff, thought this sounded interesting. "How do I get there?"

"Instead of taking a right at the end of the lane, take a left and go eight and a half miles east. At the next stop sign, go south a half mile on Highway 27, then turn east on a gravel road by the big Deer Meadows Outfitters sign. Follow the signs on the gravel road to the apple orchard and grave. It's a few miles back in there."

Jack said, "Thanks! I'll check it out—and thanks again for the tour this morning and the sandwiches!" He hoisted them in a salute goodbye as he placed a foot on the bike pedal. "Oh, I almost forgot. Do you happen to know a man named Farley Hayes?"

Wyatt scratched his chin in thought, then replied, "No, can't say that I do."

"Just checking," Jack said as he rode off.

Jack negotiated the patchwork lane back to the road and paused there to make a choice. A right would take him back to his camp at Smith Lake, and left would take him on a long ride to look at a grave. The hot July sun overhead made his decision for him- it was back to camp and a shade tree beside the pretty blue lake.

He rode seven miles of asphalt back to his campsite, eating his dinner on the way. Back at camp, he pulled his sleeping bag out and stretched it out on the shaded picnic table where he could get some air movement yet avoid the ants and chiggers. In a few minutes, he was making up for his lack of sleep.

When the heat subsided that evening, Jack took a walk through the sparse forest above the lake. The sweet aroma of pine was new to this city kid. The gentle summer breeze flowing through the needles as he trekked through the soft sand detached him from the absurd pretenses that tend to control the mind. The wide-open spaces broadened his field of vision as he thought about his mom back in Chicago, how she sacrificed so many things in her life to give him a good childhood. He didn't fully comprehend a mother's love. He wondered if he would be able to show that kind of selfless love to his own someday. Maybe looking beyond himself to love others is the real meaning of life.

    He strolled around the perimeter of the public land, then took the road back to camp. He was thankful for the two sandwiches his cowboy friend made that morning since he was getting low on food. He portioned out some granola bars, leaving enough for breakfast the next day. He studied his map to plan out the next day's ride, including a Sandoz grave visit. If he took Highway 27 down to Ellsworth, maybe he could find a store to stock up on granola bars, then ride back west to the Crescent Lake National Wildlife Refuge turnoff. This area looked to be in the Sandhills' southwest corner, where he would begin his long journey back east.

    Later that night, he braved the mosquitoes and took his customary midnight dip in the lake to wash off the summer sweat. Sleep always came quickly with a clean, water-cooled body. These "moon dives" were sure to become a cherished memory later in life.

    Jack broke camp at the crack of dawn and was soon making his last circuit around the lake. He bid farewell to the community of pelicans and cormorants out on the island as he headed south down the highway.

    Three miles later, he turned onto the cut across

to Highway 27, which took him past Wyatt's lane. This thirteen-mile stretch started on an expansive meadow but soon squeezed in between hills that became larger as he went east. Fat grouse sat in pine trees along the road and flew off with a noisy chuckle when he got too close. He was amazed at the size of the steep-faced dunes', some over two hundred feet high, that gentled to a stop next to the road. He rode past a small lake with what appeared to be an old homestead; then, he came to the highway.

Half-mile south, where the highway skirts the east face of a giant hill, Jack spotted the large Deer Meadows Outfitters sign next to a couple of houses. He turned east onto Trail 365, where another sign read, Mari's Grave and Sandoz Fruit Farm.

This road ran alongside a picturesque lake teeming with ducks. Near the east end, Jack rode past a ranch where he spotted a lanky cowboy working on a blue tractor. The road curved around a hill on the north and continued east, past a dark green alfalfa field. Then he spotted a wood sculpted sign that said, Mari Sandoz Memorial Drive next to a road that led over the hill to the north. Riding through a crack in the hills, he passed another sign with arrows pointing northwest to the grave and east to the orchard.

Jack took the north fork and rode around the west end of a meadow to a square fence on a steep face's talus slope. A rusty bench and a single stone marker which simply read Mari Sandoz, 1896-1966 lay in the barbed-wire enclosure. "Wow," he thought half aloud, "their gravestones are as unpretentious as their lives."

He looked across the meadow to the southeast, where the large apple orchard grew, and he wondered if there was a story behind it. He would have to research that later; today, he had many miles to ride.

He retraced his path back to the highway and turned south. Barely getting up to speed, he spotted another historical marker beside the road, where he pulled off and read about Mari Sandoz, the author. The sign described Mari's skills as a writer and historian of the western plains. The last line read—"how man shaped the plains country, and how it shaped him." This observation made sense to Jack, who was personally experiencing the sculpting hands of this unique land.

The next eight miles were by far the most difficult of Jack's long bicycle journey. He traveled against the grain of some of the tallest, steepest dunes in the entire Sandhills. He could rest while he coasted down one steep incline, only to start up the next. He learned that the east-west roads which followed the natural valleys were a lot more fun.

Then the road finally escaped the nasty seas and leveled onto expansive meadows with big, blue lakes. He was now in the closed basin area of the western Sandhills. Here, the water doesn't flow in any direction, except up. Evaporation creates highly alkaline waters-so high that only brine shrimp can live. These tiny marine creatures, in turn, attract shorebirds like long-legged avocets in their fall migrations. White rings of sulfur-smelling carbonates mark the shorelines. Potassium carbonate, or potash, was mined from some of these lakes during the first World War.

The American Avocet

Jack pedaled south through the lake country and eventually arrived at tiny Ellsworth, population 38. He was about to panic for food before he spotted Morgan's Cowpoke Haven.

He parked his bike at the hitching rack out front and cautiously opened the front door. Peering in, he saw a counter with a cash register, so he stepped inside. Footsteps clicked from the back, and immediately a huge dog came around the corner, heading quickly in his direction. Just as Jack backed against the door in a protective posture, a pistol brandishing man followed, yelling, "Watch out! He might lick ya to death! Go lay down, Bruce."

The dog turned and went behind the counter, leaving just Jack and the man with a gun.

"Is there anything I can help you with?" the man

asked in a gravelly voice.

Jack took his eyes off the gun for a second to glance around the store. Seeing some regular store items, he looked back at the man laying the pistol on the counter. "I was just hoping to buy some food, I guess."

"That's good... you don't look old enough to buy a handgun anyway," the man replied. "What kind of food are ya lookin' for?"

"Anything. I'm starved."

"We have sandwiches and chips, pop and candy bars, whatever you like," he offered, pointing at a refrigerator.

Jack walked over to the glass-fronted cooler and eyed the stacks of prepackaged sandwiches. Then he glanced over at the rustic old bar with stools along the south wall.

"Do you mind if I eat them here?" he asked, pointing at the bar.

"That's what it's for," the man replied.

Jack grabbed a handful of sandwiches, three bags of chips, and three bottles of water. Then he headed over to pay for them.

"Go ahead and eat first... you might want more!" the man chuckled.

"Oh, thanks!" Jack sat down and ripped open his first sandwich. Four bites, and it was down. He reached for the second and third ones, devouring them like a starved coyote. Then he twisted the cap off a water bottle and took a big chug before tearing into his potato chips.

"Ya eat pretty well for a skinny kid," the man judged.

"Yeah, I was pretty hungry. You wouldn't happen

to have any granola bars?"

The man chuckled again, "I do like a man with an appetite. Yeah, I just got a fresh box of em in. How many would you like?"

"How big is the box?"

"This big," he said as he held it up.

"That's perfect. I'll take the whole box."

"That's what I thought. Anything else?"

"No, I don't have room for anything else on my bike."

The man peered out the front door. "Yer riding a bicycle? No wonder yer so hungry. Where ya headed?"

"Crescent Lake National Wildlife Refuge."

"Good googly moogly, it's a way down there... and there ain't no place to eat. Hope that box of granola bars is enough!"

"So do I."

Jack finished his lunch and got up to pay. Bruce also got up from his nap behind the bar. The man did some figuring in his head, then asked, "Does twenty dollars sound all right?"

Jack did some quick figures in his head and also came up with around twenty dollars. "Sure," as he pulled his billfold out and paid him. "One other thing, you don't know Farley Hayes?"

"Farley Hayes... why are you askin'?"

Jack's eyes must have gotten large because the man just chuckled and said, "Sorry, Never heard of 'im."

"Oh well, thanks for lunch!"

"You're welcome. Thank you—Bruce! Stay in here. It's too hot out there for a diabetic dog—Good luck with your bicycling!"

Jack stepped back into the oppressive heat,

consulted his map, and hopped back on his bike. He crossed a couple of large railroad tracks and turned onto Highway 2, heading west again.

※ Highway 2, also known as the Sandhills Journey Scenic Byway, shadows the railroad through the natural valleys. Years after the train punched through the hills, the state built Potash highway alongside to accommodate the onrushing automobiles. When the potash industry died, folks suggested a name change to Kincaid Highway or Northwest Yellowstone Highway. In 1926 it became part of Highway 2, which traverses five hundred eleven miles in a disconnected fashion from Iowa to the South Dakota border near Crawford.

Jack pedaled across the long, level flats typical of the closed basin area of the Sandhills. He rode past alkaline lakes that left white rings around the fence posts where they spilled into the road ditches. He spotted an antelope herd grazing in a large green meadow between the lakes. All was quiet until a coal train came along. The Burlington Northern reminded him of home and the raised Chicago Transit Authority trams that rumbled incessantly around its Chicago spiderweb. This train was considerably louder with its diesel engines and piercing horn blasts at the sparse crossings. Any noise sounded amplified after living a couple of weeks in nature's quiet.

Before he reached Lakeside, a brown sign along the highway pointed south reading *Crescent Lake National Wildlife Refuge, 28 miles*. He'd ridden sixty miles since leaving Smith Lake and didn't know if he could handle another thirty, so he decided to go as far as he could, then set up camp somewhere along the way.

Jack pulled onto the graveled road, which

concerned him a great deal. He didn't know if his tires would hold out on however many hundred miles' gravel to get back to a highway. He remembered his good Samaritan cowboy, who gave him a ride earlier and decided to take the risk.

He passed a couple of ranch places and biked across large flats. Three miles down the road, he came to an auto gate at the Garden County line. He got off his bike and pushed it over the steel bars that keep cattle from crossing. Here, he faced a "good news, bad news" situation. He was now on pavement but in open range, which means that he had to share the road with cows. He wondered how the big animals would react to a kid on a bicycle; he hoped they would run away like the antelope.

As he rode south, lakes became more numerous, and sometimes the road squiggled between them on narrow passages. Then, in the middle of another long flat, to Jack's dismay, was a large herd of big black cows scattered about the roadway. His heart rate increased as he slowed his approach, not knowing what to expect. He pictured an old-time western, where a herd of cows stampedes unsuspecting cowboys, leaving behind death and destruction. This obstacle he didn't foresee.

Jack pulled to a stop about a hundred yards from the cows and tried to figure out what to do. He could wait them out and hope they saw greener grass somewhere else, but they didn't seem to be in any hurry to go anywhere. Movie star cowboys hoop and holler and wave their hats at the herd to get them to move. But he didn't have a hat, and the last thing he wanted to do was draw attention to himself and possibly make them mad. He was in a pickle.

Then, he heard a car coming from behind. Maybe, perchance, the vehicle would spook the cows away, and he could pass through safely. The car slowed as it passed Jack and then braked to a stop in front of him. After a few seconds, the reverse lights came on, and it backed up to where he was sitting. The passenger window rolled down, and the driver's female voice asked, "Aren't you the guy from Chicago?"

Of all the wild things he'd witnessed in the last couple of days, this one topped them all. How could a girl in this remote part of the world possibly know him? He fumbled for an answer, "Uh, yeah… but how… "

"My friend and I stopped to talk to you at the rodeo arena in O'Neill, remember?"

Inside, Jack nearly fainted. Outside, he tried to act retrospective. "Oh yeah! You were with- what's her name?"

"My friend, Savannah."

"Yeah, that's right!" Jack did his best not to appear flabbergasted.

"What are you doing out here?" the girl inquired.

"Uh, me? Oh, I was just waiting for those cows to get off the road."

"What for?"

"Uh, I guess I'm not sure… are they okay with bicycles?"

He could hear a stifled giggle from inside the car. "I don't know; they might take after you."

"Seriously?"

"No, I was just kidding," she replied with a laugh. "They shouldn't bother you. Just keep riding, and they'll get out of your way. If you want, I can drive ahead and bust a path for you."

"That would be great!" Jack exclaimed.
"I guess I didn't introduce myself; I'm Dusty Collins. Where are you headed?"

"Crescent Lake, but I don't know if I'll make it that far tonight. Is there a place I could camp ahead?"

"No, but you could stay at our place. It's about ten miles down the road; it's called the Wolf Lake Ranch. There's a sign in our driveway."

"Thanks! I might do that," Jack replied gratefully.

"Okay, see you later then." Dusty took off down the road giving the cows a honk as she drove through, with Jack riding as fast as his tired legs would go behind her. When they made it past the herd, Jack's guardian angel vanished into the distance.

9. RANCH LIFE

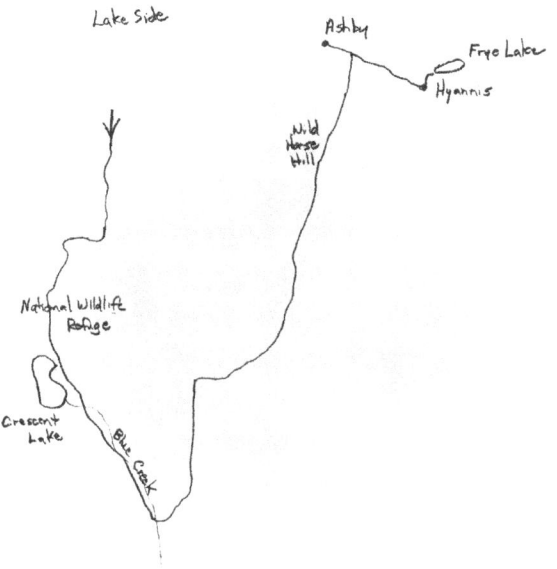

On that warm summer evening, Jack rode the last leg of his eighty-mile day with renewed energy. His encounter with the cowgirl boosted his morale enough to make these miles seem as effortless as the first.

He rode by a ranch house at the base of a giant hill where late evening mule deer browsed around the buildings. He found it odd that wild animals would venture so close to human surroundings; perhaps there's a symbiotic relationship between man and deer.

He rode over a pass in the hills and down onto a broad valley with expansive cattail marshes. The rushes were extra tall and lush, like bamboo forests in the meadow's low spots. Whitetail deer waded through the dark green grass between the road and cattails. With this area looking like a Cambodian microcosm, Jack half expected to see a water buffalo grazing with the deer.

A Sandhills sunset

The road curved around an old homestead marked by elm trees and some outbuildings and up an incline that offered an incredible view of the cattail valley that stretched miles in both directions. It descended slowly toward a sharp corner where a Wolf Lake Ranch sign described the large hacienda beyond.

Jack pulled into the driveway, struck by the sheer size of the house and barn, strategically set on a rise overlooking the valley. He sent several ringneck pheasants scurrying across the shortly cropped meadow grass into the safety of their nighttime cattail roosts. A half dozen sleek horses trotted up to the fence to get a closer look at this stranger, who matched their stares with a wary eye. The paved drive turned at the main home and circled back in front of a couple of bunkhouses, forming a cul de sac with a well-manicured lawn in the center.

He parked his bike, took off his helmet, and was pondering a reasonable approach to the house when he heard, "Hello, you must be the bike traveler."

A tall, wiry cowboy was walking toward him from the bunkhouses. He reached out a hand and introduced himself: "Pete Collins," as he gave Jack's arm a firm side to side exercise.

"I'm Jack Harris," he replied with a hidden grimace. "Are you Dusty's father?"

"Yeah, she said we might have a visitor tonight," he replied. "Where do you usually spend the night?"

"I have a pup tent… all I need is a place to set it up," Jack replied.

"Our bunkhouses are full right now, but you are welcome to use the bathroom in the far one," Pete offered. "You can set your tent wherever you like."

"Thanks, that would be great!' Jack exclaimed.

Pete looked Jack up and down and concluded, "You look like you could use some home cookin… why don't you join us for breakfast?"

Jack jumped at this offer, "I'd love to… I'm getting pretty tired of granola bars."

"I bet you are," Pete replied. "Just ring that doorbell at 5:30 in the morning," he said, pointing at a side door.

With that, the cowboy headed for his door, and Jack rode over to the second bunkhouse. He parked and started to unpack his tent when the bunk's screen door opened, and a young man stepped out. "You must be the biker. Pete just told us that we might be sharing our quarters tonight," he announced. "I'm James," he said, reaching out for a handshake.

"Hi, I'm Jack," he replied, returning the noticeably gentler grasp.

"I'm from Colorado, and my coworker, Austin's from South Dakota. We're here for a couple of months, learning the ranching trade."

"That's cool," Jack replied. "That sounds like something that I wouldn't mind doing myself."

The two exchanged brief backgrounds as Jack set up his tent and dug out his toothbrush.

"Shower's open," Austin proclaimed as he came out to meet Jack. They shook hands; then Jack said he would take them up on that hot shower.

It felt good to be squeaky clean again after so many days in the wild. Afterward, Jack sat and talked with the two interns until total darkness. Then he headed for bed after his new friends assured him that they would wake him for breakfast.

Jack tried to sleep that night, wrestling with the old nemesis that haunted him more than ever. Purpose in life seemed to be close at hand, hidden somewhere in these hills like a diamond in the rough. He drifted off, vowing not to leave until he found it.

At the first hint of light, Jack woke to footsteps nearing his tent. "Hey Jack, it's time to get up," James announced softly. "Are you awake?"

"Yeah, I'm awake... thanks," Jack replied. Stretching and moaning in pain as a cramp shot up the back of his leg, he crawled out of the sack and stumbled into the bunkhouse to throw cold water on his face and comb his hair for breakfast. He stood and stared at the scene in the bathroom mirror—if his mom could only see her forlorn, unshaven pup now.

Making himself as presentable as possible, he walked with the other two ranch hands to the main house for breakfast. Entering the garage, they went through another door and up a flight of stairs to a large dining room. Pete offered them coffee and orange juice as they sat around the table to make plans for the day.

Jack glanced in the kitchen, where a lady captured his eye. She was short of stature but agile like her husband. She had blonde hair and wore a western shirt and blue jeans. But catching his fancy were the spurs strapped to her boots. They made a jingling noise when she walked across the floor and entered the dining room.

"Hi, you must be Jack," she said. "I'm Jessie, Pete's wife."

"Pleased to meet you, ma'am." Jack didn't know where the word ma'am came from but it sounded appropriate for the situation.

Jessie set down a plate of pancakes and chinked back to the kitchen for the sausage and eggs. They dug into breakfast, occasionally breaking the ting of forks on china with a remark.

"Gonna be another hot one today," Pete deduced. "Where are you headed on your bike?"

Jack looked up from his pancakes and replied, "Crescent Lake National Wildlife Refuge... is there a place to camp there?"

"No, you have to be off the refuge by dark. Crescent Lake isn't part of the refuge, but I don't think there's a campground. The next place south would be

Oshkosh."

"Is that still in the Sandhills?"

"No, you run out of the hills a little way south of the refuge."

"Is there a road going east, toward Hyannis?"

"Yeah, the south Ashby Road comes out down there, but I might have to draw you a map." Pete pulled out a pen and drew out directions that filled both sides of a napkin.

"Thanks," Jack said as he folded the map and tucked it into his pocket.

He thanked them for their gracious hospitality, then bid them farewell. As he walked back to his tent, he felt his scraggly whiskers and decided that it was time to shave. The cowboys that he'd met so far have been clean-shaven, except for a few mustaches. To fit in out here, he needed boots, jeans, and a mustache. Looking down at his attire, he shook his head; it was no wonder why the locals saw him as an outsider.

As he stood shaving at the bathroom mirror, he left his mustache to see if it made him look tough. The sparse hairs under his nose reminded him of a line in an army movie that he once watched: "If you smeared milk on that pathetic thing, a kitten would lick it clean off." He decided to finish the job.

The morning sun was filtering through the yard trees as he packed his tent for another journey leg. He hoped to see Dusty before leaving, but she didn't join them for breakfast, so he would have to go without thanking her for the invite. As he rode out of the yard, though, he didn't notice the curtains part slightly in the upstairs window.

The horses galloped over to say goodbye as

he rode out the lane. The pheasants were back on the meadow, with their dark copper bodies and long tails shining against the bright green grass. With the sun's low angle casting a cinematic feel, he couldn't decide which was prettier, morning or evening in the Sandhills.

Back on the trail, he headed west across the cattail valley to a hill range that rose from the giant marshland. The road followed the hill's base up a valley finger, where it squeezed in tight to a tall sandhill bluff to skirt around another large lake and marsh. Upon this bluff, known as Maverick Hill, resides a well-known golden eagle that perches high on the peak, observing its marshy domain. Jack admired the gigantic, statue-like bird as he rode below.

He biked through a narrow pass and onto another large flat dotted with lakes. The road continued in a southwesterly direction for a few miles, past a couple of ranch houses. Soon after turning left at a tee, he came to a large sign stating, Crescent Lake National Wildlife Refuge. He was entering a 46,000-acre government-managed wildlife breeding grounds established in 1931.

At an information stop, he read about the various bird species that live there. Ducks, geese, grouse, pheasants, bald eagles, and herons were names that he recognized. Long-billed curlew, loggerhead shrike, and bittern were new to him. He wondered how many he would see as he biked across the refuge.

He stopped at each sign to read the interesting facts about flora and fauna in the Sandhills. One stated that a rare plant called Hayden's penstemon grows nowhere else, only in the sandy blowouts here and a spot in Wyoming. The vegetation variety is so unique here that the Sandhills region is a distinct prairie type. Another sign pointed out a heron rookery on Crane Lake, where the long-legged birds build slapdash nests in treetops to have their young. Jack tried to imagine this big, gangly shorebird perched in a tree; somehow, it didn't seem possible. The further he went, the more amazed he was at the diverse life in these dunes.

Much of his five-mile ride through the thin midsection of the refuge took him through the area closed to public access, which meant that he couldn't park and wander off the road on foot. The deer in this area seemed to know that they were safe, barely glancing at him as he quietly slid by. He rode past the headquarters, situated on a gorgeous little lake that reminded him of Golden Pond. Next, he came to a large lake next to the road where a sign read, Island Lake. Curious, he rode down the trail to the boat ramp to check it out.

He walked out on a fishing pier and studied the water. It was brownish-green with very little clarity. He paused for a minute on the dock and enjoyed the peaceful sound of gentle waves flowing by. It reminded him of evenings on Lake Michigan.

Back on the road, he soon hit the refuge's south boundary. Then he came to Crescent Lake, Nebraska's largest natural lake at 982 acres. When the road dipped next to the lake, he parked again and walked down to check it out. The water was turbid here also, so he got back on his bike and continued down the road.

Blue Creek's headwaters flowed from the lake's southeast corner, channeling down a dug canal and under the road, which now turned to gravel. A few miles later, he pedaled by a large spring that increased the creek's volume considerably. As he progressed southward, he noticed a distinct change in the landscape. It looked like the sand had washed out of this valley and down to the Platte River, exposing a finer, flat land soil below.

Jack was now cycling through a favorite Native American lodging area. The large, freshwater springs fed Blue Creek, providing year-round open water for Indians and the bison they hunted. The well-worn travel route from the Flat Water (Platte) to the Running Water (Niobrara) allowed Brule, Oglala, Cheyenne, Comanche, and Plains Apache to enter their cherished Sandhill bison hunting grounds from this southwest portal.

A few miles before Blue Creek joins the Platte River, the Battle of Ash Hollow took place in 1855. This "Blue Water Battle," or "Harney's Massacre," extinguished the fire ignited earlier when a cow wandered from a Mormon emigrant where a Brule Sioux shot it. In retaliation, Lt. John Lawrence Gratten and thirty soldiers left Ft. Laramie to arrest the Indian thief, High Forehead. In the confrontation, one of the army soldiers shot and killed Chief Conquering Bear, starting a battle that left Gratten and his thirty men dead. President Franklin Pierce then appointed the War Department to avenge the Gratten Massacre. The department ordered General William S. Harney and one-tenth of the United States Army to mount the Sioux Expedition. On September 3rd, Harney and his troops attacked a Brule village along the creek, killing eighty-six Indians and capturing seventy women and children. Harney earned the vile nickname "Squaw Killer" when the press learned the staggering number of women who died in the battle.

Jack continued down Blue Creek, where the road entered someone's yard. He found it interesting that public roads in places become part of a private residence. Winding between the buildings, Jack eventually came out the other side. A couple of miles farther, he turned left at a fork, crossed the creek, and climbed back into the hills. He reached the farthest point of his journey and was now headed back toward his home in the east.

Three miles in, the road thankfully turned to pavement again. He headed straight north on a rare Sandhills road without a curve. Instead of diverting around the hills, it went right over the top. Jack was getting his workout on this hot summer day.

The pastureland had now gone a few days without rain, but the hills were still bright green. Sand has a sponge-like quality, drawing water from the vast storage below to keep the roots moist. Jack stopped on the highest hilltops to catch his breath and take in the spectacular sea of green. The Chicago River, dyed green on St. Patrick's Day is quite a sight, but it was no match for this.

The road finally curved at the end of a seven and a half-mile straightaway, where he pedaled past a hunting club. The route took a northeasterly path, following valleys leading to passageways into the next. This terrain cycle continued for the next thirty-two miles taking Jack deep through the downstream sand waves that undulate away from the Sandhill's northwest origin.

He passed a few ranch places along the way, some

named with large signs, others sat quietly back in a grove of trees, minding their own business. A couple of buildings looked like they may have been a church or schoolhouse at one time. He tried to imagine living in this world so different from his and how it would affect his outlook on life. Something inside told him that he was about to find out.

A few miles short of his connection with Highway 2, Jack pedaled through the deep shadow of a hulking sand mountain. He rode on the narrow ribbon of oil skirting the sand talus that flowed out from the cat-stepped, three hundred-foot bluffs. The hill's sheer size was enough to take the strut out of any swashbuckling Sandhiller. Later, he learned that this is Wild Horse hill and has some interesting theories about its labeling.

Then, he topped a rise and rode by a sign that beckoned a major highway ahead. Seconds later, he rolled to a stop at the broad-shouldered super-slab known as Highway 2. "Ah, civilization again," he muttered as he pulled out his map to check directions. He determined that Hyannis was seven and a half miles to the east, and Ashby was a mile and a half west. The sun was low, and he'd biked over seventy miles that day, so he turned west to see if he could find a place to stay in the nearby town.

Ashby is the first town on the east side of the elevation divide at the Grant/Garden County line, separating the western closed basin area from the Sandhills' eastern slope. Here, the water starts flowing east, giving birth to the Snake, North, and Middle Loups, and later the Dismal, Calamus, Elkhorn, and Cedar rivers.

Jack turned off Highway 2, crossed the railroad tracks, and pedaled into the little town, looking for a park. As dusk settled in, he wheeled down Main Street and wound up at the Ashby United Church of Christ. The vacant backyard would do for the night.

He crawled into the sack and tried to get comfortable as the full moon cast an eerie glow through his paper-thin shelter. He spent little time in a church up to this point, and so far, he'd managed to avoid his fear of this unknown realm. Sleep, which came so quickly on the nights in the wilderness, evaded him in this doubtful setting. Long, muskie-scaled fingers slid slowly across the moon's face as Jack turned to his phone for comfort. He googled the word "churchyard," hoping to put his mind to rest. One particular result was a poem that struck him personally.

> *There's a grim one-horse hearse in a jolly round trot;*
> *To the churchyard, a pauper is going I wot;*
> *The road it is rough, and the hearse has no springs,*
> *And hark to the dirge that the sad driver sings.*
> *Rattle his bones over the stones;*
> *He's only a pauper whom nobody owns.*
> *—Thomas Noel, The Pauper's Drive.*

Jack mulled over these lines and pictured himself as "the pauper whom nobody owns." Not only does nobody own him, but they also don't even know him. He could be in that casket, destined for his eternal status, as the world sang goodbye in a jesting tone. His life looked pretty insignificant as his mind finally laid itself to rest in a lull between coal trains where he drifted into a fitful slumber.

Deep in the night, Jack aroused to a different

sounding rumble. He opened his eyes to the strobe light flashes of an approaching thunderstorm. Waiting a few seconds for his adrenal gland to settle down, Jack considered his options. If this were a garden variety thunderstorm, then he could lie still and let it pass. But if it were severe, he would be much safer under a roof. He remembered the fury of the storm that drove him under the bridge at Long Pine. His light pup tent would offer no protection against hail and high wind. He imagined a shredded tent, bouncing his bones across the churchyard as lightning strikes around.

Leaping into action, Jack crawled out and jerked the tent poles and stakes. Then he rolled the whole thing up in one big ball and set it on his bike. The trees started to bend under the storm's initial blast as he frantically rushed toward the nearest shelter. He rolled his bike to the church's front door and, out of desperation, tried the handle. To his amazement, the door opened, and he quickly ducked inside with all his belongings.

Jack stood behind the door and watched the chaos taking place outside. He felt secure again, with a solid roof over his head and four walls blocking the side forces—so confident that he felt the urge to curse the storm for ruining his night's sleep, but mindful of his surroundings, he tempered his oaths with forced piety.

After the storm passed and the rain subsided, Jack faced a dilemma. He could either reconstruct his tent out in the wet sand or stay here and wait till dawn. Opting for convenience, he unrolled the wadded-up tent on the dark foyer floor and stretched again, begging the mercy of the sandman.

Jack tossed and turned on the hard church floor

for a couple of hours, then decided that he had enough. Light or not, he was getting out of there. Jack didn't dare turn on the lights for fear that someone might come to investigate, so he groped around in the predawn murk to pack his gear. With the aid of a small flashlight, he managed to get everything stowed, and the agitated young biker exited the little country church as quietly as possible.

In the early light of dawn, he glanced at the tree limb-strewn backyard and sighed in relief at his decision to seek shelter. Jack negotiated the new water puddles on Main street, crossed the railroad tracks, and turned onto Highway 2, biking toward the brightening eastern horizon. Ultra-fresh air that comes with a new day coupled with the recent rainstorm filled Jack's lungs as he pedaled the smooth highway. It felt like the dawn of a new chapter in his life.

The nine-mile ride to Hyannis stimulated thoughts of reflection and soul searching. He approached Savannah's hometown, hoping to amend his awkward O'Neill encounter with her, but odds were stacked against him finding her in an area spread out like this. Then he thought about the two apprentices back at Wolf Lake and their zeal for ranch life. He had never experienced that kind of enthusiasm toward a job and wondered how it felt. By the time he rolled into Hyannis, his desire for ranch life and a thinning billfold made him resolute in his decision to find work.

The bright summer sun reflected off the roadside puddles as he biked past a feed store and a trailer sales establishment on the western outskirts. Shortly, he was in the residential area where he looked across the tracks and eyed a mansion with a red-tiled roof, surrounded by large spruce trees and a well-manicured hedge. It looked like a governor's residence. A couple of blocks farther, he rode by a two-story house with a white spindled porch and sign that said "Whisperin Angel Inn." Next, he passed a long lap-sided hardware store that nearly touched the highway curb. Across the street was the Sandhills Oil gas station. This inviting establishment looked like a good stop for breakfast.

Jack coasted past a cowboy, filling his truck for the day ahead, and parked his bike next to the station. He walked into the convenience store and inhaled the welcome aromas of sausage and coffee. A cowboy standing at the counter glanced in his direction, giving Jack a quick once-over. Looking around, he felt more out of place here than anywhere thus far. Cowboys were in the aisles and seated at tables drinking their morning coffee. They all seemed to take an interest in this skinny-legged city kid.

Jack walked past a group of seated onlookers en route to the men's room and reached for the bathroom door. Before he could grab it, though, the door swung in, and he found himself face to face with the tallest, rangiest cowboy of the Sandhills. In the millisecond that Jack used to step out of the way, he took a mental snapshot of this man's features. Boots protruded from the bottom of well-worn leather chaps with silver snaps on the sides. He wore a long-sleeved western shirt complete with a bandanna around his neck. Above his square chin was a handlebar mustache that turned white on the curled tips. Below his black hat was a pair of piercing dark brown eyes that stared silently at the stunned Jack as he stepped aside and let the cowboy pass.

Later, glancing in the bathroom mirror, he decided it was time to lose the bike helmet and shorts. What looks normal in Chicago sticks out like a sore thumb here. It was time for him to assimilate into the area's culture.

He grabbed a bottle of juice and a hot breakfast sandwich at the deli and mosied up to the counter. The lady running the register smiled at him and rang up his purchases. As he handed her the cash, he worked up the nerve to ask about employment.

"Do you know where I can inquire about a job?" he asked.

"Working here?" she asked.

"No, on a ranch," he replied.

The lady passed the inquiry on to the other gals working behind the counter, and they all turned to eye Jack from head to toe. Doubtful looks came over their faces. "No, I sure don't," said the first one.

"Thanks anyway," Jack said as he turned to go sit down.

"Buck Jackson," came a late reply from somewhere in the back. An older lady walked up to the counter and looked Jack over. "Yep, he's the guy you need to talk to. I can get you his phone number."

Jack, sparked by this new information, anxiously punched the man's name and number into his phone as the lady read it to him from the store's computer. This information could be his big break.

He sat at a booth and downed his breakfast, choosing the correct words to use in a phone conversation with his prospective employer. Then he bit the bullet and made the call.

"Hello?" came a lady's voice.

"Is this the Buck Jackson residence?" Jack inquired.

"Yes, it is. May I help you?" the kindly voice replied.

"This is Jack Harris, and I'm inquiring about a ranching job. Do you have anything available?"

"You will have to talk to my husband about that. He's not in now, but I can have him call you later. Can I take your number?"

Jack gave her his phone number using his most professional-sounding voice and thanked her for her troubles. He felt a shiver of excitement as he hung up the phone. There was something in Mrs. Jackson's tone that gave him hope.

As Jack walked by the front counter on his way out, he inquired about a campground in the area. "Frye Lake a mile north of town," was their unanimous answer.

"Thanks for all your help," he exclaimed as he stepped out the door.

Jack had time to kill as he waited for a phone call, so he pedaled around town to get a feel for the place. A block east, he turned right and started up a steep grade marked Main Avenue. On the right was an old three-story hotel and bar. On the left was a bank, a grocery store, then another bank. Then, he passed a post office and, of all things, a windmill in the middle of the street. Main Avenue dead-ended a block and a half off the highway at a brick building that appeared to be a library.

Circling back past the windmill, he turned right and rode past the Grant County Courthouse, where he turned right again and pedaled up the hill past an elementary school. The street curved to the right, turning into a two-track lane headed west along the south rim of town. As he rode, he imagined the fun he would've had riding down the steep streets as a kid. At the west end, he coasted down Sherman Avenue to the highway.

The residences were very well kept, with beautiful trees landscaping the neatly mowed lawns. Jack figured this to be a town of affluence; later, he learned that Hyannis was once considered the wealthiest town in America.

Jack consulted his map and saw that Frye Lake was a mile north on Highway 61. He crossed the railroad tracks where President Teddy Roosevelt stood on the train and addressed local cowboys en route to his favorite hunting grounds out west.

Biking past a sign that said Merriman 67 miles, Jack remembered all those miles ago when he spent the day riding around that tiny town. Then he passed an airport with a paved runway and thought how different this was from the constant flow of jet airliners that descended toward O'Hare over his apartment back home.

After a couple of bends in the highway, he spied a wooden sign similar to the other public lakes where he'd stayed. He turned onto the gravel road and followed it a half-mile to the western shore of Frye Lake. Here, he found only a graveled boat launch and a few willow trees. It looked like he would have to rough it.

He parked at the ramp and walked under some overhanging willows down to the water. Unlike the Crescent Lake Refuge, the water here was crystal clear and inviting. The lake was very picturesque, rimmed with trees and large hills beyond. He couldn't wait to test the fishing and, later on, the swimming. First, he needed to make camp, though.

The road made a loop to the south, next to a restroom. Here, a single large tree offered some shade in a mowed area between the lake and road. This spot looked good to pitch his tent. As he made camp, he thought about the storm that hit earlier that morning and if this tree would protect him from wind and hail. He figured that he could duck into the restroom if necessary.

With camp made, he constructed his fishing rod and walked over to the boat launch to try his luck. He quickly hooked a small bass in the open pool formed where boats came and left. He could see other openings in the moss beds beyond his casting range, so he took off his shoes and waded out to them. The cool water felt refreshing after his long biking days. Jack found yet another little piece of paradise in this vast unexploited green desert.

Before long, he started fighting drowsiness. His harrowing experiences during the night left him several hours short of sleep. He placed his rod and phone on a tuft of grass next to the water back at shore. Then he stretched out in the shallow water with his head on the beach and soon drifted into blissful slumber.

In the land of Nod, Jack found himself journeying through an endless maze of unreachable water sources. He was dying of thirst, yet he could never quite get the life-giving cup to his lips. As he staggered from the windmills to a water fountain, he became weaker by the minute. Next, he was flat out on the ground with two men standing over him. One guy asked, "Is he dead?" To this, his buddy replied, "No, I can see him breathin'."

Jack woke with a start, squinting up at two figures stooped over him. When he finally got his bearings about him, he muttered, "I guess I fell asleep." He sheepishly sat up and pulled himself out of the water, shaking off his stupor.

"We were afraid you were dead," One man confessed, breaking the awkward silence. "We needed to put our boat in, but you were layin' on the ramp."

Jack turned and looked at the boat poised to launch behind the fishermen. "I should've found a better spot to take a nap. This probably looked pretty bad."

"Yeah. Oh well, it'll give us something to talk about later," the fisherman chuckled.

Jack stood and watched them unload their boat, and he steadied the bow as they crawled in. One guy must have felt pity for this forlorn-looking shore fisherman and offered, "Yer welcome to come out with us if you want."

Jack looked at him and asked, "Seriously?"

"Sure, hop in. We've got plenty of worms," he replied.

Jack grabbed his rod and phone and crawled over the front as he pushed off from shore. "Thanks a lot! I've never fished from a boat."

The cowboy-hatted fisherman in the back cranked the old gas engine, and they were soon chugging across the lake to their secret honey hole. The man running the outboard looked over to a landmark on shore and cut the motor. "Anchors out!" he said as he grabbed a rusty piece of rail tied to a rope and dropped it overboard. "Yer's is right behind ya," he said, pointing to a rope tied to the bow. Jack picked up the nondescript hunk of cast iron at the end of the rope and heaved it over the side.

The two fishermen baited their hooks with hunks of nightcrawler and dropped them over the side. Then they sat back to see what their shanghaied crazy boy was going to do. Jack, wanting to impress them with his fishing prowess, cast his jig across the water. It landed on a moss island and stuck there. He tugged until he thought the line would snap, then it finally pulled loose, and he reeled in a coontail strand.

"Ya wanna worm?" the middle man offered, sliding the foam container his way.

"Yeah, that might be better," replied Jack.

"Where ya from?" he asked.

"Chicago," replied Jack.

The straw-hatted fisherman considered this surprising answer as he reeled in to check his bait. "Yer a ways from home," he concluded.

"Yeah, it's quite a ways," Jack replied.

"How'd ya end up here?"

For once, Jack had a definite answer to this question. "I'm hoping to work for Buck Jackson. Do you know him?"

"Yeah, I know Buck... makes sense; you goin' to work for 'im."

This statement perplexed Jack. "Why does it make sense?" he asked.

"I don't know... Ol Buck kind of has a heart for people like…"

"People like me?" asked Jack.

"Don't take this wrong; Buck likes to take greenhorn city slickers and teach 'em the cowboy way.

It's kind of his mission, so to speak." Jack pondered this information and decided that it sounded like good news. He liked fishing from a boat; it seemed to spark conversations that otherwise would never happen. They talked about everything from last night's storm to what restaurant serves the best hamburgers. By the end of the afternoon, Jack didn't feel like an outsider anymore.

They managed to catch a few nice perch, which they dropped in a basket over the side. The host cowboys decided it was time to go home and do their evening chores, so Jack hoisted his anchor, and they motored back to shore. He helped them load their boat and thanked them for the great afternoon.

"Good luck with your employment," one hollered as they drove away.

Jack walked back to his campsite, feeling good about life. All that talk about hamburgers earlier made him hungry. He hopped on his bike and headed into town to the highly recommended Hyannis Hotel and Restaurant.

Jack steered onto the sidewalk and parked at the restaurant's front door, which was spitting distance from the cars idling past on Highway 2. Through the door, he stepped into an old-fashioned saloon, where he half expected to see Miss Kitty and Festus standing up to the bar. He walked over to a table and sat down to gawk at the décor. The entire room was paneled with weathered barn wood, giving it a natural, rustic feel. A pool table stood at one end, and a doorway leading to more dining booths at the other end. Everything, including the diners, looked western except him; he vowed to be wearing cowboy boots and jeans the next time he came in.

A waitress came to his table and asked if he wanted anything to drink. He ordered a Coke, knowing that his old basketball coach would wag his finger at him. He figured it was time to break out of his old ways and embrace the new.

A few minutes later, she brought his iced drink and asked if he was ready to order. He pointed at the long list of specialty burgers and asked, "Do you have any recommendations?"

"They're all good... one of the favorites is the french dip... it's made from shaved prime rib," the lady replied.

"That sounds good. I'll take that," said Jack.

Minutes later, the waitress brought Jack's order, which he had to restrain himself from devouring like a wolf. He had never tasted such tender, perfectly aged beef, dipped in natural au jus. He made a second vow- to order this sometime when he wasn't so hungry, to see if it genuinely tasted this good.

When he finished his meal, he sidled up to the bar and paid his tab. Then he walked past an old, seated gentleman to the pool table, where he decided to rack the balls for a game of solitaire. He, at last, found a familiar element in Nebraska.

"Where're you from, young feller?" he heard from the curious onlooker as he methodically pocketed each ball.

Jack glanced in the old man's direction and replied, "Chicago."

After Jack dropped another ball, the man countered, "Are you a pool hustler?"

Jack laughed and answered, "No, I just play for

fun."

"Who taught you how to shoot like that... Minnesota Fats?"

Jack laughed again, this time covering the fact that he didn't know who Minnesota Fats was. Figuring that he must have been some pool shark, he replied, "I learned on my own at a pool hall near our apartment."

"Chicago," the man mused, "that's a pretty rough place... at least it was back in Al Capone's day."

Jack considered his hometown's notorious history and wondered if outsiders like this old fellow thought it was still like that. Al Capone's mobsters disappeared along with prohibition at the end of the roaring '20s. This man surely didn't figure Chicago was still like that.

"That was a long time ago," said Jack. Then he added, "I bet this town saw some rowdy days too."

"You bet it did," the man replied. "When this town started, the law was laid down by anyone willing to use his fist or six-gun."

"Wow, just like in the old westerns," Jack replied as he looked around the room. "Is this an original building?"

"Yep, built in 1898. It was considered the fanciest hotel in the west back then." The man paused as if he were savoring the taste of the good old days. Then he said with an almost regretful tone, "About the only rowdy thing left here is that pool table yer playin' on."

Jack figured that times had changed here just like Chicago. Gone are the mobster-controlled speakeasies back home and the frontier law (or lack of) out here in the west. "Our chocolate past has kind of gone vanilla," he concluded as he dropped the 8-ball in a corner pocket.

This mention of ice cream sounded pretty good to Jack, so he excused himself from the gentleman, went back to the bar, and ordered a dish to top off his dining experience. He glanced back at the older man as he enjoyed his dessert and wondered about his life history. The deep wrinkles in his face indicated struggle and understanding that only comes from a fully lived life. Someday, he hoped that he could prove the same.

Jack stepped into the warm July evening and mounted his bike for the ride back to the lake. He had a full tummy, and now only a phone call from Buck Jackson could top off his day. He checked his phone about every ten minutes to see if he missed a call.

Back at his campsite, he stretched out in his shaded tent and caught up with his mom about the last days' events. She seemed excited when he said he might have a job interview with a rancher named Buck Jackson. At first, she was quiet but then sounded very happy for him. She told him that whatever he did, she backed him one hundred percent.

Jack's conversation with his mom and earlier with the old fellow in the saloon started him thinking about life's big picture. He hoped that his life would present an era that someday, folks will look upon and smile. His days may not see the taming of the west, infamous gangsters, or world wars, but indeed, something big will happen. At this moment, he felt like he was barely past the starting line in life's marathon; maybe at the finish, he will sport wrinkles as deep as his old friend's.

The tone of an incoming phone call roused him from his thoughts. "Hello?" he answered expectantly.

"Yes, is this Jack Harris?" came a dulcet voice from the other end.

"Yes, this is Jack."

"This is Buck Jackson. I'm returning your inquiry about a job."

"Yes, you were recommended by a lady at the gas station today. She said that I should call you about the kind of work that I'm looking for. Hopefully, ranch work?"

"Well, she's correct. We live on a ranch and there's always work to be done. Do you want to come out to interview for a job?"

"That would be great!"

"Okay, we live about ten miles from Hyannis. Can you be here at 8:00 in the morning?"

"I sure can. I just need directions to your house," replied Jack.

Buck gave him explicit directions as he scribbled them out on an empty page in Farley's journal. "You shouldn't get too lost because there aren't many roads to choose from out here," Buck said.

"Okay, I'll be there in the morning then," said Jack.

"See you in the morning, goodbye," said Buck.

As Jack hung up the phone, it felt like he just turned the page to a new, defining chapter in life. Nineteen-year-olds struggle with direction as they go off to college, join the military, or in his case, wander the Sandhills, looking for purpose. Boys usually, in some fashion, follow their father's footsteps in life, but in his case, this wasn't an option. He would have to blaze his trail, using Farley's notebook for a compass. A chorus of bullfrogs hummed him to sleep in his final night, camping under the stars.

The following day, Jack stopped at Sandhills Oil for a sausage and egg biscuit and to make himself presentable for the job interview. Standing in front of the bathroom mirror, he parted his hair this way and that but just couldn't achieve the rugged, cowboy look. He hoped that Mr. Jackson was as gracious as the two fishermen described.

He consulted his hand-scribbled map and headed out, relying on his newly found sense of direction. He didn't have to check the sun's position in the sky to navigate in Chicago. He grew up learning streets and avenues and how to negotiate them on his bicycle. If he got off course, he simply took a side street to come back. Taking the wrong road out here would mean missing his destination by at least ten miles.

Out of town, he turned onto a one-lane blacktop road. He wound through the hills in the warm morning sun, studying the road ahead for Buck's turnoff. Then, where the road stretched across the middle of a large meadow, he spied a simple white sign with "Blue Diamond Ranch, Buck and Sarah Jackson."

He turned onto the lane curving around a mirror-smooth lake to the ranch headquarters tucked beneath a towering hill beyond. Ducks quacked monotonously in their cattail-lined hideaways off the open water. As he drew closer to the buildings, he could see horses milling about in the open meadow. This ranch looked like the feature photo on a July calendar page with its barn-red buildings trimmed in white.

Jack weaved around some water holes as he pedaled into the yard, where a large shaggy white dog and a couple of border collies suddenly spotted him. The large dog gave a cavernous warning bark that sent shivers down Jack's spine. The three dogs had him surrounded before he had a chance to think up any sort of defense. His bare arms and legs probably resembled freshly plucked drumsticks and wings dangling from a two-wheeled meat hook. He envisioned the massive dog grabbing him with its powerful jaws and dragging his limp body up the hill to eat at his leisure. As he stood straddling his bike with the pack of hungry wolves circling him, he heard a man's voice and the dogs immediately retreated.

Jack watched the dogs run to the barn, where a gray-haired cowboy stood at the open door, pointing their way inside. The man shut the door behind them and started walking his way.

"Sorry about that," he apologized as he walked up to the shaken lad. "Are you Jack?"

"Yuh-yes," Jack replied, trying to get his wits about him.

"I'm Buck, glad to meet you," the lean old cowboy said as he reached for a handshake. "I didn't realize that you were traveling by bicycle."

Jack stuck a limp hand out and placed it in Buck's firm, knowing grasp, "Yeah, I should've told you last night. Glad to meet you too."

"Don't worry about those dogs. Their bark is much worse than their bite. Come on up to the house, and I'll introduce you to Sarah."

Jack rode alongside the long gait of the tall man as they made their way up the drive to the house. Unlike the red outbuildings, the ranch-style home featured white lap siding and a green steel roof. Dark green shutters adorned the large picture window facing the front yard.

Jack followed Buck into the open overhead door of the attached two-car garage. They walked by a car inside to another door leading into the house. Through this door, they entered what Buck referred to as a "mudroom," with a washer and dryer, sink, and coat rack filled with winter clothes. They walked through this room into a large open area that contained the kitchen, dining, and living rooms.

Mrs. Jackson walked over from the kitchen and introduced herself, "Hi, I'm Sarah, Buck's wife. Nice to meet you, Jack."

Jack shook her hand, noticing her bright eyes and slender figure under her short locks of gray hair. "Nice to meet you too," replied Jack.

Buck motioned to the dining room table and said, "We may as well sit down. Do you care for some coffee or water?"

"A glass of water would be fine, thank you," replied Jack as he took a seat.

Sarah brought Jack a glass of water, then poured cups of steaming coffee, carried them to the table, set one in front of Buck, and sat down with the other.

Buck took a sip, then asked, "So what brings you here, looking for work?"

Jack, by now, was well versed with his answer, telling the old couple how his quest started in Chicago in search of Farley Hayes. Then he described some of the adventures that he'd experienced on his bicycle loop around the Sandhills. He ended by saying that he'd pretty much given up on finding Farley but instead wanted to try ranch life for a while.

When he finished talking, Buck looked at his wife and broke into a grin. She smiled back, and then he turned to Jack with his side of the story. "Lived here all my life. I went to school with Sarah in Hyannis and married her sixty years ago. Ranching is the only way of life that we know. We couldn't have children of our own, but we've had lots of ranch help come and go over the years. Some were serious cowboys; others just needed to get away from their normal lives. We've even had exchange students from other countries come live with us. We are currently without help, so if you still want the job, we pay fifteen hundred dollars a month, plus room and board."

Jack's eyes lit up with Buck's generous offer. "I would love to give it a try!" he exclaimed.

"Okay, you have a couple of options where to room. You can either live in a spare bedroom in this house or in an old bunkhouse that you may have to share with a couple of mice."

Jack, not a fan of rodents, didn't have to give much thought to this choice. "If it's okay, I think I'd rather live in this house."

"Good choice," Sarah said with a smile. "I'll show you around," as she got up from the table.

She led Jack through the kitchen and living room. "You're welcome to make yourself at home," as she pointed to the comfy chairs adjacent to the large picture window. A stone fireplace divided the living room from the hallway leading to the bedrooms. "This will be your bathroom," she said as she pointed to the first door. "We have a master bath in our room," she explained as they walked down the hall. "And this will be your room." She led him into a spacious bedroom with a couple of windows: one with a view of the big hill to the northwest and the other facing southwest. "The closet and dresser are yours," she said as she concluded her tour.

As they walked back to the dining room, Jack pictured his life's belongings taking such a small corner of that bedroom closet. It made him realize how meager his lot was. But something inside was whispering that significance doesn't lie in material things. This loving couple was willing to give him a chance regardless of his standing in life.

Buck met them back at the kitchen and offered to take Jack outdoors to show him the heart of the ranch, which roamed on hooves, grazing the tall summer grass. "Ranches exist on livestock," he said as they walked down the driveway toward the barn and corrals. "Our whole lives center around the cow herd. If we keep them healthy and producing calves, then we can continue to live here, doing what we love."

When they reached the barn, Buck took hold of the door handle and slid it open as Jack cowered behind. "You dogs be good," he commanded as they leaped out into the yard to meet the new stranger. "The big one's Jake," Buck said, reaching down to give his head a tussle. "He looks pretty intimidating, but he's just a big teddy bear. The two cow dogs are Rex and Missy," who came and sat at his feet when they heard their names. "These guys do most of the work when it's time to move the herd." Jack gingerly reached out and patted each on the head to make acquaintance.

Next, Buck led Jack over to the horse pasture, which wasn't far from the barn. "Have you ridden a horse?" Buck asked as the beautiful animals came trotting over to his call.

"No, but I'd like to learn," Jack replied tentatively.

Buck sensed Jack's uneasiness around the big animals and said, "That can be for another day. Let's go for a little ride to see the cows."

They walked across the road to a building with large overhead doors. "This is our tractor shed and shop. I probably spend more time here than anywhere, repairing breakdowns and building things," Buck said.

"What kind of things do you build?" Jack asked curiously.

"You might be surprised," Buck replied with a chuckle. "I'll show you when we get back. Let's go check the cows."

They crawled into the ranch-modified pickup truck, and Buck backed it out of the shed, where the two border collies leaped onto the truck bed. He drove out of the yard and onto a trail that skirted the base of the extensive hill range. They went past fenced-off areas that Buck called bale yards. "We have to keep the bales behind fences; otherwise, the cattle will get to them when they're not supposed to. It doesn't stop the deer, though."

Jack was surprised at this statement. "Do deer eat hay bales?" he asked.

"Yeah, they can be pretty destructive," Buck replied. "Their jumping ability gives them the freedom to roam wherever they like. In the summer, they get into our garden. In the fall, the bucks destroy our trees with their antlers—you may have noticed the wire panels we have around the spruce trees in the front yard. Then in the winter and spring, they ravage our hay."

Jack remembered the mule deer that he saw in the ranch yard a few evenings ago. This discussion answered why deer live in symbiosis with humans; it's all about their food preference.

Up ahead, Jack spotted a closed gate across the trail. Thankfully, he had some experience with this, and he quickly opened his door when Buck rolled to a stop. Jack jumped out, anxious to show off his gate opening skills, and strode up to the imposing post and barbed wire structure. He let it down like a pro, then drug the abnormally long gate aside for Buck to pass. But when he tried to close it, the heft of the extra wire was more than he could handle. Try as he might, he couldn't pull the gate tight enough to hook the post into the bottom loop. After a considerable—and embarrassing struggle, Buck walked up and gave him a hand. "Don't worry," he said. "Sarah struggles with this one too."

They returned to the truck, where the men and their dogs continued their trek deep into the hills. "The pastures look good this summer," Buck observed. "Some years, we get lots of rain, and the hay meadows become lakes. But when we can't hay the low spots, the extra grass in the hills makes up for it. In the dry years, like 2012, the water recedes enough that we can hay the wet meadows—another reason why this is one of the best cattle grazing lands in the world."

After a couple of miles bouncing across meadows mounded by pocket gophers, they left the valley and climbed into a high pass. The trail became much sandier as it wound between the dunes and yuccas. They bisected the cratered ridge and topped out on a gently rounded slope that had a view forever in all directions. The rolling knobs reached out to a faint, hazy line that separated earth from sky. Buck parked the truck and shut the engine off.

"This seems to be everyone's favorite spot," Buck stated with a reflective tone. Jack glanced over at the old rancher and watched a lifetime of memories wash over his distinctive face. Something told Jack that there was more to this spot than just the spectacular view. He sensed something more significant here, something that he silently made his quest to discover.

After a few minutes, Buck broke the silence, "Can you see the cows down there?"

Jack snapped out of his deep thought and scanned the hills before them. "Yes, I think so," he replied as he made out some tiny black dots on an adjacent hill. "Is that them down there?"

"Yep, let's go see how they're doing," Buck said as he fired the truck up again. They idled down the gentler north slope to the bottom, where Buck followed the fading trail toward a windmill. He parked and got out. "Go get a drink," he told the dogs, prompting them to jump down and run to the tank. Buck told Jack to grab a sack of mineral from the pickup bed and pour it into a feeder. "This is like daily vitamins for cows. Gives them all the minerals they need to stay healthy," he explained.

Buck looked up at the windmill that started spinning in the slight summer breeze. "I hope you're not afraid of heights,'" he mused. "Sometime during the dog days of August, we need to change the oil in these... and I'm getting a little too old to be crawling up them."

Jack walked over and eyed the zigzag ladder rungs. "Doesn't look bad to me... I'm used to Chicago skyscrapers!" he laughed.

They returned to the truck and continued north. Soon they approached some cows who looked up from eating to see the meaning of this intrusion. They seemed to recognize the vehicle as friendly and walked toward them when the truck stopped. "We feed cake to them in the winter with this truck. That's why they come to investigate," said Buck.

Jack, intrigued by this, asked, "What kind of cake do you feed them?"

Buck laughed and replied, "Not chocolate for sure... they're range cubes made of cottonseed oil, pressed into chunks about the size of your thumb. They're high in protein which helps the cows digest the native grass out here. We also feed distiller's grain and alfalfa bales to accomplish the same thing."

A couple of cows came up to the pickup window with their calves close behind. "This time of year, we have to watch for fly problems," Buck said. "Horn and stable flies suck their blood and drive them crazy if they get too thick. Face flies get in their eyes and can cause pinkeye."

"What can you do about the flies?" queried Jack.

"There's not a perfect solution," Buck replied. "We can use insecticide fly tags in their ears, apply a pour-on insecticide on their backs, or feed them mineral with a pass-through larvacide that stops fly growth in the manure where the eggs hatch."

Jack was amazed by the science involved in raising cattle as he looked the cows over. "How can you tell if the flies are bothering them?" he asked.

"Horn flies are easy to spot on their backs, where they prefer to bite the cows. Stable flies prefer to bite their legs, so the cows will bunch up or stand in water to get away from them," replied Buck. "Flies can make a cow's life pretty miserable."

They drove on, making a big circle and checking

the other windmills in the pasture. The cows all seemed sleek and content, so they started home. Jack soaked in Buck's lifetime of knowledge about livestock and ranching life. Any uncertainties that he had toward living out here were quickly melting away in the company of this amiable man behind the wheel.

Back at the ranch place, Buck pulled up to the house. "May as well get you settled in," he said, eyeing Jack's heavily laden bicycle. "Grab your stuff and come on in. We can store your bike in the garage."

Jack crawled out and started unpacking his belongings, which he carried to his new room and dumped on the bed to arrange in the roomy closet. Minutes later, he walked back to the savory-smelling kitchen to await his next assignment.

"Are you ready for dinner?" Sarah asked. Jack glanced at his watch; it was only noon. Then it dawned on him that Nebraskans may have a different way of saying lunch and dinner.

"Yes, it smells delicious!" Jack exclaimed.

"It'll be ready in a few minutes if you want to wash up and cool off a while."

Buck was sitting in the living room, browsing through a ranching magazine, when Jack returned from the bathroom. He sat down and picked up a copy of American Cattlemen to browse through as he waited for dinner. He smiled inside; what if his mom caught him reading literature such as this?

"Dinner's on," stated Sarah as she set a steaming bowl of mashed potatoes on the dining room table. Jack jumped up and waited at the table for seating orders. "You can sit there," Sarah said, pointing at a chair to the left of the table head. "We're kind of in a rut as to where we sit around here."

They all sat down, then did something entirely unfamiliar to Jack. The couple bowed their heads, closed their eyes, and Buck prayed, "Heavenly Father, we are grateful for the bounty which you've blessed us. We ask for the strength of body and mind in our daily tasks and forgive us when we fail You. In Jesus' name, we pray, amen." Somewhere in the middle of Buck's prayer, Jack followed suit and closed his eyes. Praying before a meal was something that he'd seen on television but had never experienced personally. He figured that this was another local custom to learn.

Sarah said, "Help yourself," as she picked up the bowl of potatoes and started them around. A platter of steaks sat before Jack, and he slid a large one onto his plate and handed it across the table. "The lettuce is fresh from the garden," she added. "What kind of salad dressing do you prefer?"

Jack eyed the various bottles and asked, "What kind is that?" pointing at an unfamiliar one.

Sarah looked at the bottle that he was pointing at and replied, "That's a local favorite, invented by a lady named Dorothy Lynch, from St. Paul, Nebraska."

Jack poured a sample of the orange-colored dressing on his lettuce and tasted it. "Uhm, this is good," he surmised as he continued to pour it over the remaining greens.

He watched Buck mash a depression into his potatoes before spooning brown gravy over them. Looking like an excellent plan, Jack followed suit, saving room for the corn and a homemade dinner roll next to the steak, which took two-thirds of his plate. Then he dug into the hearty home-cooked meal.

Jack encountered a new sensation as he enjoyed the delicious meal with the wise and devout couple. The sandy slopes outside offered a pleasant ambiance, but the warmness around this table was even more enchanting. It felt like a critical piece of life's puzzle just dropped into place.

"Save room for some pie," Sarah insisted as she got up to bring in dessert. She returned a few minutes later with three plates, each packing a large piece of pie topped with vanilla ice cream. Jack sized up the tempting treat now sitting before him. "Do you like rhubarb?" she inquired. He flashed through his short life span and drew a blank on rhubarb.

"I guess I don't know for sure... I've never tried it," he replied. He slid his fork into the pie and cut off a bite, examining the filling, which resembled punch-colored celery. He eased the dainty morsel into his mouth and rolled it around his tongue a couple of times, testing the unique sweet flavor. "This is very good," he discerned. He finished the dessert with the same enthusiasm as the main course, savoring every bite of the home-cooked meal.

Later, Buck suggested that they retire to an easy chair for a few minutes to let their stomachs settle. This idea sounded good as Jack laid his hand on his straining tummy. "I don't know if I've ever eaten so much delicious food at one time," he groaned.

After a brief siesta, Buck said, "Let's go out to the shop, and I'll show you some projects that I'm working on."

Back in the arid summer sun, the dogs accompanied them down to the shop, where they walked through the large, overhead doorway. Sand from wind and vehicle wheels partially covered the concrete floor where the tractor sat. They walked across the parking stalls and entered a door that opened into Buck's workshop.

They stepped into the room, which smelled of hardwoods and varnish. A large wooden table sat in the center, where lights hung from the ceiling. A table saw straddled a mound of sawdust next to it. Various machines and hand tools lay on benches along the walls beneath cubby holes that held nails, screws, and bolts. Paint cans lined a large section of one wall. Jack slowly walked around the shop and gazed at the curious array of unfamiliar implements. He could tell that Buck spent a lifetime in this place.

"Everyone is born with a creative side," Buck said, breaking the curious silence. "I guess mine is building things from wood." He gazed at the raw oak bench resting on a pair of sawhorses in the shaft of light from the window. "This one's just about ready for stain and varnish."

Jack walked over for a closer look. The two-seater bench had a high back with an intricate carving of a spirited-looking horse, a long mane flowing in the wind. The horse's eyes entranced him, daring him to look aside. "This is incredible," he offered with genuine admiration.

Buck grinned and thanked him for the compliment. "You're welcome to do a project of your own if you like. This shop is a pretty good place to spend the bad weather days." Buck paused, then added, "But it's a sunny summer day, and I'm sure you have a lot of exploring to do. Why don't you take the dogs for a little walk in the hills this afternoon? It's a great way to get acquainted—with the dogs and the land."

Jack sprung at this proposal, and soon he was hiking up a two-track trail, talking awkwardly to his new friends, Rex and Missy. They walked the undulating "road" until it split off onto a new one. Then they took this one to the next Y, where they paused to decide which way to go. The one going to the right appeared to head toward a distant high hill, so they opted for it. Soon, Jack was hopelessly lost but figured he could always follow his footsteps in the hot, soft sand back to the house.

Then the dogs took off after a jackrabbit. Jack watched in wonder as the enormous rabbit glided effortlessly over the ground in long leaps and bounds, staying well ahead of his pursuers. In a flash, the dogs were gone, leaving Jack alone in this sandy wilderness. He did a slow pivot on the trail, looking for a familiar landmark, but saw only hills and yuccas. Then he tried out his untested loudest voice and yelled, "Rex!" "Missy!" at the top of his lungs. He watched with anticipation the spot where the dogs disappeared over the hill, but they didn't show. His only option now was to retrace his steps back to the ranch—without the dogs.

As he plodded along through the sand, he wondered how Buck would take the news of his lost dogs. Maybe this was an awful thing. Maybe bad enough that he would get fired on his first day. The farther he walked, the deeper the hole he envisioned to be in, so he decided to turn back and go looking for the dogs. As he turned, though, he spotted the two long-haired beachcombers racing down the trail toward him. Seconds later, the three reunited in a ball of affectionate jubilation. They were now friends for life. After a minute of nuzzling and back-scratching, Jack stood up from the frolic and announced, "Come on guys, we're going home." "Home…" he liked the sound of that.

10. URBAN COWBOY

Gold needs not to be painted. - Matthew Henry

Jack settled nicely into his new life on the Blue Diamond Ranch. His boss was much different than the ones back in Chicago. Buck treated him with understanding, almost as if the old rancher raised him from childhood. He called him "Buck," but inside, he thought of him as Grandpa... or, dare even, Dad. For the first time in his life, he experienced the special father/son relationship he craved.

After several days learning ranch chores, Jack was excited when Buck announced that he and Sarah needed to go to Alliance for repairs and some shopping and wondered if he wanted to go along.

"Is there a store where I can buy some boots and jeans?" he asked with anticipation.

"Yep, Bomgaars should have everything you need, and we're going there anyway," Buck replied.

"Great!" replied Jack. "I can't wait to try on some cowboy clothes."

Buck grinned his widest grin and chuckled to himself. "I can hardly wait to see what all that red hair looks like under a Stetson hat."

From their ranch near Hyannis, a trip to a larger

town meant traveling 60 miles west to Alliance, or 75 miles south to Ogallala, or 110 miles southeast to North Platte. They made the hour-long drive, retracing some of highway 2 that Jack cycled earlier. As they wound over the passes and sped along the long valleys, Buck named each ranch along the way as if he knew each man personally. Jack was amazed that people living 30 miles away were still considered neighbors.

Buck pointed out the remains of the old potash factories near Antioch. "This was a boomtown during World War I," he reflected. "Would you believe that 2,000 people lived here back then?"

Jack looked to both sides of the highway and saw only a cattle feedlot and a couple of old houses. "No, I can't even imagine it," he replied."Where did they all live?"

"Whatever living arrangements they had was very temporary, as you can see. There isn't a trace of a city remaining," Buck replied.

A few miles west, they went around a sharp bend at the top of a hill and were met with a long, flat straight stretch of highway. "We just drove out of the Sandhills," Buck announced. Jack looked around at the flat farm ground and was amazed at the sudden change in topography. It was like passing from an imaginary realm into real life again. This land now looked much like the farm ground around his hometown of Chicago, only with the lighter colored soil and thinner, drier air associated with the high plains.

With the hills still in view in the rearview mirror, they passed the Alliance Municipal Airport, which once served as an army airfield. A minute later, they drove into the city of 8,000 people, which like so many other towns along the Highway 2 corridor, was named by a railroad superintendent back in the 1880s. "Before the railroad, this town was called Grand Lake," Buck said. "Too bad they changed it... the east end of this 290-mile stretch is Grand Island. It makes it sound like the train is traveling across a sea of grass."

They drove through downtown on the broad, bricked streets to the farm store where Jack anxiously awaited his new clothes. When they entered the large store, which smelled of feed and new rubber, Sarah offered to help Jack while Buck went for his supplies. They made their way to the clothing department and started with the boots.

"The main thing to look for in boots is comfort," explained Sarah. "The showiest ones aren't necessarily the best. We need to try several on before you decide."

Jack moved slowly down the boot aisle, breathing in the aroma of new leather. Every size 12 boot beckoned him to try it on, so that's just what he did. Pulling the first one on, he was surprised by the tightness around his foot and lower calf. These were much different than the tennis shoes that he had worn all his life. He wondered how they could ever be as comfortable as his old shoes.

"Boots have a break-in period before they fit well," Sarah explained. "The leather will conform to your foot after three or four weeks."

Jack settled on a pair of square-toed boots like the cowboy apprentices back at the Wolf Lake Ranch were wearing. If they worked for them, then they should work for him.

Next, they pushed their cart to the blue jeans rack, where they started looking for his 30" waist size.

He wasn't sure what his inseam was, so he just started trying them on. When he came out of the dressing room with the first pair, Sarah laughed and said, "They are fine if you're expecting high water. Let's try on some 34's."

After the jeans, they went to look at shirts. "Most cowboys wear long-sleeved shirts, even in the summer. They keep the mosquitoes and deer flies from biting your arms; plus, they keep you from sunburning". They picked out various shirts in the tall size and moved on to the hats.

The cowboy hats were the part that Jack most anticipated. He couldn't wait to see how much it would change his looks. He grabbed a black stetson off the shelf and donned it in front of the mirror. It didn't look terrible with his red hair, but it didn't quite look right.

"It's a little big for you," Sarah offered. "And you probably want to go with a straw hat this summer. They're much cooler. Here, try this one," she said, pulling a light-colored hat off the shelf. He pulled it on and felt the snugness around its brim.

"Much better," he said. "Fits nice... and it doesn't look bad either, does it?"

Sarah gave it a thoughtful once-over. "You know, with a haircut, you might just pass as a real cowboy," she said with a smile and a wink.

They picked up some boot socks and underwear to finish his list, then Sarah left to do some shopping of her own. Jack wandered up the aisles of power equipment and curious items that he had never seen in the stores back in Chicago: colorful halters and sacks of sweet smelling feed, pickup mud flaps, and horse fly sprays. He was immersed in this strange new array of products when Buck spotted him and asked if he was ready to check out. "Yeah, I'm ready," he replied. " I was just looking at all the neat stuff."

Buck and Sarah had a couple more stops to make while in town, then they went to a restaurant for "dinner," as they call the noon meal in these parts. The cooking was good but no match for Sarah's. Soon, they were back on the road, heading east into the hills and home.

Later, with the day's work done, Jack tried on his new duds in front of the bedroom mirror. Studying the urban cowboy that stared back at him, he wondered about flipping roles and moving to Chicago from here. Would it be as awkward trying on new city clothes? One thing for sure, if he rode down Michigan Avenue wearing this, he would feel just as unsuited as he did in the Hyannis gas station wearing his Chicago attire. He decided that it was going to take some time to assimilate into this new culture.

Buck let out a low whistle, and Sarah grinned when he strolled into the family room, showing off his new clothes. "Wow, Jack, you look like a real cowboy!" Sarah exclaimed.

"Do you really think so?" Jack asked unsurely.

"Yep, just like a cowboy," Buck agreed with a kind smile.

"One thing looks really out of place, though. I think it's my hair. Do you think a haircut would help?" asked Jack.

"Well, there's one way to find out," Buck said, glancing over at his wife. "Sarah's a pretty good barber... been cutting my hair all our married lives."

"You could cut my hair?" queried Jack.

"Sure," answered Sarah. "But you'll want to change out of your new clothes first. I don't want to get clippings all over them."

Jack retreated to his room, came out wearing his old clothes, and proceeded to get his haircut. A half-hour later, standing in front of the mirror and admiring his new look, he couldn't wait to go to town and fit in. More importantly, Jack was one step away from pursuing that cowgirl that captivated his thoughts and imagination. After learning how to ride a horse, he would reintroduce himself to Savannah.

All sorts of ranch upkeeping tasks filled the dog days of August. As Buck promised, they spent a few days changing the oil in the windmill gearboxes. Jack crawled up the towers and performed the maintenance while Buck stood below, watching with an anxious eye. Buck had him check all the nuts holding the fan blades for tightness before he crawled back down. The Nebraska winds can get pretty ferocious.

Twenty-eight-gauge steel adorns the exteriors of most Sandhill barns. Once applied, a building rides out years of summer storms and winter blizzards. The Blue Diamond ranch was an exception, though. Buck kept plenty of paintbrushes, with sizes to fit any task. When someone looked for ranch work, he always had weathered siding needing a fresh coat of paint. If the prospective help turned up their nose at this menial task and moved on to the next ranch, he just smiled and wished them well.

Jack learned the fine art of painting that summer. He started by scraping the garden shed and giving it a fresh coat of red. He then moved on to bigger things; the tractor shed/shop took several days, then he tackled the barn.

During this painting crusade, Jack's mind wandered through an equine dreamland. Unlike kids growing up in the Sandhills, horses were not part of his childhood. He shuddered at the thought of clinging for dear life to a thousand pounds of muscle as it galloped at highway speed, then having it buck his gangly body twenty feet high, on its airborne trajectory toward a landfall filled with broken bones and flailing hooves. Only one thing would prompt him to take such a risk; a knight in shining armor looks not so gallant when riding a bicycle.

One day, as Buck stopped to check on his progress, Jack mustered the courage to ask the question: "Can you teach me to ride a horse?"

Buck knew his people as well as he knew horses. This riding lesson would challenge even his vast experience in the field. Placing a red-headed greenhorn atop a ranch horse is like sneaking up to jerk the tail of a sleeping coyote. You just don't know what to expect. But he liked this kid and could sense his youthful sincerity.

"Yeah, I can teach you to ride," he said. "Just don't expect to turn into a cowboy overnight," he said with a playful wink.

Buck eased Jack into the world of horses by first acquainting them with each other. Sandhill kids learn how to ride a horse right after they learn to walk and talk. Horses are as much a part of their lives as eating pizza and reading bedtime stories. Jack grew up without so much as a dog, cat, or hamster. His closest encounter with a horse was watching the staff groom ponies at

Chicago's Lincoln Park Zoo. He would have to start at a toddler level.

Early one morning, while the late summer fog still shrouded the surrounding hilltops, Buck accompanied Jack to the horse pasture. They stopped at the tack room, grabbed a halter and lead rope, and headed down the sandy trail.

"First, you must develop a trust with your horse," he said as they plodded along. "A horse is like a dog; they view a stranger with a wary eye. You need to spend some time getting to know him on ground level first."

They came to a fence and crawled over the barbed wire. Then Buck let out a loud whistle and yelled, "Bert! Charlieeee!" The sound of his voice carried across the calm, marshy air, and soon a half dozen horses came trotting in from their favorite nighttime haunt on the big hill overlooking the meadow. As they drew near, they slowed to a cautious halt, then circled slowly around this curious newcomer, making funny snorts from their noses. Buck talked to them with the kind of voice that a diplomat would use on a newborn granddaughter. The horses slowly moved closer as he crooned to them. Then Buck pointed to a beautiful sorrel mare.

"That's Lucy. Her bloodline comes from one of the most famous stallions in the Sandhills and possibly North America—Two Eyed Jack. He lived on the Pitzer ranch down by Ericson."

Jack stood like a statue as the horses drew near. He noted their eyes and thought of the carving on the bench in the woodshop. He now realized that Buck got his inspiration straight from the horse's face.

"Charlie, come," Buck commanded with a

collected tone. "The gray is our best horse to learn on." He eased up to the old gelding with an outstretched arm. The horse focused one eye on Jack and the other on Buck's hand. "Also, like dogs, they respond well to treats," he said as the horse nibbled the apple-flavored snack from his palm. Buck started rubbing the white smoke hair on the horse's neck, first with his hand, then with the halter. With a deft movement, Buck had the halter over Charlie's muzzle and pulled over his ears. Once secured, Buck handed the end of the lead rope to Jack.

"What should I do if he runs?" Jack nervously asked as he grasped the rope.

"Let go," Buck replied with a grin.

Jack held the rope as if he were holding the tail of a snake. Charlie stood still while Buck talked and patted his big neck. The horse would often turn to leave, but the halter changed his mind as he felt resistance from Jack. After a minute, Buck suggested that Jack should step closer. "Talk to him as you approach... and don't show him you're nervous."

Jack quietly heeded Buck's instruction and shortened the rope as he took baby steps toward the unsure horse. "Good horse... good horse... good horse," Jack uttered in loud whispers. Soon he was standing close enough to reach out and touch him.

"Now rub his neck, just like I did," said Buck, who had backed off a few steps.

Jack reached out slowly and placed his hand gently on the big animal's neck. Surprisingly, the horse stood still while he ran his hand under its mane down toward the shoulder. He thought of the movie Avatar, where the Na'vi natives of Pandora bond with direhorses through neural whips on their bodies. He was bonding with this old horse named Charlie through the touch of his hand and soft talk.

"That's it," said Buck. "Now, let's see if you can lead him." He turned and headed toward home while making a clicking sound with his mouth and commanding, "Come." The horse started forward, and Buck quickly prompted Jack to stay beside him. "Horses are smart like dogs and have excellent hearing," Buck explained as the trio walked along. "They learn simple voice commands, which is one way for us to communicate with them."

This bit of information briefly diverted Jack from the heady feeling of leading a large animal by a rope. "There are other ways to talk to horses?" he asked breathlessly.

"Yeah, but we'll learn those later," Buck replied. "We need to learn to walk before we fly."

They led the horse up to the gate where they crossed earlier, and then Buck emitted a drawn-out "Whoa." The horse stopped behind them, and the old cowboy walked back and fed it another treat before taking off its halter. "Good boy!" he said as he rubbed the base of its neck. Then he said "Okay" and gave the shoulder a parting tap. Upon hearing this, the horse instantly departed to rejoin his companions.

"Wow!" Jack exclaimed. "That horse is really smart! How long did it take to teach him?"

Buck chuckled, "He was trained professionally a long time ago… but I'm sure it didn't take him long." They stood and gazed at the string of horses for a minute, then crossed the fence to return to their daily chores.

Jack resumed his painting projects with renewed energy. Each morning, he and Buck went to the horse pasture to work with Charlie. Sometimes Jack even went solo with a pocket full of horse treats for insurance. In a few days, he was able to call each horse by name, and they came running. The equines slowly accepted him into their gang. As he built his relationship with the old horse, he could feel changes in himself. He was allowing another living being into his life to share his fears and disappointments. Charlie, being the ever attentive listener, was learning the heart and soul of this young Chicagoan.

However, ahead loomed the unavoidable initiation into cowboydom. Jack was going to have to crawl in the saddle and ride.

Then the day arrived. Buck broke the news during breakfast when he paused between bites of fried taters and eggs and asked, "Are you ready to see if those new boots fit a stirrup?"

Jack looked up, almost choking on a tater, and replied, "Yes sir!" with bluffing confidence that even a poor poker player could see through.

Sarah looked at Jack with knowing eyes and said with assurance, "Of course he's ready. He and Charlie are quite the pair!"

Jack smiled weakly at her encouraging words and finished chewing the last bite of what seemed like his final meal. This day surmounted his previous acts of courage by a long shot. But zero hour had arrived, and he resolved to conquer his fear. "Yep, I have a feeling Charlie and I are going to make history today," he said, masking his uneasiness.

The following chain of events happened in a blur.

Out in the fresh morning air, Charlie came running for his routine morning treat. Buck haltered him, and then they walked to the tack room to brush him down. Jack watched closely as the old cowboy prepared the horse to ride. With all the burrs brushed out, Buck placed a clean saddle pad in the swale of its back. Then he gently swung the leather saddle across and nestled it onto the blanket. Reaching under the horse, Buck pulled the girth and flank cinches tight and fastened the heavy leather straps. Then he had Jack stand an arm's length from the horse's side while he stretched a stirrup out to his armpit.

"We need to fit the stirrups to your long legs, and this is the best way to do it before you get in the saddle."

Next, he ran his hand down each leg, picking up the hoof to examine. "We don't shoe our ranch horses, but the hooves need trimming every six weeks. The soft sand doesn't naturally chip away at the excess length like on harder ground. It's kind of like comparing the fingernails of a typist to those of a bricklayer."

The old cowboy reminded Jack of an airplane pilot, going through his preflight inspection before launching into the wild blue yonder. When he was confident that all was in order, he made a final trip into the tack room and picked out a bridle. He handed Jack the contraption of leather and steel and said, "Bring this. Let's head to the round pen for a little warm-up."

Buck grabbed a lunge whip standing next to the door, then snapped a long line to the horse's halter. "Come," he said as they headed to the pen. Jack followed along as if the order was also for him.

"Stay out here," Buck said as he opened the steel gate to enter the sandy enclosure.

"Okay," said Jack as he swung the bridle over his shoulder to rest his hands on the square bars of the pen.

Jack watched as Buck stood next to the horse and had him do various movements with a touch on the shoulder and tugs on the rope. He had the horse back away by tapping the line, then urged the big animal to walk forward in a big circle at the end of the lunge line. Buck stopped the horse and turned him counterclockwise with subtle commands and a shake from the whip. Soon he had the horse trotting in rings around him, changing directions every few rounds. Jack stood amazed at the command and obedience playing out before him.

"Whoa," said Buck, and the horse came to a halt, panting from the gentle workout. "Okay, come on in," he said, glancing over at Jack.

Drawing a deep breath and releasing it quickly, Jack ventured into the pen. He carried the bridle and reins to Buck, who exchanged them for the horse's halter. With the bridle in place and the bit positioned in the back of Charlie's mouth, he held the left rein out for Jack to grasp.

"Hold the rein and his mane with your left hand and put your left foot into the stirrup. Now grab the back of the saddle with your right hand and hop off your right foot, pulling yourself up and into the saddle."

Jack did as directed, and to his amazement, he found himself sitting astride the horse. Suddenly, he felt ten feet tall. Buck gave Jack some quick instructions on how to hold the reins and sit in the saddle properly. Then he led him through the basics of voice and leg commands to tell the horse what to do. "Just remember, Charlie needs to know that you are calm and in charge at all times. Give him a pat on the neck when he does well."

Jack learned how to make the horse go forward and back up, turn left and right, and stop in the confines of the pen. When he was confident with walking, Buck taught him how to move into a trot and then a lope. With Buck's expertise, Jack gained confidence quickly. He felt as if he were riding an intelligent, muscle-powered bicycle.

After a half-hour, Buck had him stop and dismount. "That will do for today," he said. "Next time, you can take him for a walk down the lane."

They led Charlie back to the tack room, where Buck took his saddle off and exchanged the bridle for a halter and lead rope. Then he had Jack brush the warm summer sweat from Charlie's coat. "Take care of your horse, and he will take care of you," he said.

When the horse cooled down, Buck untied the lead rope from the hitching post and handed it to Jack. "Here, take him back to the horse pasture."

Jack took the rope and said, "Come." The horse obeyed and started after him.

"Bring his halter when you come back," Buck added as they ambled off.

The old cowboy stood for a moment in the tack room door and watched the young man and his horse walk down the lane. A pleased look came across his weathered face, knowing that he took part in the shaping of another youngster. His legacy would live onward.

11. YOUNG LOVE

First love is a little foolish and a lot of curiosity.
— George Bernard Shaw

The late summer mornings were subtly changing. Dawn came a little later each day and was refreshingly cool. Invisible water vapor transpiring from the grassy hills and meadows mixed with night air, producing a fog that obscured the early morning vista on the Blue Diamond ranch. But soon, the intense prairie sun started burning holes in the opaque haze, spotlighting particular dunes that were otherwise just another part of the hilly sameness. This dream-like scene momentarily awed Jack into a religious rush. Remembering a poem that Farley transcribed in his notebook, he dug it out to read the handwritten words.

Awed

To slowly breaking dawn,
His waking eyes were drawn
To the coming of the day.
To his rear being chased,
By the day he embraced,
The night was driven away.

With the darkness in wain,
A gently rolling plain
Appeared through vanishing mist.
The sun's heat was a threat
To tall grasses still wet,
That dew could not resist.

As the chill of the night
Warmed from the sunlight,
He tarried a while to look.
For the view that he saw,
He felt nothing but awe,
That could not come from a book.

On prairie unbroken,
The heavens have spoken,
Without the need of a word.
As the dewdrops glistened,
He sat there and listened,
Pleased with the silence he heard.

Ending his wordless chat,
He slowly tipped his hat,
Still reluctant to go.
He was truly spell-bound
On this enchanted ground,
That few have the fortune to know.

From the back of his horse,
He acknowledged the source
Of peace, on the path he trod.
It was his special place,
Where he came face to face
With the signature of God.

–*Kip E. Sorlie*

As Jack read these words, he sensed a revelation drawing near in his ongoing search for life's hidden meaning. Something bigger than Chicago, Lake Michigan, or even the Sandhills loomed out there. The hills whispered hints to Jack, clues to solve his bewilderment.

But another question firmly gripped Jack's mind. He'd lived on this ranch with Savannah so close, yet unseen. He decided to question Sarah about the cowgirl's whereabouts but didn't know how to introduce the subject. Then, one day he was helping wash dishes and somehow worked up the nerve to inquire about her.

"When I was riding across Nebraska, I met a girl on a horse, and she said she was from Hyannis," he admitted with feigned nonchalance. "Her name is Savannah. You wouldn't by chance know her?"

Sarah was a little surprised by Jack's question. "I know a girl by that name, but where did you meet her?" she asked with a perplexed look.

"I can't remember the name of the town, but it was far away. She said she was practicing rodeo."

"That sounds like the girl I know all right—Savannah West. She's a neighbor of ours. I think she's a senior at Hyannis this year."

Jack's heart rate increased with this news. He didn't want Sarah to think that he'd been thinking about the blue-eyed girl with blonde locks all summer, so he shifted the conversation.

"Is rodeo really a sport?" he asked.

"It certainly is out here," Sarah replied. "High schools offer rodeo just like football or basketball. The state finals are held in Hastings every June." *really?*

Jack weighed this information against his naive and negative remark to Savannah about rodeo. If only he could take back those words. But he'd done the damage, and now he must make amends.

A neighbor, Jack thought to himself. What luck! But how could he meet her again?

"If her last name is West, does that mean she lives on the West Ranch?" he pondered aloud.

Sarah chuckled and replied, "No, it's called the Round Lake Ranch. It's about ten miles south on our road."

Hearing this, Jack immediately started devising a plan. If she lived beyond the Blue Diamond ranch, she must travel past to get to town. He just needed to figure out her schedule.

"How do students get to school out here?" he asked. "It seems like an awful lot of miles to travel every day."

"Yes, they do have lots of driving time," Sarah concurred. "Some kids live over fifty miles from school. Parents drive them to the main highway, where the school bus picks them up and lets 'em off each day. Kids are anxious to turn fourteen, so they can get a school permit and drive themselves."

"Wow! That's so much different than Chicago," Jack exclaimed. "We don't need cars to get to school."

"Do you have a driver's license?" Sarah inquired, surprised.

"No, and neither do most of my friends," Jack replied. "Many of the older people I know don't even own a car."

"Boy, that IS different," Sarah exclaimed. "We couldn't survive out here without vehicles... unless we went back to riding horses."

Speaking of horses, Jack's key player in his scheme to meet Savannah was good old Charlie. He imagined himself astride the big gray, trotting down the road when a car approaches from the direction of Hyannis. Just before the horse and car meet, the car blows a tire and limps to a stop. The driver's door opens and out steps the fair-haired maiden with a look of distress rattling her perfect features. When she discovers the flat tire, her hand hovers about her mouth, the way females around the globe nonverbally express the words, "Oh my goodness!" Just then, her knight in shining armor prances to a stop beside the car and analyzes the situation. Having no experience in changing tires, her rescuer says, "Looks like you need a lift." Then hoisting her onto the horse, the two ride off into the sunset together.

"Will you ever get a driver's license?" Sarah asked, snapping him out of his pleasant daydream.

"Huh? Oh, I don't know, I guess," he replied unwittingly. Strangely, he never really contemplated getting a driver's license.

Jack considered all of Sarah's words and then came up with one final question, "So what time of day does school get out in Nebraska?"

Sarah gave him a sideways look as she handed him the last pan to dry. "I'm guessing around 3:30 in the afternoon." She started to ask why but thought better of it; there was something about how Jack danced around the conversation that kept her from pressing the issue.

Maybe the poor boy was in love.

    The next few days, Jack hurried through his daily chores so that when 3:30 rolled around, he saddled old Charlie for an afternoon ride. Wearing his new cowboy attire, he mounted up and headed out the lane. At first, he would stop at the county road, let the horse rest a bit, and then ride back home. A few days of this emboldened him to venture out onto the one-lane road. Each day, he would take his ride a little later and go a little further. When a car or pickup came along, he would lead Charlie into the ditch, as Buck instructed him. He would wave wildly at the passers-by, who sadly only turned out to be ranchers. With each passing day, he doubted more the success of his plan.
    One Thursday afternoon in the middle of September, the young but determined cowboy was riding his old horse back from his turnaround point a couple of miles south of the lane. He was enjoying the squeak of leather and the smell of sunflowers in the warm sun. The rhythm of Charlie's steps was lulling Jack into a dream-like stupor. Complex life outside these endless hills had long since dissolved into the sand, leaving Jack in a state of near-perfect peace. Topping a rise, he noticed an oncoming vehicle in the distance. He coaxed Charlie into the ditch as usual and halted in a tangle of wildflowers.

A Sandhills expressway

As the car neared, he noticed that it was a brown compact pickup truck. The driver was the only occupant and seemed too small to be another rancher. The truck slowed enough to give Jack a good look at the blonde-haired young lady behind the wheel. It was Savannah! The girl of his dreams just turned up in real life.

At a loss for anything else to do, Jack started flailing his arms wildly after her casual wave in passing. She must have noticed his abnormal gesturing in the rearview mirror as she was driving away because her brake lights lit up, and she rolled to a stop. Jack's pulse quickened as he watched the truck back up to his patiently waiting horse.

"Do you need something," the young driver inquired out her open window. Her ice-blue eyes had the exact cutting, yet human, virtue that had haunted him all summer.

Jack searched for words but could only grin as he waited for her to recognize him. After a few awkward seconds, though, he realized that she wasn't going to. Then an awful fear washed over him. What if it looked like he set up this whole elaborate rendezvous to meet her again? Would she think that he's some sort of weird stalker? Then, he had an idea.

"No... I was just taking my horse for a walk," he finally replied. "He's kind of new to me since I got here," he said with self-assured nonchalance as if he'd been riding horses all his life. "I was just swatting at a bumblebee as you drove past, and you must have thought that I was waving at you," he said, sounding amused at her confusion. "Sorry I troubled you, heh, heh."

"Oh, that's okay—my bad," Savannah said with a smile. "See ya later." Then she let out the clutch on her Ford, and just like that, she was gone again.

Jack sat and watched in disbelief as the truck disappeared into the hills. He just blew his second chance at befriending this fascinating girl. Either fate was against him or his stupidity; he couldn't decide which. Then he urged his horse back onto the road and headed home.

The roller coaster ride of emotions that he had just experienced caused a great deal of soul-searching as they walked along. He thought about how the expectation of seeing Savannah again drove him in his grueling bicycle ride across Nebraska. He wondered if he could have done it without that hope. It for sure added some flavor to his journey.

He thought about how he could have said things differently. If only she could have recognized him without his prompting. Maybe the haircut threw her off. She sure didn't seem to share his yearning to meet again. Perhaps she did recognize him but was playing unfamiliar too. There were so many possibilities. If he let it, this situation could drive him mad. No, he decided from now on he would lay low and let her do the chasing.

The following Saturday, Buck gave Jack the day off to do whatever he wished. Jack decided to go for another ride; this time, he would venture farther south than he'd ever gone. He told himself that he wasn't pursuing Savannah again, but like a magnet stuck to steel, he couldn't get her off his mind.

A few miles down the blacktop, Jack could hear a car approaching from behind. He turned and about lost his balance when he saw it was the brown Ford Ranger again. It was coming from the direction of town and headed south. He quickly steered the horse into the west ditch to let her by. She barely glanced at him as she barreled past with a quick wave.

"Wow, she must be in a hurry this morning," Jack mumbled to himself as he slowly lowered his unseen wave. This third meeting made the other two seem not so dismal. "We're going the wrong direction with this relationship," he muttered.

Twenty minutes later, Jack topped a pass through some massive hills and followed the road down into a picturesque hay meadow. Harvesters had the hay baled and neatly placed in a fenced-off area near the road. The short regrowth in the field was bright green and scattered with Canada geese and white-tail deer.

A herd of mule deer watched with interest from the ridge to the west. They didn't seem affected by the horse and rider way down below, feeling secure on their high, rugged escape. But Jack didn't notice when the deer suddenly stood at attention facing south, their oversized ears detecting an alarming sound.

Jack rode on, unaware of the danger, headed his way. But soon, he could hear it too. It sounded like an engine with no muffler, racing at a high, steady rpm. It was also getting louder by the second, so he surmised that it was coming toward him. The mule deer ceased being curious and bounded away. Out in the hay meadow, the white-tails did likewise. Even Charlie was getting edgy. They were abandoned and exposed in the wide-open valley to whatever this was.

Then Jack saw it. An airplane crested the hill directly above the road ahead. It was flying low and coming fast. Panic gripped him to the point of paralysis. He sensed that something terrible was about to happen but could do nothing as the plane zeroed in on him like a P-51 fighter plane coming in on a strafing run.

The subsequent chain of events blurred past, starting with Charlie bolting just before the plane roared over. Jack held on for a couple of seconds but then found himself hurtling through space with nothing but blacktop somewhere down below for a landing zone. He braced for the impact, which knocked him semi-conscious as he rolled and skidded to a stop in a bloody heap.

He'd experienced some bike wrecks in his life but nothing like this. At first, he lay still and took a mental inventory of his body. His thinking wasn't clear, so it took a while to sort things out. His blue jeans saved much of the skin on his legs. But his hands, arms, and face were a mess. Thankfully, he had movement in all his extremities. Next, he ran his blood-spattered fingers over his gangly arms and legs, feeling for broken bones. Before he could get into a sitting position, the airplane circled and was heading back for him. The serene Sand Hills had suddenly turned into a scene from a horror movie.

Jack laid low as the plane flew past a short distance to the west. Then he watched it bank around and cut its engine back for another approach, this time to the east of the road. Surprisingly, the plane settled in and touched down in the green meadow adjacent to the road. It taxied on big tires across the gopher mounded grass and parked on the other side of the fence, just a few feet away.

Jack watched with apprehension as the pilot cut the engine and let down a door on the right side of the plane. He didn't know if this guy was here to help or do more harm. His concern turned to amazement, though, when the pilot jumped to the ground with youthful spring and form. It was Savannah! She ran from her plane to the fence which she deftly traversed, and within seconds she was kneeling beside Jack.

"Are you all right?" she asked nervously and out of breath, peering at Jack with anxious eyes.

Jack thought for a second, torn between displaying agony or toughness, then looked up at his rescuer and replied, "I think so."

"Oh my goodness, your face!" She exclaimed with her hand to her mouth. "I'm so sorry. I didn't mean for anything like this to happen."

Jack gingerly touched his bloodied face and felt

the piles of skin shoved from its usual place by black asphalt. He grimaced in pain as his raw fingers grated on the irritated nerve endings in his face. "I must look like a mess."

"Do you think anything's broken?" she asked with earnest compassion.

Jack thought for a second, then replied, "My pride, for sure."

Savannah looked over at a willow tree in the ditch nearby and asked, "Would you feel better in the shade?"

"Maybe."

"Here, let me help you up." She knelt behind him and gently slid her arms under his armpits until she could clasp her hands in the middle of his chest. With her lifting power and a sudden burst of energy that flowed through Jack's body, they were able to stand up. They shuffled together across the road to the tree, where she helped him back down into the soft sand and shade. "This is more comfortable," she said as she sat down beside him.

After they caught their breath, Jack broke the calming stillness. "I didn't know that you could fly an airplane."

Savannah welcomed the change in subject, taking it as a sign that she didn't fully maim this pitiful cowboy imposter, and he was no longer bluffing ignorance. "So you know who I am?"

"Yes, I know you," Jack replied sheepishly.

Savannah smiled at his belated but sincere honesty. "Yeah, I've been flying three or four years now."

Jack did the math in his still spinning head and replied with disbelief, "You learned to fly a plane when you were fifteen?"

"Well, I may have started learning before that. But I didn't get my license until I was sixteen."

This information was almost more than he could swallow. The girl has probably been riding a horse since she was a toddler, driving a pickup truck to school, and now this. Childhood in Nebraska is so different.

"How, or should I ask why, did you learn to fly?"

Savannah thought for a moment, then replied, "Different reasons, I guess. My great-grandpa bought an airplane a long time ago before there were good roads. Back then, ranchers used them to check their cows and fly out of the hills on business. We've had airplanes in the family ever since."

"I guess I can see why an airplane would be handy out here," Jack said. "But it seems like a strange thing for a girl to do."

"Do you know what an aviatrix is?"

"No."

"It's a female pilot. There have been some pretty famous ones from this area. Have you ever heard of Amelia Earhart?"

"Yeah, I think so."

"She was born in Kansas, not far from the Nebraska line. She was the first female to fly solo across the Atlantic Ocean. How about Evelyn Sharp. Ever hear of her?"

"No."

"She was another famous pilot who grew up in Ord, near the southeast corner of the Sandhills. I read a book about her when I was little, and she sort of became my hero."

"How was she famous?"

"She learned to fly when she was a teenager

during the Great Depression. Then she got her transport license at the Lincoln Airplane and Flying School, where Charles Lindbergh took his first flight. You've probably heard of him too."

"Yeah."

"Anyway, Evelyn became famous, flying people around at such a young age. She even got letters from Clark Gable and Eleanor Roosevelt."

"Wow, that's pretty impressive."

"Yeah, then she flew warplanes across the United States during World War II. Unfortunately, that's how she died. Her P-38 fighter plane lost power and crashed in Pennsylvania. She was only twenty-four years old."

"That's sad."

"It's sad, but she lived her dream life. I admire her for that."

"Sounds like she found what she…" Jack stopped mid-sentence, not ready to share his private struggle. The pause prompted a delicate interlude in the conversation. Savannah sensed a longing in Jack's voice but didn't want to meddle. She found this guy from the big city quite curious.

"That airplane looks pretty new," Jack surmised, gazing at the nifty white flying machine.

"The old Super Cub? I think it's like a 1970 model. It just looks new because we put a different skin on it a few years ago."

"Airplanes have skin?"

"Yeah, it's a fabric stretched over a steel frame. It gets kind of ratty over the years and needs to be replaced."

"Kind of like the skin on my face and arms?"

Savannah grimaced at this quip and replied,

"Yeah, kind of like that... except it doesn't grow back naturally."

"So, do other ranchers use airplanes too?"

"Quite a few. Flying is just part of life out here. I knew an area rancher who was also a pilot for Southwest Airlines."

Jack found this quite interesting. He tried to picture a cowboy sauntering into his house and emerging a little while later, wearing an airline captain's uniform. Talk about two different worlds! "I can't even imagine," he replied.

"If you find that hard to swallow, then you really won't believe what his father did."

"Oh?" By now, Jack could expect almost anything. "What's that?"

"Back in the old days, he landed his airplane on a train car."

"He what?"

"He landed his plane on a train."

"That's what I thought you said... You're kidding, right?"

"No. He enjoyed doing crazy stuff with his airplane."

"How is it even possible to land an airplane on a train?"

"He must have had a strong headwind and a fast-moving train... and a whole lot of nerve."

"Wow, I can't even imagine it. Cowboy aviators, or in your case, a cowgirl aviator, or should I say aviatrix?" Jack glanced over and caught Savannah's wide-eyed grin at his attempt to label her. He thought about how different she was from the city girls back home. There was none of the big-city streetwise indifference. Instead, she spoke with straightforward, honest modesty. There was something fresh about this free-spirited girl. She seemed to possess a peculiar kind of strength from living a lively present rather than a problematic past. Could it be that a person growing up in this wilderness can find wisdom in innocence?

Then he remembered his present situation. He was recovering in the cool sand under a willow tree because of an ornery stunt by this delightful girl sitting beside him.

"So, why did you try to kill me?"

Savannah, surprised by the sudden allegation, contemplated her plea a few seconds, then replied, "I'm really sorry for this mess I got you in. I thought I would teach you a lesson in humility, and as it turned out, I'm the one repenting."

"Why did you think I needed to be humbled?"

Again, Savannah thought over Jack's question before replying, "It goes back to your remark last summer. The one about rodeo not being a true sport. That kind of stuck in my craw. Then, a few days ago, when you acted like a high and mighty cowboy out on the road, when anyone could tell you barely stayed on your horse. I thought I could teach you a lesson, but it backfired on me."

"So you recognized me out on the road the other day?"

"Yeah, my friend Dusty told me that you rode your bicycle to her place a while back. She said that you were heading in this direction. People in town are talking about the guy from the big city working for Buck Jackson. News gets around out here."

"Yeah, it's amazing how neighbors know each

other. Where I come from, everyone pretty much keeps to themselves."

It occurred to Jack that Savannah apologized for her actions, but he still hadn't begged forgiveness for the thoughtless remark he made to her back in O'Neill. He'd been kicking himself all summer for it, and now he finally got a chance to redeem himself. "I, uh... I'm sorry for saying that rodeo isn't a real sport. I grew up playing basketball. I didn't know anything about rodeo."

"That's okay. We have basketball too, but instead of shooting hoops in my spare time growing up, I practiced roping."

"That's actually pretty cool. I don't know how you do it. I mean, riding a horse and roping a calf at the same time. That sounds impossible."

"It does take a lot of practice."

Jack hesitated before his next request, not sure how Savannah would react. "Could I uh, come watch one of your rodeos sometime?"

Savannah's blue eyes sparkled with delight. "Yeah, that would be good. We're having a high school rodeo in Broken Bow next weekend."

"How far away is Broken Bow?"

"It's not too far, somewhere between one and two hundred miles, I think."

"Oh, wow."

Savannah suddenly remembered Jack's mode of transportation. "You're not going to ride your bike all the way there and back, are you?"

"No, probably not. I might ask Buck and Sarah if they would like to go."

"Oh, that's a good idea. They would enjoy that."

"Yeah, Buck knows a lot about horses. He taught

me how to ride Charlie." Jack suddenly remembered that the last time he saw his horse, it was galloping away, with him suspended in the air behind. "I wonder where my horse went."

Savannah stood and looked in all directions for Charlie but couldn't spot him. "I'm afraid he may have run all the way home. They do that sometimes."

"Great, now what am I going to do?" Jack uttered.

"I'll take you home. It's the least I can do after putting you in this fix."

"You mean in the airplane?" Jack asked with a sudden new wave of anxiety.

"No, I don't think you're up to that. Besides, I don't know if there is a good place to land in Buck's yard. I'll fly home and get my truck. Will you be alright while I'm gone?"

"Yeah, I'm fine."

"Okay, I'll see you in a little bit." Savannah patted Jack's shoulder, then walked back to her plane. Jack watched in wonder as she crawled in and cranked the engine back to life. Soon, she was taxiing to her take-off spot in the meadow, where she turned into the gentle breeze and gunned it for a quick lift-off. Then she was gone.

When the distant drone of the plane faded away, Jack sat in the stillness of the remote meadow once again. He used the quiet to contemplate this strange, new twist in life. His long-anticipated meeting with Savannah went nothing like planned. He wouldn't have ever chosen this sort of thing. But even with all the pain and humiliation, he managed to gain sort of a date with her; watching her from the grandstand at a rodeo would have to do.

Twenty minutes later, Savannah showed up in her truck. Jack got up and slowly straightened his sore frame as she rolled to a stop on the blacktop. He shuffled to the passenger door before she could get out to help. He tried to match her grit with a bit of toughness of his own. He opened the passenger door and crawled in, stifling a groan as his joints howled in disdain.

"Are you doing okay?" Savannah inquired with patient compassion.

"Yeah, I'm fine," he replied.

The ride home was quiet. Jack finally broke the uncomfortable silence with some attempted humor when they turned in the drive at the Blue Diamond ranch. "Next time I see an airplane in the sky, I'm going to take cover real fast!"

Savannah chuckled at this, then turned serious again. "I'm afraid I may be grounded for a long time when my dad finds out about this."

Jack reflected on her forlorn-sounding statement. He suddenly felt regret for his part in the situation. Maybe there was something that he could do to help.

"Does your dad have to find out about it?"

Savannah shot him a sideways look, then replied with a question, "What do you mean?"

"I mean, if you don't tell him about it, how will he ever know?"

"Oh, I'm sure he'll know as soon as this story gets out."

"But what if the story doesn't get out?"

"News travels fast out here, remember?"

"Not if nobody tells it in the first place."

Savannah considered this possibility for a

second, then said, "What about your face? How will you explain that to Buck and Sarah?"

"I'll tell them that something must have spooked Charlie, then I fell off at full speed, and he ran all the way home. Then you came along and gave me a ride. It's all pretty much the truth."

"I guess that is kinda the way it took place," Savannah agreed. "The only thing is, if my dad asks about it, I'm going to have to tell him what really happened."

"I understand. Let's just hope he doesn't ask."

"My folks and little brothers are at a cattle sale today, so maybe no one saw me take off."

"Good... this could just be our little secret."

Just then, they pulled into the yard, relieved to see Charlie standing by the gate into the horse pasture. Savannah parked in front of the house to let Jack out. "Tell Buck and Sarah hi for me," she said as he gingerly crawled out.

"I'll do that. Hope to see you in the rodeo at Broken Bow next week!" he said with as much gusto as he could muster.

"Yeah, see ya." she replied. Then she drove off.

A week later, Jack watched the hills roll by as the trio motored down Highway 2 en route to Broken Bow. He smiled on his good fortune to work for such obliging folks as the Jacksons. Over dinner one day, he had slipped the fact that Savannah was to compete in a rodeo and that he wouldn't mind attending one sometime. They gave each other a grin and replied, "Well then, let's do it!"

Not far out of Hyannis, Jack noticed a side road to the north that said Monahan.

"What's Monahan?" he asked.

"It's a ranch," Buck replied. "One of the largest family-owned ranches in the country."

"How big is it?"

"Around 130,000 acres."

"That sounds big." Jack, curious how big, Googled the size of Chicago—234 sq. miles.

"How many acres are in a square mile?'"

"Six hundred and forty."

He did the math on his phone and then let out a low whistle.

"Wow, you could almost fit seven/eighths of Chicago in that ranch."

Soon they came to the tiny town of Whitman. Buck described this as a "poke and plum town—you poke your head out the window, and you're plum through town," he quipped. "This was once a wild and wooly cattle shipping point for the railroad."

Later, they passed a historical marker that described the bygone town of Hecla. Then they slowed through Mullen, which, like Hyannis, appeared to have some modest commerce. A few miles east, they passed a sign pointing to the hidden town of Seneca.

"That was once a rest stop for the ranchers attending their cattle on the trains bound for Omaha. The town diner served up hefty steaks to the hungry cowboys."

Further east, they drove down a big hill into the picturesque Middle Loup valley. Jack marveled at the tidy ranch houses nestled above the blue river water snaking through the green grass bottomland. A few miles downriver, they slowed again for the town of Thedford.

"This is a progressive town for the Sandhills," Buck remarked. "It's on the crossroads of Highways 2 and 83. It even has a Dollar General store."

A few miles downstream from Thedford, Jack gazed across the river valley to the west at a couple of hills that seemed to have one side slid off.

"What happened to those hills?" he asked.

Buck looked in the direction he pointed and replied, "The river is cutting into the hill, exposing the pure sand that lies beneath the grass. Erosion sites like that expose interesting clues to the history of the Sandhills. You might find Indian arrowheads or bison tracks that are thousands of years old."

Before arriving at the next town of Halsey, they passed some pine-forested hills that rose south of the river.

"Over there is the Nebraska National Forest. Years ago, it was the largest artificial forest in the world."

Jack looked with wonder at the dark green pines that contrasted sharply with the endless sage, tan, and rust colors that saturate the autumn Sandhills.

"Those are all hand-planted?" Jack asked in disbelief.

"Yep, around 20,000 acres, I believe."

Jack took out his phone again and punched in some numbers. After a few minutes, he announced his findings. "You could put twenty-four New York City Central Parks in that forest. That's a lot of trees to plant by hand."

"Yes, it is." Buck pointed out some fields and greenhouses near the main entrance. "They refrigerate seeds unique to the different forests out west and supply the trees to replant after forest fires and beetle kills. It's the oldest federal tree nursery in the United States."

Then, they entered the small town of Halsey. It, too, had the appearance of a community that is content with the lifestyle of yesteryear. Soon, they were back up to speed with a single row of massive cottonwoods lining the east ditch and the railroad tracks and river to the west.

"We're now passing the old Shinn Turkey Ranch," Buck announced as they drove by rows of galvanized steel barns. "Those sheds once housed thousands of turkeys destined for Thanksgiving dinner tables across the states. Now, there's only a flock of wild turkeys living amongst the cottonwoods."

A few minutes later, they slowed to fifty miles per hour as the highway turned south and crossed the Middle Loup. Jack eyed the sparse houses alongside and then spotted a schoolhouse with a football field. A sign on the brick building said SANDHILLS PUBLIC SCHOOLS.

"This is Dunning," Buck explained. "It sits between the Middle Loup and Dismal rivers, just before they join."

They crossed another bridge with a sign saying Dismal River, and Jack pondered this unusual name. "Why is it called the Dismal River?"

Buck shrugged and replied, "Nobody seems to know the answer to that. French trappers named the Loup rivers after the Pawnee Indians who lived along its banks. They were known as the Wolf People, and 'Loup' is the french word for wolf."

The highway departed the river valley and

climbed into the gently rolling southern Sandhills. Cattle grazed in lush, green meadows that surrounded clear water duck ponds. Shortly after entering Custer County, the road straightened out, and Jack sensed a change in topography as they slowed for the town of Anselmo. Suddenly, there was an irrigated cornfield, then another, and another.

"Anselmo is the southern border town for the Sandhills on this highway," Buck said. "We're in farm country now."

Jack studied the hills and saw a definite difference. They no longer had the familiar rounded undulations. Instead, they were more masculine, with hard lines marking the eroded clay on the hill faces. Fields of ripening corn and beans filled the valley floor between the hard-land hill ranges. A strange new air came in through Jack's open window. The musty odor of maturing corn replaced the sweet smell of sunflowers. He watched as they drove past massive grain bins and well-kept farmsteads. They went through a town called Merna, and then, completing their one hundred thirty-two-mile journey from Hyannis, they rounded a bend and rolled into the most significant city that he'd seen since their trip to Alliance.

"Wow, a Taco John's... and a Dairy Queen!" exclaimed Jack. He'd been away from familiar fast-food restaurants long enough that what was once commonplace now looked so savory. A marquee sign along the highway welcomed the high school rodeo athletes to Broken Bow.

"Broken Bow—that's another interesting name. I bet it has some meaning behind it, too," Jack mused.

"If I remember right," replied Buck, "the settler

that started the first post office in this area submitted several names for the new town, and they were all rejected. Then he remembered about an Indian bow that someone found nearby and submitted that for a name. They must have liked it."

Large, seasoned trees lined each side of the highway as they entered the residential area. Churches of various titles interspersed the well-groomed homes. Jack noticed a stately old three-story brick and stone edifice centered in a block of green grass just before they arrived at the first stoplight. Chiseled in the stone lintel that spanned across two massive columns were the words: *CUSTER COUNTY COURTHOUSE.*

At the stoplight, Jack marveled at the bustling spectacle that lay before him. A picturesque city square rimmed with vintage street lights beckoned newcomers to its adornments. Broad sidewalks led from each corner through beautiful trees to their destination. There, in the center, stood a most charming gazebo. Steps led up a short flight of stairs to the shaded stage where youngsters acted as princes and princesses in their little castle.

"Saturday morning on the square... some things will never change," Sarah sighed with a hint of recollection. "Seems like a different lifetime ago."

Jack felt a pang of yearning as they drove away from the square, continuing their way past brick and clapboard houses built in a bygone era. At a third stoplight, they entered a long stretch of commercial buildings. His stomach growled loudly at the Pizza Hut sign.

"What do you say we stop for dinner before we head out to the fairgrounds?" asked Buck.

"Sounds good to me!" exclaimed Jack, wondering if they heard his internal grumblings.

"Have you ever eaten a runza?"

"A what?"

"A runza."

"No, I never heard of one."

"Well then, I guess it's about time for you to learn," Buck replied. "How about you, Sarah, are you up to a runza?"

"Sure, I haven't had a runza in a long while."

They turned in and found a parking space at the bustling little restaurant. Inside, young servers greeted them with well-trained courtesy. They each ordered runza meals, filled their drinks, and found a seat in the sunlit dining room. Jack took a bite from what looked like a sizable homemade bun and was surprised to discover a delicious mixture of hamburger and cabbage inside.

"This is good," he announced after a couple of bites. "Different than anything I've ever eaten."

"It's an old German flavor but invented in Nebraska," Sarah replied. "We love them."

They enjoyed their meal, then loaded back into the car to drive a few blocks east to the Custer County fairgrounds. Nearing the entrance, Jack spied rows of horse trailers lining the parking lots. He felt a little shiver of excitement as he thought about Savannah preparing for her event. Jack wondered if she was nervous with anticipation or calm as a cucumber. He couldn't picture her in any manner other than her trademark quiet poise.

They paid a small fee at the grandstand entrance, and the gate tender handed them a schedule of events.

Jack quickly scanned the program, looking for clues to Savannah's whereabouts.

"Is there a particular event that you want to see?" the lady asked.

Jack's face blushed a faint red. "Well, as a matter of fact, I have a friend who is competing," he replied as he stared at the roster.

"What events is he competing in?"

"Actually, it's a she."

"Oh, I see," the lady said with a wink aimed at Sarah.

By now, Jack's face was as red as his hair. The gate lady must have sensed his uneasiness because she quit the revelry and pointed to the west. "Pole bending and barrel racing are in the west barn. You can walk from here or drive if you prefer."

Sarah laughed and returned the wink, "We're young; we can walk."

They strode toward the large steel building, admiring the fancy horse trailers parked neatly around the grounds.

"Things are a lot different these days," Buck said as they walked along. "Horses used to be the means of travel. Then cowboys figured out how to put a cage in the back of a pickup to transport their horses. Around 1960, pull-behind horse trailers started showing up on the ranches, and now look at them," pointing at a sleek model nearby. "Horse trailers with air-conditioned living quarters up front for the cowboys."

Jack gazed at the white trailers trimmed in chrome and thought how different this was from the movie depiction of rugged cowboys squatting around a campfire with rain channeling out of their hat brims and into the tin coffee cups cradled in their weathered hands.

"Wow, this is cool," Jack exclaimed. "I had no idea that rodeo was such a serious sport."

Horses and riders were meandering around the end of the barn, waiting their turn to compete. Jack eyed each one from a distance, looking for the familiar blonde hair under a white hat, but he didn't spot his "friend." They entered the barn through a large doorway and found a good spot on the bleachers inside.

"Pole bending, this is my favorite event!" Sarah exclaimed as they sat down.

Jack looked at the six poles placed in a line down the center of the arena. "What do they do with the poles?" he asked.

"The gals race around them," Sarah replied. "You'll see in a minute."

Shortly, a rider entered on one end of the barn and took off like a shot toward the last pole, spurs flailing. Suddenly, the horse spun on a dime around the stick and started a weaving two-step dance back through the others. At the first pole, it whirled around and started back through them again. Then the rider cut a quick circle around the far one and spurred her horse back to the starting line, riding so fast that she barely touched the saddle. Jack was in awe.

"Wow! How do they get a horse to do that?"

"Lots of training and practice," Buck replied. "Do you think you could do that with old Charlie?"

"No way! At least not that fast anyway," Jack exclaimed.

One by one, the cowgirls entered the barn and ran the poles like pros. The best times were in the twenty-two to the twenty-four-second range. He learned that if a barrier got knocked over, it was a five-second penalty, kind of like committing a foul in basketball. The girls even had numbers on their backs like basketball.

"Why do they have three-digit numbers?" Jack asked out of curiosity.

"The first digit tells what year of high school they're in, and the other two are their assigned number, like in football or basketball," Buck replied.

Jack eyed each new pole bender entering the arena, but Savannah wasn't appearing. Once again, he found himself watching and waiting for her. He finally resigned to the fact that this wasn't one of Savannah's sports.

Then something caught his eye. In the shaft of light that came through the open barn door, he saw a glimpse of something familiar. It reminded him of his first gander at a real, live cowgirl back in O'Neill and the glint of gold under her white Stetson. She rode in with the same spirited confidence as the aviatrix that nearly did him in a week ago. He was so exhilarated at the moment that he barely heard the words, ". . . Savannah West from Hyannis." blare across the loudspeaker.

"Well, how about that!" Buck exclaimed. "This gal lives right down the road from us."

Sarah leaned forward and snuck a glance at Jack. She smiled at his sudden alertness; he looked as if the only two things left in this world were this horse and rider.

Young Savannah lined up her palomino with the poles and spurred it into flight. The two became one as the two blondes sped across the arena. Jack was riveted to her eyes and hands as she deftly controlled her steed through the course. She rode as if she were hotly pursuing a German fighter with her P-51 Mustang. Twenty-two seconds later, she broke the time barrier at the finish line and quickly braked her ride to a cooldown walk. She checked her time on the board and looked pleased with her second-place ranking. Then she was gone again.

"Boy, rodeo events don't last very long, do they?" Jack sighed.

"Nope," replied Buck. "Most of the other events are even shorter."

As the final riders made their runs, Jack compared this fascinating sport with basketball. He couldn't find much in common. The entire game lasts only seconds. There are no hardwood floors, no roars from the crowd when a ball gets dunked, no high fives, and no taunting the opponents. Just a lifetime of training pinpointed down to a few seconds of silent speed and expertise.

"This isn't really a team sport, is it?" Jack surmised as the last contestant finished her ride.

"Most of the events are individual, but we'll get to see some team roping, which is one of my favorites," Buck replied.

As a blue-jean-clad crew started setting up the barn for the next event, the old ranch couple and Jack headed out to see what was happening in the outdoor arena. They meandered through the trailers to the grandstands overlooking the steel panel enclosure below. Jack took a seat next to Buck and began to study his surroundings. Large banners displaying sponsor names bordered the grounds. The southerly breeze fluttered a vast American flag near the entrance road. Rugged hills rose beyond the flag, encompassing this central Nebraska town like the walls of a fort. There was something safe about this place.

"Looks like you will get to see some steer wrestling," Buck announced with a sly grin aimed at Jack. "Maybe this will satisfy your need for a little contact in your sport."

Jack envisioned two steers going at each other like a couple of heavyweight wrestlers. But when the chute gate flew open, only one steer came rushing out, followed closely on each side by young cowboys at full gallop. Seconds later, one of the cowboys leaned off his flying steed and onto the steer's pounding shoulder, leaving the saddle while grasping horns with each hand. His boots plowed dirt while he pulled with all his might to turn the steer into his torso. Amazingly, the one hundred-eighty pound kid and five hundred pound beast were soon lying side by side, flat on their backs in the dirt. Then they both jumped up and went their separate ways. The cowboy checked his time on the scoreboard as he caught his horse and rode back out of the arena.

Buck looked over to see Jack's reaction to this event. Jack was dumbfounded.

"How? What? Why do they do that?" were the words that he finally managed.

"That's how you catch a runaway steer without a rope," Buck answered with a grin.

Jack pondered the sight that he just witnessed as the next contestant readied his horse beside the chute. Rodeo required skilled horsemanship and a great deal of strength and athleticism, not to mention extraordinary courage.

"This is amazing," he uttered after each five-second attempt to subdue the rushing animal.

The next event was breakaway roping. Jack was surprised to learn this was a girl's event. Then he remembered Savannah's words back in O'Neill, describing their practice on the dummy steer dragged around the arena. She, for sure, would be competing in this event.

The gals readied their horses much like the steer wrestlers but were alone in their attempt to capture the fleeing steer. A line stretched across in front of the horse to ensure that it didn't get a head start. When the calf left the chute, it broke the timing rope, which snapped across in front of the horse. If the horse broke the rope barrier instead of the calf, a ten-second penalty was added to the score. When the contestant roped the calf in the ensuing chase, she would bring her horse to an immediate stop, causing her rope to "break away" from her saddle horn when the calf kept running. The time stopped when the end of the rope adorned with a white flag flew from the horse.

"There's a lot of things that have to go right to get a qualifying time in the roping events," Buck explained.

Jack nodded in agreement after watching several girls make their runs. If a rope missed the calf, there was no time. If it ended up around the calf's head, there was no time. Then, there was the ten-second penalty for leaving the starting position a split second too soon.

"Wow, it's a victory just to get a score," Jack exclaimed as a contestant smiled with relief after her qualifying run.

"A whole lifetime of practice goes into a five-second test," Buck concurred.

Savannah made her appearance midway through

the event. She rode in, readied her looped rope, and backed her horse tight against the backstop. With a stern look of determination, she nodded at the chute operator, and the threesome took off like a shot out of a cannon. In an eye blink, Savannah roped the calf, and the horse slid to a halt.

"A great qualifying run for Savannah West out of Hyannis, Nebraska... looks like a time of three-point eighty-seven seconds!" proclaimed the announcer as the young lady rode out of the arena nodding in appreciation to the onlooker's applause.

"I'll be back in a minute," Jack said as he stood up, looking as if he had some urgent business. Buck paid no attention to his sudden departure, but Sarah watched him leave with mild interest. She had an idea where he was going.

Jack used his lanky frame to peer over the pens to keep track of the white Stetson as it moved in a northerly direction through the maze of trailers. He wondered if he could head her off like that day back in O'Neill. She seemed to be riding toward a large steel barn north of the indoor arena. As she entered the east end of the barn, he decided to find another entrance, so it didn't look like he was intentionally following her. He took off at a brisk walk but was soon trotting when he realized how long the barn was. What seemed like a quarter of a mile later, he arrived at the other end of the barn, slightly out of breath but still able to appear nonchalant as he slowed to a walk near the large entrance.

The smell of hay and horses engulfed Jack as he stepped into the massive barn. The light coming from the door on the other end looked tiny, even though it was large enough to drive a semi-truck through and then another one alongside. He had to pause a second and take in the view. An endless row of gates lined the long central corridor. Horses stood patiently behind many of the gates, watching the cowboys and girls walk past. The stalled animals eyed Jack with a wary eye as if he were an alien in their equestrian world.

Savannah was dismounted and tending to her horse when Jack happened along. She did a classic double-take when she glanced up at the gangly, straw-hatted stranger. Breaking into a smile, she gave him a warm greeting.

"Hey, you made it!" she declared. Then her face grew more serious when she recalled their last encounter. "Are you recovered from your fall last week?"

"Yeah, I'm all healed up now," Jack replied with an awkward smile.

"That's good," Savannah said with a sigh of relief. "Are you here with Buck and Sarah?"

"Yeah."

An awkward silence hung over the two as they searched to find common ground between their polar opposite stories. Jack frantically sought out a question that made sense to a western cowgirl but came up empty. Savannah used the lull in conversation to turn her attention back to her horse. Jack watched as she ran a brush down its sides and legs to remove any mud and dirt picked up in the breakaway run. She gently talked as she caressed the animal's creamy tan coat.

"What's his name?" Jack finally uttered.

"Sparky."

"That's a cool name," Jack replied. "How did he get

it?"

Savannah smiled as she recalled the naming of her horse. "When it was a young colt, it would run across the sand with its blonde mane and tail flowing. The sun glinted off its hair like it was streaming sparks behind."

"That's a neat story," Jack affirmed. "He's a beautiful horse."

"Thanks," replied Savannah as she finished up the grooming and shut the big animal into its stall. Then she added, "Would you and Buck and Sarah like to come to visit our fire tonight?"

Jack, perplexed, asked, "Fire?"

"Yeah, we always have a fire to sit around and tell stories on rodeo nights."

"Sure, that sounds like fun!" Jack exclaimed. "How will we find you?"

"Come with me. I'll show you where we're staying."

The two walked from the barn and down the road between the myriad of campers. Savannah answered Jack's questions as they walked along. His inquiries made her realize how much she took for granted her cowboy way. It struck her that this guy would be answering her naive questions if they were instead walking down the streets of Chicago. She wondered what it would be like to live in a foreign environment suddenly.

"Why did you come here?" she asked.

Jack, taken off guard, grew quiet. He still didn't have a good answer to this persistent question. Why did he come here?

"I'm not sure," he replied after a fashion. "My

life's a bit of a puzzle. Something inside told me it was time to search out a missing piece, and that voice said Nebraska."

Then, Savannah grew introspective. Something Jack said struck a chord with her also. Even though she didn't have a great desire to go there, she often wondered what life would be like in the big city. She admired his ambition and courage to leave the only life he knew to come out here and search for purpose.

She flashed Jack a kindred smile and said, "I think I know what you mean."

12. MIKHAIL

Mikhail — Russian name meaning "like God."

The autumn hills went through a color transformation as frosty nights became the norm. The green grass of summer gradually turned to warm shades of brown, ranging from rust-red to goldenrod. The tall, waving seed heads of sand bluestem and prairie sandreed reminded Jack of the flowing mane and tail of Savannah's palomino. In the end, only three green plants were remaining: the yuccas scattered throughout the choppiest dunes, some scattered patches of cool-season grass on the south bases of the big hills, and the rye planted earlier for winter forage. From the rye field emerged a food source for the cattle and a theological awakening in Jack's life.

Back in September, Jack helped Buck plant the field of cereal rye. The forty-acre field lay on the south half of the meadow on a flat area that was slightly higher than the valley floor. Except for all the gopher mounds, the "cropland" was relatively farmable compared to the rest of the ranch. Buck explained the history of the field to Jack as they prepared to plant the seed.

"The Kincaider that lived here back in the early

1900s was the first to turn the sod in this valley. He was trying to make a go of it for his family on his six hundred-forty acres of free land. He probably tried raising corn, and who knows what out there. After a few years of futility, he decided that the old Indian saying was right, 'Grass no good upside down.'"

Jack remembered the remains of the Kincaider place that the ranch hand showed him the morning of the mirage. This sort of thing fascinated him.

"Is there anything left from his time?" Jack asked eagerly.

"He planted the cottonwood grove behind the house. Do the trees look a hundred years old?"

Jack studied the trees as if he saw them for the first time. They looked as if they lived a hard life but managed to stand tall through the years.

"The soddy that he and his family lived in is gone, but if you look close enough, you can find remnants of his day, like the old horse-drawn implements left here to rust away."

The two stood and gazed at the place, picturing how it must have been in the early years before the trees, barns, and corrals. Jack found it difficult to place himself in the scenario with the mindset that he would have to make a living for his family with nothing but a couple of horses pulling crude iron through the sand.

"It must've been really tough," he muttered out loud.

"Yeah, it was tough back then. That's why the family left to find an easier life," Buck replied. Then he snapped his fingers and added, "Now I'll show you how we plant the field today."

The two walked to the tractor barn where Buck

fired up the old Farmall, backed it up to a cone-shaped machine, and attached it to the three-point hitch.

"This looks like a cement mixer," Jack said, remembering the construction crews working on sidewalks back in Chicago.

Buck chuckled and replied, "No, it's a hopper spreader. We'll fill it with rye seed and go plant the field."

Buck then backed the ranch truck up to a large pallet of seed sacks, and they loaded some onto the bed.

"You want to follow me out to the field?" he requested.

Jack readily complied, always looking for a chance to drive a vehicle. The tractor and truck ground through the trails and gates around the lake to the south field. When they arrived, Buck hopped off the tractor and had Jack pull up alongside. They opened some sacks and poured the small grain into the hopper.

"Wait here 'til I stop and motion for you to bring more seed," Buck instructed.

The old rancher crawled back on his tractor, found the gear he wanted, and started the power-take-off, which sent the little wheel below the hopper spout spinning fast. Then he pulled a make-shift lever which opened a gate, allowing the seed to flow out of the hopper and onto the spreader, throwing seeds like little bullets through the air. In the same instant, he let out the clutch, and off he went, bouncing across the gopher mounds.

Jack watched with great interest as Buck cut a straight line parallel with the north fence, turning around when he came to the other end and headed back his way. When he arrived back at the truck, he stopped and crawled off to refill the hopper.

"I'm shooting for one hundred pounds of seed per acre," Buck said as they poured more rye into the hopper. "It's kind of a 'guess and by golly' science with this rig, but it usually comes out close enough."

They continued planting until the pile of seed sacks in the shed was gone. Then Buck drove the tractor back to the yard to detach the hopper. Next, he hooked onto a drag harrow and motioned Jack to follow him back to the field in the truck. When they arrived, Buck crawled off the tractor.

"Now it's your turn," he said to Jack, pointing at the tractor seat.

Jack's eyes grew large. "You want me to drive?"

"Yep. All you have to do is pull this harrow back and forth over the field until all the seed is covered."

Buck showed him how to work the clutch and put the tractor in gear. He rode with him until he was confident in his ability to turn around without running over the harrow and stop when necessary. Then he showed Jack how to kill the engine.

"Never get off a tractor with the engine running," Buck admonished. "It's like getting off a running horse; you're gonna get hurt... bad."

"I can only imagine," Jack said.

Buck hopped off the back of the tractor and walked to the truck. Jack started across the field, trying his best to maintain the proper overlap with the harrow behind. Farming was a brand new experience for him, kind of like riding a horse for the first time. Before long, he was absorbed in the back and forth rhythm of fieldwork. He liked the feeling of control over the diesel horsepower under him. Most of all, he enjoyed watching the harrow knock down the gopher mounds of sand. But to his amazement, the busy critters would have another pile started on his next pass. "They're relentless," he remarked under his breath.

An hour later, Jack reached the other side of the field, and Buck drove out to see how he was doing. The harrow was doing a fine job scratching the loose sand over the exposed seed, but Buck had another trick up his sleeve.

"Here, help me flip this harrow over," Buck said. Jack followed Buck's lead and assisted him in turning the harrow upside down. "There, now you can put a smooth finish on it. This time drive north and south," motioning with his hand to drive perpendicular to his previous rounds. "This will give those gophers a little more work to do," he said with a grin. "Bring the tractor into the yard when you're done."

Jack went back to work again, dragging another layer of sand over the freshly planted seed. The young urbanite was getting a rare taste of farming in the ranching world. He finished his second pass and headed back to the yard, smoothing out the lane behind him. The tractor ground to a halt, and Jack killed the engine. Hopping to the ground, he suddenly grimaced and massaged his aching tailbone.

"Those gopher mounds are murder!" he exclaimed to his waiting boss.

"Yes they are!" said Buck with knowing eyes. "But you got 'er done. Now, all we need is some rain to bring it up.

"Do you think it will rain sometime soon?" Jack asked.

"I don't know. Rain in the Sandhills is a precious

commodity. We only get around twenty inches a year. Some years a lot less," Buck replied. "I guess it gives us another reason to pray."

A few nights later, Jack woke to the sound of rain on the roof above. He remembered Buck's words about praying for rain, and he found himself saying a little thank you inside.

Each new morning, Jack found himself wandering around the rye field, looking for signs of green life. Then he would get down on his hands and knees, pawing through the sand for sprouts, but he found not so much as a seed. "Maybe the darn gophers ate it all," he muttered to himself in dejection.

Ten days after planting, Buck asked, "Have you checked the field lately?"

"I sort of gave up on it," Jack admitted.

"You might want to go look again," Buck said with a twinkle in his eye.

Minutes later, Jack was at the field admiring thousands of tiny green shoots poking out of the sand. He wondered at his part in this miracle of life. Suddenly, everything seemed fresh and brimming with hope. It was his first experience in the art of husbandry.

The field grew greener each day as the rye stretched toward the warm autumn sun.

"That rye field is like having an insurance policy for the herd this winter," Buck explained. Cows get plenty of vitamin A from grazing green grass during the summer through a nutrient called beta-carotene. But this nutrient disappears when the grass turns brown, so we have to supplement their diet with minerals. The rye stays green even when it's cold, and we will let the cows graze on it occasionally this winter."

One morning, Jack noticed some trespassers in the rye field. A herd of mule deer found the new green growth to their liking and took up residence. This encroachment became a source of consternation to the young keeper of the field. He walked out to shoo them away at first, but it seemed like they ran into the hills to tell their friends and come back later in more significant numbers.

A curious mule deer

Over supper one evening, Jack brought up the subject of deer. "We can't just let them eat all our hard work," he asserted.

Buck responded to Jack's reckoning with a knowing smile. "Deer have an advantage over cattle when it comes to eating. They can jump fences, giving them a free choice to graze wherever they find the greenest grass. Ranchers are faced with the dilemma of what to do about the deer. Legally, we can get a depredation permit to shoot as many as we feel destroy our feed. But as you can guess, I'm not in the spirit of obliteration. I enjoy the deer. They are beautiful creatures that add to the aesthetics of the Sandhills, and they're an important part of the ecosystem. Did you know that mule deer are the only animals that eat buck brush without being poisoned?"

Jack raised his eyebrows. "No, I didn't know that."

Buck continued his deer lecture as Sarah brought to the table three slices of fresh apple pie topped with ice cream. "There's a way that the deer can atone for their trespasses, and you will have a role in it."

Now, Jack's eyebrows elevated to the middle of his forehead. "What's that?" he inquired, perplexed.

"You're gonna be a big-game hunting guide."

Jack's perplexity turned to skepticism. "A big-game hunting guide! Are you serious?"

"Yep. You're going to guide our guest hunter to his trophy buck next month."

"But I don't know anything about hunting. I brought a slingshot with me from Chicago but never had a chance to use it."

"I'll teach you what you need to know about hunting deer," Buck assured. "We still have a few weeks before the season."

Later that evening in the family room, Buck found some old Outdoor Life magazines and tossed them in front of Jack on the coffee table. "Here's some good reading," he said with a 'get cracking' tone.

Jack opened a fall edition and perused through the glossy images of big bucks and hunters with big guns. Growing up in Chicago, Jack had experience with neither guns nor deer. Now he would have to start as an infant in the world of hunting.

The following afternoon, Jack spied Buck walking his way with a scoped rifle slung across his shoulder. Except for the man behind the counter at the general store in Ellsworth, Jack had never met a man brandishing a gun. It looked like he was in for another lesson.

"Come with me," Buck said. "I'll show you how to shoot a rifle." Buck described the basic concept of a gun as they walked, knowing that Jack had no experience.

"The Chinese invented the gun a thousand years ago as a weapon of war. Four hundred years later, European royalty started using guns for sport hunting. Since then, guns have been improved and refined to fit their specific purpose. This gun is a rifle designed for hunting big game animals like deer."

"I noticed that you have other guns in the house," Jack said. "Are they for other purposes?"

"Yep," Buck replied. "The shotgun is for bird hunting. It shoots a spray of lead pellets out the barrel to hit birds on the fly. I also have a small-caliber rifle for dispatching problem critters like skunks and porcupines."

"What caliber is this rifle?" Jack inquired.

"It's a thirty-ought-six."

"What does that mean?"

"It's a thirty caliber, which means that it fires a bullet which is thirty-hundredths of an inch in diameter. The ought-six stands for 1906, the year it was developed."

"Oh, that's interesting," Jack replied. After a few

seconds to contemplate, he asked, "Do you have any guns designed to kill people?"

Buck gave Jack a sudden look of concern. "No, that sort of gun lost demand way back in the 19th century, when civil law replaced the law laid down by whoever carried the fastest gun."

"But what about the guns that I see for sale in Nebraska that look like military weapons?"

Buck thought Jack's question over, noting his level of sincerity. He was inquiring into a very touchy subject with many folks.

"Military-style semi-automatic rifles became popular with coyote hunters back in the '70s and '80s. They could shoot many bullets in a few seconds, which gave hunters an edge with fleeing animals. The problem is they are heavy to carry, so they became novelty guns. In my opinion, they are more of a security blanket than anything."

"I think I see your point," Jack concurred.

The two sportsmen arrived at their destination, a weathered piece of plywood spanning two posts in front of a sand backdrop. Buck taped a paper target to the perforated plywood, and then they marched a hundred paces away. Turning around, they looked back at the target, which now looked tiny in the distance.

"This is about the range that we take most of our shots," Buck said. " We want the bullet to hit a pinch high at a hundred yards."

Buck unfolded the walking stick that he was using. It turned out to be a tripod with a u-shaped rifle rest on top.

"Okay, now sit down with one leg under your other thigh," Buck directed. Next, he placed the tripod straddling his other leg and laid the rifle foregrip in the rest. Then he nestled the stock butt plate into his right shoulder. "This is how I want you to have your hunter shoot when it comes time. It's very stable and tends to rule out hurried shots. Now look through the scope and try to find the target."

Jack peered down the scope. "I see only black."

"Move your head closer," Buck instructed.

"Oh, yeah, I see it now."

"Can you hold the crosshairs steady on the bull's eye?"

"Yeah, pretty steady."

"Okay, let's put a shell in the chamber." Buck reached down and opened the bolt action. He dug a shell out of his pocket and slid it into the chamber. Then he rode the bolt forward, locked it down, and slid on the safety. "Now, you can pull the trigger when you feel good about hitting the target."

"Is it going to be loud?"

"Kind of, but you won't notice it that much."

Jack aimed and squeezed the trigger with a big jerk. Nothing happened, except for Buck's snickering.

"I had you pull the trigger once with the safety on to show how much you flinch. You would have pulled that shot rather badly. Now we'll try it the right way. Look back down the scope at the target."

"Okay, I'm on it."

"Now, take a long, deep breath. Let it out slowly. Take another long breath and let it out." Buck reached down and slid the safety off. "Now suck in a half breath. When the crosshairs settle dead center, ever so gently squeeze the trigger."

Jack watched the crosshairs split the bull's eye

into four equal quadrants. He gently applied pressure to the trigger until it—Kaboom! The rifle kicked into Jack's shoulder with the force of an ill-tempered mule. The sharp report sent a strange rush through his ears as if the bullet went through his head and created a wind tunnel.

"Did I hit it?" he cried.

"I don't know. Let's go take a look."

Buck took the rifle and jacked out the spent cartridge. He ensured that it was unloaded and slung it back on his shoulder. They converted the tripod back into a walking stick and trudged to the target. Jack's curiosity got the best of him, and he ran the last few yards to see where he hit.

"Wow! You're not going to believe this!" he exclaimed. "It's just a couple inches above the bull's eye!"

"Right where it's supposed to be," Buck replied. "You did as I told you, and the gun's always accurate. I'm not surprised at all." Then the giddy kid and his satisfied mentor strode back to the house.

That evening, and the ones to follow, Jack read every article he could find on deer hunting. He learned that deer have an incredible sense of smell. Their faces are shaped like one big nose. It funnels every whiff of scent up a long channel that acts as an amplifier, straight into the brain. Also, they have very keen hearing. A mule deer's extra-large ears can swivel like a radar beam, detecting minute sounds like distant human voices or heavy footsteps. They are smart enough to use other creatures to warn them of approaching danger. Mule deer use sharptail grouse as early warning devices (EWD's). Both species bed down in the same habitat out of the wind, and when grouse fly, the deer jump to alert. Jack was amazed at the hunting stories, some successful, others ending in utter disappointment. He wondered how his story would turn out.

One night while reading in the family room, it suddenly occurred to Jack that something important was missing in his deer herd. All the storied hunters were in quest of a certain buck. He counted up to twelve deer feeding in the rye, but he had yet to see one with antlers.

"Will our guest hunter be happy to shoot a doe?" he asked Buck.

"No, I'm afraid that wouldn't do," Buck replied.

"But we don't have any bucks in the herd. Will we have to go somewhere else to hunt?"

Buck smiled at Jack's observation. "Our buck will show up; the time's getting close."

"What do you mean, 'the times getting close?'"

"The annual rut, or breeding season, is drawing near. That's when the bucks break up their bachelor groups and go in search of does. We will have a buck show up, I promise," the old rancher declared.

A couple of mornings later, Jack noticed a new deer in the rye field herd as if fulfilling prophecy. It was more prominent in stature, and sunlight glinted from the impressive set of antlers on its head.

"It's a buck!" Jack exclaimed under his breath as he snuck out for a closer look. The deer were accustomed to human activity around the buildings but grew wary if one encroached upon their comfort zone. One of them spied Jack as he stole along the tumbleweed-lined fence to get closer. The alarmed deer stood at full attention with ears pricked toward him.

Seconds later, the entire herd was at full alert, looking in the general direction that their guard deer pointed. Jack, not knowing that he should freeze in place in this situation, kept creeping ahead. Seconds later, the herd bounded out of the field, jumped the fence, and bounced up the hill. They paused long enough on the hilltop to look back at their intruder, giving Jack a skyline look at the buck's headgear.

"Wow, he looks even better than the ones in the magazines!" he muttered in astonishment. His boss was right again; the buck showed up apropos. Jack couldn't wait to describe the encounter to Buck.

"There's a buck here!" he exclaimed, walking into the workshop a few minutes later.

The old craftsman looked up from his project, peering over his low-riding bifocals at the excited youngster. Jack's tone of voice was a couple of octaves higher than usual, indicating something special just happened.

"Oh really?" Buck replied.

"Yeah! I just saw him out in the rye field."

"Is he still there?"

"No, they ran over the hill when I tried to get a good look at him."

"Yeah, they tend to do that," Buck replied. "Did he have big antlers?"

"They were huge!" Jack replied. "Like the ones in the magazines... only bigger!"

Buck considered this report with cautious optimism. Even the young ones can have impressive-looking racks to someone who had never seen a live mule deer buck.

"We're looking for a mature buck with a big set of

antlers. He needs to be the perfect deer for someone to shoot and hang on their wall."

Jack thought for a second and replied, "He sure looked perfect to me."

"We'll see about that through a pair of binoculars when they come back down to feed this evening," Buck replied.

When the sun settled close to the horizon that afternoon, Buck and Jack climbed into the ranch truck and drove to the northwest corner of the rye field, where they found a good vantage point. Buck positioned the vehicle on a knoll and shut it off.

"Now, we wait," the old cowboy said. "Patience is a key element to hunting... maybe the most important one."

Jack used the quiet moments while waiting to gaze out across the green field and recall the day they planted it. It felt good knowing that he had a part in the ranching operation. The satisfaction that came with putting in a hard day's work in the fresh air and western skies was something that he would never have experienced in Chicago. Back there, it was about time clocks and deadlines. Out here, the length of the day determined starting and quitting time. Looking out over the field and seeing the freshly painted red barns in the distance gave him the feeling of contentment that he longed for not so many months ago.

"They're getting ready to come down," Buck said, breaking the silence. "See the doe up on the skyline?"

Jack snapped back into the present business and scanned the hill for deer. Sure enough, he spotted the doe. It was standing like a statue on the hilltop, staring down at the valley below.

"Yeah, I see it," Jack replied. "What's it doing?"

"She sees if the path is clear to come to the field. They're always on the lookout for danger. When she feels all is well, she'll come down, and the others will follow."

Jack watched with great interest the progression of the herd down the hill. The lead doe took its time, walking a bit, then pausing to look. When the scout reached the bottom, the stragglers threw caution to the wind and came running down the hill in her same path. They jumped the fence and immediately started browsing on the rye. Jack was busy counting the does in the field as their numbers increased by the minute.

"Wow, there's sixteen of them so far, but no buck," Jack announced.

"Look back on top," Buck said with a hint of excitement in his voice.

Jack swung his focus back up the hill and gasped at the view. There stood the buck, like the king of the mountain, looking out over his domain. "Holy Cow!" he uttered. "Look at him; he's huge!"

Jack looked over at Buck, expecting a reply of some sort, but he was intently peering through his binoculars. After a thorough inspection, Buck gave the binoculars to Jack and told him to take a look. He put the glasses to his eyes and instantly realized that they needed adjustment.

"I can't see anything."

"Squeeze or spread the binos apart to set them to your eye width," Buck said.

Jack did as instructed and soon had a clear view. He scanned across the horizon until he found the buck, looking more intimidating now that he could see all the individual tines. But then he started moving down the hill, and it became a challenge to keep him in sight. Soon, the buck joined the herd in the field, where the two onlookers sat in the truck and watched.

"That's the deer that we've been waiting for," Buck said after more study through the binoculars. "He's in the prime of his life, and he has no flaws. He's a perfect 4X4 with good brows."

"What does that mean?" Jack asked, perplexed

"He has two deep vees on each side, giving him four long tines, plus a brow tine on each antler. He has excellent mass, which is the circumference of the beams. A mature mule deer's ears usually measure twenty-two inches from tip to tip, and the inside of his antlers are at least an inch outside the ears; this should give him a twenty-four-inch inside spread. I guess that this buck will score close to one hundred-eighty inches Boone and Crockett."

Jack was amazed at Buck's antler scoring discourse. He seemed to know everything about all the creatures that roamed his ranch. Then he remembered how many decades he lived to learn all these subjects. There didn't seem to be a rival to a lifetime of hands-on experience.

"Did you once guide deer hunters?" Jack inquired.

"Yeah, until I got too old to get around in the hills on foot. Arthritis doesn't seem to get any better with age."

Jack watched the big buck graze among the does. The scene before them looked like a picture from a magazine with the setting sun reflecting off their gray coats. Their dingy white throat patches and rumps stood out like the sallow smiles on the 1970's baseball cards in his coveted collection.

The idyllic setting fell back to reality, though, when Buck asked, "Do you think you could kill that deer?"

This soul-searching question took Jack by surprise. Killing an animal, especially one as magnificent as this one, wasn't part of his thought process until now. He hadn't so much as witnessed death in a mousetrap. Sure, he cleaned and ate trout on the Long Pine, but cold-blooded fish aren't the same. These are warm-blooded mammals that breathe the same air that fills human lungs. But they were also eating the rye that he and Buck worked so hard to plant for the cattle.

"How much money is our guest going to pay to hunt this deer?" he countered.

"Oh, it will more than cover the damage that they do," Buck replied.

"It sounds like it's necessary then."

"Yep, it's pretty much destiny."

"Then I think I can do it; I mean, I can help do it."

"Good, then it's settled," Buck said decisively.

The sun dipped below the hills to the southwest, causing the crevice shadows to flee for a few minutes, then return as one big blanket of darkness. Buck fired up the truck, and they headed back to the house for a warm meal and an evening of reading before the fireplace.

The days were getting noticeably shorter as rifle deer season drew near. Jack watched the deer herd with vigilance each daybreak as they retreated up to the safety of the bowls pockmarking the big hill south of the valley. The deer would bed down in view of the binoculars on a day with south wind, somewhere up high, facing north. When the wind switched to the north, the deer sometimes crossed the valley to climb the steep face behind the place to escape the cold breeze. They always seemed to know the best spot to go for comfort and safety.

One morning, an unfamiliar buck showed up. Jack wondered what kind of reception this intruder would have. Now there were two would-be kings, but only one domain. He watched with great interest as the two circled, sizing each other up.

The bout that followed reminded Jack of a Golden Gloves boxing match in his neighborhood back in Chicago. He was there to cheer on Mikhail, a classmate who was also a skilled boxer. Mikhail learned to box in his homeland of Russia, where he endured some intense training. Then he became a foreign exchange student and ended up in Chicago. Jack felt something in common with this displaced Russian, and they hit it off. Mikhail was an imposing physical specimen, much like the buck that he'd been stalking the last few days.

Suddenly, the sound of crashing antlers broke the morning stillness. The two males locked horns and started a fierce shoving match, pushing each other all over the hillside. Jack found himself cheering for "Mikhail" to run the newcomer off the ranch. After a battle that lasted several rounds, the overpowered newby finally gave up and staggered out of sight. The champ watched him leave, standing between the enemy and what was rightfully his. He not only protected his herd, but he gained a fitting nickname.

Protecting his domain

That evening, Jack described the battle that took place on the hillside. Buck and Sarah listened intently as Jack breathlessly recounted how the two bucks locked horns and shoved each other at full speed across the slope. They had never seen him this animated. "Mikhail was doing most of the pushing. He won the fight because the other buck finally gave up and left," Jack affirmed.

Upon hearing Jack's name for the buck, Sarah asked, "How did you come to name the deer 'Mikhail'?"

Jack told them the story of his friend, the Russian boxer. They found this tale even more intriguing than the previous one. He finished the story by comparing the two valiant fighters.

"Mikhail, what an interesting nickname," Sarah said as she rose from her chair. "I'm going to get my name book."

Sarah returned in a minute and looked up what sounded like "Mekyle."

"How do you spell it," she asked, slightly confused.

"Em i kay aitch a i ell," Jack replied. "We pronounce it wrong, though. It's supposed to sound like 'mi-HAY-el.'"

Sarah found the name and broke into a smile. "Mikhail means 'like God'," she announced.

"That's appropriate," Buck acknowledged, returning the smile.

Two days before rifle season, Buck went over some last-minute deer guiding tips with Jack. He wondered inside how this greenest of greenhorns would do on his first hunting experience. Buck hoped that this year's guest hunter would be patient with the young apprentice.

"There are a few things that you need to know about being a hunting guide," he started. "I realize that I'm throwing you raw into what could be a thorny situation." Jack shot him a look of concern. "Our hunter's name is Percy Whitlock. He's coming to Nebraska for the first time in his life. He lives in Georgia, so this will be a bit of a shock to his system. That's one thing that you'll have in common with him. Beyond that, he's sixty-nine years old, and he's looking to kill his first mule deer. That's pretty much all I know about him."

"How did he find out about hunting the Blue Diamond ranch?" Jack queried.

"Our ranch is listed with a hunting agency that charges a finder's fee to link hunters with landowners."

"That's neat," Jack replied.

"He'll be here tomorrow. We'll put him up in the bunkhouse. I hope our little furry friends don't make a nuisance of themselves," he said with a wink, referring to the resident mice that manage to escape the ranch cats. "Sarah will cook enough for an extra plate at all the meals."

"So, what exactly will be my job?" Jack inquired with a hint of apprehension.

"Your job is to find Mikhail and lead Percy into position to get a good shot at him. By good shot, I mean not a running shot. The last thing we want to do is wound and chase him."

A wounded deer sounded terrible to Jack. He had a hard enough time thinking about killing Mikhail, let alone putting him through the torture of a drawn-out death. He hoped for everyone's sake it would end quickly.

"You're going to have to be sneaky," Buck continued. "Use the choppy terrain to hide your movements. Keep the sun at your back and the wind in your face." Then, after some consideration, he added, "Most of all, don't get lost!"

Jack's concerned expression grew more intense. Here was a new fear. He envisioned a frantic trek through the endless hills as the sun sinks on any hope of finding civilization. If they survived the ordeal, he would have to live with being labeled the worst hunting guide ever.

"Out here, you always need to keep track of the sun and what direction the wind is blowing. More than once, I've used the wind to find home on dark, cloudy nights, thick fog, or a raging blizzard. The sun always rises in the east and sets in the west. Fences generally run north-south and east-west. Following a fence line will keep you from walking in circles."

Jack tried to absorb all this information as his elderly mentor shelled it out. He knew so little about deer hunting that he wasn't sure of his questions.

"What happens if we kill a deer?" he asked, dreading the answer.

Buck noticed the cringe in Jack's face and broke into a grin. "If you kill the deer, come get me. We'll drive the ranch truck out to retrieve him."

"But don't we have to do something with him first?"

Buck laughed, "Yeah, I'll field dress him before we load him up."

Jack sighed in relief. The hunting stories that he read seemed to skim around that part. He had neither the knowledge nor the desire to tackle the messy job.

Friday afternoon finally arrived, and so did the hunter from Georgia. The pack of ranch hounds gave a warm reception to the rental car with Colorado plates. After they marked all the tires, they stood, bodies wagging, waiting for the car door to open. After Buck called the dogs off, the man crawled out of the rig to a warm, Nebraska handshake.

"Hi, I'm Buck. You must be Percy?"

"Yessir, how y'all doin? So did I find the right place?" the gray-bearded man replied in a curious southern drawl.

"This is the place. Welcome to the Blue Diamond ranch," Buck replied with a genuine smile. "Sorry about the dogs. They don't see a lot of strangers around here."

"I bet they don't," Percy nodded in agreement. "In

the Denver airport was 'bout the only folks I've seen in the last four hours!"

Jack heard the dogs barking and came from his chores to help the new arrival settle in. Buck introduced him when he walked up.

"Percy, this is Jack. He's going to be your hunting guide and gofer during your stay here."

Jack shook the stranger's hand with the best Sandhiller grip he could muster. "Glad to meet you."

"Most folks call me Whitty," Percy said candidly. The Georgian sized up Jack head to toe and replied, "I didn't know they made britches that long. I'm hankerin' to do some walkin', but don't know if I can keep up with yer legs!"

Jack laughed at the man's manner of speech. He could tell already that they were going to get along just fine.

They led Percy to his quarters and helped him get settled in. Then they drove him to the shooting range to check his rifle's accuracy after the plane ride. It needed a slight adjustment, but three dial-in shots fixed it. Jack wondered if the gunshots were alerting the deer somewhere on the hill above.

Buck gave Jack the remainder of the afternoon off from his chores to entertain their guest and keep an eye out for Mikhail. Jack, intrigued by his new Georgia friend, was happy to oblige. Over the last few months, he found his time conversing with Buck to be a missing piece in his life, and now he had another seasoned mentor.

Jack showed Percy around the place, describing ranch life like a veteran. The newcomer soaked in the sights and sounds with the wonder of a child on

Christmas morning. This environment stretched his cotton-belted imagination. It was as if he were stepping into the setting of a Louis L'amour book. He was particularly impressed with Jack's knowledge of horses.

"I don't know a lick about horses, but all y'all probably grew up on em out here," Percy surmised.

Jack chuckled uncomfortably, "Yeah, I guess we do..." He enjoyed his portrayal as a real cowboy, but he didn't know how long he could carry on the pretense. For the time being, though, he was a real-life Rowdy Yates. "How about we go see the chickens," he suggested before his senior companion queried further into the equine world.

"Yard birds, now there's something I can sink my teeth into," Percy replied with a chuckle.

At supper that evening, Jack sat and listened to the greybeards exchange tales from yesteryear to recent happenings in their respective parts of the world. He couldn't control his laughter when Percy said he lived so far in the south that sushi was called bait. Then, when they got up from the table, he described the meal as "so good it makes me wanna slap my mama." Jack could have soaked in the stories for hours, but Percy suddenly cut them short.

"All this jawin is better'n boilt peanuts, but what time are yuns gettin' up in the mornin'?" he asked, glancing at his watch.

Jack waited for Buck to answer, but the old cowboy just looked at him with expectant eyes. He then fully realized that he was handed the reins on this assignment.

"Uh, well, we usually eat breakfast at five-thirty," Jack replied. "Is that okay with you?"

"Five-thirty it is. What kind of clothes should I wear?" Percy asked.

Jack hadn't considered hunting clothes yet, mainly because he had never hunted. He tried to remember how the people dressed in the magazine pictures. "Just normal hunting clothes should do," he replied.

"Y'all hafta remember, it's a whole lot warmer in Georgia than it is here," Percy replied. "I don't wanta freeze to death!"

Jack, grasping the man's situation, added, "I usually pull on a pair of Carhartts when it's cold in the mornings."

"Insulated overalls then," Percy replied. "What's the temperature gonna to be?"

"Probably around twenty degrees," Jack replied.

"Holy buckets! That'll frost the frogs!" Percy exclaimed.

Jack laughed. "Oh, it shouldn't be that bad."

"If you say so. Well, if y'all will excuse me, I'm gonna hit the hay. I live a couple of time zones ahead of yuns." Percy got up to leave but turned as he walked to the door, "Thank you again ma'am, for supper. I'm so full I'm about to pop!"

Sarah replied with a smile, "Thank you. I'm glad you liked it. See you in the morning."

Percy left for the bunkhouse but poked his head back in a few seconds later with wide eyes. "There's a passel of deer right out here in yer frunchard!"

"Yeah, they like to browse on our lawn at night, and the bucks tear up the trees with their antlers," Sarah said with exasperation. "You probably noticed the high fences around our favorite trees."

"I have to shoo the deer out of the way to walk over yonder to the bunkhouse...now that's what I'm talkin' 'bout!" he declared. Then he retreated into the chilled November darkness.

Sleep evaded Jack for what seemed like hours that night as he mulled over all the possible scenarios that would unfold when day broke. He wondered if Mikhail would be with the resident herd, where they could sneak up on him to get a shot. But what if he wasn't there in the morning? What if he foresaw danger ahead and decided to withdraw back to the wilderness from which he came? The conjectures presented themselves one by one until Jack's brain finally gave up and fell to sleep.

The alarm went off at five a.m., and Jack's feet hit the floor like a soldier's in boot camp. He met the day with nervous determination, much like the day he learned to ride a horse. This would be another day to test his mettle.

Sarah cooked up a hearty breakfast with a side of grits to make their guest feel at home. Percy had to demonstrate the proper way to eat them to his yankee hosts. "Mix in a dab of butter'n a lil salt. Don't even think about puttin sugar or syrup on it," he exhorted.

When they finished breakfast, Percy looked Jack in the eye and asked, "So what's the plan, Capt'n Jack?"

"Um, I guess we'll start by looking in the field where the deer like to eat at night. Hopefully, the big buck will be there with the does," Jack replied.

Percy's eyes lit up. "Y'all have a biggun hangin around?"

"Yeah, he's like the perfect buck. I call him Mikhail."

"Y'all even call him by a highfalutin' name. He must be a sho nuff trophy."

The trio of Sandhillers smiled at Percy's animated remarks. They hoped to treat him to a welcome stay, but the guest was doing most of the entertaining so far.

Percy asked to be excused to his cabin to get dressed for the morning hunt. Jack went to the mudroom to pull on his brown duck overalls, jacket, and new winter wool cap with the fold-down ear flaps. He, for sure, wasn't going to be cold. As he finished getting dressed, Buck stepped into the room with his binoculars.

"Here, you'll need these." He helped Jack strap them to his chest with the elastic harness. "Good luck...and remember what I said about getting lost."

"I remember," Jack replied. "Well, here we go."

Jack walked over to the bunkhouse and knocked on the door. Percy bellowed, "Come on in."

He opened the door and stepped in to wait for Percy to finish dressing.

"Ah ain't never hunted in a place without trees," he said. "Mah mossy oak camo'll pry stick out like a sore thumb...but pry not nearly as bad as this here blaze orange vest."

Percy finished dressing by pulling on his orange fleece beanie cap. Then he started strapping on his hunting accessories: first, his binoculars, then a range finder, next he shoved some extra shells in his pocket. Lastly, he threw his backpack over his shoulders and clicked the snaps together in the front.

"Now, Ah just need mah gun... and mah gloves," he said. When he was finally ready, he gave Jack the thumbs up with a thickly gloved hand, and they stepped out into the crisp dawn.

The sun lingered behind the eastern hills, but the sky gradually transitioned from black to blue. The two figures walked silently through the barnyard and out the two-track trail toward the rye field. The sand, which had a thin, frozen crust from the night hours, crunched loudly in the gentle stillness. As they stole along Jack wondered how many sets of eyes were following them.

Then they arrived at a spot in the stackyard where Jack liked to hide to watch the herd. Jack led Percy into the bales, and they leaned against them, using the hay for an elbow rest to steady their binoculars. They peered across the field and saw brown bodies but needed more light to distinguish antlers. Minute by minute, the details came into view. Mikhail, unfortunately, wasn't there.

Percy was mesmerized by the interplay between the mule deer in the field. He stood and watched, giving a quiet play-by-play as if he were broadcasting the PGA tournament at Augusta.

"There's a buck out yonder," he hissed. "He's pushing that doe all over tarnation."

Jack studied the activity through his binos and realized that Percy was right. There was a young buck in the herd. He must have moved in recently because he had never seen him before. The doe acted like she wanted nothing to do with this newcomer. Another unfamiliar element now reinforced Jack's state of ignorance. What was he to do?

"Is that MacElroy, or McCully, whatever his name is?" Percy whispered.

"Mikhail. No—I've never seen that deer before," Jack whispered back.

"Is he a shooter?"

"Um, he looks much smaller than Mikhail."

"He looks purty big to me. I could shoot him'n be done right now"

The thought of having this ordeal over sounded pretty tempting to Jack. It would be so simple to sneak within range and shoot this deer. Percy would think that he was the best hunting guide ever! Then he remembered Buck's words the night that they examined Mikhail, "That's the deer we've been waiting for." Shooting this lesser deer would shatter destiny.

"No, we'll let this one go," Jack said quietly. "He's not the one we're after."

Percy thought the situation over and said with a hint of resignation, "Yer the guide."

The two hunters hid in the bales and watched the herd of mulies move up the slope to bed for the day. Then they scanned the hills in every direction for other deer. Seeing nothing, Percy broke the silence with the inevitable.

"So what now, Capt'n."

Jack had been mulling over strategies, using Buck's advice for guidelines. He remembered him saying to keep the sun at their backs and wind in their face. The sun part was easy to figure out, but the wind was calm this early in the morning. He recalled watching old westerns, where the cowboy would lick his finger and hold it up to test the wind before he took a long rifle shot. Percy watched with interest as Jack impersonated the crack-shot cowboy.

"If'n y'all want to know what direction the wind's in, back in Jawja, we jist toss a fistful of leaves in the air."

Jack looked around but didn't see any leaves.

Instead, he spied the feathery heads on a clump of sandreed. He pulled a cord of seed heads through his hand and let the chaff drift to the ground. They floated ever-so-gently to the south.

"Looks like a north wind," he said using his best Eastwood voice. "We need to walk north." Then glancing at the sun, he added, "and west." He was thankful that Buck took the time to teach him his compass directions.

"Well, let's get ta crack'n then," the anxious hunter urged.

"Okay, let's go."

Jack started them on a trek that Percy would later refer to as "The Death March." They walked across the valley, crossed the lane, and started their ascent up the nearly vertical mountain behind the buildings. Percy tried to keep up as the hill became steeper but soon ran out of gas. He stopped to catch his breath and gain some strength back in his legs of jello. Jack was halfway up the hill before he noticed that Percy was no longer with him. He turned to say something, but realized that he was alone. He lost his hunter. Now, Jack was back to being the worst guide in the world. Worried, he retraced his steps back down the hill and spotted Percy's orange cap behind a yucca. He was sitting on a catstep, looking back at the valley from whence they came.

"Whew, thought I lost you for a minute," Jack said as he hopped down onto Percy's ledge.

"I jist had ta stop 'n' catch mah breath," Percy said. "Feels like there ain't any air up hyah."

Jack sat and contemplated his first lesson in deer guiding. His legs were six inches longer and forty years younger than his walking partner. He concluded that the oldest legs should dictate the walking speed.

"Sorry about that," Jack apologized. "Guess I got a little carried away."

"That's ahright," Percy replied. "Ah thought ah was in better shape than this."

Percy stood and indicated that he was ready to go again. They continued their climb up the hill, this time pausing every few yards to get a breath. In a few minutes, they reached the rim, only to discover that their path continued upward. They stayed long enough to glass their surroundings and found that they had a much better vantage point from up high. They could now see into the bowls on the hilltop across the valley. Jack decided that the higher they got, the more likely they would spot their quarry.

"This country's purty as all get out," Percy said after he caught his breath. "Ah didn't know anything like this existed."

Jack gazed out over the vista before them and agreed. "Yeah, I didn't ee…" His voice trailed off when he realized that he almost gave away his real identity. "I mean, I didn't remember how spectacular this is to newcomers." He internally sighed relief to have come up with a quick patch to his blunder.

They continued uphill with the slowly increasing northwest wind in their faces. The deeper they penetrated the secondary rise, the lower their hope was of ever finding a peak. They would march to the highest point in view, only to spot a much higher one in the distance. They continued this exercise in futility until they overlooked an unfamiliar meadow with another hulking grass mountain beyond. Jack suddenly realized the vast expanse of hills they had to cover to try to find

Mikhail. The task ahead was going to be more difficult than he ever anticipated.

"Lawd have mercy. Look at all them hills!" Percy exclaimed.

The endless hills

Jack stood and pondered the situation for a few minutes. Where should they go from here? All his deliberating boiled down to one clear plan. They needed to turn back and retrace their steps home to Sarah's noon meal. Maybe he could talk to Buck in private and get some advice for the afternoon. "We probably better head back to the ranch now. We sure don't want to miss dinner!" he said with certainty.

"Reckon yer right about that," Percy replied. I need ta shed some clothes first, though."

"Yeah, it's warming up," Jack agreed.

Percy took off his outer coat and rolled it into a neat ball that he stuffed behind some straps on his backpack. Jack was impressed with Percy's organized hunting system. It reminded him of the hunting experts that he read about in the magazines. He wished that he had a way to carry his bulky Carhartts back to the ranch but decided it would be easier to leave them on.

Jack took note of the sun, which was now high in the southern sky. Remembering Buck's navigational advice, he led his hunter back in the direction of home. At first, Jack could see their footprints in the sandy spots, but he soon lost them and was now dependent on the wind at their backs and the late morning sun to guide them.

They were climbing again as they approached the center of the extensive range of hills. Jack continued to pause halfway up each grassy knoll to give his partner a breather. The hills here were similar to the ones on their way north but seemed unfamiliar. The deeper they penetrated the convoluted labyrinth, the higher Jack's anxiety level soared. He stood and looked in all directions at each hilltop with the pretense of looking for deer, but in reality he was trying to find a familiar landmark. As much as he hated to admit it, he was lost.

"Ahm sho glad y'all know where you're going, cause Ah have no idee where we're at," Percy gasped at one of the stops.

"Yeah, I thought I'd take a different route home in case Mikhail is out here somewhere," Jack fibbed. "We better keep going."

They trudged on, expecting each distant hill to be the one overlooking the Blue Diamond ranch place, but it only revealed more hills beyond. As they descended into a sand crater, they were startled by a flash of bodies jumping up around them. They had walked blindly into a herd of bedded deer; paralyzed, they stood and watched the flurry of scampering hooves and hides. Somewhere in the melee, Jack caught sight of antlers. His eyes followed the large buck as he trotted away behind the group. On the horizon off to the left, the buck stopped and looked back momentarily at them. Jack raised his binoculars and stood in a trance until the deer turned and disappeared behind the hill.

Mikhail

"Great day in the mornin!" Percy exclaimed. "Was that an elk?"

"No, it was Mikhail!" Jack replied in astonishment. "That's the deer we're after?"

"It has to be. There aren't any others like him around."

"Mercy me. Well, what are doin' lollygagging here when the biggest buck in Nebraska's over yonder? Let's skedaddle!"

Jack and Percy took off in the direction of the fleeing deer, revitalized by adrenaline. Percy was now hot on Jack's heels as his guide charged on with renewed hope. They soon arrived panting, at the rim where they last saw the deer. Peeking over the hilltop, they discovered a bittersweet scene. The deer were gone, but the Blue Diamond headquarters lay shimmering in the distance to the east. Jack silently sighed in relief at the welcome view.

"Well, rats. It looks like we lost them," Jack said after they scanned the surrounding hills. "Guess we'll just have to go eat dinner."

Percy sized up the situation and said, "If Ah had mah druthers, Ah'd sit raught here and let ya'll fetch me mah vittles."

"Seriously?" Jack asked.

"Nah, well, maybe a smidgen. Ahm worn slap out."

"Do you think you can make it back to the ranch?" Jack asked with pity.

"Ah reckon so. Dagnabbit, it's too bad we didn't crack off a shot at that buck."

Jack weighed Percy's remark against Buck's advice about clean kill shots. A running shot didn't seem proper.

"Yeah, it's too bad we spooked them away," he said.

He then realized that if they hadn't jumped those

deer, that they would still be walking west in the opposite direction of their destination. The wind had switched to the northeast, and the sun was on its daily track to the west, throwing Jack's compass off ninety degrees. Mikhael pointed the way home for them.

They descended the hill and trudged east along the edge of the hay meadows that skirted the lake. A pair of trumpeter swans swam warily ahead until they finally took to flight as they neared the cattails on the east end. They circled and flew closer, making their deep throaty honks. Jack stopped to watch as they flew over.

"Man, their necks are longer than all get out," Percy observed.

"Yeah, they're big birds," Jack agreed.

They walked on, spurred by the growling in their stomachs and the chance to take off their boots and rest their weary legs. As they neared the horse corrals west of the yard, a flock of pheasants flew cackling out of a sunflower patch. They startled even Jack, who regularly saw their loud eruptions.

Ringneck pheasant

"Merciful Sakes!" Percy exclaimed. "Them birds jist about made me jump plum out of mah shoes! They're kinda hard on the ole ticker."

Jack laughed loudly at his hunter's humorous wordplay. "Now I know why they call you Whitty!" he said between fits of glee. They were safely back home, and all was well again.

Sarah treated the tired hunters to a delicious noon meal, where they sat and recounted the morning's events to their gracious hosts. The Sandhillers laughed along with each story told by their southern guest. Jack sensed that rifle deer season was a yearly highlight to Buck and Sarah, and it felt good to have a part in the occasion.

After dinner, Percy thanked Sarah with his usual polite charm and then asked permission to retire to his cabin for a spell. "Ah jist need to rest mah eyes for a second," he said as he got up from the table. "See y'all later."

After Percy left, Jack told Buck about their near-disaster in the hills. Buck listened with knowing eyes. He didn't seem surprised or dismayed that they almost got lost.

"I watched you climb the hill behind the house this morning, heading northwest," Buck admitted. "When the wind switched, I suspected that it might mess with your mind a little. If you weren't back by noon, I was ready to come looking for you."

Jack felt better hearing this. He felt secure having a man with Buck's experience backing him.

"What should we do now?" he asked.

"Well, you have a general idea where the deer's at," Buck replied. "I would go sit in the valley below where you saw him this morning. He may come down to the meadow to feed at dark. I can drive you and Percy out there later this afternoon. It sounds like you've walked enough for today."

"That sounds like a great plan," Jack said. "I guess now I just wait for Percy."

Two hours later, Buck loaded the hunters up in the ranch truck, and they headed west on the two-track trail. Jack remembered a lone willow tree in the valley where they came off the hill earlier. When they arrived at the tree, Buck parked the truck, and Jack and Percy crawled out with their binos, gun, and shooting stick.

"Make sure you have plenty of clothes," Buck advised. "It can get pretty chilly when the sun goes down, and you're sitting still."

"Yessir," Percy replied. "I put on an extree layer."

"I'll come to pick you up at dark. Good luck!"

They walked over and made an ambush position under the scraggly willow tree as Buck rumbled off in the truck. Jack watched as his hunter kicked at the sand before he sat down.

"Jist gettin' rid of the cow patties," Percy explained.

"Good idea," Jack replied.

The two sat, nestled into the cold November sand, getting comfortable for the long wait. Percy leaned up against the tree and started glassing their surroundings. They had a good view of the entire hilltop across the valley to the south, but they were much closer to the north range, making it impossible to see beyond the steep front rim. If a deer came from that direction, they wouldn't see it until it was almost in range.

Waiting and watching in the solitary quiet, they became aware of life in the grassy wilderness. A coyote reared up on its hind legs at the hill base across the meadow and pounced in the soft sand, searching for voles and mice. A striped skunk rooted relentlessly in search of grubs in the grass. A family of coons wandered past like a gang of masked marauders.

"What's that shiny thing movin out there?" Percy asked quietly.

Jack looked in the direction that Percy was pointing and spotted the glistening aberration. It was moving to and fro, like a giant golden slinky. Close examination with the binoculars revealed it to be a porcupine.

"What's a porkypine doin way out here where there ain't any trees?" Percy pondered.

"I don't know," Jack replied. "Buck says that the dogs and cows sometimes get porcupine quills in their faces."

"Sounds painful," Percy replied.

The sun dipped closer to the hills, and the two hunter's anticipation grew as the "magic hour" arrived when deer appear out of nowhere. Jack watched the ridge to the north diligently, waiting for Mikhail to come and stand silhouetted on the skyline.

"There's a deer out there by the sawgrass," Percy hissed.

Jack once again looked in the direction that his hunter was watching. He could see a tan animal ambling around the cattails on the west end of the lake. He found the deer in his binoculars, and holding them steady on the shooting stick; he could see antlers.

"It's a buck," Jack proclaimed.

"Can I barree yer shootin stick?" Percy whispered. "Ahm having trouble holding mah binos steady."

"Sure, here," Jack replied as he handed the tripod over.

Percy rested his Swarovky's on the rock-solid rest and peered at the distant buck.

"It's a whitetail," he observed. "A real nice whitetail."

Jack agreed with Percy, not because he could discern the difference between whitetails and mule deer, but because he didn't want to appear ignorant.

"Yeah, it's a whitetail, alright," Jack replied.

"If Ah didn't see that huge mule buck this mornin, Ah'd be mighty tempted to shoot that'n there," Percy admitted. "He makes ahr whitetails back home look lack rabbits."

They sat and watched the whitetail sniff the ground every few yards as it walked around the lake. It was the middle of the rutting season, and this guy was on a mission to find a hot doe. The deer kept them so preoccupied that they hardly noticed that the long shadows turned to darkness, and the hunting day was over.

Soon, they could see the headlights of Buck's old ranch truck bounce up the trail toward them. They gathered their gear in the waning light and made their way back to the rendezvous point.

"Well, did you see him?" Buck asked when they arrived at the truck.

"Saw a big whitetail but didn't see hide nor hair of MacElroy," Percy replied. "Ah think we were barkin up the wrong tree tonight."

"That's alright," Buck replied. "There's always another day. Tomorrow doesn't look good, though—we've got a snowstorm coming in late tonight."

"Snow!" Percy exclaimed. "Ah didn't bring any snowshoes. What're we gonna do?"

"I guess we'll just wait to see what the conditions are like in the morning," Buck replied.

Sarah had another home-cooked meal ready for the hungry hunters back at the ranch.

Percy treated his hosts to another round of stories until he was ready to turn in for the night. He hobbled, stiff-legged to the side door, where they wished him a good night's rest.

"Ahm gonna sleep lack a baby tonight," he said as he walked out the door. "Up every hour bawling," he added coyly.

Jack woke to the alarm clock the following day

and staggered to the window to see what it looked like outside. The ground was white, and big flakes were flowing in front of the yard light. It looked like this day would bring him yet another new experience.

Percy stepped in the door at five-thirty, bifocals fogged over and big snowflakes on his stocking cap and shoulders.

"This Nebraska weather's plum crazy!" he exclaimed. "It ain't fit for man nor beast out there!"

Buck laughed at Percy's remark. "Yeah, you'll get to enjoy the whole Sandhills experience now."

The foursome huddled around the dining room table for breakfast and their daily game plan. Buck said it would be best to wait for the heavy, wind-driven snow to let up, then hunt from the cab of the ranch truck. "Maybe we'll get lucky and have Mikhail walk by."

The hoary murk of the snowstorm gradually replaced the night's blackness. The sun barely filtered through the snow and clouds to bring light to this gloomy day. Jack kept vigilance out the front window, waiting for the big red barn a hundred yards away to appear; he had learned in his little time watching deer in the Sandhills that long-range vision was paramount. If he couldn't even see a barn across the yard, then their chances of crossing paths with Mikhail was next to nil.

"Let's go for a little drive," Buck told Percy, breaking the monotony. "We'll get the truck and pick you up at the cabin."

Percy pulled on his boots and parka and disappeared into the whiteout. Buck and Jack got dressed and tramped through the accumulating snow to the tractor shed. The ranch cats peered down from their dry loft when the two cowboys stepped in the door. Buck slid open the overhead door, then started the ranch truck and cranked up the defroster.

"We'll just have to make the best of it until this snow lets up," he conceded as they backed out into the storm.

They drove to the cabin, where Percy promptly appeared with a rifle in hand. He hopped in the passenger door, and the trio proceeded out into obscurity. Jack was thankful for Buck's willingness to take the reins in this adventure. He felt secure riding along with the man who spent his life learning every trail, fence, and blowout on this vast ranch.

The old cowboy knew that hunting mule deer under these conditions was futile. He figured the herd would be tucked into a protected bowl somewhere amongst the other hundred bowls that inundated these hills. He didn't believe in using the truck to bird-dog deer out of their beds, so he stayed on the trails that passed from valley to valley, connecting the windmills.

The poor visibility disoriented Jack. He had helped Buck service all these windmills back in August, but none looked familiar now. Without the sun for a reference, he couldn't even make an educated guess as to which direction home was. Yet Buck drove on.

When they were in what Jack figured was the uttermost reaches of the ranch, he spotted darkness ahead in the otherwise world of white. As they drew nearer, he could see that they were trees. As he wondered what this could be, a gray horse came running up to the truck. "Charlie! What are you doing way out here?" he blurted when he recognized his old friend.

"Probably just looking for a handout," Buck

chuckled. "He's always the first to come begging."

Jack managed to conceal his bewilderment from Percy as he frantically analyzed the situation: They were miles from home, the horses were here—and then suddenly, as if he were in a time warp, they were driving into the yard? After a few seconds of absolute confusion, he realized that they had gone in a big circle and were now back home. After he collected his wits, he added, "Guess the horses are just a little jittery in all this snow, heh, heh."

Buck drove up to the cabin and parked the truck. "Well, that's about all we can do for now. This snow should let up later. Maybe we'll get lucky and catch them coming down to feed this afternoon."

Percy agreed. "The snow's done whupped us this mornin', sho'nuff."

"You're welcome to come over to the house to pass the time," Buck added. "We have plenty of reading material and a warm fireplace."

"I reckon that sounds like a goodanuff way ta piddle the ars away," Percy replied. "Ah'll be over in a bit."

"Jack and I need to do a few chores, but we'll be there for dinner," Buck said before driving off.

The "chores" that Buck referred to involved shovels. Jack spent the next three hours scooping snow from feed bunks and walkways while Buck hauled hay and pushed snow with the loader tractor. The snow may have made everything pretty and white, but it sure created a great deal of toil. They worked up a good appetite by the time dinner rolled around.

Sarah provided a bright spot on the otherwise dreary day by serving the hungry men a famous

Nebraska dinner. A melt-in-your-mouth beef roast carved into thick slices took center stage in a supporting cast of mashed potatoes, gravy, and corn. As if that wasn't enough, she brought a plate stacked with slices of homemade bread, still warm from the oven. She followed the bread with a butter dish and a bowl of chokecherry jam.

"Mmm," Percy sighed after taking a bite of the jelly slathered bread. "What did y'all call this jam?"

"Chokecherry," Sarah replied.

"Chokecherry?" Percy asked. "If y'all ask me, they didn't name it right. Should be called highfalutin berries,' or 'slap my momma berries.'"

Sarah giggled at Percy's observation, assuming that he was paying the jam a compliment.

"If you eat them raw off the bush, you'll understand why they call them chokecherries," Buck apprised. "For some reason, they lose their strangling power after you cook 'em."

After a dessert of peach cobbler, topped with vanilla ice cream, Percy backed his chair away from the table and let out a pleasurable groan. "Thank you for that dee-lishus meal ma'am. I'm full as a tick."

Sarah smiled with a hint of a blush. "You're welcome," she replied.

Jack rose from the table and walked over to the front window to look for any change in the weather. If anything, the wind was picking up. He wondered if they would be able to hunt at all that afternoon.

"What's hapnun out there?" Percy asked as he watched his young guide study the weather.

"Not much different, except the wind is starting to drift the snow now," Jack observed.

"We have more chores to tend to," Buck said. "Will you be alright here until later this afternoon?"

"Y'all do what ya hafta," Percy replied. "I'll be just fine in here where it's warm."

Buck and Jack ventured back out to their ranch chores while Percy napped and read hunting magazines. They worked a couple more hours, making sure that all the animals had feed and water. Jack decided that ranching in a snowstorm wasn't much fun.

The snow wasn't coming down as much as it was blowing sideways, and by midafternoon, the sun started showing through the frosty haze. Buck instructed Jack to load Percy in the ranch truck and drive to their lookout point by the rye field. "Keep the truck in four-wheel drive... and head back home before dark," he advised.

Jack trudged up his freshly scooped sidewalk and poked his head in the front door. "Are you ready to go hunting?" he asked his hunter stretched out next to the fireplace.

"Sho'nuff am," Percy replied, hitting the lever on the side of the chair, which initiated the smooth motion in which he jumped to his feet. 'I'll head over yonder and be ready in a jif."

Jack walked over to the shed, raised the overhead door, and jumped eagerly into the driver's seat. He now had the pleasure to plow a truck through snow. Buck made it look so effortless that he felt invincible.

Ten minutes later, he and Percy were stuck. He hadn't noticed the wide drift in front of them as they drove the trail out to the rye field. The truck ground to a halt, high-centered on packed snow. Jack gunned the engine after their forward momentum halted, digging the tires down into the soft sand underneath. The more power he applied, the deeper they went, like struggling in quicksand.

"I think we're stuck," Jack announced presently.

"I reckon so too," Percy agreed, breaking his tense speechlessness.

Jack tried to open his door to get out and study the situation, but it jammed against the snowdrift. Then he opened the window and slithered his lanky frame out. Hopping down, Jack broke through the wind-packed crust and sunk in over his knees. Now he was floundering around outside the truck, with Percy watching in horror.

"Lawd, have mercy! What'll we do now?" Percy shrieked from inside the cab.

Jack stopped thrashing about, and after a few seconds of thought, he drew a deep breath. There was only one option. "I'm gonna go get Buck," he concluded with as much confidence as he could muster. "Just hang tight till I get back."

"I ain't goin' nowhere," Percy conceded.

Jack wallowed out of the drift and headed back down his tracks to the yard. He couldn't believe his terrible luck as a tenderfoot hunting guide. So far, he'd gotten lost, scared away the deer, got hit by a blizzard, and now he's hopelessly stuck in a snowdrift. What else could go wrong? He figured that his luck would have to change sometime.

Buck was moving a bale of hay when he spotted Jack trudging his way with arms flailing. Wondering what this was about, he turned the tractor toward him and opened the throttle. Seconds later, they met up, and Buck swung the cab door open. "What's up?" he asked with a look of concern.

Between gasps of breath, Jack explained his dilemma. "I left Percy in the truck... and walked back... We're stuck."

"Hop up. Let's go," Buck commanded.

In a few minutes, they arrived at the scene of the debacle. Buck turned the tractor around and backed it within a few yards of the truck's back bumper. Then he told Jack to drag the log chain that he carried on the cab floor to hook over the pickup's ball hitch. Buck crawled out and attached the other end of the chain to a clevis on the tractor. "Get back in the truck, start it up, and put it in reverse. Give me a thumbs up when you're ready. I'll pull you back until you're out of the drift. Then I'll stop, and you need to stop too, so you don't run into the tractor. Okay?"

These orders sounded easy enough to Jack. "Yeah, I got this."

Jack crawled back through the window and did as instructed. A minute later, they were pulled free, and he jumped back out to unhook the chain. Then he thanked his boss for coming to their rescue.

"No problem," Buck said. "Next time you come to a big drift, drive around it."

Jack returned to the truck and continued his short journey to the field with the attentive eyes of his southern copilot pointing out drifts ahead. Soon they were at the overlook with the defroster blasting, peering through the windshield at the frigid world outside. The warm air flowing from the heater, combined with the rocking of the truck in the wind, gently lulled the two hunters into a state of rest. Jack, physically spent from scooping snow and his recent run for help, dozed off on the job. His partner, refreshed from his long hours in front of the fireplace, kept vigil.

The sun, dipping near the western horizon, was somewhat obscured by the airborne ice, giving it a pinkish glow. Underneath this, some tiny forms came scurrying down the north face and onto the snow-covered meadow.

"Over yonder's some deer," Percy declared, rousing Jack from his nap.

Jack quickly gained his senses and brought the binoculars to his blurry eyes. "Yeah, looks like a whole bunch of them," he replied.

The herd of mule deer was in the middle of the broad meadow about a half-mile to the west. Nothing stood between the hunters and deer but an endless pattern of snowdrifts across the frozen lake.

"I think I see horns on one of 'em," Percy observed.

Jack studied the distant animals and caught a glint of antler reflecting off the setting sun. As the heavy-bodied deer turned its head to and fro, his rack became very apparent. "It's Mikhail," he replied intently.

"Yep, that's the same buck we saw up in the hills yesterday," Percy agreed. "He's one fetching deer."

The two hunters sat in the warmth of the truck and glassed as the big buck directed his followers across the frozen valley and into a hidden swale. They were so engrossed in the action that they didn't notice they were losing light.

"We better head for home," Jack surmised. "We don't want to get stuck out here in the dark."

"That's for darn sure," Percy replied.

Jack followed his tracks back to the place with no further incident and dropped Percy off at his cabin. "See ya for supper," he said before he left to park the truck.

"Yup, I'll be over there in a lick," Percy replied.

That evening, they ate a heaping bowl of chili soup and discussed plans for the next day. Buck informed them that the weather would be much more agreeable for hunting. He said it with a confident gleam in his eye as if he knew something was about to happen.

On the third day, Jack rose from bed with a new resolve. Buck's sureness the night before helped him forget all the catastrophes thus far and gave him the same fight-to-win attitude that his high school basketball coach used to inspire his team. "Today's the day," he said quietly to himself as he got dressed for breakfast.

The sun rose on an arctic landscape, illuminating trillions of ice crystals suspended in space. The ultra-calm air stung the nose and lungs, stifling the breath of their southern guest.

"I di'nt know air could get this cold," Percy said as he pulled a wool gaiter up over his quivering face.

"Yeah, it's pretty cold this morning," Jack replied as they trudged off in the direction of the previous night's deer sighting. They decided to walk west and try to spot Mikhail again before the deer bedded down for the day. When they topped a short rise in the trail, Jack stopped and knelt. He spotted the herd starting their way up the slope across the meadow. "There they are," he said quietly.

The two hunters knelt on the wind-crusted snow and glassed the deer, looking for antlers. They didn't have to look long to spot them. "There he is," Percy mumbled through his gaiter.

"Yeah, they're pretty far away," Jack surmised.

"They're headed up the hill to the south. Let's watch and see what they do." The two watched until the deer disappeared into a deep bowl up high on the hill. "Okay, they're out of view now. Let's go."

They stood up and brushed the frozen powder from their knees. The route across the meadow was treacherous, with hidden water springs under the drifts waiting to drench hunting boots that broke through the frozen crust. Jack led his hunter across the marshy minefield, giving a wide berth to cattail patches that rimmed the water bogs. Jack breathed a sigh of relief when they reached the fence at the base of the abutting hill. Now all they had to do was climb the snow-covered mountain and find Mikhail and his friends without being winded, heard, or seen by the wary animals.

They worked up the more gently sloping north face, stopping to gulp frigid air every few steps. Thankfully, the storm's north wind swept up this hill face, leaving only a hardened skiff of snow in the grass. Jack guessed they were scaling the hill a couple of hundred yards east of Mikhail's path, remembering Buck's advice about staying between the sun and the deer.

At the top of the first rise, they peeked into the swale beyond and found only a few scattered yuccas. "We need to keep climbing," Jack directed. Percy silently complied with his young guide's leading.

One by one, they checked each bowl as they ascended the snow-packed ridge. As they neared the peak, Jack's pulse accelerated, not from exertion but a sense of proximity to their prey. He could feel his heart pounding blood to every extremity of his body as they inched up to the highest bowl on the hill.

Jack suddenly crouched and turned back to his hunter. "They're here!" he hissed as he motioned him to get down.

Percy's frosted eyelashes widened in the tiny slit between his parka hood and wool gaiter. He hunched down and instinctively swung the rifle off his back and jacked the bolt back, watching the bright brass shell pop into place. Then he slowly slid the bolt forward, ensuring that the shell was indeed in the chamber and ready to send downrange. Then he slid the safety back on and looked at Jack for the next move.

Jack eased back up to peer at the herd milling about on the sunny hillside across the bowl. He guessed them to be around one-hundred-fifty yards away- well inside Percy's shooting range. His face and binoculars were about the same freezing temperature by now, so they didn't fog up next to his eyes. He scanned the herd of does, looking for Mikhail, but couldn't find him. Then he noticed one lying down next to a yucca. There he was, looking content, surrounded by his vigilant guards.

Jack's heart was pumping at its upper limit by now, like an old locomotive at full steam and yet unmoving. Against all these stimuli, he slowly lowered his head below the horizon and turned to his tense partner. "He's lying down in the middle of the does," he whispered with a quivering voice.

Percy, the experienced hunter, took over at this point. He spread out the three-legged shooting stick and slithered forward in the snow until he was high enough to view the herd. Slowly setting up the tripod, he rose to his knees. Cradling his rifle in the rest, he peered through the scope for what seemed like an eternity.

Then Jack heard the click of the safety. Seconds later, a sharp report shattered the morning stillness, followed by the dull thud of a one-hundred-fifty grain bullet slamming into Mikhail's chest.

"Got 'im!" Percy exclaimed. "He's down."

Jack stood up to watch the herd scattered anxiously around the hillside. The deer acted confused by the situation. Should they run from the two humans invading their hill or stay with their leader? One by one, they reluctantly disappeared over the skyline until only Mikhail remained, motionless under his thorny yucca.

"We did it," Percy said, holding his heavily mittened hand out to shake Jack's. "That was awesome!"

Jack returned the exuberant handshake with equal vigor. He was happy for his hunter's success, yet he couldn't help but feel sadness for losing his fallen comrade. It was a bittersweet moment for the fledgling hunting guide.

The two crossed the deep bowl and climbed effortlessly up to their trophy. "Lawd, have mercy, look at the size of them antlers!" Percy exclaimed. "I ain't never… dagnabbit… I'm plum tickled as all get out! Yer one heckuva huntin' guide!"

"Congratulations," Jack gushed. "I guess it worked out this time."

As Percy pored over his prize, Jack remembered Buck's instruction to get him when the hunt was over. "Will you be alright here while I go get Buck to haul the deer back to the house?"

"Sho'nuff… whatever ya say capt'n," Percy replied. "I'll be right here when y'all get back."

Jack took off in a long-legged trot down the hill toward the ranch house in the distance. As he traversed the snow drifted undulations, he thought about the storybook event that just took place. How would he relay it to his boss? Should he feign toughness and show no regret for the loss of Mikhail? He was pretty sure that Buck would wonder how he handled his first experience with a kill. He decided to wait and let the stage dictate his words.

As he crossed the meadow, taking care to stay in their previous footsteps, he spied Buck ahead, waiting for him. Soon he arrived at the truck and jumped into the passenger seat. "We got 'im," he said breathlessly.

"I heard the shot and watched for you to come down the hill," Buck said. "When I just heard one shot, I figured it was good news. Multiple shots are never a good sign."

Buck dropped the truck in gear and skillfully drove around the valley to the south hill range. "How was the hunt?" he inquired.

"It went well," Jack replied.

Buck, detecting the hesitation in Jack's voice, pried deeper. "So, do you want to be a hunting guide now?"

Jack brooded over Buck's question as they traversed the drifts in the trail. He wasn't sure how to handle his mixed feelings about the fresh kill. On the one hand, he felt like he was doing a service to Percy and the ranch. He helped their Georgia friend accomplish his personal goal of harvesting a trophy mule deer for his wall back home. He also aided in compensating for all the winter feed that the deer were eating. But deep inside, he felt sorrow for taking the life of such a magnificent animal.

"I'm not sure," he replied.

The old and wise cowboy took advantage of this teachable moment to broaden the scope of his young apprentice. "You know, we are soon going to celebrate Christmas...and this spring we will observe another holiday called Easter. What you just experienced this morning is a great analogy to why we celebrate those two holidays."

Jack waited with curiosity aroused, but his boss said no more. He had a way of prompting a person to think for themselves, thoughts of deep persuasion. Now, the bewildered young pilgrim had a strange new mystery to settle.

13. WINTER

Sometimes silence speaks the loudest. - Unknown

When the earth tilts away from the sun, weather in the Sandhills becomes as fickle as a coddled crybaby. A day could start with a temperature in the single digits, climb to forty degrees by noon, then a Canadian clipper could roll through and drop the wind chill down below zero by nightfall. The occasional snows don't linger long in the arid wind, evaporating into puffy clouds that flit off toward Kansas. The only thing sure about Nebraska's weather is change.

Christmas and New Years Day zipped past, like the engines on a Burlington Northern rumbling through the hills, pulling an endless string of short days and long winter nights. Jack spent most of January helping keep the livestock fed and watered. As the hay bale yards dwindled, the ice chunks piled higher around the water tanks. The long, monotonous part of winter had arrived.

The frost penetrated deep into the ground, turning the soft sand to stone. The lake where ducks, geese, and swans spent most of their year was now firm real estate that, when it snowed, blended in with the rest of the meadow. The Blue Diamond ranch now had a brown and white bleakness to it.

One evening after supper Buck surprised Jack with a question. "Have you ever been ice fishing?"

Jack gave the old cowboy a perplexed look. "Ice fishing?"

"Yeah, you know, where you drill holes in the ice and fish through them," Buck replied.

"No. Is that something that you do out here?"

"Yep, fact is, most of us Sandhillers spend more time fishing on the ice than out of a boat."

"I had no idea. I thought maybe the fish hibernated when it got this cold."

"They might slow down a bit, but they don't quit eating," Buck replied. "Would you be game to give it a try?"

Jack's eyes lit up. Fishing sounded like a fun way to break the tedium of winter. "Sure!" he replied.

"It's supposed to be pretty decent weather in a couple of days. We'll go give it a whirl," Buck said.

The next evening Buck carried a pail into the living room and set it down by his chair. An assortment of tiny fishing rods stuck out the top, catching Jack's eye. He watched with interest as Buck pulled each one out and inspected them.

"Those are funny-looking fishing poles," Jack observed. "What kind of fish do you catch with them?"

Buck held a rod up and explained how it worked. "I call this a jigging stick. You noticed that it doesn't have a reel on it? Instead, it has two little wooden dowels that the line wraps around on the handle. It weighs almost nothing so that you can detect the slightest bites. It's designed to catch panfish, like bluegills and perch, but I've landed some pike and bass on them also."

Buck handed the rod to Jack to look over. "Wow, it doesn't weigh anything. It doesn't seem like it would handle a big fish." He then proceeded to tell Buck the story of the pike that he caught at Merritt Reservoir the previous summer. Buck listened to his tale of the momentous battle with a knowing smile.

"A pike that big will simply swim away and snap this light line, that is, if he doesn't bite the line off with his sharp teeth first," Buck said.

The old fisherman checked the knots connecting the teardrop lures to the line by pinching the tiny hooks between his fingers and pulling them taut. If one snapped off, he retied it, using the same palomar knot that Jack learned back at Pine Creek. Then he pulled some small clear plastic containers from the bucket and opened each one, displaying to Jack the various shapes and colors of the teeny lures used to catch fish through the ice.

"Looks like our tackle's in order," Buck said. "We'll load up the sled and ice auger after chores in the morning. Sounds like tomorrow's our day."

Sarah made a hearty breakfast the following day. "It's a long time til supper, doing what you guys are doin' today," she explained. "I'll have some sandwiches ready for you also."

Jack hurried through his morning chores, anxious to get on the road. He hadn't been fishing since he started at the ranch, so he couldn't wait to feel a tug on his line. When he finished, he walked to the tractor shed where Buck was making room in the ranch truck for the ice fishing gear.

"You're just in time to help me load the sled," Buck said when he saw Jack. They hefted the craft made of plywood and 2x2's onto the truck bed and strapped it on. Then Buck laid a gas-powered auger in the sled and tossed a couple of five-gallon buckets into the cab where they wouldn't blow out. "Okay, that just about does it. We'll stop at the house and grab our lunch and the fishing rods."

Soon, they were on the road to Hyannis. Buck pulled into the gas station when they arrived in town, where he handed Jack a twenty-dollar bill. "Go in and ask for a tub of wax worms."

Jack took the money and entered the store, where the crew showered him with the usual friendly greetings. "Hi Jack, how's the job going?" the lady behind the counter asked.

"It's going fine," Jack replied.

"How are Buck and Sarah?"

"They're doing fine also. Buck sent me in to get some wax worms."

"Ah, you're going ice fishing! You lucky duck. You know yer going with the best ice fisherman in the county, don't you?"

"No, Buck didn't tell me that."

"Well, now you know. The worms are over in the little white fridge," she said, pointing to the front window.

Jack walked over, pulled a small tub from the refrigerator, then carried it up and set it on the counter. He watched, perplexed when the lady opened the lid and peeked inside.

"Just checking to see if they're alive. That'll be twelve dollars." Jack handed her the cash, and she made the change. "Where are you headed?"

"I don't know. Buck didn't tell me."

"Fishermen never tell you where they're going or where they've been," the lady chuckled. "Good luck today!"

"Thanks," Jack replied as he walked to the door.

As soon as Jack hopped in, Buck turned the truck onto Highway 2 and headed east out of town. "Where are we going?" Jack inquired.

"The Valentine National Wildlife Refuge."

"How far is that?"

"Far enough," Buck replied. " You just as well make yourself comfortable."

The two cowboys cruised the highway, which curved along the valley pinched between massive hill ranges. Jack noticed whitetail deer scattered out on the other side of the railroad, grubbing for tender grass under the thinning patches of snow. They didn't seem to mind that the sun was shining, and they were out in the wide open. Jack's hunting experience back in November gave him a new appreciation for the deer's habits.

They slowed for Whitman, then quickly revved back to speed, and they shortly passed a sign that said they were entering a different county. "That's a funny name," Jack said. "How did they come up with Hooker county?"

"They named it after a civil war general," Buck replied. "Most of the counties in the Sandhills came in the quarter-century after the Civil War, so they used the names of famous Union officers, like Custer, Grant, Garfield, Logan, Sheridan, and Thomas."

"I guess that makes sense," Jack figured.

Buck turned north when they arrived in Mullen. They drove through the enterprising little town and were soon on Highway 97 headed north. A few miles up the road, they coasted down a steep descent and crossed the Middle Loup River. Then they immediately climbed back up the north side and were back in the hills again. "This is an interesting section of the Sandhills," Buck explained. "Twenty miles either side of this highway, the river valleys from the Dismal down south to the Snake up north are much deeper than anywhere else."

"Why is that?" Jack inquired.

"Geologists claim that the earth's crust is heaving on this line, causing the rivers to cut deeper into the ground over the years. I guess it makes sense when you think about it," Buck replied.

The road continued north, traversing the seemingly endless hill ranges until it dropped into another deep valley. "This is the North Loup River," Buck explained. At the top of the far ridge, the road started an east, north, east stair-step pattern that continued for miles until they came to a large meadow where they turned onto the Kennedy Road. "Had we stayed on the highway, we would soon be at Merritt Reservoir, where you caught the big pike," Buck said, nodding toward a large hill to the north. "We could ice fish there also, but I prefer the shallow, natural lakes on the refuge."

A mile east on the gravel road, they crossed a small stream that flowed to the north. "That's Gordon Creek," Buck said. "Believe it or not, the upper end of this drainage is out in Sheridan County, in the valley behind Marie Sandoz's grave. Downstream, it flows into the Niobrara River below the Highway 97 bridge. That's a distance of about seventy miles as the crow flies."

Large cottonwood trees lined the county road, creating a narrow channel barely wide enough for two cars to meet. Buck drove several more miles until they passed a large brown sign welcoming them to the Valentine National Wildlife Refuge. "Well, here we are," Buck exclaimed. "A seventy-two thousand-acre outdoor paradise and almost twenty percent is water. The only problem here is deciding which lake to fish."

They drove past a sign pointing south to Rice, Duck, West Long, and Pelican lakes, and then Jack spotted a large lake through the trees on his side of the truck. "Hackberry Lake," Buck announced. "We'll fish this one, but down on the other end."

No sooner than they went by the refuge headquarters on Hackberry, they passed another sign pointing to Watts Lake on the left. "These are all good fishing lakes," Buck explained, "But I always seem to gravitate to the east end of Hackberry. Maybe because someone caught the state record yellow perch here back in eighty-four."

"A state record, wow!" Jack exclaimed.

"Yeah, wouldn't that be something," Buck mused. "But how about a world record? One of those was caught here on the refuge also."

"A world record fish right here?" Jack inquired, wide-eyed.

"Yep, an angler caught the world record bluegill for ice-fishing on Pelican Lake," Buck replied.

By now, Jack could hardly contain himself. He envisioned doing battle with hefty fish through a saucer-sized hole in the ice.

Buck turned off the blacktop onto a sand and rock trail that wound through the dunes. They were soon driving along the lake again, making their way to the east end. They parked on the boat ramp next to a large cottonwood and got out to stretch their legs.

"Looks like the fish are biting," Buck surmised, eyeing the variety of rigs in the parking lot. "Especially if the locals are here," he said, pointing to a sixty-six county plate on another well-worn ranch truck. *Cherry County plate*

They unloaded the sled and stashed the auger and buckets for the trek on the ice. Before venturing onto the lake, they dressed in insulated coveralls and waterproof boots. Then Buck sat on the sled's seat and pulled rubber straps onto the bottom of his shoes. "Here," he said, tossing Jack a pair. "Put these cleats on to give you some traction."

Buck did a quick inventory of their equipment, then he started onto the ice, with Jack close behind, pulling the sled. The old fisherman made a beeline for a nondescript point in the middle of the lake, marching past assorted sleds and shelters with heavily dressed anglers tending their poles. Jack wondered at a hand-painted sign on the side of a plywood enclosed sled that said *Snow Snake Medicine Sold Here*.

When Buck neared the spot he was looking for, he turned and searched with seasoned eyes for the distant landmarks to triangulate his location. When he pinpointed it, he pulled the old gas-powered auger from the sled and started jerking the starter rope until it fired to life. The old pro bored a circle of paired holes and shut it back down in what seemed like seconds. Next, he kicked the pile of ice shavings away from each opening and cleaned them out with a metal scoop. He pulled the sled up to a pair of holes, sat down on the seat, and grabbed a fishing pole.

"I'll show you how to work these poles," Buck said as he unhooked the tiny lure from the peg on the handle. "The most important thing is to keep a good worm on the hook." He opened the waxworm container and picked out a tiny white grub. "Thread the worm on the hook like this," he said, gently pulling the bait onto the hook until only the point was showing. "The next thing to watch is your depth." He dropped the baited lure into the hole and unwound the line off the pegs. "When your line kinks, then you know you hit bottom. Then you want to raise it a few inches and suspend it there."

Jack closely watched the old expert do everything again on his second pole. "I always fish two lines, mostly because I have two hands to work them. Give the lures a jiggle once in a while and keep your eyes on the line. The fish usually bite very gingerly. If you feel any resistance, set the hook and pull the fish slowly up out of the hole using the pole. Never grab the line with your hands."

Buck poured some worms into an empty container and gave it to Jack. "Put this in one of the empty buckets, and you can use it for a seat." He picked out two poles and directed him to another set of holes to fish in. Jack anxiously prepared his hooks and lowered them into the clear, cold water. Finally, he was fishing again!

Early anticipation wore away as the minutes raced by. At first, he expected the fish to attack his bait like a pack of voracious piranhas. When that didn't happen, he figured that he needed to change his presentation. He tried wiggling the bait a little—nothing. He raised and lowered his offerings, searching for the correct depth—still nothing. He glanced over at Buck to see if he was doing any better. The veteran stared down his holes with patient determination, luring the fish to his locale with a sort of aquatic telepathy.

After twenty minutes of futile concentration, Jack's patience began to wane. He couldn't help but notice a fellow angler across the way, pulling fish out of his hole with regularity. Watching him battle fish after fish, he couldn't take it any longer. He had to see how the man was doing it.

"Would it be okay if I went and talked to that man over there?" he asked Buck, pointing at the lone fisherman.

Buck looked over at the man, who was fighting another one and nodded approval. "Sure. He must be doing something right. Make sure and secure your poles before you leave."

Jack stood and looked for a way to anchor the little fishing sticks. He decided to put them under the bucket, but it didn't weigh enough to stay put, so he scooped some ice shavings in for ballast. "There, that should do it," he said, and he departed.

The lucky fisherman was sitting on an old homemade sled about fifty yards away. The closer he got, the older he looked. When he arrived, the wrinkled old man turned and said "Howdy" in a squeaky voice.

"Hi," Jack replied, noting the man's antiquity. He also snuck a peek into his five-gallon bucket teeming with large bluegills. "I noticed that you were catching fish and wondered what you were doing differently."

"Well, sonny," the elderly gent creaked, "the whole secret is, you have to hold the bait perfectly still."

Jack looked down at the man's hands that were

quivering uncontrollably. Then he glanced back up at his sincere eyes. "Thanks, I'll give that a try," he replied with a smile.

"Good luck, young fellar," the old man said as Jack turned to head back to his poles.

"Thanks again. You too," Jack replied as he clomped off.

When he got back to his holes, he noticed something amiss. "One of my poles is gone!" he exclaimed.

"Yeah, I heard it go but couldn't get over there in time to save it," Buck said. "I guess that fish was waiting for you to leave."

"You mean a fish took it?"

"Yep, it happens, but only when you're not paying attention."

"I'm sorry about your pole; I'll replace it."

"Don't worry about it, as I said, it happens. Get another pole. We have plenty. Did you learn anything from that man over there?"

"Yeah, we need to shake the lures like crazy," Jack replied as he drew a replacement fishing stick from the bucket.

"Oh really?" Buck asked, sounding somewhat surprised.

"Yep, that must be the secret," Jack replied.

"Well, you go ahead and shake. I'm going to try a new spot," Buck said as he got up, grabbed the auger, and headed west. In a few minutes, he had some new holes bored and cleared of ice. Then he walked back, got the sled, and trudged out to the new location. Jack pulled his lines out and followed him.

"We may have discovered what I was looking for,"

Buck said as he positioned the sled next to a pair of holes. "I hit some green cabbage with the auger. Bluegill like the little green worms that live in these leaves." He held up the strand of water cabbage that the auger pulled out for Jack to inspect.

Jack looked closely at the aquatic weed and spotted the creatures. "Yeah, I see them. They're like little transparent slugs."

The two fishermen set up shop and dropped their lines in with renewed hope. Soon, Buck let out a yelp and slid a slab bluegill out on the ice. "That's what we came after," he said with a boyish excitement new to Jack. Buck spooned some ice water from one of the holes into an empty bucket and dropped the flopping fish in. "There's number one. We have a ways to go to catch our daily limit."

"How many is our limit?" Jack asked.

"Fifteen each. We only need twenty-nine more. You'd better get busy."

Jack checked his lines to ensure that they were off the bottom. Then he tried to emulate the old angler's nervous tremor, making the lures shimmy like a cheerleader's pom-poms. Jack quickly tired from this and took a few seconds to let his hands rest. But when he resumed, he felt resistance in his right hand. Heeding Buck's instructions, he set the hook and felt the tug of a good fish. Dropping the left pole, he slowly applied pressure to the fish, which swam in big circles on its way up to the hole. When the fish finally appeared, he couldn't believe his eyes. This bluegill was twice the size of any that he caught at Merritt last summer. He quickly slid his hand under the fish and scooped it out on the ice. Now he knew why Buck had a rare excitement in his voice.

"Holy cow! Look at the size of this bluegill I caught!" Jack exclaimed. He tried to pick up the fish to show Buck, but one hand wasn't enough. He could palm a basketball, but not this bluegill. Grasping it in both hands, he carried it over to show Buck, dragging the pole along behind.

"Yep, that's a good one," Buck affirmed. "Put some water in the other empty bucket to keep him fresh until we get home."

Jack unhooked the fish and did as instructed. Soon he was back in business, shaking the poles like a set of maracas. His newfound strategy worked on a couple more fish, but his hands finally tired, and he settled into a gentler presentation with the same results. Perhaps it wasn't the violent action the fish wanted; maybe the answer was all about location.

With a few fish in the buckets, the two hungry fishermen took a little break and dug into their lunch. Sarah was right; they had worked up an appetite. The roast beef sandwiches and chips with a slight hint of fish from their fingers tasted mighty good.

They stayed in this spot all afternoon, picking up occasional bluegill or perch, most of them too small to keep. Jack set the hook on one that nearly pulled the rod out of his hand with a sharp burst of speed, only to break off. Buck informed him that there were also pike in this lake, and he just briefly hooked one. He also said that the fishing would slow down for a while because the pike probably scared their panfish away. Jack used this lull in the action to snap a few photos of the peaceful panorama surrounding them. The wind was so slight that between distant conversations that wafted across the ice, he could only hear silence- the kind that created a stimulating rush to the brain. This day, for sure, would be a memory that he'd cherish forever.

Way too soon, the sun dipped near the hills on the south side of the lake. "Okay, it's time for the five o'clock flurry," Buck announced.

"What's the five o'clock flurry?" Jack asked.

"It's the last half hour of daylight when the fish go on a crazy feed. It doesn't always happen, but when it does, you're in for some unforgettable action."

"That sounds like fun," Jack agreed. He did a quick count of fish in his bucket and figured he was about halfway to his daily limit. It didn't seem possible to double his catch in the last thirty minutes, but Buck's prediction gave him hope.

Suddenly, he hooked a fish on each rod. He managed to pull them both out, and when he looked over to see if Buck was watching, he discovered his mentor fighting a fish. The next few minutes, he was busier than a one-armed wallpaper hanger with hives. The hungry fish made a bumbling idiot out of him, tangling his lines into a hopeless birdnest. Somehow though, he ended up with his daily limit.

"The flurry's gonna have to end," Buck said. "We have to leave the refuge by dark."

They quickly stowed their gear in the sled and joined the throng of anglers pulling their sleds toward the boat ramp. In a matter of minutes, the lake was barren, and the only sign of humans was the train of headlights snaking west on the auto trail. Buck and Jack parted ways with the others when they came to the blacktop road. The obvious direction to go was east, toward the only significant town within a hundred miles. With its motels and fine eating establishments, Valentine is a mecca for tired, hungry ice-fishermen. They, instead, headed into the dark recesses of the interior Sandhills. Jack settled back for the long drive home, lazy and gratified from their glorious day on the refuge.

"Well, what do you think of ice fishing?" Buck inquired.

"It was great!" Jack replied. "This might be the best day of my life."

Jack couldn't see it in the dark cab, but the old cowboy had a grin as wide as a Nebraska horizon. He, too, was gratified with the day, but even more by this statement. Nothing could be sweeter to a man who was pouring his life into a youngster than to hear such a positive, heartfelt response to his efforts.

"About your life," Buck ensued, "Are you finding what you came from Chicago to look for?"

Jack pondered this question a few seconds, then replied, "Yeah, I guess in a way I have. Life was getting pretty complicated back home. Looking back, I was like an orphaned puppy, unsure and afraid of what lay ahead."

"Fear is one of the handles of the soul, for sure," Buck agreed. "It gets a good grip on us at times."

"Life out here in the Sandhills is so pristine," Jack continued. "It takes a person back to the basics, without all the distractions of the rest of the world. I feel like I'm able to see myself as a soul, and not just some random number."

"Yeah, we lead a pretty simple life, but it's a good life," Buck concurred.

Jack remembered the sign that they passed in

the bus after crossing the Missouri river stating that they were entering Nebraska, the Good Life. He thought about all the places he'd seen and people he met. "Yeah, it's a good life out here," he replied.

Reliving his trek from Chicago as they drove deeper into the dusky hills, his mysterious notebook came to mind. "Farley Hayes was the main reason I came to Nebraska," Jack continued, sounding deep in thought. "He wrote all kinds of things about life that fascinated me. I just wanted to find him and encounter those things first hand. It turns out; I got the experience and probably won't ever meet him."

"Oh, you never know," Buck said with another unseen smile. "Someday, he may just show up."

The two tired fishermen talked about life without inhibition for the duration of their trip home. Something about the rolling drive promoted an intimate discussion that wouldn't happen in a normal setting. They told fascinating stories from their earlier years. Jack was amazed by the wild tales of horses and cowboys. Buck took great interest in the stories of the urban childhood that Jack lived. They talked of teen crushes, near-death experiences, and theology. All the free-flowing speech sadly ended, though, when they drove into the home ranch.

"Now the fun begins," Buck said as they pulled up to the garage. "Let's see if we can find a bowl of soup before we start cleaning the fish."

Sarah had a pot of chili on the stove that satisfied their hunger and warmed the body right out to the fingertips. After supper, they set up a table in the garage and started in on the fish. Jack watched in wonder at Buck's deft fingers, magically transforming whole fish into perfect fillets that they washed and packed into freezer bags, taking great care to remove all the air before sealing them.

"There, now we have some fresh fish, straight from the ice-cold water to enjoy," Buck announced as they finished cleaning up. "I'll guarantee you'll never eat better tasting."

"I can't wait to try them," Jack replied, admiring the neatly labeled bags of fillets as he carried them to the deep freeze.

After a hot shower, Jack melted into his soft bed in a peaceful, tired bliss. He quickly drifted off to sleep with visions of giant bluegills dancing in his head. Every day should be as fine as this.

14. DAWNING

Spring in the Sandhills comes like a revolving door, connecting Canada, the Rocky Mountains, the desert South West, and the Gulf of Mexico. The weather on any given day depends on which way the door is pointing. Air from Canada is still frigid from the long winter. Chinook winds flowing down the eastern slopes of the Rockies quickly warm the air. Low-pressure systems from the southwest mix with moist Gulf air, producing heavy, wet snows that cripple the spring calving. Daily plans change quickly with the weather.

The cowherd on the Blue Diamond made it through the winter, thanks to diligent attention from Buck and his urban cowhand. The stockpile of winter feed looked as if it would hold out until the new grass emerged in May. The cows were round now, carrying eighty-plus pound calves in their bellies, ready to give birth any day. Calving season for ranchers compares to planting season for farmers or market week for a clothing retailer. It's time to resupply the stock that they sold off last season to keep the operation going.

After supper one evening, Buck dug a DVD out of the rack under the television and tossed it to Jack. "Here, pop this in the player," he said. "It's a cowboy poet who talks a lot about calving. You may find it interesting."

Jack looked at the cover on the DVD case and smiled. It was a photo of a cowboy up on a stepladder, placing letters on a marquee sign. He was nervously looking back over his shoulder, like a kid stealing from a cookie jar. The sign read *R.P. SMITH LIVE*. Jack inserted the disc, titled *CAUGHT IN THE ACT*, sat down on the couch, and hit play.

The video started out showing a cowboy that he figured to be R.P. Smith on a horse, with a dog at his side, checking calves in a beautiful green pasture. Jack watched with interest as R.P. got off his horse and caught a newborn to put a tag in its ear. The calf's mother stood tensely by as the man worked. The dog watched, ready to protect his master if the cow decided to charge. The whole process was over quickly, and he got back on his horse to ride back to the ranch place down in the valley. Once in the yard, he unsaddled his horse and hurried to the house where he changed clothes and emerged wearing some fancy go-to-town duds. He sped to a city where he ran through a backstage door as the announcer introduced him to the crowd. The next shot was of him beginning his oratory before an auditorium filled with eager onlookers.

Jack listened intently to R.P.'s stories, interspersed with poems he had written to illustrate his experiences as a cowboy. He talked of rodeos, kids, and his wife. The poet described an adventure where he and his dad dove into a water cistern to fix a leak. He had a way with words and facial expressions that brought the stories to life. But the final poem was the one that left the biggest impression. As the poem unfolded, he realized that this story could hit very close to home.

Finale

Birth, witnessed in that barn in the hundreds, I suppose. Each one an affirmation of the vocation he had chose. They came in for a reason. They were not there by chance. If help was needed, he would be there; that's the way he ran his ranch. This should be an easy one; a heifer with back feet showin. She hadn't been pushin very long and he had no way of knowin. How the night would play out and that fate would tip its hand, and it probably wouldn't have mattered, though it's hard to understand. Tonight he used the pullers, not like his younger days, when he would stretch his sinews; those were a young man's ways. And tonight he worked alone; no one in the house to call. He had missed her all the time, when she passed on in the fall. The winter long, cold and lonely, the cattle helped him cope. It was springtime now, and spring always brings new hope. His mind was on the heifer now; the calf's hips were coming through. Speed was all that mattered; to tarry would not do. The calf wasn't comin easy; against the puller he did strain. With each click of the handle; calculation in his brain, the time that had elapsed since the calf's cord had been broke. At last, the heifer gave him up, but there was no gasp or choke. The calf was quickly in the air; by its back feet he was swung. Two pounds of calf to three of man; til dizziness had wrung, the ability to swing not even

one round more, they landed in a pile on the stall straw-covered floor. He placed his ear on the calf's side, a cowboy's stethoscope. Now he had a slimy ear, and a little bit of hope. He knelt down at the calf's head, held its mouth shut with his hand, and blew into its nostrils, til he saw the ribs expand. Then he pushed the ribs back down and then again he blew, until he was exhausted, he'd done all he could do. He placed his ear back on the ribcage and listened for the heart, and he heard a steady beating, the beating of a new life's start. Then his world went silent; Lord it must have hit him fast. Who knew the breath he pushed into that calf, would be his very last. Somehow it seemed fitting, his passing in those cedar walls, instead of walls of brick, draped glass, and antiseptic halls. I'm sure that some would not agree, do not share my belief, would say he paid too high a price for just another head of beef. Look close, see the reflection of something greater there? He is our God, we are the people of his pasture, and the flock under His care. Psalm 95:7
　　　　　—R.P. Smith

As the screen went dark, Jack thought about his old boss. He could easily be the man in the poem. He could picture Buck out there in the barn trying desperately to save a calf's life. How quickly death could take Buck, leaving him alone in this world again. Then he thought about the poem's closing lines and how much this analogy resembled Buck's remarks after Percy shot Mikhail. He'd done his homework and decided it was time to act.

"I need Jesus," he said half under his breath.

Buck and Sarah looked over at Jack as if his red hair were on fire. "You what?" Buck asked.

"I need Jesus in my life," Jack said a little louder.

Buck could see the seriousness in Jack's eyes. The young man that he took under his wing and quietly mentored all these months had reached a critical juncture in his life. Thankfully, he decided to take the road less traveled but with an excellent destination.

"Well, Jack, we're pleased to hear you say that, aren't we Sarah," Buck said, smiling at his wife.

"Why, yes!" Sarah exclaimed. "Those are about the sweetest words I've ever heard!" Unable to control herself, she got out of her chair, walked over to Jack, and threw her arms around him, hugging him with all her might. "You just made the best decision of your life," she said eye to eye with him.

"I feel the same- that I just made a big decision that answers an awful lot of tough questions," Jack replied with a relieved tone.

Jack joined Buck and Sarah each Sunday morning on their weekly drives to church from that point on. He soon got over his fears of the unknown behind the sanctuary walls, realizing that churchgoers were just like everyone else. Oh sure, there are always the self-righteous, the hypocritical, and the paranoid, but Jack quickly picked them out and avoided them. His attention was directed more toward the spiffy cowgirl with golden locks and ice blue eyes sitting across the aisle. Savannah gave him a huge, welcoming smile when they caught each other's glance. This church thing was going to be alright, he concluded.

Calving season soon came in full force. Buck and Jack took turns on the night rounds, getting up at two a.m. to check for cows in labor. It made for really long days when the cows calved at night.

When a cow was having trouble, they drove her to the barn and put her in a headgate. Then Buck set a calf puller which resembled a high lift jack in place. The jack's bottom was a u-shaped metal bar, called a breechen, that went against the cow's back end, just below the calf. A strap went up over the cow's back to hold the puller in place. Buck then pulled long plastic gloves on and lubed them up. Ensuring that the head and front feet were coming first, he looped a pulling chain around each front hoof and brought them back to hook on the ratchet. Then he instructed Jack to hold the outer end of the puller rod while ratcheting the handle. The chains pulled first one leg, then the other with each pump of the handle. They would wait a minute for dilation if it pulled too hard while Buck rubbed more lubricant around the tight spots. Then Buck instructed Jack to lower his end of the puller to the ground, which aided in pulling leverage. Then he would raise it back up and crank it again. A shoulder at a time, the calf would emerge, then the rest came quickly. Once on the ground, Buck ensured that the calf was breathing, then he put an ear tag in for identification, and they dragged it into a pen where the mother joined it to lick it clean and get it up for its first suck of milk.

One morning Jack noticed that Buck was spending a lot of time on the phone. The concern in the old cowboy's voice was troubling him. "Is something wrong?" he asked after the conversation.

"Yeah, we have a sick calf needing professional care; it might be a staph infection," he replied. "I'd like to take it to our regular vet, but he's overrun with sick calves, so we'll have to haul it to Arthur. Could you and Sarah take it when you finish your chores?"

Jack lurched at this plan. He begged for chances to take advantage of his new learner's permit. He quickly finished his chores and then helped load the sick calf into the trunk of the car. Without so much as a spin of the wheels in the gravel, they were off.

Sarah guided her young driver across the route to Highway 61. When they arrived, he turned south on the smooth ribbon of asphalt leading to Arthur. After traversing seemingly endless miles of giant hills, they passed the Sandhills Auto and Tractor Garage and then the junction of Highway 92. They were on the outskirts of Arthur, the illustrious county seat and only town of Nebraska's youngest county. The next place of business was their destination, the Sandhills Veterinary Clinic.

"I'll go in and see where they want him," Sarah said.

Jack got out and opened the trunk to see how their sick little passenger fared on the drive. The calf seemed content with its situation, dire as it was. The vet came out and took the patient off their hands, telling Sarah that they would have to keep him a day or two and they would call when he was ready to go back home.

"Okay," Sarah replied. "We sure hope the little fellow pulls through."

They got back in the car, and Sarah directed Jack to drive into town for supplies. "We may as well eat dinner while we're here since it's about noon. Before we eat, though, why don't we drive down some side streets. I can show you some interesting buildings, and you can get some practice city driving for when you go back to visit Chicago," she said with a wink.

"That sounds like a good idea," Jack replied with a grin.

First, they drove past a sign that said Chuck Wagon Meats. "The butcher shop," Sarah announced. "Turn left onto Elm Street." Jack took the next left, and they drove south down a street lined with neatly kept houses, occasional horse trailers, and parks. "Take another left before you get to the brick church." Jack turned off on Heath Street, and they went east past neatly fenced yards and houses to the end of the street, where they came to a large white building. "Stop here a minute." Jack pulled up to the stop sign and peered at the structure to their left. A sign above the door read, *"PILGRIM HOLINESS CHURCH, built of baled straw 1928."*

Jack remembered the straw bale grocery store run by high schoolers in Cody, where he stopped on his bike ride. "Wow, those bales must last a long time," he said. "That church is almost a hundred years old!"

"Take a right here," Sarah instructed. They drove down Cedar Street, past a swimming pool to the end of the road. "Take another right, and I'll show you the school." Jack drove down Marshall street, where a football field appeared through a break in the cedars. Then they drove past a large brick building. "This is Arthur County High School. They're kind of famous for their good six-man football teams."

A half-block west of the school, Sarah pointed to a square wood-framed building in the middle of a park. "That's the original Arthur County Courthouse. It's famous for being the smallest courthouse in the nation.

They came to a stop sign back at Highway 61, otherwise known as Fir Street. "Take a right, and we'll cruise the main drag," Sarah laughed with a playful fist pump. They turned on to the main street and drove through town slowly, gawking at the nostalgic buildings that reminded Jack of a western movie set. They drove past the rustic Sandhills State Bank, which wasn't much larger than the ATMs back in Chicago. Next to it was a rambling weathered wood structure with cedar posts supporting a full-length porch. Above was a facade bearing the name, *Bunkhouse Bar and Grill*, spelled out in hand-hewn logs. Three tattered flags waved overhead: a white Arthur County, a blue Nebraska state flag, and a red Cornhusker. Next to this building was the Wolf Den Market using much the same rustic architectural style. Next came the well-weathered Rose Saddlery with hitching rails out front. As they drove north, they passed various small business buildings from yesteryear that looked to be vacant now. Then the commerce section turned to residential, and Sarah told Jack to make a u-turn in a wide spot that seemed made for that purpose. They drove back into town, and Sarah had Jack park in front of the Grocery store.

"Are you hungry?" she asked as she opened her door to get out.

"Sure am," Jack replied, stepping out and taking a whiff of hamburgers frying. "That smells really good!"

They walked to the Bunkhouse entrance and stepped inside, feeling the whirl of senses brought on by aroma to make a stomach growl and interior decor that felt like the Long Branch Saloon down in Dodge City. They sat at a table and soon had a friendly waitress at their side, taking their orders. "Today's special is roast beef, mashed potatoes, green beans, a white roll, and peach pie."

"I'll have a half order of the special," Sarah said while Jack deliberated. The special sounded good, but a big, juicy hamburger made with local Nebraska beef was hard to pass up.

"I'll have a hamburger," he decided.

In a few minutes, the waitress came back with their steaming meals, and Sarah gave thanks to God before they ate. Jack echoed her "amen," and they dug in.

"This might be the best hamburger I've ever eaten," Jack said between bites.

"Mine's very good too," Sarah replied.

Sarah slid her peach pie over to her ravenous cowhand. "Here, you need this more than I do."

"Are you sure?" Jack asked, eyeing the pie.

"Yep, I'm full."

When they finished eating, Sarah went up to the bar and paid for the meals; then, they headed back outside. "I need a few groceries. Do you mind waiting?" she asked.

"No, I might walk over and look at the old courthouse," Jack replied.

They parted ways, and Jack walked across the street and headed south toward a city block consisting mainly of lawn and trees. The old courthouse sat in the middle of the park. Jack walked over and studied the white, wood-framed structure. It was twenty-six feet square, with a hip roof. The scalloped fascia and a picket-fenced square on the peak were the only ornamental features. A stone's throw to the east was another small building. Jack walked over and read the plaque on the side, describing it as the county jail. It looked as if an inmate could easily beat his way out with a hammer.

As Jack wandered around the grounds, he couldn't help but visualize how things were when all this was new. The railroad doesn't link Arthur to the rest of the world like the towns up north. Organizers selected it as the county seat because of its central location in the newly formed county back in 1913. Road builders didn't complete Highways 61 and 92 until several years later. It was indeed a frontier town, made up of cattlemen and Kincaiders. He smiled when he realized that even the rough and tumble men of the west needed a community structure.

Jack spotted Sarah coming out of the Wolf Den Market, so he hurried across the street and helped her stow the groceries in the back seat.

"We just have one more stop to make," Sarah said as they got in to leave. "Head on down the highway to Crusty's Feed Store. Buck has a list of things for me."

They drove south, then west out of town, past the fairgrounds where Jack spotted a rodeo arena. "The Sandhills have rodeo arenas like Chicago has basketball courts," he determined.

"Yeah, every town has one," Sarah chuckled. "Take the next right off the highway."

Jack turned off and parked in front of Crusty's, where they got out and went inside. Sarah gave the man their list of calving supplies, and he quickly rounded everything up for her. They stowed the goods in the trunk and were soon back on the road home. As they drove through town one last time, Jack made a mental image to take home with him. He never wanted to forget the special aura about it.

That day with Sarah was much like the day that he spent with Buck ice fishing. They conversed about things that probably never would have come up at the kitchen table or while napping in front of the fireplace.

There was something about the quiet hum of the car driving down the lonesome highway, with the peaceful hills drifting past that freed the mind and tongue. Jack knew that this day would be one to think about and smile.

Spring eventually won the battle with winter and the calving season drew to an end. Marsh birds that flew south last fall were slowly reappearing. Frogs that lay dormant in the muck at the bottom of the lake came back to life and started their incessant chirping. As each day came and went, the sounds of spring increased, like a crescendo leading to the climax.

Possibly the most anticipated event on a cattle ranch is branding day. When calving season's over, cowboys sort the newborns off their mommas to get branded, castrated and vaccinated. This job requires many skilled hands. It's the day when the neighbors come together to work, socialize, and feast.

Buck and his neighbors figure out a schedule so that the branding crews make it to each ranch in a timely fashion. Somehow, the ranchers of the Sandhills pull this off in short order each year, leaving no herd unbranded.

Buck set a date for the Blue Diamond branding on Saturday, the fourth of May. He and Jack worked to get the corrals ready for the sorting and branding, clearing tumbleweeds, tubs, and various other debris from the ground, leaving it as smooth as a rodeo arena. They arranged panels so that they had a handy sorting gate to swing open and shut quickly.

Jack was learning the branding process on the days leading up to the fourth on the surrounding ranches. He wasn't quick enough with old Charlie to ride and rope, but he learned to throw calves like a pro. His long arms could reach over even the most mature calves and grab their flanks, lifting them off the ground and coming down with his wiry knee on the pinned animal. The locals were so impressed that when a cowboy called him "Red Chicago," the name stuck. They even shortened it to R.C. in the heat of the action.

Saturday, the fourth of May finally came, and the Blue Diamond herd was ready. Buck led them with hay into a small pasture near the holding pens the day before. Cowboys pulling horse trailers started showing up around 7:30 a.m. Buck welcomed each one as they pulled in and told them the game plan.

Jack hurried through his morning chores so he could help with the sorting. Buck told him he would be handling the gates. Shortly after 8:00, the horsemen headed out to the pasture to bring the cows in. Rex and Missy, the well-trained border collies, went along, staying even with the horses and twenty yards to the side. They seemed to know exactly when to go and when to stop. In a few minutes, cowboys had the bawling cows, and their yellow-tagged calves gently herded into the large holding pen, and Jack shut the panel gate behind them. Next came the job of sorting the calves from the cows. A line of steel panels divided the holding pen in half. Jack's job now was to operate the swinging panel in this dividing fence. The calves needed to stay put while the cowboys sorted the cows off and brought them through the gate into the other holding pen. If a calf came with the cow, Jack quickly shut the gate and did not let them pass. The cowboys were experts at cutting the cows off from the calves, making Jack's job easier. When the last cow came through, only a couple of calves had escaped. That's when a cowboy brandishing a rope rode through the gate and caught the escapees, dragging them back to join their peers.

Buck had all the calf working utensils ready outside the pen by now. A propane-fired branding pot filled with irons stood within reach. The vaccine waited in a cooler, and the syringes lay on a towel on the bed of the truck. He placed a package of surgical castrating knives in a tray next to the vaccine guns. He'd fired up the torch so the irons would be ready to go.

"Okay, looks like we're ready," Buck hollered for everyone to hear.

Jack let the ropers through the gate into the calves, and the action began. In seconds the mounted cowboys dragged their catches to the wrestlers, who threw and pinned them securely with a man on each end, stretching the calf out. Jack, otherwise known as R.C., joined in on the wrestling. With several teams holding and multiple vaccinators, branders, and castrators, the process went quickly.

Somewhere in the heat of the operation, Jack noticed a new roper in the corral. He immediately recognized the palomino, the hat, and the blonde hair. Savannah must have slipped in unnoticed. His attention diverted from the business at hand to the roping action.

"Hey, R.C., the calf's done; you can let "im up now," his partner muttered.

"Sorry," Jack apologized. "I must've been daydreaming."

Jack gravitated to the calf on the end of Savannah's rope. "Hi, I didn't know you were coming!"

he said to the cowgirl.

"Hi, Jack! Yeah, today's Saturday, and what's better than this on a day off?"

"Yeah, you're right about that," Jack agreed. "Thanks for coming!"

"You're welcome," Savannah replied. "Uh, I think your helper's waiting."

Jack looked over at his waiting partner and flushed red. "Sorry, I guess I forgot what we were doing."

"Focus, R.C.," he mumbled.

Jack grabbed the calf and threw it with as much manly skill as he could muster. Then he loosened Savannah's rope from the back hoof and offered it back to her.

"What does R.C. stand for?" she asked as she coiled her rope.

Before he could answer, his holding partner replied, "Red Chicago, it's his wrestling name."

"Oh, I see," Savannah replied. "I like that."

The branding went on like clockwork that morning until Buck's voice rang above the bawling cows. "Time for dinner!" He announced to the tired, hungry cowboys. The action ceased when the last calf was turned free, and the wrestlers dusted the sand off their pants. The ropers dismounted, and everyone started the welcome walk to the house and the mudroom sink, where they took turns washing off the morning's residue.

Sarah and some neighbor ladies had a spread set up in the garage that put royal feasts to shame. Fried chicken and barbequed beef sandwiches waited in large heating ovens next to a cauldron of mashed potatoes topped with melted butter. Veggies included corn, green beans, and candied carrots. Then came the trays of hot, homemade buns with several choices of jelly and jams. Pies of many colors: peach, apple, and chokecherry, to name a few, filled the dessert table.

The cowboys filed through the lunch line and walked back out to the tables set up in the driveway. Loaning out their tables for branding dinners is a local ministry of Sandhill churches. They sat down to good food, good conversation, and a chance to rest aching muscles.

Way too soon, the siesta was over, and they plodded through the sand back to the corral. Buck fired up the burner, and in minutes the irons were hot again. The ropers each picked out an unbranded calf at Buck's command and had it captured with a sharp swing. They were back in business for the afternoon.

As the unbranded calves became harder to find, the cowboys let some of the worked ones out to join their mothers. The bawling cows came running to the gate and sniffed at them, looking for their babies. Amazingly, it didn't take them long to pair up again.

Around 3:00 in the afternoon, Jack got up with a groan and looked around for another captured calf. The ropers were sifting through the calves, looking for unbranded ones, but were finding none. After a thorough search, one of them announced, "That's it."

Buck shut down the branding pot and had Jack open the panel gate. "Watch them run out and make sure we didn't miss one," he advised.

Jack did as told, and the ropers drove the calves slowly out of the pen. The cows raised their mooing intensity by several decibels when they saw their babies coming for them. They ran the last calf out, and Jack closed the gate behind the horses.

Buck personally thanked each helper before they walked and rode back to their trucks. Jack focused on Savannah. He ran and caught up with her as she was riding toward her pickup and trailer.

"Thanks again for coming today," he said, walking briskly to keep up.

"You're welcome," Savannah replied, smiling at him. "Sorry that I'm in a hurry to leave. We have our senior prom tonight, and my date is picking me up at 5:00."

Jack considered this explanation with mixed emotions. She was apologizing to him for being in a hurry. She worked all afternoon in a smelly herd of cattle, knowing that this was her prom night. He admired her determination. But the part about her date for the prom threw a wet blanket on the fire.

"That's okay," he replied, trying to sound upbeat. "I hope you have a wonderful time tonight."

"Thanks, it should be fun."

They reached Savannah's truck parked with the others on the side of the ranch lane. Jack helped her load her horse and saw her off as she turned her rig around to head out the road.

"See ya R.C.!" she hollered from her window as she drove off.

Jack waved slowly and said under his breath, "Yeah, see ya."

He stood and questioned how many more times he would stand and watch her leave. Just then, he saw her brake lights come on. She slowed but didn't stop. As he pondered this, he saw the reason why. She was meeting an oncoming car on the narrow lane. The two vehicles passed each other, one leaving, the other coming. Curious, Jack stood and waited for the sedan to drive in.

The car pulled up and stopped next to Jack. The door opened, and to Jack's utter astonishment, out stepped his mom!

"Mom! What in the world?" was all he could say.

"Hi, Jack! Wow, look at you!" she said as she rushed over and gave her son a big hug. "Whew," she exclaimed, waving her hand in front of her nose. "You smell like money!"

"That's the same thing Farley said about cow manure," Jack said. "Did you read his journal too?"

"Sort of," Shelly replied. "They must not have told you."

"Who must not have told me what?" Jack asked, perplexed.

"Buck and Sarah didn't tell you who Farley is."

"No... How do you know Buck and Sarah?"

"It's kind of a long story. But seeing you here like this- I guess it's time to tell you." Shelly turned and looked back out the lane and smiled like it was a long-lost friend. "I need to stretch my legs after that drive. Let's go for a little walk."

The two shuffled slowly out the lane while Shelly opened her soul to her bewildered son.

"I've been hiding some things from you, Jack, but I did it for your benefit. Twenty years ago, an unwed, pregnant girl came to this very ranch to get away from her troubles. Buck and Sarah, being loving people who couldn't have children of their own, took in young, troubled youth and tried to help them restore their lives."

"That girl was you?" Jack ventured.

"Yes, it was me. I got Buck's name and number from a counselor. They took me in and helped me through a tough time in my life. I'm ashamed to say that you probably wouldn't be here today if it weren't for them. They talked me into delivering my child and raising him to manhood."

Shelly looked over at her son for a remark, but Jack was speechless.

"After I had you, I decided to start fresh in life and move to Chicago. I got a good job doing what I love, writing. I never met a guy to marry and be a father to you, so I did an underhanded thing. I wanted a man like Buck to teach you manly things, so I pretended to be Buck, with a fictitious name."

"Farley Hayes," Jack deduced again.

"Yes, Farley Hayes. I was Farley's ghostwriter. I even learned to print like a man. I wrote some stories that Buck told me, and some from his hired hand, but mostly, I wrote from my heart what I learned while living in the Sandhills. I thought maybe it would teach you some things too. But you decided to come here and experience them for yourself. I was hesitant, but then I remembered myself at your age. I decided to turn you loose and let the Sandhills do its thing. You can imagine my surprise when you called and said you got a job working for Buck Jackson. I thought, what are the odds? But then I decided to play dumb to see the outcome. My curiosity got the best of me, though, and I contacted Sarah a couple of months ago. She said that they figured out who you were on the first day that you showed up here, but sensing that you may be unaware of certain facts in your family history, they didn't pry into the matter. I couldn't wait to come see you and thank the Jacksons for all they've done so they told me to come to the May branding- when spring makes the Sandhills come alive."

The treasure found

Jack now had the completed puzzle laid out before him. The past seemed so clear now; the present was under the gentle control of his surroundings, and he anticipated what lay ahead with youthful gusto.

Mother and son walked now, in grateful silence, listening to the frogs, the marsh birds, and the cows. They savored this moment in God's country—in a land called the Sandhills.

ACKNOWLEDGEMENTS

My sincere thanks to those who provided inspiration and information in the writing of this book. It probably all began with *Old Jules*, by Mari Sandoz. I was fortunate enough to read it in high school and again in college under an English professor named Helen Stauffer, who also happened to author *Mari Sandoz: Story Catcher of the Plains*.

Years later, I took up guiding hunters and anglers in the Sandhills, where I stayed on ranches and met many of the characters who became the role players in this story. Out of courtesy, I gave these ranches and people fictitious names to protect their privacy.

I especially want to thank poets R.P. Smith and

Kip Sorlie for letting me use some of their amazing artistry with words. Jeff O'Donnell provided many historical facts from his books, *Luther North Frontier Scout* and *Amazing Tales of the Old West*. A good part of the science came from *An Atlas of the Sand Hills* provided by the University of Nebraska.

I probably enjoyed gathering information for this book the most through face-to-face interviews. Tim McAbee and Buck Buckles were a wealth of information concerning ranching in the Sandhills. Bob Rooney and Adrian Boykin helped immensely in developing my main character. Shailey McAbee shared her expertise in rodeo.

Four people graciously accepted the task of proofreading this book. Megan Hempstead looked for continuity of the story. Darwin Hunt read it with the discerning eyes of a retired school teacher. Tim McAbee searched for errors in ranching practices and rodeo. I am especially indebted to Vicki Kraeger, who did the final edit.

Finally, I want to thank Mitch Hunt with Huntrex for equipping the technology to write this eighty-eight thousand word novel with as little aggravation as possible. For me, writing a book is like a snail climbing Mt. Everest. Mitch made the impossible happen.

None of this would've happened, though, without the time I spent enjoying the Sandhills. Thank you, Teri, for encouraging your husband, when life becomes a harried rut, to hitch on to the old boat and head to the place that I call the land of the living- the incredible Nebraska Sandhills.

Made in the USA
Monee, IL
03 February 2025

11456329R00198